THE
EMPTY SET

THE
EMPTY SET

The Iowa Trilogy
Book 2

Tommy Murray

Joe McTigue Full-Court Press

Other Books by Tommy Murray

The Iowa Trilogy

Bridging generations of heartbreak and triumph in small-town
Iowa, The Iowa Trilogy explores the crossings of time,
belonging, legacy, death—and what comes next.

Fathers, Sons, and the Holy Ghosts of Baseball (2017)
The Empty Set (2025)
Let That Be All (planned for 2027)

For permission requests, contact Joe McTigue Full Court Press at fatherssonsandholyghostsofbb@gmail.com.

The author's note includes the spoken word piece "In the Memory of Injustice" with permission from Tou SaiKo Lee, first performed on April 24, 2009.

ISBN: 979-8-9992781-0-4 (print), 979-8-9992781-1-1 (ebook)
Library of Congress Catalog Number: 2025912868

Editing by Angela Wiechmann

Proofreading, cover design, interior design, and ebook conversion by Kris Kobe

The Empty Set honors and blesses the memory of my former students at (Patrick) Henry High School (now Camden High School) in Minneapolis, especially Alex Xiong, Mandela Jackson, and Jordan Hughes. Jordan Hughes, the all-time basketball scoring leader at Henry High School, and fellow Henry Patriots Alex Xiong and Mandela Jackson, all lead now and forever in ways not reflected in record books and box scores. All live on as long as we say their names and tell their stories.

This story also celebrates the women in my life who taught me when to hold on and when to let go: my grandmothers, Bessie and Mary; my grandmother-in-law, Elmira; my mother, Janette; my mother-in-law, Helen; my wife, Mary Ann; my daughters, Danielle (mother of my first grandchild, Daisy), and Christina; my sisters, Mary Beth, Jean, Peggy, Frances Eileen, Ann, Kitty, and Molly; and my sisters-in-law, Colleen, Peggy, Kathy, Veronica, and Julie.

In *The Empty Set*, a dragon-tail symbol separates storyline transitions. This design is common in *paj ntaub* (flower cloth), a traditional Hmong art form. In Hmong culture, the dragon holds negative and positive symbolic meanings, associated with strength and power.

The full dragon-tail design on the back cover is a computer illustration recreation of an appliqué and reverse-appliqué artwork. Each quadrant of the design is made up of a heart with a dragon tail motif inside. In the original artwork, each heart is decorated with couched herringbone stitches to create fences around the dragon tails. In the red channels of the hearts, ladder stitches are used to hold the appliqué down. Small triangle appliqués decorate each side to act like a frame.

Original artwork by Mai Thao, 1990, 35 x 35 centimeters

Source photo by Noah Vang; item at the Hmong Archives

Used with permission from the Hmong Cultural Center in Saint Paul, Minnesota.

3745 Humboldt Avenue North
Minneapolis, MN 55412
Christmas Eve 2018

Joe Mauer
Minnesota Twins
Target Field
1 Twins Way
Minneapolis, MN 55403

Dear Joe,

PLEASE SAVE ME AND MY LITTLE FAMILY.

I am Michael Joseph Moriarity. Michael, for God's strongest archangel. Joseph, for you, Joe Mauer, the Minnesota Twins GOAT. But everyone calls me Empty—the nickname Harden gave me—everyone besides my little family and Pa Dao. Pa Dao is my part-time mom, friend, and full-time shaman. Harden? He's fam—my inspiration.

Harden nicknamed himself after Houston Rockets point guard James Harden. My Harden plays the point in my life. He teaches me what's more terrifying than death: not living while you're alive. Once, we stood on the Lowry Avenue Bridge and threw worry stones into the Mississippi. The ripples spread and faded. "When you die on North," Harden said, referring to the Northside of Minneapolis, "your memory is forgotten before the ripple passes away. Live while you're alive. This is all we got."

In my favorite movie, *Field of Dreams*, a spirit whispers, "If you build it, they will come." Pa Dao says, "If you say the words, the spirits will come. The spirits live forever." She explains that Hmong words have power. "Words have history and family," she says. "They can come to life. Speaking them can build up and heal or tear down and kill." Mom believed this too. So do I.

Pa Dao says, "Spirits never leave the posts they're tied to, their birthplace and grave. They guard them for eternity."

Harden responded with a basketball analogy about the afterlife: "You have to switch up from man-to-man to zone defense." His words grounded me. Even in death, there's a game to play, and defense wins every game.

Now the spirits of Mom and Harden play man, up on me, twisting and turning inside me. Their last breaths and blood jolt my heartbeat one hundred thousand times a day. Neither rests in peace; instead, they restlessly battle to guide me. I hold them tight until I'm big enough to fill the emptiness they left.

Emptiness isn't nothingness. It's space waiting, the potential to be filled with something, everything. I am empty with the loss of Mom and Harden, yet brimming with my life that's left to live.

Pa Dao teaches me a horror more terrifying than not living while you're alive: "Not dying after you die." She helps spirits move on to where they're supposed to go. She teaches me that even the dead—especially the dead—"must learn to hold on." And they must, as Harden said, "let shit go."

My dad, Puff, doesn't talk much, unless it's about you, sports, or fixing our 2004 Ford Crown Victoria, which we call Vicky. "Joe Mauer knows when to let go and hold on better than anyone," Puff says. "He always evaluates the first pitch, lets it go, keeps his eye on the next pitch, and holds on. That's how you should handle life and death."

I'm writing to you in the bedroom I share with my big brother, John. I'm alone, as usual. Also, as usual, John is with Puff in our TV room, where they absorb ESPN while spinning dials and rolling dice in baseball board games like Strat-O-Matic Baseball, Dynasty League Baseball, and their favorite, All-Star Baseball. I watch them from the bleachers instead of the field, removed but comforted.

Their passion is about more than baseball and board games; it's about holding on and letting go and learning when to do each. Baseball is the sacred ritual that helps us do that. It keeps life from rolling between our legs and into the outfield or from dropping out of our glove at the end of a sky-high pop-up.

The sun set an hour ago, at 4:30. The purple heron in my beveled stained-glass window now streams darkness. Earlier today, it came to life with sunlight and broke the light into rainbows across my bedroom wall. The heron is like my little family, waiting for something more, something that will bring us back to life.

I've never met you, but Puff has. He scouted for the Twins and followed you in high school. Since then, Puff has listened, watched, and provided play-by-play and color commentary about you. Whenever you came to bat—all 6,930 times—Puff sat up on the couch, reporting to John and me.

"Watch how Joe Mauer works this pitcher. See how he keeps his head down during his swing? Eyes on the ball. Joe Mauer's a comet streaking across the sky we'll never see again."

Or, "A golem is a protector, born from the earth when hope is lost. Joe Mauer is our golem. Every time he steps to the plate, he carries the weight of our hopes on his shoulders."

Every time you positioned yourself in the batter's box, Puff muttered a prayer to transform you into a golem to crush our enemies. It worked.

Remember your walk-off home run against the Red Sox last year? Puff summoned you that night with these words—the same words I say now: "God bless Joe Mauer."

This is a letter from one of your biggest fans, but it's not fan mail. I might be a faceless fan in the crowd to you, but to my little family, you are the face in the crowd. I write for you to save my little family of Puff, John, and me.

Puff holds on to every Twins game like his old Louisville Slugger. He holds on to you even harder, with all his might—the way he holds John and me, afraid to let go.

Puff made sure I grew up with you, starting when I was born, in 2004, the same year the Twins brought you up from the minors. Our family photos, which are now gone, showed me propped on Puff's lap, watching you play. Puff's face was lit up like a kid's on Christmas morning. Mine, too, in the hope and excitement of something great to happen in the future.

Whenever I get a team uniform in any sport, I pick your number, my lucky number, seven. I'm right-handed, like you, but Puff made me bat lefty, like you.

"It'll help you get to first base faster," Puff teased. "You need all the help you can get with speed. For you, slowliness is holiness."

We pray for you and to you, and not just in the bottom of the ninth. Though you played your last game a few months ago, Puff says we need to hold on to you—study you.

Puff prayed for me to be you. I did play baseball, but I was garbage. I never became Joe Mauer. I became Mom. I look like her and take after her. I hung around her so much that Puff called me Mama's Boy.

"Moms hold their kids close," Puff told John and me after Mom's funeral. "Dads let them go, pushing them on to live their own lives. It's the natural order, even if it hurts."

"Does it hurt you?" I said.

He looked away so we wouldn't see his expression. "Every day. I'm sorry, but don't look for Mom in me."

Unfortunately, Puff looks for Mom in me, but she's not there either. As a rising Hmong shaman, Pa Dao knows where and how to find Mom. Pa Dao instructed me to light an incense stick at a temporary altar near our front door to honor Mom.

"The smoke smells of the simple thatched hut on the mountain in Laos where Mai entered the world," Pa Dao says. "Her placenta, buried there, marks where she must return upon death."

As I light the incense, the most painful words in "The Empty Set"—the personal narrative I wrote for my sophomore English class at Minneapolis Thomas Jefferson High School, here on the Northside—escape my notebook pages and get carried away in the wispy, sweet, and sour smoke that drenches the time between my inspire and expire. At this moment, I, too, die and journey back with Mom to everyone and everywhere I have lived. That journey, along with every Hmong expression Pa Dao teaches me, pulls me deeper into a culture I barely understand. Though the journey centers and anchors me, it does so in water way over my head. Like Mom, I drown. But I bounce back to life again.

John bounces back, too, after the tornado, brain surgery, radiation, and chemotherapy. He's not done with cancer. "Every brain tumor has a name and specific threat," Dr. Mendoza, his neurologist, explained. "John's astrocytoma will come back. It might come back in six months, six years, or sixty years. But it always comes back with a vengeance. Meanwhile," he joked, "be sure to look both ways at intersections."

Puff's real name is Patrick. He earned his nickname on the mound, puffing his cheeks into balloons before each pitch. Before he rocked and fired the ball, his cheeks would burst, making a *pow* sound that terrified anyone batting against him. Once he let go of the ball, no one, including Puff, knew where it would go.

He still holds his breath when he's nervous. But these days, he forgets to let go. Since the tornado, I've caught him beet red and nearly faint three times. Humans take twenty thousand breaths per day. I worry I won't be there the next time to remind him to breathe.

I call Mom and Harden back to life by saying their names and writing their stories. This personal narrative is as much their stories as it is mine, and how I balance their deaths with my life to move on. Or as Harden would say, "Keep on steppin'." That's my legacy—to free their spirits, swirling inside me, so they will live eternally in each word of "The Empty Set."

But I need your help to call Puff and John back. I need you to read "The Empty Set," which I've included with this letter. It's about holding on and letting go at the same time. Afterward, I hope you'll come out to our Northside home, as you came out to conference on the mound. I hope you'll talk to us and help to save us. Help us hold on to each other. Help Puff find his way. Help John step back on the mound again. Help me be the catcher he needs. And help us let go of the first pitch and hold on for the next.

Sincerely,

Michael "Empty" Moriarity

Minneapolis Thomas Jefferson High School

"The Empty Set"
Personal Narrative

Michael "Empty" Moriarity, Grade 10
English, Period One
Mr. Lane, Teacher
December 24, 2018

— CHAPTER ONE —

Turnover

Puff says we should never go back to Cottage Park, Iowa. Not even look back. "You can't go home again," he warns, his voice tinged with a bitterness I probably won't understand until much later. But I argue, "You can't know where you're going until you know where you've been."

For my little family, home isn't a place. It's a memory, a ghost that shadows us no matter how far away we go. Against Puff's advice, I find myself drawn back in time, remembering home—where I have no home—180 miles south of the Northside of Minneapolis on Highway 169.

I picture Joe Mauer's baseball card showcased on my childhood dresser. The card's edges are worn and bent from years of examination. Next to it sat Puff's rookie preview cards from his time with the Birmingham Barons, the White Sox's farm team. The cards featured Puff's wild red hair gushing from under his cap, cocked to the right. He pitched there for three years until he threw his arm out and never got it back, settling for "a Gumby arm like a wet noodle." Puff retired from playing baseball, but not the game. He scouted for the Twins, where he followed Joe Mauer at Cretin High School in Saint Paul. The back of the cards listed Puff's stats and birthplace—Cottage Park, just like mine.

Cottage Park is a blink of a town sixteen miles north of Algona on Highway 169. Coming into town from the north, the first sign you see is a weathered wooden billboard. Washed-out letters read

Cottage Park—A Mighty Small Town." T.J. Jones—our insurance agent, one of the few outsiders who moved to Cottage Park as a teenager, and one of the even fewer outsiders who stayed—amends it, "Vanishing, not on any maps, and—like the other little towns in northwest Iowa—stubbornly holding on to two bars, a Catholic church, and a baseball field."

Puff, who left Cottage Park twice "for good," says Cottage Park plays up above its size, expects to win every contest, and "doesn't accept excuses when it loses."

He brought Mom to Cottage Park the second time he returned. They had married in Saint Paul but had a falling out with Mom's family and moved to Cottage Park, about as far away from the Hmong community as possible.

Puff and Mom were opposites in every way. He was older, very white, and a redneck. Mom was younger, Hmong, and reserved. Puff is a gigantic cottonwood tree. Mom was a tiny, elegant, but gritty orchid. She stood five feet on her tiptoes and never weighed over a hundred pounds, even when pregnant. Mom told my little family, "You'd never survive in Laos." Life there rewards the strongest and hardest workers.

Mom carried John for nine months in her womb. With such a tiny woman, he had no wiggle room to spin and turn to prepare for birth. He grew stuck in the breech position, and when the doctor carved him out via cesarean section, he weighed ten pounds and four ounces.

Recently, Joe Mauer was blessed with his first son. I'm sure he has hopes for that boy. I'd tell him to be careful what you pray for— God has a sense of humor. Puff prayed for a big son who could play baseball. A pitcher. The first time John reached for a baseball, he did so with his left hand. Puff's eyes lit up. "Left-handed," Puff said. "Worth his weight in gold."

God also granted Puff an additional cherry on top: John inherited Mom's eyes—sharp and piercing. No one outside our little family noticed Mom's eyes, which were embedded in the face of a tiny, soft-spoken Hmong woman. But those same prison-inmate eyes in John, even as a toddler, terrified Puff.

From then on, John grew faster than any other kid in Cottage Park. He grew so big and rugged that other fathers wouldn't allow him to play football or baseball with their same-aged, normal-sized sons. "It's not fair," one of them muttered as John dominated. "He's going to hurt someone out there."

By seventh grade, John started for our North Kossuth High School varsity teams in football, basketball, and baseball. In eighth grade, he dominated high school sports in the little towns across northwest Iowa.

As a freshman, John's six-foot-seven frame carried 265 pounds of solid muscle. But his emotional development lagged behind his physical growth. He had no friends outside our little family.

Instead, John befriended animals in the nearby rivers, creeks, pools, and swamps that form the Union Slough. The slough was our home away from home. More accurately, it wasn't too far from home but far enough away from basketball courts and football fields.

Mom feared the slough. She believed dragons lurked beneath the shallow waters, waiting to pull John under and away to their kingdom. She made me go with him to keep watch. Through John, I, too, became friends with animals—and, eventually, with John himself.

On one of my first visits to the slough with John, he pointed to a tiny trickling that fed the creek. We followed the winding water one hundred yards through tall grass to its source. There, on an open patch of dry gravel the size and shape of a pitcher's mound, John knelt before a crystal-clear spring that bubbled up and leaked to begin the watery trail. Then he stretched out on his stomach until his head lay over the water, and he plunged his head below. John disappeared for a full three seconds before pulling up and away, screaming, howling, and laughing. He shook his head like a dog. Water sprayed in every direction.

"Your turn," he said. "And drink the water. It's sweet."

I, too, knelt before the spring and stretched over it. Four feet below, water burst through a sand floor, churning the sand.

"You can't think about it," John said. "You just have to do it. And keep your mouth open." He rolled his hand for me to go on.

I turned back and sank my head into water so cold I thought it was hot. I jerked my head out and also sprang to my feet, coughing.

"I'm dying!" I spat, sputtered, and laughed.

Funny, but I'd never felt more alive.

The same for John, who teased, "You lasted one second."

Unlike Mom, Puff believed the dragons and all other creatures in the slough were friendly. He encouraged us to hike through the upland oaks, brushy silver maples, and green ash trees to the cotton-woods on Buffalo Creek and to paddle our kayaks to the Des Moines River's East Fork.

During our adventures, John never spoke unless to point out the animals we encountered: deer, otters, muskrats, minks, and skunks. His silence made me uncomfortable. But I discovered that his still-ness was a rest in his nature song.

John did speak up whenever we encountered a certain angry opossum. When she hissed and snarled, John would offer the same cheerful greeting: "Oh, hi, Puff."

Snapping turtles also failed to appreciate John's greetings or lifesaving gestures. Whenever one crossed 360th Street, he'd pick up the wayward traveler, carry it safely to the other side of the street, and pat its shell goodbye. Each turtle responded by twisting, turning, and shooting sharp jaws to bite off a finger.

John and I once brought home a snapping turtle. We called him Chunkasaurus. He was the size of a manhole cover. Mom discovered him right away and jabbed him with a stick until his jaws snapped out and locked onto the stick, then she lopped off his head with her Hmong knife. She tossed the stick into her garden with Chunkasaurus's head still attached. Then she sliced, sawed, and scooped his still-squirming flesh away from his shell and transformed the gooey collection into a stew. We never tried the stew or brought home another turtle.

We brought home a lot of fish from the slough, even the carp that everyone else in Cottage Park left on the shore to die. We brought plants home too. Mom taught us to collect Solomon's seal, stinging nettle, wild onion, fiddlehead fern, garlic mustard, and dandelion leaves. We also brought home raspberries, gooseberries, mulberries, and ground-cherries. And Mom taught us to hunt for and identify mushrooms; she taught us that one mistake could put you on lifelong dialysis or in a casket.

We also cared for abandoned animals—rabbits, raccoons, and even a fox. Once, we nursed a wounded great horned owl in our bedroom. Puff always set the animals free within a day.

Mom fed us any animals that crossed her path, including deer, raccoons, and squirrels. One time she came face-to-face with a territorial wild turkey lurking at our back door. She retreated into the house just long enough to grab a baseball bat. For the first time in her life, she swung that bat. That night, we ate roasted turkey for supper.

Mom cooked pure Hmong dishes we could never pronounce correctly. Other times, she made American dishes we had no trouble saying: hot dogs, potato chips, apple pie, and Blue Bunny butter-brickle ice cream. We never left a single crumb on our plates.

During his freshman year, John switched from tight end to quarterback. He could fling a football fifty yards even with defenders wrapped around his ankles. Not that it mattered. His teammates couldn't catch such an intercontinental missile—or they'd fumble it away as they were tackled.

Puff and the football coach begged John to wrestle in his sophomore year. The holdup was basketball. The seasons overlapped. When the basketball coach relented, John could wrestle so long as he didn't miss any basketball games or practices.

John never learned wrestling rules and strategies. As soon as the referee signaled to start, he marched onto the mat, slapped down his opponent's stiff arm, spun around back, and locked his arms around the guy's stomach. Then he threw the glorified tackling dummy over a leg or lifted him high, twirling him around like the Kossuth County Fair swing ride until the guy longed to be put on the mat and pinned.

As a sophomore, I wanted to be like John—the best at a sport, let alone the best at several sports. People expect more from you when you're the best. It's not enough to produce golden eggs. Each egg must have diamonds encrusted across its shell. Still, I wanted to be like him. But I was afraid of the ball in baseball and of the contact in football.

Over the years, I spent thousands of hours practicing with our solemn burnt-toast-colored rubber Spalding basketball. When I finished ninth grade, Puff said, "The only good thing about being a freshman is you become a sophomore." He told me to focus on my strengths, which were all in basketball. "You can shoot," he said. "And you're a decent height," referring to the fact that I wasn't as tall as John but still above average in my class at North Kossuth. "And you're smart."

That's when he gave me Hawk, a jubilant, old-school red-white-and-blue carousel-striped American Basketball Association (ABA) leather Wilson to track backspin.

"You're not supposed to use a leather basketball on an outdoor court," Puff said. "But in your case, we'll make an exception. You're worth it." He tossed me Hawk and stepped back, arms crossed. "Prove it."

I dribbled twice, pulled up, and sank a shot from the corner. Puff chuckled as he walked back into the house. Hawk has stuck by my side ever since.

I christened Hawk the day we moved to the Northside, when I discovered a cool book in our neighborhood Little Free Library: *Foul! The Connie Hawkins Story*. Originally from Brooklyn, Connie Hawkins enrolled at Iowa. He never played there but starred for the Harlem Globetrotters, the ABA, and the NBA. That's why I call my first basketball Hawk.

Basketball became the string between the tin cans Puff used to talk with me. And as my freshman year ended, he sent a message down the line.

"If you keep working on your shot," he said, "you could skip junior varsity and go straight to varsity with Big Bad John. But that can only happen if you practice by yourself . . . a lot."

They say it takes ten thousand hours to master a skill. Unfortunately, I had only 2,184 hours from early June through the end of August, so I compressed each practice hour into a dog hour—hyper-hard work drenched in sweat.

Hawk and I practiced every day on the driveway court Puff had built for us. From breakfast to bedtime, my Chucks sinkholed as I made ten thousand shots. The nylon net loosened and wore down until only skeletal threads swung from the rim.

On August 1, I climbed a stepladder to replace the net. I was high enough to look down through the rim. Basketball players always look up at the glossy orange rim but never look down inside its enormous space. The rim became Hawk's home. I stretched my arm out to it on each shot, extending my right hand into the cylinder from as far as thirty feet away to tuck Hawk inside its gracious hug.

I learned to make all my shots. If I missed one, I stuck in that spot until I made amends by sinking five shots in a row to repair and restore a broken universe.

After the first week of August, I incorporated new degrees of difficulty. I shot while kneeling on one or both knees. I shot while sitting or lying (forward or backward) on the scorching concrete. I shot after bouncing Hawk off my head, fist, or knee. I shot after bouncing him backward between my legs, up into the welcoming rim. Soon, I expected to make those trick shots as well.

I beat everyone in Cottage Park in our shooting games: Twenty-One, H-O-R-S-E, Shoot Until You Miss, and my favorite, Around the World. I made three-pointers all night long. I'd never miss two in a row.

On August 24, my little family played basketball together after supper. Puff took John and me outside at night on our garage half-court, with measured and drawn free-throw and three-point lines. He set his antique boom box to Joe Mauer's Twins game, tied with the Oakland A's in Minneapolis at one apiece.

While Joe Mauer batted leadoff as the designated hitter, Puff positioned me in the corner with Hawk. Puff guarded John low in the post. Over and over again, I passed Hawk to John, who took Puff to the hole and punished him. Then Puff fronted John, forcing me to arch a pass to John for a wide-open dunk. At other times, Puff took Hawk, threw him at me, then screamed and jumped with arms thrashing to block my shot. Each time, I drilled a perfect swish.

At ten o'clock, the Twins game ended. We lost 7 to 1. Joe Mauer had gone only 1 for 4 at the plate. But there was a little good news: That one hit had bumped him past Rod Carew to second place on the Twins' all-time hit list with 2,086.

Static interrupted the postgame analysis show.

"There's a storm between here and the Twin Cities," Puff said. "Let's go."

We began our retreat inside. Fat brown moths circled the buttery glow of our lonely garage light. Crickets and cicadas clicked and screeched around us. We wiped gnats off our sweaty arms and legs and swatted mosquitoes.

"Imagine that you two are attacking an enemy castle," Puff said. "Big Bad John is the battering ram, banging away at the gate. If they try to stop him"—he pounded my chest before turning to John—"then Michael will catapult a long shot." Now he pounded John's chest. "And if they try to guard Michael, Big Bad John will march through the gate and dunk. You two will be unstoppable this year," he said between heavy breaths. "You own this time and world. We can't lose."

At our back door, I lobbed Hawk in one long, last shot between the telephone wires that hung from the relay pole from our garage to our house. Hawk rainbowed toward the sky and back to earth against the shooter's square paint before bulleting through the rim dreamcatcher, snuggling and rocking gently in a tight new nylon net. I let him happily sway in his hammock overnight.

I went to sleep that night as the best basketball player in Cottage Park, besides John.

I awoke to an explosion. No clock, no glimmer of moon or sun marked the day's ending or beginning.

Instead, I found myself trapped in the remains of our bedroom, under our collapsed house. John covered me face down like a blanket in his perspiration's sour perfume. We had sunk beneath a mangled mess of dust, plaster, shingles, wires, boards, and mattresses—a shifting dual burial vault.

Thunder shook, settled, and crammed us tighter together. Heavy rain splattered above and dripped through the sludge into my mouth.

I spit the dirty water out, but more dribbled into the open air pocket around me.

I called John's name, then screamed, but John's body on mine forced my words to seep as a whisper. "Wake up."

John did not awaken.

I used all my might to push against him. Nothing happened. I remembered wrestlers pinned beneath him in terror—big, strong guys, one hundred pounds heavier than me, helpless, waiting for a referee to count off their time in defeat.

I jerked from one side to the other, numb. Maybe paralyzed. Any effort to move only restricted further breathing. My eyes opened and closed. In each case, the world went dark.

I wanted to live, but the thought of fighting only to lose was unbearable. As I sank deeper into the wreckage, the darkness began to crush me.

Then Mom appeared—Mom as I had never seen her. She was a little girl, but old enough to run for her life from the communist soldiers invading her mountain village in northern Laos. Mom and her brother and their parents raced across mountains to the lowland jungle, with soldiers relentlessly trailing behind. They'd been running for weeks, but they finally stopped at the deep, swiftly running Mekong River, which separated Laos from Thailand. They needed a way to cross.

Two boys my age drove a Thai longboat under a sliver of moon. They maneuvered the boat onto the riverbank, where they negotiated terms to deliver Mom's family across the river. The family had to give up all their possessions, including three silver bars. After the transfer, the boys welcomed Mom's family aboard.

But midway across the Mekong, the boat paused. The boy piloting the boat pounced on my six-year-old mother and held her. He pointed a pistol at her temple and cocked it.

"I will kill her unless all of you get out," he announced. "No negotiation. Now!"

Though strong and agile in the mountains, Hmong often struggled to swim. In helplessness and terror, Mom's family understood that their lives must end for hers to continue.

Hmong men always go first. Beginning with Mom's father—my grandfather—the rest of the family members slipped one by one from the darkness into the darker underwater. They were immediately surrounded by immense lumbering dragons, who greeted and guided them, not pulled, farther below to rest and tumble along with the current upon the Mekong floor.

Mom, too, moved to the boat's edge to join them, but the Thai bandits ordered her to stay behind.

The Thai bandits delivered Mom to Thailand, dumping her on the shore. She wandered, crying and starving, until Thai soldiers discovered and transported her to a nearby Hmong refugee camp. There she reunited with relatives, her uncle Pa Kao Vang and his family.

She grew up with that family until she married an older man from her refugee camp in Thailand and came to America with him. My big family followed.

Then the vision shifted. Mom transfigured into an adult, fighting for her life—and losing. She thrashed in the water, gasping for breath, swallowing and being swallowed by it, not in the Mekong River but in our slough. Mom floundered in its warm, cloudy water. Ducks and geese cried out as she descended into silt and muck.

I prayed for her to let go, for her life to end. I prayed for her suffering to end.

I could not—cannot—escape Mom, how her flailing stirred the silt and muck into a dragon that she settled amidst. The dragon wrapped one wing around Mom; with the other, it bundled me with her. At that moment, I was no longer afraid. As darkness covered us, I didn't feel peace but rather surrender and a flicker of hope that even in our darkest moment, we are never alone.

— CHAPTER TWO —

Hail Mary

After rumbling prayers and feverish resuscitation, I came to life. I blinked my eyes and breathed deeply. I found myself in an ambulance, surrounded by EMTs and neighbors.

"Thank you," I announced.

The EMT sitting alongside me burst into tears. Others cheered.

I sat up, but the EMTs told me to lie back and rest. I looked at a dark sky and asked the time.

"Four forty," the EMT said.

As I lay there, people fed me snippets of information.

"A tornado wiped out your home."

"Big Bad John's in an ambulance on his way to the Mayo Clinic Hospital."

"Puff's still searching for your mom."

After a few minutes, I eased off the gurney, left the ambulance, and took my first few steps. Our two-story, three-bedroom home had disintegrated into an open space bordered by three walls. Our century-old red oak tree, which had held rusty-red leaves all winter, had let go of its hold on the ground and now lay across the foundation, crushing and spearing our home's remnants.

The tornado had hit with brutal force, shredding our house and scattering scraps across tidy streets and yards. Five seconds later, it swept off over a bordering soybean field and dispersed into the slough.

There were people everywhere with flashlights, generators, floodlights, chainsaws, and shovels.

Puff was covered with filth and scratches. On his hands and knees upon the rubble, Puff clawed away wreckage, passing each piece of debris down the human chain that transported it all to piles in our front yard.

"Hold on, Mai!" Puff wailed before digging in and scooping away another load. "We're coming for you! Almost there!"

Generators and chainsaws whined over his shouts. Our neighbors tore the tree into pieces and hauled them away.

That's how Puff had found John and then me. He'd cleared away clutter until he discovered a red, bloodied scalp. Like pallbearers, six men had reached down, lifted John, rotated him onto his back, set him on a locked-arm stretcher, and speed-walked him to a waiting ambulance's rear hatch.

I now joined the human chain, carrying debris away. But the more splintered boards and plaster chunks I uncovered, the more certain I became that we wouldn't find Mom at the bottom. I had *seen* her death, not just dreamed it.

She was in the slough.

My friend Ricky Jones repositioned a lantern to light up my way as I stumbled from the rubble.

"Ricky," I said, "I know where to find Mom."

I started running, with Ricky right behind me. We followed the tornado's destruction, zigzagging the soybean field that rose over a gentle hill overlooking the slough. Canadian geese circled overhead in dawn's first dim light; their V formation pointed to Mom. In the distance, a lone trumpeter swan honked.

I ran down the hill and waded into the warm water. Cool mud squished between my toes as I sloshed waist-deep along the shore. From higher up on the bank, Ricky scanned the scene, looking for Mom.

Twenty minutes later, we spotted a tuft of hair sticking above the water, twenty-five yards ahead—Mom's trademark ponytail.

Ricky sped down to the shore while I charged forward in the water. As I sank into the silt, I reached out and brought Mom close, lifting her head and shoulders above the water.

"Sorry, Michael . . ." Ricky said as we locked arms underneath Mom. He mumbled a reverent curse.

We heaved Mom a few feet at a time to a cattail patch where deer had pressed tall grass into a soft bed. We laid her there, crumpled, and gulped air beside her.

Mom's glassy eyes were locked open. I pressed my fingers to her eyelids, trying to keep from shaking. The last piece of her had slipped away to never return.

As my breath returned, I waved a heavy arm toward the house. "Go get Puff."

Ricky ran away.

Mom was wearing underpants and Puff's White Sox T-shirt that covered to her knees. Silt covered the T-shirt, and a dozen leeches were sucking her arms, legs, and face. I hugged her, cold to my touch, then pinched off the leeches and tossed them back into the slough. I removed my T-shirt and covered her legs, stiff, like the garden hose when we brought it in for winter.

Mom's muscular tone had wrinkled, softened, and bloated. Her skin color, glowing brown, had paled to gray. Green and yellow bruises dulled her face. A thumb-sized red gash festered across her neck.

I sat with her until Puff drove Vicky as close as possible to us and jumped out. No one else had come with him. Vicky shivered for a moment after the ignition shut off.

Puff ran toward us, fell to his knees, and cradled Mom. I leaned her toward him. He kissed her scalp and held her close.

"I'm sorry, Mai," he moaned, his voice breaking. "I . . . I never should have brought you here. I thought leaving . . . Saint Paul would give you a fresh start. But I . . . took you farther away from everything you knew. I failed. We lost you."

Puff slipped off his wedding ring, held it against Mom's cold fingers, and pressed it over the only finger it fit—her thumb. He sobbed.

I ran back to Vicky to retrieve the blanket we kept in her trunk for emergencies. I returned to Mom and Puff and set the blanket alongside them on the grass.

"We should head back to town," I said. "People will start to worry."

Puff gazed beyond Mom, across the slough. We sat in silence, letting time pass as it always does in Cottage Park—so slow it sleeps, forever, or until something wakes it.

"Need more time?" I asked.

Puff stared at nothing. "We should keep moving."

He hung his head, closed his eyes, and waited. His shoulders dropped before he leaned Mom into the blanket, situating her shoulders first and then repositioning her head, which had flopped to one side. I straightened Mom's legs and lifted the blanket on my end.

Puff stopped me. "I can carry Mom myself," he said.

He muscled under the blanket—one arm under her shoulders, the other under her knees—and genuflected up, carrying Mom to Vicky's passenger side. I opened the front door, and Puff set her in and buckled her seat belt.

She'd always sat in the back seat with me, from the time she first strapped me in a car seat. We'd discovered Cottage Park and northwest Iowa together from our back seat.

Mom slid toward the door as I climbed into the back seat.

"Hold her steady, Michael," Puff said, his voice softer and more patient than ever. "She always held us together. Now it's our turn."

I stabilized Mom as Vicky swayed back and forth over bumps and holes on the path to the road. When Puff stopped Vicky at the blacktop, Mom leaned forward, and I guided her back.

From behind big glass doors, Mr. Stengler watched us pull into the looping driveway in front of Stengler's Funeral Home. Known for always wearing a suit and tie, he was now in his work clothes—an older pair of suit pants and a formal white shirt without a tie. He stepped from the entrance and motioned for Puff to park alongside a gurney.

"I'm sorry for your loss," Mr. Stengler said as Puff and I got out. "It's no consolation, but truer words were never spoken: The good die young. Mai left us too soon."

"Yeah." Puff's shoulders sank. "Now we give her to you?"

"We'll take care of Mai from now on," Mr. Stengler said.

Puff opened the passenger door, unbuckled Mom, slid his arms under her, and lifted her from Vicky. He took two steps backward, turned, and tenderly placed her on the gurney.

The blanket separated, exposing Mom's face. In the short time since I'd found her, she had whitened like snow. She was no longer Mom—more statue than human.

Puff covered her again.

"I'll keep you for only a moment," Mr. Stengler said. "We're going to prepare Mai so she's beautiful for the funeral. What would you like her to wear for the open casket?"

Puff stood by for Mom's answer.

Mr. Stengler said, "I know nothing is left of your house, but did Mai have a favorite outfit? Blouse? Skirt? Pants with a nice sweater? We often dress people in what they wore to church."

He waited until it was clear Puff wouldn't respond, then he looked at me.

"Mom wore a peach-colored shirt and light-gray pants for my confirmation in March," I said.

"That's helpful," Mr. Stengler said. "I can have Mrs. Stengler pick up a dress in Algona." He looked to Puff. "Okay?"

Puff brushed his hand toward me. "I guess Michael would know."

"The Ladies Guild is putting you up in the rectory," Mr. Stengler said.

Holy Trinity had abandoned the rectory since Father Ryan, Cottage Park's last full-time priest, had died at Puff's state championship game his junior year.

"They've already cleaned and stocked the kitchen," Mr. Stengler continued. "There's a wallet on the kitchen table with money until your insurance helps you on your feet again. People will drop off casseroles and meals all day. There's nothing else you can do here or anywhere else." He was counseling now as a close but stern friend. "Get over to the rectory, eat good food, and rest. I realize you don't want to do that, but be smart."

"Uh . . ." Puff said. His jaw quivered. His bottom lip stuck out.

Mr. Stengler trembled. Like most in Cottage Park, he was over seventy-five years old. He'd been friends with Grandpa Moriarity. He and the other old men in Cottage Park feared showing grief. Such expressions triggered them to lose control, especially if they saw tears. Cottage Park men don't cry, at least not in public.

Mr. Stengler focused on me, though he spoke to Puff. "No, no, no—let's move on now, Patrick," he said as if shooing a little boy home for supper.

He watched for me to take Puff away. But I couldn't move either.

Mr. Stengler moved first, pressing the automatic door opener to the funeral home. Both doors opened wide. He leaned toward the gurney and pushed Mom away from us, saying, "Everyone will remember Mai's beauty."

It took a few minutes, but Puff eventually followed Mr. Stengler's advice to proceed to the rectory. That was the only part of the advice he obeyed. Instead of resting there and eating breakfast, Puff parked in front, left the engine running, and raced inside. Upon his quick return, he tossed a wallet swollen with neighbors' cash onto the dashboard.

Puff drove Vicky back onto Main Street, past Stengler's Funeral Home, and onto Highway 169, heading north toward Rochester. We drove over the speed limit, hitting seventy miles per hour, as fast as Vicky would take us before she tremored.

After crossing from Iowa into Minnesota, Puff slowed to the speed limit in Elmore—a town smaller than Cottage Park. His blood-shot eyes oozed salty tears, wetting dried white stream beds on red, burnt skin. Sweat and dirt matted Puff's hair except for a few wild strands.

"I can't drive another mile," he said, bugging his eyes to force the eyelids from closing. "Too far gone to go on. Can you take over?"

I hesitated. Puff would let me drive Vicky around Cottage Park, where there were rarely any other moving cars. No way could I ever drive on Highway 169 or face oncoming traffic.

"But I haven't taken driver's ed," I said. "The police might catch me up here."

Puff swerved off Highway 169 into a neighborhood dotted with green ash trees; their leaves shimmered as they basked in sunlight. He stopped Vicky under the cool, dark shade of one tree and shut off the engine. As Vicky reluctantly rumbled off to sleep, so did Puff, reclining his seat as far back as possible.

I also fell into a deep sleep.

It seemed like the next day, but three hours later, Puff gently rocked me awake. "Let's go see Big Bad John."

I scouted my new surroundings. We had arrived at the Mayo Clinic Hospital parking ramp.

"We need to bolt," Puff said.

We burst from Vicky in the same Iowa Hawkeyes T-shirts and basketball shorts that we'd worn to bed, through a tornado that had buried us under the rubble of our house, and while we retrieved Mom from the slough. Our sandals, which neighbors had provided, weren't in much better shape.

We clopped across the parking lot and headed inside to the information desk, where Puff asked the fastest way to Big Bad John Moriarity's room. The woman behind the desk gave us directions.

We took the elevator to the fourth floor and ran down the hallway to room 4414. Puff cracked open the door and peeked inside.

A nurse stood over John, adjusting the plastic tubing in his nose, which connected him to a nearby oxygen tank. A black blood pressure cuff fit snugly on his right arm, underneath a micro-dotted patient gown with billowy sleeves. The gown appeared to be in its seventh reincarnation. Two bags hanging from a pole dripped clear liquid into him. A control panel with digital numbers kept score and sounded periodic and scary alerts of blood pressure, heart rate, and oxygen levels.

The nurse introduced herself as Carole.

"A tornado," she said, shaking her head. "I'm glad you're safe and here for John. Now we watch, wait, and give him time to rest." She adjusted a blanket around John. "May I help you while we wait?"

"Yes," Puff replied. "Contact a priest. And we need two rosaries as soon as possible."

"The beads on the chain . . ." Carole said, translating for herself. She shut the door behind her.

We stood at John's bedside, one on each side. A purple blotch surrounded an egg-sized lump protruding from his right temple. Jagged black stitching spread five inches across the right side of his scalp. He lay still, his red hair glowing against ghostly skin.

A few minutes later, Carole knocked and stepped in. "It might be a while before we can locate Father McAlpin. But I did find one rosary." She handed the rosary to Puff, the beads slipping from her palm and piling in his, like an hourglass. She scooted back outside.

As the door closed behind her, he called out, "Don't forget that priest," without taking his eyes off John.

Puff circled his rosary above John's head, twisting the beads in the light until they shone like bloody Christmas tree bulbs.

"Here we go, Big Bad John," he said as if igniting a seventh-inning come-from-behind rally. "Irish monks invented the rosary. But they prayed one hundred fifty prayers. So, today we'll triple our Hail Marys. And we won't stop until you're well again."

Puff blessed himself with the rosary's crucifix. "In the name of the Father, Son, and Holy Ghost, amen." He recited the introductory prayers: the Apostles' Creed, an Our Father, three Hail Marys, a Glory Be, and the first of the five Sorrowful Mysteries.

Puff said that the mysteries—especially the Sorrowful Mysteries, which we knew best from the Stations of the Cross on Good Friday at Holy Trinity—were like bases on a baseball field, leading us onward, leading us home. He also told us, "You're never supposed to look back when running those bases."

But Puff did look back on this day.

"The First Sorrowful Mystery: The Agony in the Garden," he began. "Today is not the first time I've waited for you to come to life. I waited in a hospital room sixteen years ago, while your mom struggled in labor for twenty-three hours of excruciating pain. You came to us then. You'll come to us again."

Puff's rosary spread across the blanket, which rose and lowered with John's breath like whitecaps splashing onto the slough shore before a storm. He recited Hail Marys, one after another, rapid-fire. A finger popped from Puff's fist for each one. He pinched a red crystal bead apart from the decade and closed his fists again when all fingers had risen.

I couldn't keep up with Puff's complicated way of counting, so I focused on my responses to Puff's steady calls. I lost track of time, unsure of where we were in the count until Puff followed a Hail Mary with a Glory Be and the Second Sorrowful Mystery.

"The Scourging at the Pillar. Standing out as the best wasn't easy. Other teams couldn't break you physically, so they tried and failed to break you mentally."

Into the next decade we went. Back and forth, Puff and I played catch with the words of prayers. Through it all, Carole entered the room every twenty minutes to monitor machines and fluff up pillows or adjust blankets. As we prayed, I floated away like a balloon, tethering only once Puff surpassed another decade and announced the next mystery, The Crowning with Thorns.

"No freshman ever made all-conference. But no freshman played on varsity for their seventh- and eighth-grade years. You never complained—not once."

By the time we meditated on the Fourth Sorrowful Mystery: The Carrying of the Cross, I robotically recited the words. The words and I drifted away and popped, unconnected to each other or anything else.

"Jesus's cross was heavy, but he carried it," Puff said to John. "You carried your cross without any grousing. You're a man now. We're proud of you."

I had never carried a cross of any kind. Until the tornado, Puff and Mom had served up life for me like her feasts—spread out on festive platters. My only care in the world was to get back home for a meal, which I was often late for. All I had to do was sit back and enjoy the feasts, which I did.

Puff took a deep breath and exhaled haltingly at the Fifth Sorrowful Mystery: The Crucifixion. Instead of beginning the Hail Marys, he beheld John.

"The Crucifixion begins the Resurrection. We've hit rock bottom. It's time we rise again."

Puff waited again.

After a few minutes, John twisted in his bed, and color returned to his face. He opened his eyes, focused on the ceiling, and turned to Puff and me before closing his eyes again.

I took his limp hand and blurted, "I love you, John."

Puff pocketed the rosary and placed his hand over mine, still holding John's. With his other hand, Puff pressed a button for assistance.

"You're okay, Big Bad John," he cooed. "It's time to open your eyes."

Carole hustled back in to join us. "Very good," she said, standing over John. "You're in a hospital with your family." She stepped back.

John blinked and opened his eyes—narrow, angry eyes that softened to round, sad eyes. "Mom's dead," he said, closing his eyes again, to slam a door and lock out further words. Tears flashed across his cheeks.

Carole left to get the doctor, and we waited until John reopened his eyes. He kept them open while Puff explained the events of the preceding twenty-four hours.

"A tornado gutted us," he said. "Everything is gone. Mom too. All we have now is each other, right here."

We held John for a long time and only let go of his hand and stepped away when Dr. Chen entered. She shone a light in his eyes and asked him to look in all directions without moving his head. Then she checked his grip by placing her tiny hand into his and teasing him. "Come on—you can squeeze harder than that!"

After a few reflex tests, Dr. Chen asked John to repeat five words: *baby, monkey, perfume, sunset,* and *wagon*. Next, she proceeded to pepper him with school questions: favorite subjects, extracurriculars, and sports. She asked about the date. Then she tested his memory from the night before.

Even though his speech had always been slow, it took him a long time to remember the day of the week and the month—and he had no idea of the time or the date. Neither did I.

When John failed to recall the tornado or the basketball session we'd had with Puff in the driveway, she asked him to repeat the five words from earlier.

John thought hard. *"Baby . . . wagon . . . monkey . . ."* He wavered. Tears dripped down his cheeks.

"Sunset and *perfume,"* Puff interjected. "He'll remember them eventually. First, he needs to warm up."

"Let's have you sit up," Dr. Chen said, studying how John moved. She waited until John's dizziness cleared before resuming questions. "What's your favorite TV show?"

John waited for Puff to answer.

"He doesn't spend time on TV unless it's sports," Puff said. "He's busy all day exploring the slough or playing his sports."

"Okay, now let's have you stand up," Dr. Chen said.

John struggled out of bed. He was barely upright before Dr. Chen continued with more instructions. "Close your eyes," she said. "Balance on one foot . . . Now the other . . . Turn in a circle . . . Now step over to the door and back."

John swayed and trembled through the sequence, occasionally sniffling and pinching or grinding away tears. Eventually, he'd clammed up, pretending not to hear her questions and instructions.

"He's going to be fine," Puff said. "Isn't he? He can do all these tasks perfectly. But first, he needs to eat a big meal. He hasn't eaten since supper last night. And he needs more rest."

"You can go back to bed," Dr. Chen said. Once John settled, she pointed to the stitching on his scalp. "A brain injury on the right side will affect his performance on his left. John, tell us how the tornado changed you."

She focused on John, who waited for Puff and me to respond for him.

"He's naturally quiet," Puff said. "He doesn't say much unless we drag it out of him."

"We can help, John," I said, "but you know yourself better than we do."

He continued to look at us.

Until that moment, I'd never noticed how dependent John was on us to speak for him. He'd been that way all his life. But as he struggled to find the words, I realized the tornado had changed something deeper—something neither of us could name.

"I'd say that's plenty of info for now," Puff said to Dr. Chen. He turned to John. "Take a break now. We'll get you a nice meal—two nice meals for all you've been through." Puff turned back to Dr. Chen. "You're welcome to come back again once we feed him."

"We'll do more testing," Dr. Chen said, "and start John with physical and occupational therapy."

As Dr. Chen closed the door behind her, I wished she had asked John one more question.

How did he know Mom had passed?

— CHAPTER THREE —

Fadeaway

Two days after the tornado, Puff dumped soggy Wheaties and leftover milk out of his plastic cereal bowl into the rectory kitchen sink. Next, he set the bowl, a toast plate, and a spoon on top of yesterday's dirty dishes. Then he returned to the table, reached inside the Wheaties box featuring Kyrie Irving, and scrunched the plastic lining shut by jamming it deep into the flakes. He tried to push the box between the Cheerios and Rice Krispies in the cupboard, but the shelves were overflowing with donated food. Finding no room or energy to make room, he left the Wheaties on the counter.

There was no room in my mind for an explanation of *Why us? Why Mom?*

I sat at the table, picking at scrambled eggs. The tiny kitchen had the stale smell of decades of sloppy joes and burnt coffee; their odors were baked into the peeling wallpaper and cracked linoleum. Those scents—and the past—had survived the scrubbing efforts of Mr. Clean and the parish women.

"I have to visit Big Bad John," Puff said, backing toward the door. "You okay staying behind to wrap up business for us?"

"If I have to," I said.

My little family's "business" overwhelmed me like bugs splattering on a smeared windshield I could no longer see beyond. This was the kind of thing Puff had previously and thankfully considered "adult issues." But now, for the first time in his life, Puff needed me. I had to help him. Even though I could barely take care of myself.

"Mr. Burnette visited again yesterday," I said as Puff backed toward the door to leave.

The ancient owner, publisher, editor, and writer for the *Cottage Park Chronicle* needed Mom's obituary to announce her wake and funeral arrangements. Cottage Park was accustomed to older people's steady passing. They ran down like old gassed-out lawnmowers. But Mom's death was a shock. The obituary required Puff's immediate attention.

Puff returned to the table, pulled out a chair, and sat. The wooden chair stretched and crackled under his weight. For a few moments, only Puff's labored breathing filled the kitchen. He yawned as he looked through his new billfold.

"Daddyup?" I said.

Mom had told me my first word was "Daddyup." It was a word of my invention—and intention. I'd call to Puff and stretch my arms for him to lift me up near him. He's always come for me, so I've never stopped calling out to him that way.

Puff's listless eyes focused. "Time for me to go. Big Bad John gets ornery if I'm not there with him." He looked at me. "You're a good writer. Could you write the obituary?" Before I said no, Puff tacked on another job. "Can you also connect with Father Gerardo for me? He wants to plan Mom's funeral."

Father Gerardo, the new exchange priest from the Philippines, coordinated church services between Holy Trinity and three Catholic churches in nearby towns. Puff removed a notebook and pen from his pocket, then tore out a scrap of paper with the priest's phone number and handed it to me.

"Thanks for doing all this," Puff said. He pressed on my fork's sharp prongs until it balanced, then teetered it until the handle clapped against the tabletop. "We should discuss Mom's family in Saint Paul. One more contact I need you to make."

I winced. I couldn't juggle one more problem.

"Being an adult means doing things you don't want to," he said. "Ready or not, you're an adult now. And I'll be honest—I don't want to call Mom's uncle, who is basically your grandfather. I can't. We don't get along and never will. I can't go down that road again. You'll have to contact him."

"I've never said a word to anyone from Mom's family," I said. "Every time I asked Mom to tell me their story, she said, 'Someday you'll meet them.'"

That day had come.

"Mom's uncle raised her from the time he took her in at the refugee camp back in Thailand," Puff said. "He needs to know the funeral details. You're the only one who can reach out to him. All this might work. You have no history with them. Besides, you're part Hmong. Maybe all Hmong, for how much you hung around your mom. Your grandfather might accept you."

I concealed my reaction, but I failed to hide my response. "I doubt it."

"Just let them know about the funeral," Puff said. "He's not going to show up anyway. He wrote us off a long time ago. Your mom and I invited him to come to our wedding. He refused to have any part in it—or us."

He aimed his pen at his open notebook. He wrote my grandfather's name, PA KAO VANG, on the paper, then added ZONG/ZOO.

"I lost all his contact information in the tornado," Puff said. "You'll have to do a little investigative work at the library to find his number. Ruth Miller will help you. There'll be a million Vangs. But there can't be many Pa Kao Vangs with a wife named Zoo. Zoo—which is pronounced 'Zong'—is his first wife. They're on Magnolia Avenue East, Saint Paul. That will help narrow it down."

Puff tore out the page and handed it to me.

"You can do this?" he said. "They'd never take a call from me."

The answer was no, but I buried that word before I buried Mom.

"Call John's room at the hospital if other stuff comes up."

Puff stood from the table, pushed his chair back, and walked away. The screen door slammed shut as it closed behind him.

At the Cottage Park Library, I searched Vang listings on the computer for a few minutes before Ruth Miller, the librarian, plopped down next to me, as she did with anyone at the library. She had no family of her own. She barged into any situation, whether you needed her help or not. Ruth Miller was older than the library and older than any book in the library except for the Bible. Like everyone else in Cottage Park, she knew my search history before I sat at the computer. She also had at least three books, which she had picked out for me, waiting whenever I visited.

That day, though, there were no books. She fussed and adjusted her chair close to me until her leg touched mine. "Computers are not my forte," she said, patting my hand. "Back in my day, we used typewriters. But I'll help as much as I can."

She sat on the edge of her chair, leaning forward to the computer, resisting her urge to take control as we whittled the search engine's Pa Vangs to our best guess for my Grandpa Pa Kao. Then she shushed two little boys playing a game at the next computer and handed me her phone.

"Dial the number," Ruth Miller ordered. "I'll stay here with you." She called to her assistant, who stood at the front desk, in a loud whisper. "I'm helping Michael Moriarity contact his Hmong grandfather. Absolutely no interruptions."

The phone rang four times before an older woman answered, "Hello!" followed by a cheery up-and-down three-note song. "*Koj yog leej twg?*" Then more Hmong words filled the air, making me feel far away from Saint Paul. I was departing for Laos and Thailand.

Pa Dao would later teach me that "*Koj yog leej twg?*" means "Who are you?" Despite not knowing that, I somehow answered correctly. "I'm Michael Moriarity, calling from Cottage Park, Iowa, to talk about my mother, Mai Vang. Can Mr. Pa Kao Vang come to the phone?"

The woman dropped the phone on the counter. Hmong music played in the background—a lively, nasal voice accompanying what Mom had called "Laos country music." She listened to it in her Hmong room. Puff called it "nauseatingly addictive."

The radio switched off, and a group chattered in rapid smidgens, all in Hmong, as they gathered around the kitchen phone.

Ruth Miller oversaw me as I waited. "Be patient," she said. "And say your mother's name slowly so they'll understand."

After a few moments, a much younger male voice responded in English. "Hello. I know you're looking for Pa Kao Vang. My name is Tou. My grandfather's English is not very good, and my Hmong is not very good either. But I can explain what you say to him. Can I call back on my phone and put you on speaker?"

We hung up. A few seconds later, Tou called back.

"My grandmother said you mentioned Mai Vang," Tou said. He sounded a few years older than me. "There are a few Mai Vangs," Tou said. "Could you clarify how you think we might be related? Who's her father?"

Ruth Miller opened her phone to the speaker. She shooed the boys from their computer game, and the library hushed.

"Mai was my mother," I said. "Her parents and big brother drowned crossing the Mekong River from Laos to Thailand. She survived. I believe she found her way to her uncle Pa Kao Vang, and his family raised her."

"You've connected to the right home," Tou said. "Mai is my auntie. How can we help you?"

Ruth Miller nudged me to talk.

"Mom died in a tornado here in Cottage Park, Iowa, on Saturday morning."

Crying and sobbing began before Tou finished his translation. After a long silence, Tou cleared his throat. "We all feel badly now," he said. "My grandparents might not respond right away."

Yet Tou's grandfather—Grandpa Vang—did respond. Tou carefully interpreted his sentiments.

"We are sorry to hear this news," Tou said. "We feel so bad for you. It is a terrible time. But we want you to know you still have us. We will be here for you. We love you. We are here to grieve with you."

This stranger, this part of my family I didn't know, was offering me something I'd never known to ask for: a place to belong.

Ruth Miller removed her eyeglasses and held a tissue over her eyes. Her assistant left her post at the front desk and dashed a Kleenex box to us. I took a tissue and wiped my eyes. Grandpa Vang's words were comforting, yet his grief and despair were additional anchors that dragged me out into deep water.

After a few minutes, Grandpa Vang asked another question, which Tou relayed, "Is your father alive?"

"Yes," I said. "But he's at a hospital, caring for my brother. He's so busy he asked me to contact you."

Tou interpreted again. "As a sign of respect, your father should have called me."

"My father wants to invite you to the funeral this Saturday at eleven a.m. in Cottage Park," I said.

Tou conversed in Hmong for a few minutes. When the conversation quieted, he said, "Will there be a Hmong funeral?"

Ruth Miller dropped the tissue from her face, poked me, and whispered loudly, "Tell them Father Gerardo is from the Philippines. He'll do his best to make the funeral as Hmong as possible."

"We will try our best to have a Hmong funeral," I said. "Our priest is good at listening to families."

Grandpa Vang cleared his throat and spoke again. Tears mingled in his words.

"Grandfather says Mai was lost while she lived and is even more lost in death," Tou said. "He says, 'I've come around the world to a land that promised me happiness. Instead, I've lost everything. My Hmong words are old. My grandchildren do not know them. They do not know me. I am alone. I am done.'"

It was a long time before anyone spoke. Instead, crying continued at the other end.

Ruth Miller prodded for closure. "Ask if they can come to the funeral."

Before I could ask, Tou ended the silence. "Thank you for calling us," he said. "I'll keep talking to my grandparents. We'll see if it's maybe possible to come to your town for the funeral."

After a moment of silence, the line disconnected.

I stared at the library computer's blank screen for the next hour, unprepared for how to begin Mom's obituary. She was tight-lipped regarding her past. She never shared her biographical information, such as her age or birthday. She wasn't sure of it herself. So, we celebrated her birthday on a day she liked, Saint Patrick's Day.

Whenever I had nagged her to tell her story, she'd ignored me, saying, "It's none of your business." I was used to that response, the unofficial motto for everyone in Cottage Park except Ruth Miller.

Now, telling Mom's story was entirely my business.

Most of what I did know had come from Puff—the pieces he'd gleaned about her early life and the pieces of their shared story. And of course, I knew about her life in Cottage Park—the pieces I shared with her.

I gathered Puff's stories and my memories, found an obituary format online to reference, and wrote,

> *Mai Vang Moriarity died unexpectedly from a tornado on Saturday, August 25, 2018, in Cottage Park. Born in Laos, Mai escaped from there as a little girl in the late 1970s to the Ban Vinai Refugee Camp in Thailand. She was adopted and grew up in the camp until immigrating to Saint Paul, Minnesota, in 1992, where she briefly attended Saint Paul public schools.*
>
> *Mai actively participated at Holy Trinity Church and in the Altar Linen Society and Church Cleaning Ministry for several years. She took pride in her garden and enjoyed making traditional Hmong family meals from scratch. Whenever anybody needed a hand, they called her first.*
>
> *Funeral services are Tuesday, August 28, at 11:00 a.m. at Holy Trinity Catholic Church in Cottage Park. Burial follows in Resurrection Cemetery.*
>
> *Preceding her in death were one brother and both parents. She is survived by her adopted father, Pa Kao Vang of Saint Paul, Minnesota, and his extended family in Thailand and America. Mai is also survived by her husband, Patrick Moriarity, and sons, John and Michael.*

No photo would grace this obituary. Our little family never took photos, especially Mom's. She'd reproached us, covered her face, and scooted away when we tried.

The *Chronicle* publishes free obituaries of any length. Most families write endlessly for their loved ones. Babies who died in childbirth received longer write-ups than I wrote for Mom.

After staring at my words for another hour, I added three lines to the ending:

In giving, she received. Mai gave her all. She leaves us with more riches than we can ever collect and carry on.

— CHAPTER FOUR —

Fast Break

Father Gerardo's voice rang out in the silence of the church. "Everyone grieves differently," he began his homily. "Respect the unique, personal response each of us has to loss, especially tragic loss."

The funeral lasted one hour, but it stretched on like a lifetime, nearly an eternity. Afterward, men shook my soft hand with their firm, calloused hands, their eyes avoiding mine. Women dabbed at their faces with tissues, patting aside mascara-polluted tears that streaked like the wet ink of a rain-soaked issue of the *Chronicle*. The air was thick with the scent of flowers and grief.

The Catholic Daughters prepared the usual funeral luncheon in the old Holy Trinity High School cafeteria: ham sandwiches in powdered white buns, potato salad, macaroni salad, coleslaw, red Jell-O with marshmallows, fruit cocktail salad, brownies, cookies, Rice Krispie bars, and powdered lemonade.

Puff sleepwalked through the funeral and reception, his eyes vacant, his hands jiggling. He kept glancing at the door, as if Mom might walk in with a tater tot hotdish for the potluck. But she didn't come. Puff heard only silence where her voice had once been.

He barreled through the fog of grief to get back to John. That's how Puff is about his sons. He'll do anything for us. Mom had handled the housework, meals, and dishes; bought and cleaned our clothes; and swept, mopped, and vacuumed the floors. She had also dusted the furniture and done all the work inside our house. And she had taken care of her garden. Puff worked, but only outside the home.

Inside, he had been dependent on Mom to do everything and hold the family together.

Puff did odd jobs umping or reffing games John and I were in. It gave us enough money to pay the bills. Mom took care of everything else, including Puff. She took care of Puff like he was another child. He was like the other fathers in Cottage Park. Their wives, too, took care of everything for them. Women ran the show in Cottage Park.

The problem wasn't that Puff changed after Mom's death. It was just the opposite. He never changed at all. He became more dependent on someone to care for him. And that someone was me.

Puff touched down a few days after the funeral. After spending the day at Mayo, he arrived back at the rectory after midnight. He sunk into the weathered leather La-Z-Boy rocker-recliner and shifted the side lever like an emergency brake until it released the footrest and the chair sprang into a reclined position. The La-Z-Boy had doubled as Puff's bed since we'd moved into the rectory.

A cool breeze lifted the sunlight-stained white lace drapes and carried the scent of rain. I closed the window, went to the fridge, and gathered a cold Grain Belt bottle and a tall frosty glass from the freezer. Puff thanked me—his words dripped like the cold sweat sliding down the bottle he emptied into the glass. Bubbles streamed from the glass bottom until they nuzzled into thick white foam at the top.

"The doctors say we're lucky Big Bad John survived the tornado," Puff said.

He guzzled a long swig, wiped foam from his lips, and set the glass on the end table partnered with his La-Z-Boy. The glass stenciled a sweat circle among a thousand other rings that betrayed the table's age and drinking history.

"He's going to require rehab and therapy," Puff continued. "There's no definite prognosis that he'll regain his balance and grip."

Puff undid the top three buttons on his short-sleeved shirt and tugged a finger into and around the collar to loosen it. He continued to fidget with the collar until he finally removed the shirt and covered himself with it like a blanket. After a few moments, he massaged his right palm heel over his heart.

We stared at the empty cabinet space where a TV set had once been.

After a while, Puff said, "I told your mom I was sorry for bringing her here. I made a mistake raising you boys in this town." He closed his eyes to change the channel to a story with a brighter future. "People only leave Cottage Park. No one comes back here. We have to leave. There's nothing for us here. No house. John's up in Minnesota. All we can do is take the insurance money and start over."

Puff didn't wait for my response. If he had, we'd still live in Cottage Park. I couldn't imagine a world outside of Cottage Park.

"We'd be cursed to stay anywhere near here," he said. "Or anywhere that resembles Iowa." He closed and reopened his eyes for a second. "Life moves on. Hopefully forward." He turned from the cabinet space to me. "We need to keep moving on and hope the bad times never catch up to us again."

I awoke the following morning in the rectory's second-floor bedroom to someone or something beating on the back door so hard the black-and-white Sacred Heart print above my bed throbbed. The right-handed Jesus with the faintest golden halo watched over me. His left hand cupped and exposed his heart, entwined in thorns. His right hand offered the same friendly two-finger salute that Iowa farmers use to greet fellow drivers on the highway.

As the pounding intensified, I jumped from the bed and threw on jeans and a T-shirt. "Hold on!" I hollered as I hopped down bare wooden stairs two at a time. I ran through the living room to the front door.

T.J. Jones—our local insurance agent and my friend Ricky's father—was standing outside. Forty years earlier, T.J. and Puff had played on the Holy Trinity baseball teams that won back-to-back summer state tournaments. Cottage Park regards those alumni as heroes. We honor them like veterans. I opened the door.

"Puff told me you'd still be asleep," T.J. said, his balding, thinning gray hair tied back in a limp ponytail hanging down his neck. He held a long box containing assorted Orlowski's Family Grocery donuts and long johns. "I'm sorry to wake you."

I waved him inside. We headed for the kitchen.

T.J. opened the refrigerator door and peered inside. "Milk or orange juice?"

"Both," I said.

He poured two glasses for me, rounded up paper towels and a plate, and set them before me. "All yours," he said, sweeping his hands generously over the pastries. "Save one or two for Puff," he added as he sat opposite me. His eyes were kind but serious. This wasn't just a social visit.

I selected chocolate long johns first, putting two on my plate. As I took a big bite, T.J. announced the purpose of the visit.

"In case you aren't aware, Puff put you in charge of helping my agency create an inventory for everything the tornado took away—a huge job with major responsibility."

I groaned, and dread filled my face.

"Now, I'll help you," T.J. said. "But your situation is unique. In all my years in the business, I've never seen a house or any real estate in such devastation. Everything is gone except the garage. We're supposed to take pictures and discuss each lost item, but my company and the mayor don't want anyone near the site. Too dangerous. What's left is roped off until they bulldoze the whole area as soon as possible."

T.J. opened his briefcase and handed me a printed list of common household items in a standard house, organized by room.

"Since you're a minor, if anyone ever contacts you from my headquarters, tell them Puff participated at every step during the process. Got it?"

I had become one of the rabbits Mom captured with homemade Hmong traps in her garden, but I signaled a thumbs-up.

"Picture us walking through your home with a movie camera, recording every object. That's the level of detail we need."

T.J. pretended to hold a movie camera with his hands, and panned like he was filming on a movie set.

"Once we document what was in each room, I'll work with headquarters to receive the highest possible price for each item. They'd fire me for saying this, so never tell anyone, but I'll calculate everything as being far better quality than the originals."

I motioned to lock my lips and throw away the key.

"Good," T.J. said. "Let's begin with the family room. I recall one nice couch, a loveseat, a recliner, two end tables, a beautiful wall lamp, and two smaller lamps on end tables. Were there two or three windows?"

I agreed at three.

"Those windows all had drapes," he said. "I remember a big throw rug. Any decorative items? Family pictures? Artwork? Porcelain figurines?"

"Nope." I wiped my lips and reached for a chocolate cake donut. T.J. poured me more milk.

"Moving on," T.J. said, "to the living room."

Again, he recited a list of standard items. I confirmed another couch, two formal chairs, two lamps, carpeting, drapes, and a framed print of Cottage Park's Memorial Field.

Then I remembered one fixture from our home that no one else in Cottage Park possessed: a pale-green jade Chinese Buddha, bald, with a huge smile and eyes creased in joy, sitting in a relaxed lotus position. His enormous belly had hung over onto the floor. He'd rested under a plastic Tiffany-style lamp on an end table.

As a toddler, I once tried to pick him up. Mom corrected me.

"Never move Buddha," she said. "This is his home." She took my fingers and delicately rubbed Buddha's stomach. "Rub Buddha's tummy for good luck." I did it every day after that, hoping it would keep Mom safe. But even good luck, too, shall pass.

"Mom's prized possession from Thailand," I said, "a jade Chinese Buddha, a little bit bigger than a baseball."

"Well," T.J. said, "I'll mark 'one solid jade Buddha.' But I'm guessing we won't find a replacement at the Kmart in Algona." He made a note on his inventory. "Where did Mai come by that?"

Instead of answering that question, I recalled John's strategy for finding morel mushrooms: "Wherever there's one," he'd say, "there are more nearby. You have to slow down and look around." He'd position himself on all fours to scan the immediate area.

I practiced the same technique. I'd found one of Mom's Hmong artifacts in my memory, so now I searched for more. It worked.

"Back to the living room," I said. "Two Hmong story cloths in fancy silver frames."

I held up my arms and stretched my hands to indicate the length of each cloth—one blue, one green. Both detailed her family's exodus from Laos, one step or two inches ahead of soldiers, racing to the Mekong, which boiled with dragons. Across the river lay buses, a refugee camp, and silver airplanes to bring the Hmong around the world.

"Let's do the dining room too," I said. "Mom had a tea set in our china cabinet with six miniature teacups, a skinny teapot, and a serving tray, all gold and dotted with rubies."

"Got it." T.J. jotted it down.

We moved through the kitchen quickly—table, chairs, toaster, microwave, mixer, plates, bowls, refrigerator. But I paused as I remembered more Hmong artifacts. Suddenly, they were everywhere.

"Mom had a huge pot on our stovetop. We never used it. We just moved it around when we needed the burner space. She also had a big wooden mortar with a pestle for making papaya salad whenever she came across fresh papayas—which seldom happened in Cottage Park or Algona. And knives like miniature swords that aren't available in stores around here."

T.J. scribbled notes. "Let's discuss the master bedroom. Puff will come into a king-sized bed from this tragedy. Next, we've got bedroom accessories: dressers, nightstands, mirrors, and drapes." He waited for me to contribute.

"Hmong brooms," I said. "Straw branches splayed at the end into fiber threads. Mom kept one in her bedroom."

"And the other bedroom—you boys' room. Two beds, two closets, and two dressers."

I thought of my artifacts. "Baseball trophies and baseballs covered our dressers—including the home run ball Joe Mauer hit into a classroom at Cretin. And two balls Puff had pitched in four state championship games."

"Priceless," T.J. said. "All gone. Just like Holy Trinity School." He stroked his ponytail. "Cottage Park is fading away. Memorial Field will be next."

Memorial Field, where I'd played a thousand games all day and night, was growing old and abandoned. There weren't enough boys to play little league anymore.

"Can I mention our plants?" I asked.

"Fire away," T.J. said.

"On John's dresser, Mom had two bamboo stalks growing in rainwater in a clear glass vase."

"I can't . . ." T.J. said, shaking his head. "I mean, where would we find those around here? The guys at corporate won't believe this case." He scanned his list again. "Back to bedrooms. Any other rooms upstairs?"

"Mom's workroom. It had a bed we never used, a window with drapes, and wood flooring with a rug. Mom retreated there to play Hmong music, do needlework on Hmong story cloths, and organize her Hmong keepsakes. She also had a sewing machine there for sewing Hmong clothing. Hmong dresses filled her closet—they were brightly colored, beaded, pleated, and wrapped in plastic casings. She had a jewelry box in there too."

I moved my hands to gesture the size.

"It held her traditional silver earrings, bracelets, rings, and a breastplate. She also had a stand holding delicate silver chains with medals—like the ones sold after Mass at Holy Trinity. One medal featured a coin-sized General Vang Pao encased in glass." I anticipated T.J.'s questions. "I don't know where she bought her Hmong-themed items or how much they cost."

T.J. paused. "I never saw your mom wear those outfits," he said. "Or her Hmong jewelry."

"Neither did I. Not even around the house. She safeguarded her Hmong items for a reason. Maybe she was saving them for Hmong weddings and funerals. But she never went to either one."

"Anything else to document?"

I said nothing. How could we document Mom or her possessions? How do you document a home with parents, children, secrets,
smells, bumps, bruises, and love?

T.J. handed me a business card. "If anything else comes to mind,
call me. I'll process all this, and we can cut a nice check."

T.J. rose, and I walked him to the door.

"Puff told me that you three will be moving away soon," he said.
"We'll miss you."

I stared at T.J. I couldn't believe Puff had told him about the
move. People in Cottage Park don't say goodbyes.

T.J. opened the screen door, stepped down cement steps into
sultry sunlight, then looked back at me.

"This move might do you good," he said. "You'll experience new
places and meet new faces." He looked down at his briefcase, then
back at me. "I moved around as a kid. I came to Cottage Park a year
older than you. When I first arrived, I shut the door and closed myself
off to Cottage Park. Opening that door"—he took a deep
breath—"was the best move I ever made. It saved my life. I hope your
move will do the same for you."

A massive bulldozer scooped our home from a hole into dump trucks
one week later. All the items I'd described to T.J.—those that hadn't
been swept away—ended up in the Kossuth County Landfill alongside countless memories.

Puff and I waited for the bulldozer to level the ground and cover
the hole neatly. No evidence existed that anyone had ever lived there,
except for the garage.

Puff had grown up in that house. After his parents moved to a
smaller, more accessible one-story home down the street, they
followed Cottage Park's custom and gifted their home to the rare
child who had stayed or returned to town. After housing three generations, our home had passed away.

Now it was our time to depart from Cottage Park.

Puff held on extra-long as he turned the ignition. Vicky sputtered to life, her engine wet-coughing like a chain smoker with emphysema.

Puff holds on extra-long with Vicky in many ways. He won't ever let her go, even though he easily could have bought a new car for all the repair bills she's racked up over the years.

He doesn't maintain her according to any schedule. He only pays her attention after a warning light glows on her dashboard, and then he takes her to Mr. Krampet at the Service Garage. Even then, Puff won't act unless Mr. Krampet *insists* a repair is needed. Usually, Puff brings Vicky back home, and we live with her new ailment.

And we'll keep living with her ailments until the day Puff sees her—in his words—"bleed out her fluids and drop her parts on the street or highway behind us."

As Vicky quivered and stretched, Puff entered the garage one last time, reemerging with two snow shovels to toss into Vicky's trunk.

"Let's go," Puff said, sliding behind the wheel. "Aren't you going to bring along your buddy?" He nodded above us to Hawk, who still rested in the hoop from the night we hooped before the tornado.

I had been so busy preparing for Mom's funeral and our move that I had no time for anything else, including Hawk. I took a running jump and snatched Hawk from the net. I buckled him into the back-seat, where I sat when Mom was alive. I rode shotgun with Puff behind the wheel.

"Funny," Puff said, though no laugh followed. "Two shovels and your basketball." He squinted. "What do you call something you take to remember a place by? 'A souvenir?'" Puff reversed down the drive-way. "Or a keepsake?"

"A souvenir is something you bring back from a trip," I said. "A keepsake is tied to a relationship and has great value. Hawk is my keepsake."

"Either way," Puff said. "That's all we're taking from Cottage Park. Say your goodbyes to everything else."

Vicky murmured, hiccupped, and belched white exhaust as Puff put her in drive and pulled out onto Elm Street. She didn't want to leave either.

"We don't stop for nothing," he said. "And we're not coming back. It'll be easier if you don't look at anyone as we leave."

Hands white-knuckling the steering wheel and eyes straight ahead, he stepped on the gas faster than usual.

I couldn't heed Puff's advice. I had to look. I lowered the window and nestled my chin on the rubber window cover. The balmy breeze rustled my hair during my last gaze at my slowpoke town.

It was six o'clock, so Elaine Powers was ending her hour-long perpetual adoration shift at Holy Trinity and ringing the Angelus bell to alert Cottage Park to pray and spread goodwill.

Bikes and trikes were catching their breath on lawns where played-out kids had dropped them after riding all day. Big friendly mongrels, that everybody knew, were now stretching and reclining on front lawns after roaming the town all day.

The elderly were parking golf carts in garages where cars had once been stabled. In an hour, they and everyone else in Cottage Park would line up at Memorial Field for the nightly baseball game. The lights were already shining.

Mourning doves were flitting onto telephone wires, like notes on a scale, to catch the soft sunrays of summer's whispered *So long*.

I would miss Cottage Park—but not the raw stench of hog manure that the breeze delivered from the confinement farm of windowless metal sheds north of town.

We drove onto Main Street, which was closed for the day except for Orlowski's Family Grocery, and the Lipstick Bar, where dull pink neon lights illuminated the word OPEN, but there were no other signs of life inside.

We drove five blocks east to northbound Highway 169.

Puff jerked down his overhead visor to block out Cottage Park more than to block out the evening sunlight of summer's end.

"Our windshield is bigger than our rearview mirror for a reason," he warned. "We're supposed to be looking forward."

Vicky's rearview mirror—held together by silver duct tape—bobble-headed in agreement.

As we accelerated, I raised my window. Puff's shoulders slacked, and he braced against the steering wheel tighter.

"Don't look back," he said.

But on our way to seventy miles per hour, we looked back at two signs as we said our own *so long* to Cottage Park. The signs marked Cottage Park's proud baseball heritage—all the times our Holy Trinity and American Legion teams had won championships.

Puff winced. "You and Big Bad John would have put a couple more state championships on that billboard. Now we'll have to win those championships in Minnesota." His jaw locked in resolve.

"Like Joe Mauer," I said.

Puff bowed. "God bless Joe Mauer."

He looked back up quickly to give the road his attention. His words hung in the air. He inhaled as an unspoken plea echoed the ache in my gut. I nodded, though he wasn't looking at me. His eyes were locked on the road.

"Still . . ." he exhaled, giving voice to that plea, "bring me back home to Mom when I die."

— CHAPTER FIVE —

Traveling

Under a black-and-blue bruised sky with ivory rain falling always just ahead of us, Puff and I wound our way up Highway 169, merged onto Interstate 90, and finally connected to Interstate 35. We searched for motels south of the Twin Cities, finding a lonely Super 8 with a few cars in the parking lot.

Once we checked into our room, Puff collapsed onto his bed, calling Mayo to check on John. He waved me over to sit with him when he connected to the station nurse on John's unit. Then he cradled the receiver between us and adjusted the volume so we could listen.

"How's Big Bad John doing today?" Puff said, his voice mingling hope and dread.

"John checked himself out of a therapy session this afternoon," the nurse snapped. "Now he's in the hallway, threatening to march outside and hitchhike to the Twin Cities. And with John's size, we would have to call for six or seven grown men to restrain him. We can't afford to wrestle with him—not with his head injury."

"Big Bad John's not easy to live with once he's made up his mind on a matter," Puff said.

"Mr. Moriarity, this is not a matter of a stubborn personality or age. Poor decision-making is a symptom of brain injury. John is an injured teenager who needs attention and support. We're all concerned about these MRIs. The doctors and the neurosurgery unit want more testing. He can't be responsible for managing his life during this time. He won't make the right choices." She sighed heavily. "We need your support to ensure he's on the road to recovery and not standing on a blacktop with his thumb out, hitchhiking in the dark. Talk to him."

"I get it," Puff said. "Can you put him on?"

"Yes, but before I do, this is where we can reach you?"

"Right," Puff said. "Room 117 at the Super 8 in Burnsville."

"Uh-oh," she said. "He's arguing with staff right now. Hold on. I'll ask him to speak with you."

We waited a long minute before hearing John's voice in the background. He was talking before he even lifted the phone.

"I want out," he said. "I'm not a kid. I don't need babysitters who want to teach me to color again."

"I need time," Puff said. "We're looking for a place in Minneapolis. I can't drive down there tonight. I can't."

"Okay," John said. "I warned you."

Puff lifted the receiver closer and held it to his mouth but then froze. John's defiance had stolen his voice.

I took the receiver from Puff. "Let me talk to him," I mouthed.

Puff eyed me warily.

"John," I said, "we know it's hard. We appreciate you following your treatment plan. We can do this. We can—"

"These creeps have me doing baby stuff," John interrupted.

"They're professionals establishing a baseline," I said. "That's their job—finding and building a program around your strengths. You've heard the expression 'It's not brain surgery'? Well, this time it is. You're at the best hospital in the world. Follow Mayo's program."

John sighed a dramatic exhale. "Maybe I'll hitchhike back to Cottage Park. Or should I meet you guys in Minneapolis?"

Puff reached for the phone, but I begged him off.

"We can't come today," I told John, my voice steady. "We'll come tomorrow. But you have to stay at Mayo until then."

"I'll give you until three p.m. tomorrow," he said.

He hung up without letting me respond.

I handed the receiver back to Puff. He held it like a run-over puppy before setting it back on the base.

"This won't be easy," he said.

We arrived at Mayo five minutes to three the next day, Labor Day. John stood outside his room, holding a grocery sack that carried his Hawkeyes T-shirt and football shorts.

Before we could leave, a social worker insisted we huddle with John's caregivers—a physical therapist, an occupational therapist, and a care nurse. The team encouraged John to stay for one more week. Usually, they explained, patients with injuries as severe as John's stayed much longer. The team looked to us to chime in, but Puff and I knew better than to try to change John's mind.

"No one doubts your strength," the social worker told John as we concluded the meeting. "But true strength knows its limits and when to accept support. We highly recommend the Courage Kenny Rehabilitation Institute in Golden Valley. It's superb for building on your strengths."

"We're already planning to look for homes nearby there," Puff said, "for Big Bad John's sake."

"Good. And follow through to receive support services in your next school," the social worker said. She handed us a folder containing brochures on support services and John's medical records.

Puff thanked her.

An awkward silence hovered between the things the social worker had just said and the things we were afraid to say. The silence continued to cloud my little family as we headed for Vicky and drove north, back to our motel.

On the way there, we listened to Joe Mauer and the Twins against the Astros. The crack of the bat and the roar of the crowd filled the car. For Puff, baseball and Joe Mauer were a lifeline—a rope that pulled him to safety when everything around him, including his family, was falling apart.

Joe Mauer had two hits and two strikeouts. After each strikeout, Puff announced, "That's a travesty. Dumb umpires. They're not lining up correctly for low-and-outside balls. No one has a better eye for a strike than Joe Mauer."

With two hands on the wheel and our little family, Puff steered us to a new life.

We drove with the windows down, the wind whipping through the car in a failed attempt to cleanse the stench of sweat and desperation clinging to us. A dead skunk lying on the side of the road added to the stench and reminded me of my little family—trapped in a cycle of rot and decaying dreams.

To make matters worse, the Astros beat us 4 to 1, twelve hundred miles away in Houston. Though Joe Mauer slugged two hits in five at-bats, the loss was our eighth in the last ten games.

We were all falling.

The next morning, Puff asked the front desk for the yellow pages to search for Realtors. The twenty-something-year-old guy behind the desk had never heard of the yellow pages. But he did allow Puff to look over his shoulder as he Googled Realtor listings for Minneapolis and its western suburbs. Puff stopped him to study an ad for Mary Berry, a woman wearing a big smile and holding a large bowl filled with fresh raspberries. Below her picture, a slogan boasted I ONLY PICK THE BEST!

Puff quickly dialed Mary Berry's number. After connecting with her, Puff explained we needed a house near the Courage Kenny Rehabilitation Institute in Golden Valley. He made no effort to hide his desperation.

"We need a place to call home—fast. Money's not an issue. I've got an insurance payout coming. What time can we meet this morning?"

Puff took out his pocket notepad and black BIC pen and scribbled a time.

"We're not from here," he continued. "Give your directions to my son, Michael." He handed me the receiver, the notepad, and the pen. "Write it down so we don't get lost."

The first action I had to take was to convince Mary Berry that I didn't have a cell phone and couldn't simply input her location and follow the online directions. When she came to believe me, she patiently offered a series of can't-miss landmarks with accompanying turns until I visualized our arrival, including a warning to slow down for a speed bump before pulling into the parking lot.

We piled into Vicky—Puff at the wheel, John riding shotgun, and me in the back seat with the directions, explaining, pointing, and repeating when to make each turn. Mary Berry's directions were perfect.

As soon as we parked at Mary Berry's office, Puff popped out and bolted inside like this would be our best shot to get our little family back on track.

Mary Berry greeted us with a big smile and a firm handshake. "Welcome to Minneapolis!" she gushed.

Puff cut through small talk. "I know school started today. We're already behind the eight ball. The clock is running. I want these boys in school as soon as possible."

Mary Berry's smile faded as she primped the front, back, and sides of her wavy pixie cut, the layers and blond highlights lining up for battle. She snapped open her postings notebook.

"We have plenty of homes to visit. It's my job to introduce you to neighborhoods, alert you to traffic issues, and place your location near shopping areas and good schools."

Puff pointed at John. "Location is priority A, number one to us. Our new home has to be near the Courage Kenny Rehabilitation Institute."

"Do you care whether you have a view, are up on a hill, or are backed up against nature?" Mary Berry asked. "Any particular house style you want to see?"

Puff hunched his shoulders. "Something simple. Any style will do if there are three bedrooms. Of course, good neighbors would be nice."

Mary Berry drove us around in a black 2018 Mercedes. John and I sank into cool, smooth black leather back seats that smelled and looked brand-new. The neighborhoods blurred by, each one a prospective start, but none of them felt right. Puff's face wrinkled in worry; he was likely thinking the same.

But the harder we searched for a home, the farther we strayed from a home. We knew it wasn't in those neighborhoods but in our memory. It was the only home we'd ever known—the home where there was no home, in Cottage Park.

For the next day and a half, Mary Berry drove us around, explaining the pros and cons of every type of house in our price range: Cape Cod, Colonial, French country, Tudor, Victorian, foursquare, American craftsman, cottage, Mediterranean, ranch, and modern.

To Puff, though, they had one glaring weakness—they weren't our old, hand-me-down home in Cottage Park. And they were all outside our price range, even with the insurance payout.

"I can't pay that money for this house," he responded glumly each time.

"I empathize," Mary Berry said after the fifteenth viewing and Puff's fifteenth glum response. "Moving is one of the great stressors in life. It takes incredible time and patience."

Even Mary Berry's enthusiasm had sagged. I could tell that our escalating dejection had worn her down.

"Maybe we should take a break from looking at houses for now," she said, pulling up to a stoplight.

Puff panicked. "No, no—I'll lower my standards. We can't quit. Let's keep going. My gosh, the boys have missed so much school."

Mary Berry mustered a big professional smile. "Listen, we're not going to quit. We're going to take a break."

She U-turned into a KFC lot and parked her car. "I have an idea. My old high school teacher is looking to rent her bottom unit. It's furnished. You can move right in if you like it—and if she likes you. She lives upstairs. Let's run over there and take a look. After you're situated there, you and I can keep an eye out for the right house. That will buy us time to consider a few foreclosures in your price range."

Puff slip-slidingly objected, "If we have to."

Fifteen minutes later, we parked at 3745 Humboldt Avenue North, in front of a spacious two-story rectangular brown stucco, more like a ship than a house. It appeared that an airplane had dropped the duplex between two ramblers, with only enough space for one person to pass between them. Below each window sat a flower box with bushy red geraniums and impatiens.

Neighbors on each side awaited us as we headed for the front doors. Curtains closed on the left after a woman spotted me looking at her through her picture window.

On the right, a shirtless man in sagging Bermuda shorts raised his cane in greeting. "Welcome to the Northside!" he called, his voice raspy and earnest. He tipped a hummingbird feeder upside down and hung it from a hook. Red nectar bubbled like a lava lamp. "Hummers are heading south," he said proudly. "I refill this bottle every three days."

Mary Berry knocked on the door to the lower unit. We waited until Mrs. Flowers opened the door wide and halfway scolded us to leave our shoes on and come inside. She hugged us as we entered, as did her intoxicating perfume—lush peonies.

On North, where everything starts with color, Mrs. Flowers has no color or all the colors. She's mixed, but a mix of all the students she's hugged at Minneapolis Thomas Jefferson High School. She's the oldest person there, our grandma.

"Keep going to the kitchen," Mrs. Flowers said, "and sit at the table. I know you all are hungry. Yesterday I made a nice mixed-fruit jam from Concord grapes, currants, and raspberries. Everything came from the garden. It'll taste wonderful on the banana bread I pulled from the oven an hour ago."

Pulling items out of a picnic basket set on the table, Mrs. Flowers sliced everyone a thick slab of warm banana bread with a chunk of butter, then dolloped jam on the side. She even had milk for me and John and coffee for Mary Berry.

For the next few minutes, Mrs. Flowers explained her garden, as Mom would have. She listed which plants had thrived and which had disappointed, speculated on the origin of her unique volunteer vegetable plants, and detailed how she prevented raccoons from coming up out of storm sewers and getting into her sweet corn.

"Mr. Moriarity," she said, interrupting herself, "do you have any people up here in Minnesota?"

"No," Puff answered. "We're the first. I hope we can stay here. It turns out our insurance compensation for our home in Cottage Park may not be enough to pay for a house like it up here."

"You'll find a home," Mrs. Flowers said. "You can't help but find home on the Northside."

As Puff described our house-hunting travails, Mrs. Flowers opened the blinds to take in her backyard garden. Six moonbeam chickens, round as soccer balls, rolled through skeletal, yellowed tomato plants, absent leaves that had long fallen away. Scrawny green tomatoes, hard as rocks, clung to withered, drooping vines. Bloated pumpkins, as round and orange as harvest moons, spread out around them.

"Keep talking," Mrs. Flowers said as she hurried into the TV room and opened the curtains. But Puff stopped, fatigued of talking about the places we couldn't afford to live in.

From where I sat at the kitchen table, I saw beyond the TV room, outside the picture window, past Humboldt Avenue North, to where Folwell Park welcomed us. It was a sporting Garden of Eden containing four softball/baseball fields plus tennis courts. No kids played at the park, but perhaps more activity was happening inside the Folwell Recreation Center. We'd passed it on our way to the duplex when Puff spotted the connected outdoor basketball court with fiberglass backboards.

"My goodness," Mrs. Flowers said as she returned to the kitchen. "You're all half asleep." She eyed Mary Berry. "They're done hunting down houses today, and I will not let them go back and stay in a horrible motel another night." She turned to Puff. "You all are staying right here tonight," she insisted.

"We could never impose," Puff said. "But Mary Berry did say you might be interested in renting this unit?"

"Why, yes, I am," Mrs. Flowers said. "Come on—let me show you the rest of it." She waited until we finished our last bites before standing and waving for us to follow her.

We entered the TV room. Two mammoth brown leather couches lay before a big-screen TV. The couches were comfortable and inviting, like the fingers on an old-fashioned catcher's mitt. Puff unloaded into one. He took the remote, switched on the TV, and sped through channels until he found ESPN. He locked onto that channel but muted it. I knew he would not want to leave that channel or the couch again.

"I don't spend time on TV," Mrs. Flowers said. "The previous couple did, so I left the cable hooked up. Would you like it to stay that way?"

Puff eyed us. The vote was unanimous.

"Yes, please," Puff said.

"Follow me," Mrs. Flowers said, "to see the other rooms."

Puff reluctantly reached for me. I towed him up, and we followed Mrs. Flowers to a bedroom. The room's high ceiling made it feel vast, unlike our cramped bedroom back home.

"The other couple made this a guest bedroom," she said.

John and I sat on our beds. I bounced on my floppy mattress, and the box springs squeaked like an orchestra tuning up before a performance.

Like the other rooms in the duplex, our room featured a beveled stained-glass design. Other rooms had flower designs, but ours was the purple heron. With tall stick legs, it stretched like a ballerina and lit up in neon blues, whites, and greens in the afternoon sun.

"You can easily move one of the beds down the hallway," Mrs. Flowers said as we followed her to a smaller bedroom. "Or this can be office space or storage. You decide."

We glanced at the room, then kept moving to a narrow bathroom. Like everything else, it had been maintained, in Mrs. Flowers's words, "to hold up as it did when it was built in the 1890s."

"All the woodwork, doors, and cabinetry," she explained, "had been harvested up north and floated down the Mississippi. Back in the day, the lumbermen walked across the river, thick with logs, from one side to the other." Mrs. Flowers smudged her toe into the floor's black-and-white checkerboard tile. "Original." She knocked on the brown marble sink and ran her hand along the lacquered black walnut countertop. "You could never replace this today."

Puff's master bedroom featured a king-sized brass bed with oversized decorative pillows along with ample space for the rocking chair to sit alongside the window.

"I'm afraid this will be too nice for us," Puff said. "How much do you want a month?"

"Well, I planned to ask for twelve hundred dollars," Mrs. Flowers said.

"Would you accept eleven hundred?" Puff said. "Until we can find a house to buy?"

Mrs. Flowers thought for a moment. "As long as you and your boys help me with house chores: mowing, raking, shoveling, and a few odd jobs and errands from time to time. I'll be eighty years old in November."

"Deal," Puff said. "The boys will do any jobs you need."

"All right," Mrs. Flowers said. "While you and Mary return for your car, the boys can pull weeds and pick mustard greens for our meal tonight."

That night, I was standing at our kitchen sink, washing the dirt off mustard greens, when Mrs. Flowers knocked on the back door a half hour before supper. Puff and John were dozing in their respective beds.

Mrs. Flowers carried a picnic basket in one hand and a vase in the other. "Put this on the table, Michael," she instructed, handing me the basket. "Then come help me pick some hydrangeas for your centerpiece."

When I joined Mrs. Flowers outside, she was studying the big hydrangea bushes that smothered the side of the duplex. She pointed to the fullest flowers for me to snip and place in her vase. After we filled the vase, we returned inside, and she placed it as a centerpiece.

I set the table while she explained the function of each shelf, drawer, and cabinet in the kitchen.

"Sorry," Puff said, walking into the kitchen from his bedroom, where he'd retired as soon as he'd returned with Vicky. "I guess sleep is catching up to me." He sat at the table and yawned long and loud.

We worked around him until Mrs. Flowers called him over to replace her at the stir-frying post. Before she left him, she dolloped a spatula of peanut butter and a heaping tablespoon of Chinese hot chili sauce onto the greens.

"Mix it all together," Mrs. Flowers directed, handing him a long wooden spoon.

I helped Mrs. Flowers unpack the picnic basket, which included a pot roast, mashed potatoes, and a green bean casserole, all swaddled in dish towels. There were also mason jars of sweet and dill pickles.

Mrs. Flowers surveyed the food and table settings, then announced, "We're ready to eat." She handed Puff a bowl and a jar of peanuts. "Sprinkle a handful of peanuts across the greens and carry this bowl to the table. Michael, go call John."

"He's sleeping," Puff said.

"Oh." Mrs. Flowers froze up, miffed.

"We let Big Bad John do as he wants," Puff said. "And he loves his sleep."

"But the food is hot," Mrs. Flowers said. "Everything is ready to eat now. We're all together. Can't he sleep tonight?" She waited for Puff to answer. "Well?"

"I suppose," Puff said. He tipped his head toward our bedroom to signal that I should awaken John.

A much happier Mrs. Flowers greeted John and me when we returned. She insisted we take our seats, then she circled the table, carrying steaming-hot bowls and platters. She scooped piles of mustard greens and garden-fresh mashed potatoes onto our plates.

"Yukon Golds!" Mrs. Flowers boasted about the potatoes.

She served herself last, then bowed. "Who would like to lead us in prayer?"

Puff directed me to proceed. I said grace, and after a hurried blessing, we ate. My little family gobbled like dogs, not looking up as we steam-shoveled food into our mouths, chewing, swallowing, and requesting more.

Mrs. Flowers finished first. She took her plate to the sink, then sat to watch us eat. After a few minutes, she left the table for her upstairs unit. When she returned, she carried a wine bottle and two wineglasses.

"I bottle my wine," Mrs. Flowers said, hitching her head toward the backyard garden and the Concord grapes that grew throughout a trellis on the garage. "From the fruit of the vine."

She popped the cork and poured Puff a glass. He thanked her, and they clinked glasses. Puff chugged half his share.

"To your new home," Mrs. Flowers said, raising her glass. "Home is where your heart is. I hope your heart is in this home and with your new neighbors."

We all raised our glasses to the toast and drank.

"I'll introduce our neighbors tomorrow," Mrs. Flowers said. "I don't want to alarm you, but our neighborhood can pop off in any direction. I'd say we're between extremes."

"But everything we've seen so far looks like Cottage Park," Puff said.

"Minneapolis is a city of prosperity," Mrs. Flowers said, "but there's an undercurrent of severe discrepancy on the Northside that's difficult to see. You have to look back into history to learn how Blacks and Jews were separated and segregated here through redlining. Follow the money—or lack thereof—in income, homeownership, unemployment, education, and poverty."

Puff took a long gulp of wine, and Mrs. Flowers refilled his glass.

"Have you heard of generational wealth?" she continued. "Our families of color inherit no wealth, only deep, never-ending generational debt manifested in neighborhoods with drug houses, assaults, burglaries, vandalism, and tagging—mostly across the lows. But we're also not far from the highs of white families with money and stability, where those issues are less prevalent. It helps that we've established a strong neighborhood watch group. Do you have a computer or a phone?"

"Not yet," Puff said.

"You'll need a computer," Mrs. Flowers said. "If cost is a problem, we can get you a free refurbished model to connect online. I'll show you how to track gunfire and stay updated in online forums."

I gathered empty plates and bowls from the table and carried them to the sink. Mrs. Flowers patted my arm as I returned to the table.

"I wish you could have moved here twenty-five years ago, when we were safer," she said. "Or thirty-five years earlier, when we were actually safe. Back in the era of two-parent families, a father typically earned enough to buy a home, and the mother could afford to stay home. Now I don't know what we'll do with crime."

She chugged more wine.

"Part of me says you can't help people who won't help themselves. But the bigger part of me believes that many of those criminals are children, and it's not too late to reach them. We *have to* help them." She turned to John and me. "They are the wilting fruit of branches grown from twisted trees with long, deep roots in chemical dependency, institutionalized racism, mental health, illegal guns, and the wrong education."

"Let's talk schools," Puff said. "I need to enroll these boys by tomorrow. I know a few schools up this way, but where do kids go to high school around here?"

"You can go to school wherever you want," Mrs. Flowers said. "Our Northside public schools hemorrhage students to schools in the suburbs, charter schools, private schools, or home schools. You can access them by a free school bus. The legion of buses driving through our neighborhood is ridiculous. You certainly have choices. Don't feel forced into anything you don't like."

John and I stretched out, careful not to be rude. Then we did what we did best—we listened. Puff had always modeled it for us, and we followed his lead.

"I'm the long-call sub at Thomas Jefferson High School," Mrs. Flowers said. "I'm there every day. It's the largest school on the

Northside—the longest-operating high school in its original building in Minneapolis. After school, I'm regularly out in the homes of our sick and injured students as a homebound teacher." She added, "Of course, Thomas Jefferson is a school with its share of problems. Every school will have its problems."

"The school the boys came from didn't have problems," Puff said.

"Once upon a time, Thomas Jefferson didn't have problems either," Mrs. Flowers said. "The problems arrived after jobs and businesses went away. Good men followed those jobs, including my husband, who took off when my son was a baby. But the Northside helped raise him, and he's become a good man. I'm very proud of him. The Northside is my family now." She focused on John and me. "Are you boys getting enough to eat?"

We assured her we were full. Still, she spooned the remainder of the mashed potatoes into piles on our plates.

"I've never been to Cottage Park," Mrs. Flowers said. "But I'll bet if you get a flat tire there, a Good Samaritan pulls over immediately to help you. Am I right?"

"Every time," Puff said.

"And why do you suppose that is, John?" She narrowed her focus on John.

"Because," Puff said, "everybody—"

Mrs. Flowers raised a hand to halt Puff from speaking, then waited for John to respond. We all waited.

"Everybody knows each other," John said.

"Ah," Mrs. Flowers said. "Well, let me tell you how it works here. If you have a flat, people will pull over even faster on the Northside than they do in Cottage Park. And not just one car will pull over. I've had two or three cars come to my rescue at the same time. Even if people here don't know you, they know your problem, and they'll drop everything to stay with you until they fix it. We all have problems up here. Big ones that the community is ready to jump in and help us with. When we see another poor soul with a problem, we help them. We remember how we've been helped, and we pass it on.

There's no better place to be than the Northside if you have a problem." She winked. "You're forewarned."

Mrs. Flowers topped off Puff's wineglass. She now turned to John and me.

"There's one simple rule to succeed at Thomas Jefferson and on the Northside: Give respect, get respect. Once you get respect, you'll have loyal friends and a community for life. You'll come to love this place as I do."

"Which school is closest, though?" Puff said.

"Easy," Mrs. Flowers said. "Thomas Jefferson."

Puff's next question drilled down harder, zeroing in on a factor more vital than location or academics. "Do they have a good baseball team?"

Mrs. Flowers's words slowed after she gulped her wine. "Yes, we have a team. Last year, we had a German foreign exchange student on the team. He could really play soccer, but not so much second base. He blocked ground balls by kicking them. By the time he picked up and lobbed the ball to first base, the runner stood safe on the bag. Fly balls created an even bigger adventure."

My little family laughed.

"You've got to be kidding me," Puff said, growing serious. He rolled his eyes.

"The boys lose games, lose interest, and lose heart," Mrs. Flowers said. "Eventually, they quit the team. I like baseball. I go to all their games, but for the last two years, we've forfeited the season's last few games."

"You had me on Thomas Jefferson until now," Puff said. "Baseball is bottom-line up front for us. What's another nearby school with a team?"

"No." Mrs. Flowers put her wine down. "Plant these two boys on our team, and our Thomas Jefferson boys will come out and play. No one likes to play on a losing team. Of course, you could take the boys to another school, and that team would be better. Or you could create a team here at Thomas Jefferson and play baseball with boys hungry to win. You can help them achieve victory on a baseball field—maybe for the first time in their lives."

Puff leaned back, stunned.

"I'm serious," Mrs. Flowers said. "As two strokes and a heart attack."

Puff sat up and set his wineglass on the table. "When Big Bad John pitches," he boasted, "no team at Thomas Jefferson—and you can set up folding chairs out on the field behind him—will lose." He turned to John. "We're going to have Michael catch you."

"Sounds good," John said.

"I'm not a catcher," I piped up. "I can't catch John. He's too fast." I never could have uttered those words in Cottage Park, where the community was only as strong as its weakest link.

But my concern was lost on Puff, who stopped zooming to a future where his boys were galloping in on white horses, long enough to look at me. "You'll catch John. More than likely, you'll also have to start pitching."

I was the worst pitcher ever, even crummier than I would be trying to catch John. But no amount of logic would ever convince Puff that I was correct in my baseball self-inventory.

Puff turned to Mrs. Flowers. "Michael has been playing or watching baseball all his life, and he still doesn't get it. The catcher is the smartest player on the field because he dictates the game, decides what pitch will be thrown and where, and positions players so that if there is a hit, they can make the play. The catcher knows the future because he knows what happens next. Michael can learn how to catch Big Bad John, but you can't teach someone how to think about the game. And Big Bad John trusts Michael. Besides, Joe Mauer was a catcher—the best." Still looking at Mrs. Flowers, Puff signaled like a hitchhiker going my way. "This kid, Michael, is the smartest player on the field."

Puff's analysis of my baseball potential hit me like a judge announcing my life sentence. I was now on death row as I approached the upcoming baseball season. John and Mrs. Flowers saw the horror that etched my face. For once, I didn't know what John was thinking, but Puff was already shaking off any notion that Thomas Jefferson would ever lose another baseball game.

"I'm definitely going to help coach this Thomas Jefferson team," Puff said. His following proclamation foretold our enrollment plan and predestined accomplishments.

"You two boys can work miracles," Puff said. "And your first miracle will be a championship baseball team at Thomas Jefferson."

— CHAPTER SIX —

No Call

The next day, Friday, September 7, at 7:30 a.m., Puff navigated Vicky around a block dominated by Thomas Jefferson High School. The three-story rectangular brick building loomed over the neighborhood like a relic from another era. Its many large windows stared out in all directions over small, mostly one-story homes. The year 1926 was carved into a cornerstone, a testament to the building's nearly century-long longevity.

Puff parked Vicky in an open parking spot across the street from the school's main entrance, marked by a worn-out sign labeled as door 1.

"This is the castle I talked to you about the night of the tornado," Puff said.

John and I were bewildered.

"Remember when I said you two would capture a castle? I told you no one could defend against Michael's catapult or Big Bad John's battering ram."

We walked by a flickering electronic marquee that scrolled the wrong date, April 15, and outdated back-to-school events from August 2017. The time, 7:37 a.m., and temperature, 83 degrees, were the only accurate details.

A pellet gun or volley of rocks had dented a large tin sign at the front of door 1 that warned MINNEAPOLIS PUBLIC SCHOOLS BANS GUNS IN SCHOOL BUILDINGS AND GROUNDS. I held the door for Puff and John.

Red and gray lockers lined the hallways like terra-cotta warriors. Puff led us by them to the attendance office. It was an hour before first period. So few students were in school that when lockers clattered, the echo traveled down the hallways. The faint smell of industrial cleaner lingered in the air.

We approached an office cubicle with a sign that read ATTENDANCE CLERK and another sign at the front of the ledge that read DO NOT LEAN ON LEDGE. We stood a few feet away on a shiny wooden floor and waited until the attendance clerk swiveled in her chair.

"How can I help you?" she asked curtly. She had determined eyes, and her name tag identified her as Ms. Gomez. Her desk was cluttered with stacks of paper, a nineteen-ounce spray can of Original Scent Lysol Professional, and a digital retirement countdown timer that blinked like a votive candle: 4 years, 13 days, 6 hours, 27 minutes.

"We're the Moriaritys from Cottage Park. I want to enroll my two sons here," Puff said, his voice urgent. "They're excellent students and athletes." He handed her the folder from Mayo. "This excuses Big Bad John from gym class for a while."

Ms. Gomez pinched the folder as if it were infected before picking up her phone. "I'll give this to a social worker," she said, her expression flat. She spoke into the receiver, her words deliberate, then turned back to us. "I can schedule your enrollment appointment on"—she scrutinized a calendar on her cubicle wall—"Monday, to start your sons in school."

Puff shifted from side to side and scratched the back of his neck. His plaid shirt clung to him, damp under the arms, and his forehead glistened with sweat. He'd figured he'd complete our enrollment paperwork and send us off in time for our first class.

"Why Monday?" he said. "My boys have already missed three days of school."

"Actually," Ms. Gomez responded, "they've also missed five days from the previous week." Her tone was objective like a highway patrolman's. "Minneapolis starts before Labor Day, a week before all other schools in Minnesota. You're not the first family to trip up in that confusion. Your sons missed five days last week plus three so far this week. But I still can't schedule you for today. Two families already scheduled appointments. That's why the earliest we can work you in is Monday."

Puff's jaw tightened and his face flushed red. This was all uncharted territory. No newcomers ever came to North Kossuth. But here, his boys were being treated like problems instead of scholars.

The social worker arrived, a bendy man with a pencil tucked behind his ear and a walkie-talkie clipped to his belt. Ms. Gomez presented him with John's folder.

"That's for John's exemption from gym class for a while," Puff explained again, his voice edging with frustration.

The social worker flipped through the documents. His eyes narrowed, and he bit down hard on the pencil's eraser. "Did you read what's in this folder?"

Puff played off the question. "I skimmed it."

"Well, it's much more than a gym exemption," the social worker said. His voice was calm—too calm. "Mayo expresses legitimate concerns regarding John's head injury. They recommend a special education assessment."

He turned to Ms. Gomez, his expression grim.

"We can process Michael on Monday," he said. "Regarding John, though, it'll take time before I can pull together an assessment team to plan with him and his father. We'll have to see if our team agrees with Mayo's recommendations. He shouldn't begin school until we get everything in order."

Ms. Gomez nodded, her eyes flicking to the retirement count-down timer. Thirteen minutes had evaporated since we'd arrived.

Below the countdown timer was a picture pinned to the cubicle's fabric panel. A miniature white poodle dressed in a pink tutu with a matching pink beret was balancing on her hind legs while maintaining her focus and smile for the photographer. Handwritten at the top of the picture was the name FUFU.

The social worker unclipped his walkie-talkie and spoke into it. "Can an administrator assist us in the attendance office?" His movements were quick and precise, like a juggler.

"Unbelievable," Puff muttered. He shifted again from side to side and scratched the inside of his ear.

"What's the problem?" a harried woman snapped as she entered the office. She lowered her eyeglasses to study her suspected problem—Puff—up and down. Then she directed her frustration at her other problem—the social worker. Her name badge read DR. POLLY PORTER, PRINCIPAL.

I would later learn from Harden that she's a retired Minneapolis Public Schools principal assigned to Thomas Jefferson as an interim.

"This report from Mayo," the social worker said, handing the report to Dr. Porter.

She two-hand-stiff-armed to block his offering. "Tell me what it says."

"It recommends a special education assessment for this new student." The social worker motioned to John.

Dr. Porter's eyes did not follow. "Follow through on its recommendations. I have an appointment waiting in my office." Her lips pressed into a thin line, and she turned and left.

The social worker rolled his eyes. "Fed up," he muttered before turning to Puff. "Can I make a quick copy of this?" he asked, holding up the folder.

"You can keep it," Puff said as he walked away to door 1.

As John and I followed, I believed we'd never step foot in the Thomas Jefferson attendance office again.

I was surprised, then, when Puff delivered me back to the Thomas Jefferson attendance office on Monday morning. As Puff patiently completed the enrollment paperwork, a steady stream of students presented Ms. Gomez with excuse notes for why they'd missed Friday or needed to leave school early today.

When the paperwork was complete, Ms. Gomez handed me an excuse to class, my schedule, and a student planner. The planner was red and gray, the school colors. On the cover, the school mascot, Thomas Jefferson, pointed a musket at whoever held the planner. Ms.

Gomez instructed me to ask each teacher to initial my schedule as I entered class.

"A student volunteer will be here shortly to give you a tour and help you locate your classrooms," she said, though her tone suggested it might not happen.

I quickly reviewed my schedule with Puff before he had to go: English, choir, biology, geometry, lunch, Mandarin, and geography.

"You're going to have a great day," Puff said, fist-bumping me. His smile was forced, but his eyes flickered hope. "You'll love Thomas Jefferson. Go get 'em, Michael." Then he turned and walked out of the attendance office.

They say you come into and leave this life alone. That's also true on your first day at Thomas Jefferson. When the assigned student volunteer failed to show, I set off toward my first period alone.

I walked through dark, quiet, and cool hallways, like tunnels, on my way to room 139. Just me and the lockers. First period had already started.

When I arrived at the door of English class, I rechecked myself. I cuffed the sleeves of my new, starched white dress shirt and tucked the shirttails into my zipped blue khakis. As Puff says, "You get one chance to make a first impression".

I took a deep breath as I gripped and turned the metal door's slender, cold stainless steel handle. The handle held firm—locked.

I peered down the endless hallway, looking for an adult to help— no one. I gently knocked on the door. No one responded. A booming teacher lectured on the other side.

I quietly jiggled the handle a few times, waited a minute, and knocked again, louder. Inside, the class laughed. Still, no one came to the door.

I tried once more to yank the handle and pull the door. Not today. My only option was to head for the choir room and be on time for second hour.

I was taking my first steps in that direction when a hallway aide, even bigger than John, called out from down the hall.

"Hold on," he said as he ambled toward me, huffing to catch his breath.

I was awestruck. He was the biggest man I had ever seen. His chest stuck out like the home plate umpires in Cottage Park who wore inflatable chest protectors under their shirts.

I did hold on, because I couldn't do anything else. The man had no neck, but a large head gobbled up by mountainous shoulders. He absorbed the hallway's dim light as well as the words that filled my mind and raced to my tongue, which I bit, *Did you play in the NFL?*

"I'm Williams, and you're coming with me." I strained to hear his words. He strained to say them. "We're in Sweeps Week. We sweep the halls clean once the bell rings to start class. You late to class this far into the year—you should reflect on that for a spell in the Citizenship Room. Follow me."

"It's my first day," I said, holding up my schedule and student planner as evidence. "The attendance clerk told me to go to class. I tried, but the door's locked."

Williams frowned. "The first lesson you'll learn here is to speak up. We can't read minds."

He shivved a key into the handle. The lever swung down, and the door opened.

"Mr. Lane," Williams announced to the buttoned-up classroom, "new student for you."

I stepped through the doorway, but a short, bald, muscle-bound man in a tight-fitting T-shirt and new-looking blue jeans flexed as he hurried to block my entrance.

"Wait right there," he told me.

He glared beyond me to Williams, who was already backing away into the hallway.

"How long will you keep bringing me kids?" Mr. Lane said to Williams. He pointed at me. "He's missed nine days already, and he's late on day ten. We used to draw the line around here for taking new students at seven absences. How am I supposed to give this guy a passing grade?"

"No one seems to know," Williams said as he backed away. "I found him standing outside your door. Do what you can do." Then he stopped and looked back. "I can escort him to the Cit Room today, if you want."

"Forget it," Mr. Lane said, stepping aside just enough for me to squeeze through. His head cocked, and his eyes aimed at me, locked and loaded. "You're on strike two," he said loud enough for everyone to take note. "You've missed so many days. You come in late—"

"And you hated how Bob knocked at the door," a voice called from across the room. "You said Bob sounded like a rat scratching a loony bird lotto ticket."

I recognized that voice. It was Pat Bev. He called anyone he didn't know, or didn't want to know, Bob.

I'd seen Pat Bev at the rec center over the weekend. He and Curry, Westbrook, and LBJ were a set—Harden's set, the Harden Set. Unlike the other Harden Set members, who wore their hair freshly cut, short, and crisp, Pat Bev combed his wispy Afro straight back on the top and sides—the way Frederick Douglass presented himself in the mosaic mural at door 1.

I peeped now at Pat Bev. He was sitting as close as possible to Harden without touching him. I already knew that Harden was the center of the basketball universe at the rec center. It was clear he was the center of the school universe too. Harden's attention to his Harden Set members was vital to them in both places.

Mr. Lane stink-eyed me. "It's not fair to waltz in here late in the semester and receive a grade that corresponds with the grade of those"—he theatrically waved his arms to encompass my new classmates—"who enrolled on time and have attended since day one."

He stroked his chin, equally bald as his head, and pondered a course of action.

"I do not promise anything. However, I'll let you take a seat. But miss one more day or come late for any reason, and I do promise to give you an application for summer school." He smiled to himself. "Which, by the way, I also teach."

He gazed wistfully above the class and recited:

But to go to school in a summer morn,
O! it drives all joy away;
Under a cruel eye outworn,
The little ones spend the day

In sighing and decay.

A long inhale whistled through his nose. He exhaled silently, like trying to hold a drag from a cigarette.

"That, my sweet little headaches, is actual poetry from William Blake's 'The School Boy,' written a few years before I was born, in 1789. You're not likely to discover this beauty in rap-is-crap." He flashed back at me and pointed to a desk before him. "Now sit."

I headed for the desk, then stopped. "Oh—I forgot," I said, presenting him my schedule. "The attendance clerk said I should—"

"I don't care about or engage in that nonsense," Mr. Lane said, cutting me off. "Take your place. I mean, my God—don't you feel awful that you've wasted enough of our time today?"

"Yes, I do," I deferentially agreed.

Everyone laughed except for Mr. Lane, whose eyes pierced mine.

"Stay in your lane," he growled as I sat.

Mr. Lane marched to his desk, grabbed a stapled packet, and delivered it to me.

"It's a syllabus," he said. "Read it—not now, but later—if you want any chance to earn a passing grade and credit for this course."

Harden raised his hand. Mr. Lane acknowledged him.

"You recited that poem differently for the last new student," Harden said. "You said, 'The little ones spend the day, in sighing and *dismay.*'"

"Good catch," Mr. Lane said. "I employed artistic license—in this case, exchanging the word *decay* for *dismay*. I took the liberty to exchange a stronger word to drive home the point that you should all work your hardest to pass this class. As much as you all love Mr. Lane—and I assure you, the feeling is mutual—summer school with Mr. Lane is no one's ideal happy place."

"Isn't that a lie, though?" Harden pressed. "You're not reciting the poem truthfully."

"I'm embellishing the truth," Mr. Lane said. "Blake would understand this wretched context and appreciate the addendum. If not, I'll burn in hell for eternity."

He reviewed the aisles from top to bottom, eyeing each student.

"Trigger alert: Unfortunately, many, if not all of you, will no doubt join me there." Mr. Lane stuck up his chin as he gaped downward at the horror of hell. "And oh, I'm aware you'll stampede home and tell Mommy that mean old Mr. Lane is forcing his religion down your throat. Good. I'll give her the same response I give you: Tough toenails. There is a hell, and if I had my way, we'd have a big banner at door 1 that says ABANDON ALL HOPE, YE WHO ENTER HERE."

"And when your parents inevitably discover that Mr. Lane is prejudiced, I would ask you to share the heartwarming story of when I came to Thomas Jefferson, over thirty years ago, first as a substitute teacher. Full disclosure: Initially, I did not like Blacks. But now, after all that time, including a ten-year simultaneous graveyard stint driving the Metro 5 bus on our beloved Northside, I can truthfully proclaim, I dislike Blacks even more, and every other race and creed in equal proportion." Mr. Lane paused before exhaling in dismay. "Now, for God's sake, let's move on."

I fumbled for my pen and notebook, but I was too shook-up.

"As I was saying, the personal narrative makes up twenty-five percent of your grade." His eyes locked on me again. "You, in particular, will need one helluva personal narrative, Mr. Wise Guy." He then addressed the class. "But your personal narrative is about more than your grade. Who can tell our new friend why it's paramount?"

This time, Pat Bev raised his hand. Mr. Lane nodded at him.

"If you don't tell your story," Pat Bev said, "somebody else will. And it won't be as good as if you tell it. You don't tell your story, it never happened. You never happened. You don't exist."

"Correct," Mr. Lane said. "Storytellers rule the world. Good stories live on for as long as we tell them. As do their authors."

He checked his watch and winced at its harsh proclamation that time was frittering away. He soldiered on.

"The first component of a personal narrative is the exposition. Who are the characters in your story? Where does it take place? And what is the problem or event driving your personal narrative?"

As I sat at that front-row desk on my first day of school, I already knew the answers to those questions. My personal narrative would focus on my little family's move from Cottage Park to the

Northside. And when it was complete, I'd send it to Joe Mauer, who would rescue us.

A few nights later, after an Irish Night dinner of baked potatoes and ham, Hawk and I escaped to the rec center and shot at the outdoor baskets. Before long, cold rain sprinkled dots across the white concrete court, and those dots then connected into slippery black stars. Soon, the whole court was a black hole, drawing me in until I took cover in the gym.

I wasn't comfortable shooting in the gym. At the side baskets, I had to carefully rebound Hawk after each shot, keeping him from ricocheting into the players rocketing past me in full-court games.

The Harden Set, all between six-two and six-four, raced up and down the floor. Their sneaks cheeped across the floor like day-old broiler chicks at the Cottage Park Hatchery. Together, the Harden Set made music—nimble fingers thumping a ragtime piano melody. Those fingers tightened into a fist to smash the keys like teeth if threatened.

Two teams waited to play the winner, which was always the Harden Set. Standing beyond the out-of-bounds line, each challenger compacted his muscles into a tight jack-in-the-box, then burst high to release imaginary jump shots.

Harden spearheaded the Harden Set up the floor as fast as possible on offense. Always playing without shirts, they drove hard to the hoop for acrobatic layups, regardless of the defender's size. They never backed down.

Everyone crashed the boards for rebounds and raced down the floor to exploit mismatches. They followed with the best offense, a swarming man-to-man defense.

Pat Bev shimmied, preened, and woofed whenever he scored or forced a turnover. "I straight-up kilt Bob! Get a body bag!" Ten fists fighting together provided the cover for him to run his mouth and add trash-talk salt to fresh wounds.

Through all this, inevitable collisions resulted in foul calls and caustic disagreements concerning the player's manhood. A predictably heightened dispute occurred at the end of the game. To settle the disagreement, Harden released a shot from outside the three-point line—a prayer to the basketball gods. The shot would go in if the gods weighed in Harden's favor.

The end result of Harden's shot and chance for the return-of-the-ball salvation was a solid brick and his giving up the ball. Still, he never gave up.

The Harden Set never attempted three-pointers in their one-point-per-bucket games to 11. Unlike the real James Harden, who made three-pointers with two guys hanging on him, this Harden clanked horrific bricks off the rim or backboard, each uniquely miserable. And he was the set's best three-point shooter.

Like the others, I noted the Harden Set's abundance of good and bad play. But I had no reason to get myself drawn into that drama. While those guys exercised their jaw and tongue muscles, I shot around near the hoop.

I kept to short shots at first, shooting with my right hand only to strengthen right-hand dominance. Next, I practiced fishhooking to steer Hawk from knuckleballing and floating away. Knuckleballs cause air balls, which wither, droop, and die before reaching their destination. And to teach myself to follow my shot, I rushed to rebound Hawk before he bounced on the floor.

After an hour, Harden came over. The Harden Set was between games.

"Hey, Country," he said, both curious and challenging. "What are you trying to prove? No one comes here just to shoot around. Why don't you ever call next? All you gotta say is 'I got next.'"

"No thanks," I said. "I have my own game to work on."

"But out here," he said, tilting toward the Harden Set, who were already jawing with the challengers, "you learn if your game is for real. You're going out for the team, aren't you? Tryouts are less than two months away."

"Thursday and Friday, October twenty-fifth and twenty-sixth," I said. "It's marked on our calendar at home. That's what I'm playing for. That's my next."

Then Harden cursed my mother and called me the N-word, which I can't say or even write.

"Next game is always next," he said. "Basketball is a team sport. The real game is getting to know people, because that's the best way to get to know yourself. I'm just saying." He turned back to the court, then at me. "You better bring peeps when you play here. Loners don't last long."

He scrutinized me to make sure his message was received, then walked back to take the court. The Harden Set played their next game.

So did I.

Almost everyone stopped when Coach, the rec center manager, ended the games at ten o'clock. The exception was the Harden Set, who were allowed to play on. I would later learn that Coach was Harden's dad.

Coach wore polished black steel-toed workman's boots bigger than my size 14s. The shoestrings strained to contain his feet and gave up on any effort to cover his thick ankles and calves halfway up his boots. Faded carpenter blue jeans, meticulously pressed, also failed to cover up the long leg, thigh, and hip muscles threatening to burst through. He looked as if a sloppy bricklayer had spread extra muscle mortar between brick muscles in places I'd never seen before. His neck, as straight and thick as a fire hydrant, extended to a face as dark and rich as the soil in Mom's old garden, the same soil blanketing her grave.

I exited the gym with the others, while contemplating the ones who stayed behind, who moved as one, who fed off one another's energy. I wanted the skill, domination, and belonging that went with circling Harden in his universe. I would have sold my soul to the devil to grind with the Harden Set and discover next with them.

— CHAPTER SEVEN —

Box Out

On Monday, September 17, the Thomas Jefferson social worker called to notify us they'd finally assembled the necessary staff for John's assessment meeting, scheduled for the next morning. By that point, John had missed three weeks of school. That was no skin off his back.

What bothered him was the thick manila envelope we'd received from the school. It listed the Thomas Jefferson and district professionals who would be attending the meeting: the principal, the social worker, the school nurse, a speech clinician, an occupational therapist, a physical therapist, a special education resource teacher, and one classroom teacher.

In addition, a parent-advocacy brochure outlined John's rights during the meeting. It encouraged him to contribute his invaluable insights during the assessment and weigh in on his individual education plan, if one should be warranted.

John glimpsed at the envelope's contents and handed them to Puff, who hot-potatoed them to me. I flipped through the paperwork as we sat at the table for supper. It was Walking Taco Night.

John opened a snack-sized sack of Cool Ranch Doritos and jammed in a heap of taco-seasoned ground beef. Next, he strangled an easy-squeeze bottle of Hidden Valley Original Ranch until the dressing drooled over his beef-and-chips mix. Since moving to the Northside, we'd squeezed it on everything.

"This all looks good," I said, stuffing the papers back in the envelope and setting it on the table. "You should be pumped—along with the academic assessment, they'll do fine motor skills testing, which will show where you're at with gripping and throwing a baseball."

John said, "I'm not nuts."

"Definitely not," Puff said. "But Thomas Jefferson is our new team. How can it hurt if they want to be certain you're okay to play on their team? Let's show these people we're not hooligans."

"That principal will hound me until I go to her special classes," John said. "I don't need any help."

He set his walking taco on the table, lifted the mammoth envelope with his humongous hands, ripped it and its contents in half, then deposited the pieces into our kitchen wastebasket. Now free from the meeting's worrisome details, John devoured his walking taco and built another.

"I don't want to end up as Thomas Jefferson's official science experiment," he said, his eyes locked on the ranch bottle.

Puff rummaged through the wastebasket, hoping the paperwork could be salvaged. "I wish you hadn't done that," Puff said. Any effort to save the paperwork would be futile. He turned toward me. "I just want to do the right thing for you boys, but I can't fight this by myself. You need to sit in on that meeting with us tomorrow."

I sat back in my chair and despaired. I'd become the circus worker in charge of following the elephant, John, with a scoop shovel to clean up his poop. How do you train an elephant to clean up after itself?

Mom would have stood on a chair and shot daggers down at him. She would have made him attend the meeting, whether he wanted to or not. She carried a big stick and relished using it. Her threats were successful. She backed them up by not backing down.

Puff and I did not stand on chairs. We sat on them. And on our hands.

Now no one could make John do anything.

The next day, at 7:30 a.m., we gathered around a long table in the principal's office. Dr. Porter introduced herself first. She turned to her right to prompt the next person to continue the introductions. One by one, Thomas Jefferson staff and district representatives introduced themselves and explained their roles in the proposed assessment.

Eventually, Puff introduced himself and nudged me to continue.

"I'm Michael Moriarity—John's brother."

I looked for the introductions to continue, but Dr. Porter stopped the meeting.

"Wait a minute," she said. "I'm confused." She reviewed her notes, looked at the social worker, then me. "Are you the young man we're planning for today?"

"No," I said.

Dr. Porter's pen began tapping impatiently on her desk. "Well," she said, "where is he?"

"Waiting outside your office," I said.

"First off," Dr. Porter said, "why aren't you in class?" She waited for me to open my mouth, only to immediately cut me off. "Go to class."

She pinched out a pink hallway-pass pad, wrote on the top, then ripped away the completed pass. She handed it to me.

"And on your way," she said, "tell your brother to come in here and join us."

I half rose until Puff pulled me down.

"Michael can stay here," he said. "And John can stay where he's at too."

"Mr. Moriarity," Dr. Porter said, now locking eyes on him, "I am doing my absolute best to help with this situation. But I also need you and both of your sons to do your absolute best. Instead, you're presenting us with a perfect storm of obstacles."

"I know about perfect storms," Puff grumbled. "We survived one. This one's a sprinkle."

Dr. Porter spread her arms over the table. "We're all here today because the Mayo Clinic recommended we provide"—she rechecked her notes—"*John* with a special education assessment. He may need an individual educational plan, and he's already missed three weeks of school. We can't help him if he won't sit at the table with us."

Puff shook his head.

Dr. Porter stood with a humph, walked to her office door, and opened it. From my vantage point, John sat with his chin over his hooked wrist and the back of his hand like *The Thinker*.

"John," she said, her voice patiently low-key stern, "would you come join our meeting?"

"No," he said. "No way."

"Please," Dr. Porter said. "We want to help you, but we can't begin until we meet you."

She waited for a response, then tried again.

"You can sit by your father and your brother."

John sat up straight with his back against the wall. "I'm never coming in there. Not today. Not ever."

Dr. Porter took a deep breath. When she spoke again, her voice softened. "John, if we can't assess you, we can't help you. And if we can't help you, you'll only fall further behind. This process isn't just about today. It's about your future."

When John didn't respond, Dr. Porter stepped back from the doorway and returned to her seat.

The speech clinician spoke first.

"John may be intimidated by our group's size," he said softly. "He may also be struggling with comprehension and expression issues. Perhaps I can accommodate by sitting with him for a few minutes and—"

Dr. Porter held out her hand. "I'm not going down that road." She took another deep breath. "I know it would be preferable to have John attend his assessment meeting, but we'll have to move on without him." She waved a hand at Puff. "Mr. Moriarity, since John is a minor, we'll have you sign off on the assessment instead."

"I won't sign off on any plans unless Big Bad John agrees," Puff said.

"Make me the bad guy, if you must," she said. "I'm used to it."

Puff pushed himself upright in his chair. "Look, this whole thing is a waste of everyone's time without Big Bad John's buy-in. Why can't we skip all this and enroll him as you did Michael or any other student?"

"We must follow Mayo's direction," Dr. Porter insisted. She spread her arms across the table again. "Put yourself in our position—we're caring professionals who want to help John during this difficult time. We need you and him to work with us. He needs an assessment and likely an individual education plan."

"My son sees this process differently," Puff said. "I wish that weren't the case. Big Bad John has made up his mind, and I can't change it. I don't believe anyone else can either." He turned to the speech clinician. "Not even this nice man, here, willing to go the extra mile."

"In that case," Dr. Porter said, her tone lowering, "you can find another school more to your liking. You could even homeschool."

"Our Realtor graduated from here," Puff said, tapping the table with a determined finger. "And Mrs. Flowers said this would be a good school for my boys. We're gonna follow her advice."

"Mrs. Flowers?" Dr. Porter sucked her cheeks and soured her lips. "With all due respect, Mrs. Flowers isn't an expert on student placement."

"John has every right to consider his educational options," the social worker interrupted. "But until he makes his final choice, we're obligated to plan for his enrollment here in the least restrictive environment."

The social worker's chest slouched as if he wished to continue this discussion with Dr. Porter in private. Instead, Dr. Porter wrung her paperwork through her bony hands before backhanding his due process lesson and refocusing on Puff.

"You do understand," she said, "if we can't resolve this matter, we'll all end up in court."

Puff flipped up his palms to signal he'd let go and let God sort it out.

"Get John into classes today," Dr. Porter ordered the social worker. "I'll assign Mr. Williams to shadow him until all this is resolved."

I knew then, and still know now, that I don't vibe with Dr. Porter. No one does. They call her Old Parrothead.

Every Sunday at 7:00 p.m., she sends a robocall to all families outlining the student misbehavior she wants parents to address before the upcoming week. Puff calls the messages "upcoming incoming," meaning incoming missile fire. In the messages, she goes off on clothing, especially the lack or "incorrect" usage of it: sagging pants, basketball jerseys over bare skin, or leggings worn as pants. She also makes doomsday predictions of where we'll rot if we don't show up for school on time and aren't prepared to work hard.

She ends her one-minute calls with her hashtag: "I'll be watching you."

And now she ended our meeting by standing, circling her pointer finger toward the staff, and leaving. Whatever the gesture meant, it worked. The staff gathered their materials, stood, then silently left the room.

Before making his way out, the speech clinician turned to Puff. "Thank you for the compliment," he said. He gave a wry smile. "This will work out. You can't keep a good man like John down. He'll be back up soon. Life always goes on at Thomas Jefferson."

"There you go," Puff said, focusing on me. "Now it's up to you to make this happen. I can't leave this office until you get John started in class. You can do this." Puff's wave goodbye also served as an invitation and a turning signal toward the door, where John awaited me. I joined him.

"What's happening?" John said. "What do we do now?"

"We wait for a guy named Williams," I said. "He'll take care of us and you."

John followed me out into the hallway, where Old Parrothead was barking orders at Williams. From his pained expression, Williams appeared to pass a large kidney stone once he grasped his new role as John's one-to-one paraprofessional.

"I get that you need somebody," Williams said to Old Parrothead, "but first I need to run all this by someone at the union."

"Williams will take you to your classes," I said.

From the agonized expression on John's face, he viewed personalized oversight from Williams in the same manner.

Old Parrothead ended her meeting with Williams in the same way she had dismissed a room of teachers and staff a few minutes earlier: She gave Williams the finger, circling her pointer finger at him and toward us. She left him to find his way.

Williams trudged over. Without looking at either of us, he grumbled, "Follow me."

The three of us walked down the hall to drop me off in room 139 for English. As we walked, John and Williams ranted to themselves, but just loud enough that I could hear them—John on my left ear, Williams on my right.

John's yammering was predictable. "Watch me. I'll never set foot in a classroom here. Looks like I'll be heading back to Cottage Park to stay with Coach Woj (short for Wojtek—the wrestling coach who had invited him to live with his family until he graduated). "If that doesn't work out, I'll go to one of the schools that Mrs. Flowers mentioned."

I focused on Williams's mutterings, which were much more interesting. He also began with the same command for his future: "I graduated from here, one of four staff who still live on North. I've held this place together for twenty years. And no one listens or cares what I say. She has no idea what I do for twenty-eight dollars and seventy-six cents an hour. Morning and afternoon breaks are *always* interrupted by Code Reds because these teachers refuse to break up fights. So, why is that only *my* job? How do I house my sister and her three little kids on the measly pay they dole out here?"

Williams shivved his key into the steel door at room 139, and Mr. Lane pounced toward us.

"Stop!" Mr. Lane said, motioning us out of his room.

"Not hearing it," Williams said, holding up his own hand stop sign. "Not in the mood today. You'll have to do what you can do." Williams continued to hold up his hand and spoke before Mr. Lane could continue. He waved me on like a traffic cop and ordered, "Go!"

I scurried into the room and took my seat. The door closed behind me with Williams and John off to their first class together. For the rest of class, I worried how John would react when he found out that Williams wasn't just dropping him off at classes, but sticking by his side for the rest of the day, for days, weeks, and maybe months.

I was still preoccupied with thinking about John at the end of class when Harden caught me watching him. I turned away, hoping for a no-blood, no-foul call for mean-mugging or trippin'. Instead, Harden's fierce amber eyes narrowed and drilled through me as if I'd committed a flagrant foul. He scowled and hitched his pants—the first step in preparing to box.

"The fuck is your problem?" he said. "I'll come back there and knock your broke-ass, spooky, no-friends Frankenstein self out."

I slunk down at my desk and pretended not to hear him. But everyone in class had heard him. That's how class ended. No one wanted me.

Everyone on North was angry. No one in Cottage Park was ever angry. I wanted to go back to Cottage Park with John and live with Coach Woj, even if that meant I had to go out for wrestling.

But Harden was correct about me. The truth hurts. My olive skin had brown undertones, darker than usual because of my summer tan. My hair, fine and silky, occasionally stands on end. I was quiet, alone, different, lonesome, and tired.

I would never think of wearing a watch, ring, or earrings. My signature style is "clearance rack." Before John and I enrolled here at Thomas Jefferson, Puff had driven us to the Mall of America. We hated shopping, but we bought blue jeans, three pairs of khakis in different shades, white and blue formal dress shirts, a few plain hoodies, Joe Mauer jerseys, and cheap Vikings jerseys immortalizing benchwarmer white players. My little family didn't care much for what we wore or how we came across, with one exception: Puff insisted we be clean and keep our clothing unwrinkled.

People see right past me, but never Harden. I crave anonymity, but he assumed the spotlight, center and solo. He had a way of dazzling gradually, so the rest of us wouldn't be immediately blinded. At six-four—three inches taller than me—he routinely dunked on people. I envied how he carried himself with such dominance, even with adults.

As everyone from Mr. Lane's class joined the sea of students in the hall, Harden drummed his pencil across lockers and classroom doors to transform them into the percussion section of his Thomas Jefferson orchestra. He sang, too, a four-word song he'd created called "I Wanna Ball You."

All day, every day, he sang that song out in the halls. He varied the vocal ranges and stresses on those four words, and we accompanied each rendition.

Everybody knew Harden, but he didn't know me. Not at all.

That night, I came home from the rec center in time to catch the Twins versus the Yankees at Target Field in the top of the ninth. Puff and John ignored me when I crashed on the couch beside John.

"Hold on," I said, checking and rechecking the score. "We're beating the Yankees ten to five?" Over the years, we'd lost ten straight to the Yankees.

"Remember—it's the Twins," John warned.

Hildenberger threw a 0-1 count pitch to Gregorius, who grounded out to Polanco for the out.

"Okay, one down," Puff said, edging forward in his seat. "The reason the Twins haven't beaten the Yankees is that we don't have any playmakers besides Joe Mauer and Polanco. And good Lord, Willians Astudillo is our catcher tonight, with Joe Mauer as DH."

Hildenberger threw two quick strikes to Sánchez, then overpowered him on the third pitch. Sánchez struck out swinging.

One more out to go.

Luke Voit stepped to the plate, the last hope for the Yankees. On the first pitch, Hildenberger finally threw a ball. Two foul balls later, with a 1-2 count, Hildenberger struck him out swinging.

As the Twins congratulated one another, Puff congratulated Joe Mauer. "There's a life-changing lesson you boys can learn from Joe Mauer," he said.

"Why?" I asked. "What did he do tonight? Hasn't he been in a slump lately?"

Puff said, "An oh-for-twenty-three slump, including a strikeout in the fourth inning. But do you know what he did in the sixth against a full count?"

"I don't know," I said. "Lately he's been hitting it hard up the middle into double plays."

"No," Puff said. "He clobbered his fifth career grand slam. He concentrated on the here and now, and he connected. Joe Mauer breathes life into the Twins, Hildenberger included. And he breathes life into us. Joe Mauer makes everyone better. He makes us better. He's clutch."

Puff sat back to take in the Twins hanging on to their win, their field, and one another, lining up to shake hands and celebrate their rare success against the Yankees. Joe Mauer was at the center of the joy.

"You two are also clutch," Puff said. "You just wait—I predicted Joe Mauer's success, but I'm even more confident my boys will be successful at Thomas Jefferson."

He waved his hands to shoo us away.

"You two, off to bed. You have a big day tomorrow. You both will clobber grand slams like Joe Mauer." He leaned back, his eyes fixed on the TV, where the Twins were still celebrating. "Let Dr. Porter take us to court. We'll see who wins that game."

John's face, illuminated by the TV, also glowed with a fire that Puff had lit in him. Maybe Puff was right. Maybe we could find a way to win at Thomas Jefferson and everything else.

— CHAPTER EIGHT —

Time-Out

"This place is hell," Harden said, rubbernecking the rest of us from his cramped desk in the front row.

It was the start of my third week at Thomas Jefferson. Our fourth-hour geometry class, in room 311 on the third floor, was a slow cooker of thick, suffocating air. We waved our textbooks and notebooks and flapped our shirts to stir the stagnant air over desperate, sopping skin, hoping to breathe.

As hot as it was, Harden embodied fresh and chill. He wore immaculate low-cut white-on-white Nike Air Force 1 basketball shoes, laced to be worn untied, to cover white Nike tube socks. Those socks rode up piano-wire calves to black Nike shorts displaying a giant Swoosh that twinned the one on his white Nike T-shirt.

He called each Swoosh adorning his body a check and rapped those checks and more from a rapid-fire mic check: "Check, check, check, baby check." That was how he began his Northside rap: "Checkmark, checkmate, my check is in the bank, on the . . . North-side. North! North! North! North!"

Harden chose Nike, the Greek goddess of victory, for the simple reason that she had wings and hovered over mythical battles until she decided the victors. Nike chose Harden because he was also a frequent flier who flew throughout Thomas Jefferson, the Northside, and, most importantly, to the rim. Harden won every battle. He worshipped the NBA gods—Nike's chosen, who also flew. To Harden, the Swoosh wasn't just a logo but his approval on a contract that promised him freedom, elevation, and the ability to rise above any obstacle in his way.

Harden blinged a big white gold diamond stud on his left ear. It matched the white gold Cuban link chain, slightly larger than a collar, tight around his neck. A Dodger-blue crystal rosary draped over the link chain. His right pinky finger sported a white gold Rolex-knockoff ring with a tiny circle featuring twelve apostolic diamonds orbiting the center diamond, Jesus.

Harden stuck with the Rolex knockoff for his yellow gold diving watch, which was built to withstand deep-water pressure and gauge the remaining oxygen level in a scuba tank. He showcased it across his right wrist with a gold band. The hour hand displayed a peace sign. Both minute and hour hands locked upright—correct only at noon and midnight.

I'd asked him about the watch in geometry class a few days earlier, on Friday. That day, we had a Russian sub who barely spoke English, so everyone sat around chillin'. By that point, the standoff between Harden and me on Tuesday was ancient history. Unlike Cottage Park, the Northside has a short memory span. Harden and I were becoming more comfortable around each other, in school and especially at the rec center.

"Why wear it if it doesn't keep time?" I'd asked, pointing to his watch.

He jerked back and stifled a smirk. "You country as hell," he said. "Ball so hard, got a broke clock, Rollies that don't tick-tock."

"Huh?"

"You never heard Kanye and Jay-Z's 'Niggas in Paris'?" he asked.

"Not really," I said.

"Man, you missing out. That's the anthem. Let me school you."

He performed the entire song for the class and nailed every word and beat. We cheered when he ended.

Harden turned back to me and tapped the watch's face. "I keep the date set at four," he said. "A warning—to live life in the fourth quarter when time dribbles to an end," he explained. "That's when you find out who lives and dies for the W."

That day, today, every day—Harden embodied cool. Not even a blast furnace like room 311 could make him break a sweat.

"Come on, K-Chek," Harden now called out to Mr. Kozamchek, our teacher. "I know you're not trying to make us work today in this hell pit."

Most of us groaned in suffering agreement, except the other Hmong students, who sat ready to deploy for the lesson.

Harden sat closest to the door, which he'd negotiated with Mr. Kozamchek to keep open. The open door and adjacent seat allowed Harden to arrive to class last and exit class first. Most teachers at Thomas Jefferson kept their doors closed and locked during instruction. Harden's unique open-door policy allowed him to filter isolated breeze slivers through muggy air and hallway drama.

"I'm checking out of this plantation for real," Harden said, his wings starting to melt.

The word *plantation* was a reference to the historical Thomas Jefferson, a Virginia slaveowner who slept with his slave servant Sally Hemings for most of her life, beginning when she was fourteen (my age). She died at sixty-two (Puff's age). No provision allowed a slave girl to resist her master. No stipulation required Jefferson to care for their six children or lift her or them from slavery.

We schooled at Thomas Jefferson's house, or at least one named after him. Harden argued that this founding father shouldn't be the namesake of anything, especially not a place of learning where half the students were Black.

Harden turned back to address the class. "If Thomas Jefferson marched into this classroom now, he'd tell all your sorry Black asses to go back to the fields and work—after he'd chopped a finger or a toe from you sleepy Negroes. That's the least he would have done. Dude hated us."

At that moment, the original Thomas Jefferson unburied himself and marched into our classroom to revel in his name. Harden Black-powered his fist right between the slaveowner's eyes.

"Founding father, my ass," Harden said. "An abusive father, no doubt. He wrote in the Constitution that we earned slaveowners three-fifths of a vote equal to white men. How's that for a representative democracy? Can one of you scholars tell me how the biggest school on the Northside is named after a slaveowner asswipe like Thomas Jefferson? Come on, now . . ."

"I see you, king," said Mona Harris, a Black girl taller and stronger than me. She wore faded blue jeans punctuated with pearls and silver chain strands hanging from her knees.

I strained to read her T-shirt. It was from that weekend's celebration of life for Benny Moody.

I hadn't been on the Northside long, but I knew how these cotton obituaries worked. In Detroit Tigers script, GONE BUT NOT FORGOTTEN would banner a predictable airbrushed party photo memorializing a next-up Black son, brother, or young father—all victims of failed drug deals, jealous boyfriends, robberies, carjackings, mistaken identities, online disrespect, or random stray bullets. These young men starred in served-fresh-daily no-name tombstone headlines in the Metro section of the *Star Tribune* but never received even an honorable mention with a picture in the Obituary pages. The line for the on-deck circle to be the next sacrifice stretches up and down the avenues of the four sides of the Northside full-court hotbox: Plymouth, Penn, Lyndale, and 44th, and one—Broadway.

Harden explained away the tragic endings to their personal narratives as "stupid shit for no reason" and "being in the wrong place at the wrong time." He said the killed and the killers had one thing in common: They had no hope, nothing to live for. Then he quoted Tupac's mom: "If you can't find something to live for, you best find something to die for."

Harden regularly buried these dead. Lots of my classmates do. The girls talk about the memorials in the same manner as the long-lived ladies from Cottage Park, who view death as a blessing, an end to suffering. Both groups of mourners share matter-of-fact movie reviews of the actors: where they came from, what they wore and said, and their looks.

After a coroner's autopsy, Harden never tried to hear props for an embalmer's artistry. "What do you mean 'casket pretty'?" he said. "No kid ever looks good steamrolled in a casket."

As Mona leaned forward now, I made out Moody's sunrise stretched out on her back: November 18, 2003. His sunset was beneath the photo, though eclipsed by the back of her chair.

Mona had never spoken in class before, so I listened intently to the words rushing from her like a trumpet blast.

"People have tried to change the name for years, but any discussion gets squashed. Old white people won't ever listen."

All agreed.

She persisted, slowing, pleading. "No. I'm for real. Please believe me." She sat up straight and knocked her yellow steel asthma inhaler against her desktop like hitching a cigarette from a pack.

Harden up-nodded Mona. "Preach, sis."

But Mona reverted to her native language of sitting back and observing, so Harden stepped in and confronted Mr. Kozamchek.

"Coach K, you realize Thomas Jefferson would have punished a white teacher too. You'd have gone to jail for six months and been fined three hundred dollars. That's how they kept white folks in check back in the day—the law and big fines."

Mr. Kozamchek chewed on the knuckle of his right forefinger. He knew—we all knew—the well-beaten path of discussing a name change for Thomas Jefferson High School. The people who argued for keeping the name cited the never-ending domino effect: "What will we change next? Jefferson Street in Northeast Minneapolis? Mount Rushmore? The Jefferson Memorial? The nickel? The two-dollar bill?"

They have a point—Jefferson is everywhere. But to those geezers, all history, good and bad, should be sanctified, memorized, and memorialized, not cleansed.

"History is now," Harden announced with wonder.

He stood at attention in his official role as geometry class doorman, ushering in the ghost of the man he wanted to namesake our school.

"Good morning, Minister X," he said reverently.

Malcolm X's ghost strode in from the hallway, stepping upon and over Thomas Jefferson, still laid out from Harden's knockout punch. Harden envisioned both spirits so clearly that we saw them too. When he gestured for Malcolm X to take his position of honor at the front, Mr. Kozamchek took a step backward to give the presentation his consideration.

Cupping a hand to his ear, Harden listened intently to our new guest, then nodded and relayed the message to us.

"He's saying, 'If you stick a knife in my back nine inches and pull it out six inches, there's no progress. Pull it all the way out, that's not progress. The progress is healing the wound that the blow made. And they haven't even begun to pull the knife out, much less heal the wound.'"

"'They won't even admit the knife is there,'" Mona said, reciting the second half of the Malcolm X quotation, which she, too, had memorized. "*Shoot.*" She dragged out that expression like she was easing into a hot bath. "It is what it is." She pushed back the large black glasses that were slipping down her broad nose.

"I'm over what it is," Harden said. "I refuse to accept what it is." He viewed Mr. Kozamchek. "I'd like a big reparation check from Uncle Sam I Am Goddamn. Until then"—he focused back on Mona—"an IOU would go a long way. Believe us. Feel us. Is that asking too much?"

"That's never going to happen," Mona said. "The people in power got us all penned up here in prison."

"Buried alive in prison," Harden said. "Born to live slow on death row."

He paused, thinking whether to put a beat to that verse and keep rhyming, but he quickly slackened, winded. He resumed his point instead.

"Brother Malcolm is gone."

He lifted the rosary crucifix from his chest to his lips, kissing Jesus's nailed feet, just as Cottage Park's warped old ladies with dirty-snow, Civil War–blue-and-gray hair did after saying their prayer to Saint Michael to conclude the rosary before the 9:00 a.m. Sunday Mass at Holy Trinity.

"Why do your folks have to hate us so?" he asked, looking one last time to Mr. Kozamchek.

Mr. Kozamchek dismally shook his head in long silence. He did not look up as he spoke in shame. "For starters, I'd say ignorance and apathy. Dr. King said the opposite of love is not hate, but apathy. Fighting that two-headed monster is why I teach."

"Just living life on North is damn near impossible," Harden said. "Then we have to deal with racism—hundreds of years of it." Harden grew despondent. "I'm melting into three-fifths of a human being." He shook his head. "This heat will make you stupid. Time for me to check out of the game. Like Brother Malcolm."

But Malcolm X hadn't left. He was still in front of room 311, pacing, arms crossed, buttoning and unbuttoning his suit coat, seething.

Harden unfolded his blue bandana and prepared it like a bed-sheet or a cocoon over his hair, which on that day he had spun into stiff, twisted, straight strands sprouting like Jimmy Butler's skewers. Then he reached back to Westbrook, his enforcer, who handed him a small green bottle of Polo cologne. Harden sprayed a cloud of the cologne above himself and lowered into it until his head rested on his desk.

Mr. Kozamchek stepped into Harden's vacuum and smiled gravely. "To circle back to your initial point—yes, I will make you work today. And yes, we are in a hell pit. But this, too, shall pass."

Everyone let out another collective groan except, again, the loyal Hmong students, who waited in anticipation over their geometry textbooks and notebooks.

Mr. Kozamchek removed his phone from his pants pocket. "We kick off today, Monday, September 24, 2018, at exactly . . . 11:11 a.m., plus or minus fifteen-thousandths of a second. I'm not going to lie—it's warm today."

He slipped his phone back inside his pocket, tapped his computer's keyboard to locate the website for the National Weather Service, and clicked HEAT INDEX CALCULATOR. A square box titled CALCULATE HEAT INDEX was displayed from the overhead projector onto the whiteboard. Mr. Kozamchek circled the cursor around the first box in the calculator, TEMPERATURE.

"Does anyone want to guess the current temperature in the City of Lakes?" After a long silence, he prodded, "Anyone? No one seems to know . . . ?"

"No one seems to know" was the first half of the security blanket all Thomas Jefferson staff and students wrapped around themselves in doubt. The other half followed promptly: "I guess we'll just do what we can do." Mr. Kozamchek used it as a call-and-response, providing the first half, then waiting for my classmates to chug through the second half in unison, like Little Blue Engines.

Olive Turck, the cool white girl sitting in front who kept to herself, raised her hand and held it even after Mr. Kozamchek beckoned her.

"It's four hundred and fifty-one degrees," she said.

Mr. Kozamchek snorted. "You're off a bit."

He inputted 93 in the TEMPERATURE box, chose the bubble labeled with an F for Fahrenheit, and entered 59 in the RELATIVE HUMIDITY box. The algorithm calculated 106.

"A hundred and six degrees," he said. "That's how this heat feels for your body."

Hearing the number only intensified the lived experience. We were marinating in a Sichuan hot pot of odors: burp-and-blow aromas from everything we'd eaten for supper the night before, silent-but-deadly farts, overnight smells from clothing that had been slept in, AXE Body Spray deodorant and Victoria's Secret perfumes, and the lingering musk of marijuana that reeked like skunk.

I daydreamed as far away as possible from the nausea stalking me in room 311.

Mr. Kozamchek moved from behind his desk and strode across the room. He wore baggy Macalester College gym shorts, sandals, and a brown T-shirt picturing five American Indian chiefs. The bold caption read MY HEROES HAVE ALWAYS KILLED COWBOYS. I recognized only Geronimo and Sitting Bull.

"Today," he said, "our learning objective is to define a set, a subset, an intersection, and a union. To begin, a set is a collection of things. We'll examine times when no number will satisfy an equation. We call that set with no common members the *empty set*."

Heads submerged onto desks. Cell phones, banned in the classroom, rose from hiding places.

As Mr. Kozamchek lectured, I noted crude graffiti of a male private part on the back of the chair of Fatima Warsame, the Somali girl who sat in front of me. My finger traced over the fossilized words engraved into my desktop: PUBIC ENEMY.

I surveyed the 1920s-era compact classroom and took my own census of how Thomas Jefferson would classify us into racial categories: eleven Blacks (counting Fatima), six Hmong, two whites, three Latinos, and one American Indian.

This was only the second time Eddie Big Bear, the American Indian, had been in class. "I come to school once every couple weeks," he'd told us the first time he was in class. "That way, I stay on roll and avoid truancy court." He'd also announced, "I am the union of a Dakota dad and an Ojibwe mom, the bitterest enemies of all time."

I didn't count one student—me. Back then, I didn't fit into a category. Like Mom, I am Hmong, or trying to be Hmong. Like Puff, I am white. That means I'm mixed. And mixed up, caught between worlds that didn't quite claim me. I was a question mark in a school full of exclamation marks.

At North Kossuth High School, I'd counted as white, like almost everyone else. North Kossuth had enrolled one Black student for a short time in the '90s. Currently, there are half a dozen Latinos plus two hundred extremely white students. Every year, a handful of guys take their graduation photos in Western outfits and cowboy hats, posing by the co-op grain elevator or the railroad tracks leaving Cottage Park.

Here, we have more students in our largest class (271 freshmen) than North Kossuth has for its total enrollment. Thomas Jefferson's enrollment of 1,150 is nearly double the population of Cottage Park.

Though I counted as white in Cottage Park, it didn't mean I fit in. With a Hmong mom, I'm not all white. To complicate matters, even Mom didn't fit neatly into being Hmong. Moving to Cottage Park with Puff was as far away as any Hmong person could run from their past.

Puff's Moriaritys are the opposite of Mom's Vangs, who I would soon come to call my big family. In due time, I would learn that the Vangs never talk about death. The Moriaritys never stop talking about death. Grandma Moriarity laughed at it. She'd say, "Life is hell, then you get old, then you get shingles, and then you die and hopefully go to heaven, which is a Super Target. Whatever you need, whoever you want, is right there shopping with you."

Puff agrees with this creed until the Twins are down in the bottom of the ninth, and it's time to put on our rally caps. That's when he reminds us, "There *is* a God, and now we need to pray to her like hell."

"Michael," Mr. Kozamchek said.

That one soft word from far away ended my recess. A more insistent invitation followed.

"Mr. Moriarity."

I sat up and refocused as Mr. Kozamchek returned to the overhead projector and circled a problem with his cursor.

I studied the final equation:

$$\sqrt{(6x+5)} + 13 = 5$$

Clueless.

"Um . . ."

Should I confess ignorance?

Fatima, who spent class time drawing clocks, slid her notebook to display a lopsided clockface drawn to fill an entire page. Both arms pointed to a gigantic 12. She circled the number repeatedly.

"Twelve?" I said.

Class would dismiss at noon—twelve minutes away. Everyone chuckled, and I blushed as red as Cottage Park's solitary stoplight. My mouth dried. I couldn't swallow.

Suddenly, Harden awoke, lifted his bandana, and faced me. "It's the empty set," he said.

"Correct, sir," Mr. Kozamchek said, lofting an imaginary alley-oop pass to the desk closest to the door. "Harden gets the dime."

Harden smiled at the basketball reference and raised a fist for air knucks.

Mr. Kozamchek tapped his keyboard until the curly brackets representing the empty set appeared on the overhead—two hungry garter snakes stretching alongside each other to determine if they were long enough to swallow the other:

$$\{\,\}$$

"And why did you answer with the empty set?" Mr. Kozamchek asked him.

"There's no solution, nothing."

As Mr. Kozamchek's already-sapped face strained, Harden rushed to correct himself.

"Nothing is empty."

"Stop for a moment," Mr. Kozamchek said. "The empty set is not the same as nothing. Nothing is always something. The empty set is the space where something *could* be. The silence before the first note of a song. Potential. And the empty set is a subset of every set, including itself. Here—see for yourself."

Mr. Kozamchek grabbed a grocery sack from his desk, then emerged among us, stepping over outstretched, fallen, and fallen-asleep legs blocking the aisles. He placed a one-ounce sack of Nacho Cheese Doritos on each of our desks.

"You may now open your sack"—sacks crinkled and tore open—"but don't dig in yet."

He returned to the front, tapped his keyboard, and read the theorems on the whiteboard.

"'Every chip in this sack is red. No chips in this sack are not red.' Anyone disagree with either theorem?"

Mr. Kozamchek looked out at blank stares, salivating mouths, and fingers that itched to be contaminated by red powder.

"They are logically equivalent to each other," he continued. "Whenever one is true, the other must be true, and vice versa."

Mr. Kozamchek picked up an empty Doritos sack from his desk and blew inside until it popped open. He held it high and angled it out for us.

"What do I have here?" he asked.

"An empty sack," Olive Turck said.

"An empty *set*," Harden said.

Mr. Kozamchek's eyes lit up. A goofy smile showed his crooked teeth and further sparked his face.

"Brilliant," he said. "Notice there are no chips that aren't red in here."

"And your sack is the same as ours," Mona said.

"This sack symbolizes parentheses," Mr. Kozamchek said. "That's one more characteristic that makes this empty set a subset of your twenty-four sacks."

He wrote the equation to show that Set A, the empty set, was a subset of Set B, which contained the number 24.

"By the way," he said, "you can prove the empty set is a subset of every set by removing set members from a full sack until it, too, empties." He circled his hands outward and together, the universal sign inviting all to eat. "Now dig in."

"Aw, hell no," Harden said. "Hold on."

He spun around to command our attention, reached into his sack, extracted a chip, and held it out over the aisle as an offering.

"We don't eat until you do, K-Chek."

The rest of us copied Harden, arms stretched out and high to share a Dorito.

After a pause, Mr. Kozamchek accepted Harden's offering, then traveled up and down the aisles, collecting other offerings. By saying nothing, he said everything.

Cell phones and our worn-out restlessness disappeared. The hallway parade stilled. The Nipsey Hussle rap song reverberating from the street three floors below us quieted.

"I used to hate geometry," Olive said. "Now I'm starting to understand this junk."

"Mr. Kozamchek cares," Mona said. She waved him to retake the stage. "Go on with your bad self."

Mr. Kozamchek swallowed. "Oh. I, uh, love the empty set—for its potential. It doesn't always have to be empty. It can instantly fill to everything and change everything."

Harden extracted another chip to start another wave of offerings.

Starting with Harden, Mr. Kozamchek again proceeded through the aisles with his empty sack, collecting one chip from every student.

I offered the last chip to join the others, overflowing into his open hands.

After the final bell rang at 3:10 p.m., I scooped Hawk from my locker, then skipped and hopped down the second-floor steps. I blasted out of door 1 with other students and eyeballed parents inching forward in jittery cars.

"Yo, bro—give up the rock," NBA wannabes called from gravitational fields so intense they drew me near.

But if I were to let Hawk out of my hands, even for a moment, he would never return. These types had never experienced the joy of a genuine give-and-go—a sharp pass to your teammate, who touch-passes it back as you cut for a layup.

I blew them off, guarded Hawk, dodged the little special education buses, and crossed 43rd Street. Once in the Victory neighborhood, I freed Hawk to talk and play, dribbling him between my legs and around my back. It was easy to let Hawk go when I was alone. He always bounced back. He reminded me that what goes down will come up again. To go up, I must go down. I, too, will come up again.

After one hundred of those reminders, we reached Newton Avenue's dead end: a cemetery. I now had to choose—jaunt west a few blocks to Penn Avenue and risk getting jumped, or jump the fence and risk getting stuck or impaled on it to get through the cemetery.

I chose the cemetery. If I survived the fence, I would dribble down the road through 101,000 graves. I might not see another live person—just the dead and me.

I stood before the shoulder-height black chain link fence, hurled my backpack across, and launched Hawk over with a jump shot. Next,

I jammed my left foot into the fence to secure a toehold, then propelled myself to the top. There, I teetered on the steel bar, suspended between divisions: up/down, health/injury, and life/death.

I fell, more than jumped, into the community of saints. I at least remembered to roll like a parachute jumper as I landed on the forgiving earth. I imagined myself as an American fighter pilot shot down in Laos during the Vietnam War, with Hmong fighters, perhaps Grandpa Vang, coming to the rescue and taking me to their village to recuperate.

But instead of springing back to my feet, I lay on the warm grass and kicked up a raspy blanket of trees' tears: brown, red, orange, and green. The musky smell of earthworms underneath, creating life from death, saturated me.

Hawk and I daydreamed, gazing above as pillowy clouds mushroomed and glided into elephants tied trunk to tail, swallowing sunlight as they lumbered across a busy sky. Once the clouds outnumbered and overcame the sun, the temperature dropped. For the first time in a long time, I shivered. We gathered my backpack and made our way onto the curved roads folding over one another like intestines leading home.

Crows greeted me from a pine tree—nearly a dozen, their sharp calls cutting through the air. Their sleek, shadowy bodies were silhouetted against a gray sky. Their eyes—black, knowing—followed my every move. Half of them floated to the ground and trailed me. I knew them well.

Right before the tornado, a similar family of crows had roosted in a purple maple tree across the street from us, above Mr. Hatch's driveway. They squawked for hours and pooped white splotches onto his new blacktop.

Mr. Hatch tried to scare them, but they wouldn't fly away. Eventually, he fired his pellet gun into the family and hit one, breaking a wing. The wounded crow fluttered from the tree and smashed onto our lawn. As he flopped helplessly, the other crows besieged him, each pulling at feathers and pecking him to death. Finally, those crows left and never came back.

Puff said crows are the most intelligent birds and that they killed their fallen member before we could see one of their own in distress. Crows want the world to believe they're invincible.

But I knew better. I went out to Mom's garden and buried that crow—but not its secret: mortality.

These crows were Northside newcomers, like me. They'd moved from the suburbs around the same time I'd moved from Cottage Park. The cemetery would be their winter home.

When I first discovered them, on my walks home from school, I mimicked their caws to befriend them. That only made them further avoid me. Then I started bringing Cheetos, hoping to feed them the way people feed pigeon flocks. I scattered the pieces on the ground, but the crows wouldn't touch them.

Instead, I learned that if I approached the crows without a sound, with my head down, and with the Cheetos bursting from open palms, they would trail behind, strutting, hopping, and wobbling like the North Kossuth senior girls in their black caps and gowns on graduation day, navigating their first free steps from high school in high heels. The crows cawed approval as I distributed the cheese snacks. Once the Ziploc baggie was emptied, they would chastise me for never bringing enough.

Today I recognized, foremost, the extended family's largest member and field general, who was inspecting me as he strutted a safe distance behind. He was skeptical and never grateful to receive the last Cheeto. I call him Commander Crow. He always ate last.

Commander Crow oversaw thousands of granite and marble monuments in precise formation—stone formations standing vigilant, uneasy, and fearful. They moaned, *I should have let go*, or *I could have held on*.

Weeks later, Harden would relay to me what his grandparents had told him, that until the 1950s, the cemetery buried Blacks in a segregated section. "Separated womb to tomb," Harden said. "I used to believe death and life were separate. It turns out not even that is true—not in the United States of Amnesia."

Each day, the cemetery welcomed at least one new resident. Today's arrival was accompanied by molting black flower petals, shiny

Mylar balloons that grazed fresh dirt, a Hennessy Very Special cognac bottle, and an unopened Newport cigarette pack. Around the second curve, I spotted another fresh grave in Babyland, featuring soggy stuffed animals and withered helium balloons.

At last, the road delivered me from the cemetery. I looked both ways and crossed busy Dowling Avenue, the Northside's squeezing necktie.

Now I was back in my neighborhood, which is also a cemetery. I passed by makeshift memorials: balloons, flowers, candles, and wrinkled-and-washed-out signs leaning against trees to honor victims slain there. These memorials across the Northside grow from the victims' living blood.

I trekked a block up from Dowling to arrive home at 3745 Humboldt Avenue North, a duplex in a sketchy neighborhood between the lows and highs—like me, poised on the cemetery fence, ready to jump or fall in either direction.

I hopscotched our cement front steps and opened the left of two doors, leading to our living area. Puff lay where I'd left him in the morning, sprawled across one of two parallel couches, watching ESPN's *Pardon the Interruption*.

Since moving to the Northside, Puff has let the TV babble on for twenty-four hours a day. It's set to ESPN during our waking hours, then to public TV at bedtime as white noise to lull us to sleep—and to give burglars second thoughts about robbing us.

Puff and I barely acknowledged each other. Since the tornado, my little family has skipped such formalities.

I dropped my backpack on the kitchen table. "I'll shoot until supper," I said, holding Hawk high for Puff to see. "I'll be back to make pizzas. It's Italian Night. Don't forget John's medications."

Puff gaped at me as he always did, as if this were the first time he'd learned about John's medications.

I answered him as I always did, as if this were the first time I'd told him about John's medications. "His horse pills," I said.

Puff's eyebrows inchwormed to register the reminder.

John hated his horse pills, the gigantic antiseizure pills he had to take twice a day. He'd quit taking them for a time after we moved to the Northside. I couldn't say or do anything to change his mind—until I lied to him.

"Joe Mauer took horse pills after his first concussion," I'd said.

John had cockeyed me.

"Justin Morneau too," I'd added.

Harden once said, "Be honest all the time, especially when it hurts." But in this case, lies—and Joe Mauer's name—worked.

With the assurance that Puff would remember John's pills, I burst outside, triple-jumped back down the steps, and ran as fast as possible, dribbling down the block to jump on the one-hour shootaround at the rec center outdoor court.

If I wanted to make varsity at Thomas Jefferson and play with John, I needed to make the best of my time and work as hard as possible to improve. And I needed to break free of the house, Puff, and John—they only reminded me of Mom and how much I missed her. Out here, I could sweat Mom out of me.

I positioned myself under a hoop and set Hawk on the court to prepare for my usual pre-hooping ritual.

I stretched to try to touch my toes. Then I jogged in place boxer-style—training for a battle, throwing jabs, and doing an Ali dance. From there, I jumped as high as possible for thirty seconds.

Big men need reliable hands and fingers—soft enough to catch but hard enough to hold the rock. I passed Hawk between my legs and around my back and knees for one minute before rolling him across my arms and shoulders like the Globetrotters. My arms ached, but that's how muscles grow.

Next, I threw Hawk high and caught him behind my back. I made nine more tosses like that, each one higher than before.

I practiced pivoting off both legs into reverse layups until the moves were instinctive. I'm slow because I think.

After the warmups, I took my first shots two feet from the rim, using the backboard on either side and aiming to swish in front.

Puff says, "The world is a spinning ball. Without that spin, there would be no order. In any game with a ball, you have to spin to control it. For basketball, it's backspin."

I snapped my wrist down as Puff instructed—"Wave to your girlfriend"—to create the backspin. Hawk kissed the rim's tip with backspin and dropped dead through the net.

I then backed away to the free-throw line. Free throws are a gift. I followed seven steps.

First, I squared my feet at the line.

Second, I bounced Hawk three times, then positioned him until his air hole looked back at me. At that moment, I became one with Hawk. Only good happens in Hawk.

Third, I aligned my fingers to Hawk's air hole, into his rubber grooves, and onto his dimpled skin.

Fourth, I tucked my elbow.

Fifth, I bent my knees.

Sixth, I aimed my eyes at the rim's front tip.

Seventh, I let go, shooting with a follow-through that turned my wrist into a fishhook.

I always willed myself to make that first shot.

I took my second shot while an imaginary announcer said, "He's dribbling . . . He shoots . . . "

I scored again.

I kept shooting the string, whispering the count of every consecutive shot I made, entering the zone.

"Three."

Dribble. Deep breath. Concentrate.

"Four."

So easy I could do it with my eyes closed.

"Five."

Don't get cocky.

"Six."

Use more backspin.

"Seven." And, "Eight."

My real and imaginary talk continued until, "Twenty-eight for twenty-eight."

Hawk wove around the rim and dropped in.

Living right.

"Twenty-nine for twenty-nine."

On shot thirty-three, Hawk slipped off my hand to the right. I missed.

I stepped back to the line again, dived into the air hole, and gave the next shot my attention. I have to end every practice on a made shot.

I swished that one.

"Finished."

The Harden Set strolled onto the court as I prepared to leave, its members arrayed in skin tone from brown to Black-skinded. (With "skinded," two syllables, being how all the Black kids around here say it.) We envied Harden's light skin, a fawn's cinnamon brown.

At Thomas Jefferson, students classified other students by a reality even more meaningful than race: skin color. Everyone's color is defined, like the swatches at the paint store. The colors range from albino to dark-skinded. There's white, yellow, olive, light-skinded, brown, and Black.

The Harden Set approached me at the free-throw line, with Harden out front.

"What it is, Empty?" Harden said. He read my jittery eyes. "Anyone can jack up a free throw without pressure."

He clapped for me to pass him Hawk, so I did. After three-plus weeks of watching the Harden Set play, I knew what he would do. He took a step near the rim and took a warmup shot like he always did— shooting from nearly underneath the rim as high as he could. Hawk rose until he peaked, then nosedived back to earth like a shooting star for a score.

"It's different when you put your life on that line," he said.

He tugged a money clip stuffed with a thick wad of cash from his front pocket. Andrew Jackson, a slaveowner, peered from the top. Harden slid the Jackson from the clip, folded it, and held it to his forehead like a third eye.

"Money talks," he said. "One-to-one free throws. You and me. I'm good. You're good. You're warmed up. We shoot one at a time until you miss. I'll even go first."

"I don't got any cash on me," I said.

Harden was a left-hander, like John. Puff says, "Left-handers have a better eye than right-handers, making them better pitchers, passers, and shooters." It's true. But Harden's gift was his head game. He played everything to win. The only principle he held tighter than his love of winning was his fear of losing. He took everyone's money, marbles, and chocolate.

I knew I could take him at shooting, but I could never challenge him—not in shooting, not in anything. His swag was too much; I'd buckle under it. Swag is the art of unthinking, getting your mind out of the way so the body can take over—the art of letting go. The best in any sport, like Harden, have it. The most frustrated, like me, know that fact but can't internalize it. It's a skill you can't fake.

Harden stepped to the free-throw line with Hawk. Andrew Jackson and the money clip fell at his feet. He noodled his arms, prepared to shoot, and eyed me again.

"I don't think so," I said, edging around him.

As I did, Harden blessed himself with the sign of the cross, closed his eyes, and shot Hawk, who dutifully arced up and down through the net. Harden opened his eyes and cackled.

"And bullshit walks," he said, roasting me as I gathered Hawk. "Another time, Empty. But a word of advice: Ballers always carry a twenty."

He picked up his money clip and dismissed me with a quick wave. The Harden Set burst into laughter.

The laughter followed me as I dribbled Hawk off the court and down the sidewalk toward home.

Once inside, I found Puff attached to his couch. John was stretched out on the other couch. My little family was a silence begging to speak, a promise of what could be if someone or something filled and transformed us.

"What you on, cuz?" I said to John.

He perched, leaned forward, glanced at me, then lay back down again to return his attention to ESPN. It was easy to imagine the *Whatever* he said to himself. It was easy to imagine most of his thoughts. Talking to him was like playing chess against myself.

Puff and John both measure six feet, eight inches. Puff has shrunk to this height in sixty-two years; John has grown into it in sixteen years. Puff once said, "Every time you boys grow—and you two never stop—your old man dwindles away. My sons rise; I must set."

A shrinking frame isn't the only sign of Puff's years. His hair is thinning and balding at his crown. In contrast, John's hair is thick and coarse with natural curls, long and shining like an orphan penny—except above his right ear, which was shaved to an ivory scalp, revealing zigzag stitching from the gash he received from the tornado.

"After the stitches go away," John once said, "I'll never cut my hair again."

I preheated the oven to 450, as directed on the frozen pizza boxes. As the heat built, I emptied the dishwasher, set the table, then opened a can of raspberry-flavored peaches and set them in a bowl. I tore open a Fresh Express Caesar salad kit and drizzled the dressing packet across the greens. I laid three large Home Run Inn meat-lovers pizzas on individual pizza pans and slid the top two into our oven. I always fed John and Puff first.

When their pizzas were ready, I plated two meals and delivered them to the TV room. It was a wordless transaction, the only sound coming from *SportsCenter*.

I returned to the kitchen to prepare my meal. I ate alone at the table, thinking about the personal narrative assignment for English. What would I write? What was my story?

Once I finished eating, I went back to the TV room to gather Puff's and John's plates. I cleaned up, then headed to my room. Before doing any other homework, I collected my English notebooks, selected black on my BIC four-color ballpoint pen, and jotted ideas for my personal narrative, starting with the title.

"The Empty Set."

— CHAPTER NINE —

And One

It took me a while to learn Pa Dao's name. It also took a while for Pa Dao to know her own name and Mom's.

I sat by myself at one end of a long stainless steel table in the cafeteria, reading the *Star Tribune* sports pages. My little family had watched Joe Mauer play in the second of a three-game series against the Detroit Tigers the night before. I read the article on the victory and noted Joe Mauer's two hits in the box score.

At the other end of the table—where the Goth, LGBT, and senior Hmong girls gathered—a ruckus arose. I didn't know them, but I had seen them in the halls between classes and at the end of this very table since I came to Thomas Jefferson. You couldn't help but notice them. They were stuck together like Gorilla Glue. They didn't walk but transported together, like a slow-moving, pulsating, amoeba Slinky whose protrusions extended and retracted to constantly change shape.

One of the Hmong girls rose from her seat, earning some playful teasing from her friends.

"See you later, Fart Face," a teaser said.

I browsed up from the sports pages to catch the reaction. That girl—definitely not a Fart Face—laughed and proceeded in my direction. She wore red-plaid flannel pajama pants and white Crocs with no socks. A worn grocery sack dangled from her arm, its contents clinking softly as she walked.

I ducked back into the article and the compliments the Tigers' manager—and former Twins manager—Ron Gardenhire gave Joe Mauer on his professionalism. Puff says, "Gardy's as nice a guy as you'll ever meet." But as I sank deeper into the newspaper, I sensed the girl—and time—stopping across the table.

Eventually, the girl tugged down my newspaper, peered at it for a moment and at me for several moments. A beauty mark dotted the top right of her pouting pink lips. Her left eye lazily strayed away from her right eye's focus on me.

What's that left eye reporting while I talk to the right eye?

"Hey," she said. Her voice rose like a flute above the punishing bass drums and clanging cymbals around us. She pointed to an open seat. "Is anyone sitting here?"

"No," I said. "Feel free to join me."

"Thanks," she said. But she stood there, scrunching her face. "You're not reading a newspaper at lunch, are you? Seriously?"

"I'm just"—my words echoed in a vast cave between my ears—"trying to keep up on current events."

I gathered the newspaper sections spread across the table and shuffled them until they reassembled neatly. Then I gestured for her to join me.

After she sat, I returned to the article. The Tigers were struggling this season. They were too far behind to catch us for second place in the division standings.

"I'm Pa Dao," she said. She slid her chair close to the table and leaned forward. "You're new. And your name is Michael."

I put down the newspaper. Those were statements, not questions.

"Um, yes. My name is Michael. I'm new."

Pa Dao's willowy body arched as she dipped her head backward and twisted and wrapped her shoulder-length black hair through a rubber band, making a ponytail. A smile curled her lips, showing sparkling teeth.

"You're Hmong," she stated, her tone leaving no room for argument.

I was unsure how to respond. "Do I look Hmong?"

Pa Dao tilted her head and looked at me sideways. "Well, you don't look all that white," she said, the hint of a smile playing on her lips. "I mean, you're tall and light-skinded, but I can see Hmong in you—something in your eyes that says you're searching."

"Mom was Hmong," I said. "She passed away . . ."

"You're Hmong," she restated.

I tried to inhale but couldn't. The wreckage of our Cottage Park house was pressing my chest again. The weight of Mom's absence— her voice, her laughter, the way she'd hum while cooking—crushed me. But I hadn't just lost her. I now had to confront that part of me that was Mom, that part of me that was Hmong.

"To be honest," I said, "I don't know what I am."

"Oh my goodness," Pa Dao said. "All my life, no one has ever responded that way. You *know* who you are. Funny. Funny."

Suppressing a laugh, she hitched her head, sending her ponytail flying behind her shoulder. But the giggles still came. The harder she pressed her hand over her lips to confine them, the more her little nose pointed upward like a pig's snout.

I let down my guard and laughed too. Our Cottage Park house lifted from me.

"Okay, then," I said. "If that's so funny, who do you say that I am?"

Pa Dao collected herself and sat down. I sat up and gave her my full attention.

"From the time they can first speak," she said with authority, "Hmong children are raised to stand proudly and say, 'I am Hmong.' So, let's start again. All right, Michael. I'm Pa Dao. I am Hmong. Who are you?"

"I'm Michael, and I'm Hmong too. I guess," I said. "Should I stand?"

"No," she said. "And you're not at all convincing. We'll work on that. My mission will be complete when you understand that you are Hmong because we are Hmong." She grew thoughtful. "But first, we have other issues to fix. Like, Why do you hide behind a dumb newspaper at lunchtime? And where's your food?"

I aimed at her second question first. "Too many budgers. I kept getting pushed farther back in the line until I fell out of line. It's no biggie—not worth the bother. I eat a big breakfast instead."

Pa Dao raised both hands for me to stop. "Everybody's hungry. You must be hungry too. *Noj mov!*"

I speak a little Hmong: *hello, goodbye,* and *thank you.* But *noj mov* was an easy one. Mom said it all the time. Pa Dao was telling me to eat.

"You're hungry," she said. "*Wb noj mov.*"

She stood, grabbed her grocery sack, and walked away. She stopped at a microwave against the far wall and removed five Tupperware bowls from her sack. One by one, she inserted the bowls into the microwave and grabbed plastic silverware from a nearby tray.

While Pa Dao was busy at work, four Hmong senior girls from the other end of the table stood. Two girls on each side, they marched arm in arm like a wedding procession until they surrounded me, trapping me.

"Hi," a girl in front of me said as the others smiled. "Pa Dao is our friend." The group's spokeswoman checked the other girls, then continued. "She's more than a friend. She's our unborn child."

"We're Dysfunctional Family," the girl directly behind me said, her voice sharp and teasing. "I'm Brother, the one who says what no one else will. That's Father, the peacekeeper. Mother's the quiet one who sees everything. And Sister? She's the wildcard. You'll figure us out soon enough."

Knees brushed against me from behind as Dysfunctional Family moved even closer and enveloped me from all sides. I was being swallowed.

"I'm Father," the spokeswoman said.

She wore no makeup and only simple clothing, most likely what her older sisters or cousins had handed down. And she wore her hair in a solid ponytail banded just above her neck. Behind her eyeglasses were old eyes that had seen everything before, like a gentle hill.

"Brother," another girl announced.

She was shorter than the others, and when she moved, she bounced, looking like she had just dropped in from the sky. Brother's eyes twinkled, like she was on the verge of laughing, even though she rarely did, as I would learn. She was direct and blunt, and she would pepper her language with curse words.

"Mother," said one girl behind me.

Both she and Brother wore their hair with brightly colored barrettes and pigtails. They were also glammed out in makeup.

I turned in time to match the voice of "Sister" to the remaining girl. Sister was a Goth Hello Kitty with silver piercings in both ears and her lower lip. I got the impression it was not unusual for her to wear the sequined cat-ears headband—possibly to take the place of her ears, which were partly covered by a soft, fluffy perm surrounding her face. Like Father, she wore glasses. They were larger, round black glasses that made her look even more like a cat.

"As we said, Pa Dao is our unborn child," Mother said quietly, with obvious affection for Pa Dao. Satisfied that she had contributed and confident that she hadn't spoken out of turn or hurt someone's feelings, she withdrew again to observe the others.

"You're not really a human," Brother said, "until you become a senior."

"Pa Dao will continue the family name next year, after we are gone," Sister said. "Who knows? Maybe you will be the unborn child at that time."

"We have a question," Father said. "Brother and I have Public Speaking class with your brother." She looked at Brother, who signaled for her to continue. "Is your brother one of those school-shooter types? Is that why they have Williams near him wherever he goes?"

I was sure this was all a put-on, so I played my part. "As long as he never gets hungry, you'll be perfectly safe."

When their expressions didn't change, I second-guessed whether I had misread their sincerity, but I knew I had also won something.

"You guys!" Pa Dao whined. "Out!" she then ordered. She pointed to the end of the table.

Dysfunctional Family took one step toward their destination but stopped to gather around Pa Dao and give her a suffocating group hug. Then they moved on.

Pa Dao was out of breath when she took her seat. "They're impossible!" She took a deep breath and smiled. *"Wb noj mov.* That means, 'Let's eat rice.'"

Pa Dao placed the Tupperware containers before us and opened them. They contained long-grain rice, vegetables, and chicken chunks. She arranged two plate settings, one for her and one for me. She then came around to stand beside me and scooped rice first.

I closed my eyes and inhaled through my nose. The deeply familiar aura of lemongrass and cilantro pulled me back to Cottage Park, where Mom made these same dishes. For a moment, I was in Cottage Park again, sitting at the kitchen table while Mom stirred the pot, her hands flowing with ease. It also pulled me further back, to Thailand and Laos, where these same dishes had made Mom.

"Rice is the heart of every Hmong meal," Pa Dao said.

She nestled green stir-fried baby bok choy alongside the rice. After that, she stirred the third container, mixing chicken rough cuts in a clear broth with lemongrass and cilantro. She scooped out legs and breast meat and rested them alongside the vegetables over my rice.

"Boiled chicken," she said. "My favorite. I'll bet boiled chicken is your favorite, too, Hmong Boy."

A smile burst across my face. Pa Dao had guessed correctly. And "Hmong Boy"? That was a first. What Hmong did she see in me?

"Before we eat, I think we should say a toast," she said. "I like to mark first and last times, and this is the day we first met each other." She bowed her head for a moment before looking back at me. "Let's name a person or event we are grateful for today. I'm grateful for Niam, which means 'mom,' for packing this delicious food for us. Your turn."

I didn't know what to say. I glanced at the newspaper. "I'm grateful for the Twins' win last night over the Tigers."

Pa Dao rolled her eyes.

"Hey, a win is a win," I said.

Pa Dao backed away to her side of the table, arranged the Tupperware containers around her plate, and served herself portions from each.

"Eat," she said once her plate was ready.

I took a bite. It reminded me of Mom.

"Stop!" Pa Dao yelped. She pulled another, smaller Tupperware bowl and popped it open.

I recognized the contents immediately. "Hot chili dipping sauce," I said. "Mom made it for every meal."

Pa Dao scooped the sauce with minced hot chili peppers, cilantro, garlic, green onions, fish sauce, and lime juice. She gave me a spoonful before she took a spoonful for herself.

I ate while Pa Dao told me all about the eighteen Hmong clans and how they comprise one-third of Thomas Jefferson's enrollment. Her words bubbled out like the warm water that continuously bubbles from Thomas Jefferson's drinking fountains. She taught me all the short, choppy family names. She explained that Lee, Chang, Vue, Yang, and Xiong are popular, but the Vangs are the most numerous.

Was I Vang enough to be included in that count?

"Guess my clan name," she said. The lesson was over, and it was time for testing.

"Vue," I said.

Though the cafeteria was loud and I strained to hear Pa Dao, the girls at the end of the table somehow had no difficulty hearing our conversation. They were now interjecting as they wanted.

"Hint," Father said as she pushed away from the table. She stood with her tray and made her way to Pa Dao. "She's not a Vang, like me."

Reaching over Pa Dao, Father spooned a generous pile of rice onto her tray, then helped herself to everything else Pa Dao had brought. Her indigo T-shirt displayed large, bold lettering: VANGSTER GANGSTER. She left us to return to her seat.

Pa Dao ignored her and smiled. "Keep guessing."

From the other end of the table, a chorus of Hmong clan names sang out at once.

"She's not a Thao, like me," Mother said.

"Or a Herr, like me," Brother said.

"She's not cool enough to be a Pha," Sister said.

"They just narrowed it down," Pa Dao said to me. "Keep guessing."

"Um, Lee? Yang?" I looked up to the ceiling and tried to pull down more names. "Moua . . . Kong . . . Khang . . ."

The harder I tried and the more frustrated I became, the more Pa Dao's smile broadened. Finally, I paused and waited for her to provide another clue. Instead, she sat back smugly.

"I give up," I said.

"You're not that smart, are you?" she said. "I told you—there are only eighteen Hmong surnames. Memorize them." She thrust her hand out to shake mine, and I grasped it. "I'm Pa Dao Xiong," she said. "Pa Dao is the ancient needlework art of how Hmong people tell our story."

We ate silently until she questioned me in a new command.

"Describe your father."

"That's a loaded hot potato," Mother called out from the end of the table. "My father is a dog that sniffs around any woman of any age." She looked at the girls around her and sidebarred, "Consider yourselves warned."

"At least you've got a father in your house," Sister said. "I have a series of divorced fathers who are in and out of our house. And don't get me started on how or why some grown men throw their lives away by marrying girls our age. Yucko!"

"Or even younger," Brother said. "Be thankful the guys coming into your house don't fight with your mom. That's got to be better than having a mom and dad constantly at each other's throats."

"No," Sister said. "You can predict the fights. You can't predict the drive-bys that don't care to learn your name."

We waited until it was quiet at the end of the table, then Pa Dao signaled for me to continue.

"My dad is a white guy," I said. "Named Patrick, but everyone calls him Puff."

"*Meka*," Pa Dao said. "That's what we call white people," she added, shifting gears to slow down and measure each word. "What's your family name?"

"I should make *you* guess."

Her eyes widened. "There may be only eighteen Hmong surnames, but there are a few thousand family names for *meka*."

I smiled at her anxiety but let her fret for only a moment. "It's Moriarity."

"Uh . . ." Pa Dao said. "Hmong people can't pronounce that name. Sounds Italian."

"Sounds like *morbidity*," Sister said. "I see that one on the weight-loss commercials."

"Nope. It's one-hundred-percent FBI," I said. "Full-blooded Irish. It means 'navigator of the sea.'"

Pa Dao smiled, then grew serious. "Now let me tell you about our Hmong moms. That includes Mai."

Before I could remember if I had mentioned Mom's name, Pa Dao continued.

"Hmong moms can trace their history back to China. Once upon a time, our people lived there peacefully. We fought many battles against outsiders but had to escape to Vietnam, Laos, and Thailand. Now, we're here, in the Twin Cities and the Northside. It's always a war that pushes us away."

She stopped long enough to chew, swallow, and drink from a Hi-C Grabbin' Grape juice carton—the same flavor she'd given me.

"Now we're in a different war that pushes Hmong children from their mothers. Hmong language has no words to describe this war and how to win it. You think *you're* frustrated? Try being a Hmong mom, working her hardest to make sense of where she's landed. There's no textbook to turn to with an easy solution for the situations that confront them here. But they do their best and never give up on us. *Never.* They're going to do their best to raise good children. That's what you need to know about your mom, my mom, and all Hmong moms."

I took a sip of my Hi-C, then set it back on the table lightly. "My mom met Puff in a Thai restaurant in Saint Paul. She'd been married to an older man from the camp. They divorced, and she married my dad. They moved to Iowa and had my brother and me. Her name was Mai Vang."

Pa Dao said, "I know."

Our Cottage Park house returned. Only this time, it pressed harder on my chest and my whole being.

"I know," Pa Dao continued, "because a persistent Hmong woman named Mai Vang has woken me every morning at five o'clock for the last week. She directs me to sit with you each day and tell you her story. She says you're more likely to understand the lessons if I feed you." Pa Dao spread her hands across the containers and plates.

"Wait, wait," I said. "My mom is dead."

"She died only about a month ago, right?"

My mouth hung open. "How do you—"

"I'm a Hmong shaman." She looked at me carefully. "Is that weird to you? Do you know what that means?"

"It means she knows what she's talking about," Father said. "You better listen up."

I raised "you got me" hands in surrender.

"I connect to the spirits all around us," Pa Dao said. "They're everywhere—watching, listening, and speaking to us, to me. I hear them loudly. Thankfully, I have my shaman guides with me. They protect and teach me the ways of shamanism."

"Shaman guides?" I asked, though I wasn't sure I wanted to hear the answer.

"They're spirits too. Special kinds of spirits that help shamans."

Uneasiness bubbled in my stomach.

"Pa Dao isn't my first Hmong name," she said. "I was born Douazong, which means 'shadow.' In our culture, names carry power. I got sick when I was little, and my parents thought changing my name might protect me. I tried to hide. I was scared to be a shaman. I kept getting sick. My parents changed my name to Pa Dao, thinking the shaman guides couldn't find me anymore. But that only brought on more sickness. My parents tried everything to help me. Finally, I accepted my fate. I became a shaman."

"All of that is true," Brother said. "I remember when it happened."

Now my uneasiness turned to fear. I couldn't grasp any of it. Pa Dao and these spirits, guides, and powers? And Mom—still alive? My body tensed, readying to walk, even run, away. Yet Pa Dao spoke with such authority that I followed her like a puppy.

"Being a shaman is a hard life," she said. "I'm still learning and adapting. I'm seventeen, so I'm probably the youngest Hmong shaman in Minnesota. Unless you know of any younger shamans . . . ?" She looked at me in earnest.

I slowly shook my head. "I don't know any shamans except you."

"Oh," Sister said, "you'll get to know more shamans. But none are as good as our little unborn child."

"Shamans also help with the passage from life to death," Pa Dao said. She stopped and eyeballed me, the left eye drifting even more. "Your mother never had a proper Hmong funeral, did she?"

"No. My little family doesn't know anything about Hmong funerals. How are they different from Catholic funerals?"

"They're as different as night and day and life and death."

Pa Dao was quiet. She stared at her plate, and I stared at her, waiting. At last, she took a deep breath.

"We have a problem—a big problem," she said. "When people die, their spirits return to their ancestral home. That is, if they're guided correctly. But if the dead person's spirit gets lost, she may wander like a homeless person without a face, unable to find peace or reincarnate into another life. Stuck between two worlds. We must help Mai move on."

I remembered what Grandpa Vang had said the day I called about Mom's funeral: "Mai was lost while she lived and is even more lost in death."

Before I responded, Pa Dao glanced over her shoulder at the black wall clock. Like a safety patrol ushering kids across the street, the hour hand pointed straight up, and the minute hand pointed nearly down.

Pa Dao said, "Your mom's responsibility in life was to love her children, help her family, and live a good life. Now it's our responsibility to help her find her way home—her spiritual home, where she came from. Death brings our Hmong families together. Our health, safety, and prosperity depend on honoring those who go before us. You and I have a lot of work to do for both Mai and your family. A spirit that lingers near the family is bad luck."

Without a word, Pa Dao stood and put the plastic containers away. All around us, students rose and gathered like geese to fly south for the winter. As I came around the table, I stood face-to-face with Pa Dao for the first time. She was six inches shorter than me but very much in control.

Dysfunctional Family locked together and rolled into Pa Dao. Though I was close to Pa Dao, she was brushing up against Dysfunctional Family.

"I have strict rules on mediating between spirits and families, but Mai refuses to follow them." She sighed. "I've tried to get her to move on, but I can't budge her. I hate her for that, but I love her like Niam. Know what I mean?"

"I do."

"She's relentless."

"Like water," I said.

It made sense. Mom wouldn't move on because we needed her. I would have been more surprised if she *hadn't* stayed around.

It was my turn to eyeball Pa Dao. I'd been hoping for a sign from Mom. She sent a billboard. Now I was hooked. I'm not going to lie—I wanted to be hooked.

"Why did Mom choose you?" I said.

"Your mom is really smart," Pa Dao said. "Hmong moms know just who to match us to. And I'm a proud, traditional young woman who is dedicated to my family and determined to live by my family's rules." She recited these and the next words as if she were saying the Pledge of Allegiance. "I respect my elders. I'm kind. I'm a good Hmong daughter."

More and more students lined up and jostled for position in front of the two steel doors that were shut and blocked by the immovable force that was Williams. He stood sternly with his bulging arms crossed, like Mr. Clean, yet he bantered with the students directly before him.

Pa Dao and I joined the mix. With every step we took, I sensed the beginning of a journey.

"In Hmong culture," Pa Dao explained, talking over the crowd, "everything relates to the Hmong father or husband. But Mai came to me since you have no Hmong father to teach you your culture. That's why I need to help you. But I'm not sure what I can do to help you without you having a Hmong father. However, one thing is certain—I need to devise a plan. Mai's threatening to stay for all time until I do."

"Really? What else did she say?"

"She has a lot to say," Pa Dao said. "She's waiting for you to talk to her. At the end of a Hmong funeral, people line up to talk to the person in the casket. Did you talk to your mother at her funeral?"

"No," I said. "I wouldn't have known what to say to a dead person."

"You say the same things you say to a living person," Pa Dao said. "If you never talked to Mai when she died, who did you talk to? Your dad? Your brother? Who's helping you carry your grief?"

"No one. We don't talk a lot."

We had reached the exit. Massed together like sheep, we and the other students leaned and pushed toward the doors, waiting for the bell to ring and release us.

Careful to avoid elbowing anyone, Pa Dao pulled a Ziploc bag of Skittles from her grocery sack. She clutched a handful and took my hand.

"Open up."

Skittles filled my cupped hands until Pa Dao paused. She was waiting for me to eat before grabbing a handful for herself, so I plunked a few into my mouth. While she continued to watch, I jammed the whole handful into my mouth. At last, Pa Dao finally helped herself to a handful. I waited while she shared the rainbow candies with the many open hands reaching all around her.

"When Mom was alive," I said, leaning down to talk directly into Pa Dao's ear, "I was with her all the time. Being together was how we talked. Words interrupted that talk." I paused. "Maybe I took her for granted."

Standing close to Pa Dao, I was drawn even closer by the warm, sweet scent of vanilla in her hair. The aroma was strong enough to hold its own with the bold scents of the leftovers in her grocery sack.

But then Brother bumped me from behind. I braced myself in time to avoid crashing into Pa Dao.

"Say all that to Mai," Pa Dao said over her shoulder to me. "And say anything else you'd wished you'd said when she was alive. You need to hear those words as much as Mai."

Everything I wanted to say rushed down a mountain upon me. My eyes blurred behind stinging tears. My throat burned.

But before I could even stammer one of those thoughts, the bell rang and the cafeteria erupted into motion. Dysfunctional Family, Pa Dao, and I hung back while Williams and the crowd cleared.

Three Hmong B-boys stayed behind as well, breakdancing on a large, flattened piece of cardboard on the cafeteria floor, spinning on their backs and heads like hyper water beetles at the slough.

After a moment, we joined the lazy river and spilled along with everyone else right into the hallway.

Pa Dao locked onto Dysfunctional Family with one arm but also locked onto me with the other. "You don't have to talk to Mai right now," she said. "But whenever you do, don't hold back. She's waiting for you, Michael. You'll know what to say when the time is right."

She pulled me and Dysfunctional Family to a stop.

"But now I have a question for you," she said. "This morning, Mai told me, 'Everything is emptiness.' Does that mean anything to you?"

"I'm beginning to think so," I said, separating from her and Dysfunctional Family to head to class.

The weight of Pa Dao's words stayed with me. Our Cottage Park house continued to press and flatten me. Only this time, the house stayed in place.

— CHAPTER TEN —

Cutthroat

"Hey, Empty," Harden called out. "Ya bring your Andy Jack today?"

I stood at one end of the rec center outdoor court, and the Harden Set stood at the other. He approached half-court, pinching his fingers together like he was counting bills.

"No twenty today," I called back. I launched another shot. "I'm broke."

"Come over anyway," Harden said. "Hoop with us today."

He waited until I jogged over. As I rolled Hawk to the sideline, I looked over the Harden Set.

They wore new Nike shoes and shorts. Their shirts rested over backpacks near Hawk. The first nip of winter signaled its intentions. Despite the chill, the Harden Set's stringy muscles glistened with sweat. I wore an Iowa Hawkeyes T-shirt and baggy gray sweatpants with a rip across the knee.

This would be my first time playing with the Harden Set. It was no big deal for them. All they cared about was our shared love of the ball. But it was a big deal for me. I'd never played against Black guys before.

The white guys I'd grown up with treated basketball as just one more recreational activity, another way to kill some time and have some laughs. Like bowling. But for the Harden Set and the Black guys they played against, basketball was their calling, their business, their life. They sacrificed their lives during their play.

I'd been watching them from my bubble, safe and secure with the knowledge I could never fully belong in their world. No way could I hang with any of them—the five best hoopers my age I'd ever seen. Others paid them their proper dues with respectable ground-level and fantastic future-skyscraper expectations. The Harden Set not only accepted and understood those expectations but demanded them.

Once I took my place on their court, Harden got down to business. This was a shootaround—whoever made their shot received the rebound, to shoot again until they missed. Harden was the best of the five, fast-forwarding around the rest of us like we were stuck in wet cement. He slithered, shapeshifted, and leapfrogged in his own highlight reel.

After a few minutes, he paused when the ball bounced his way. "We finna Hustle," he said. He did not wait for agreement but instead passed me the ball. "Toss the rock."

I'd never played Hustle, though I'd watched the Harden Set play it all the time. It began with taking a shot from the top of the key.

I dribbled to the spot and prepared to shoot. The Harden Set bunched together underneath the rim to fight for a rebound. But I made my shot. They bickered as the ball danced through the net.

Harden collected the ball and threw it back to me. "Remix," he said. "Do it over."

I lined up as before and shot again. The ball left my hands on target, and I followed through, snapping my wrist downward and framing it proudly. The ball swished a second time.

Pat Bev jumped and swatted the ball before it exited the net. "What is this wack?" he said. "Go down with them," he ordered, coming over to replace me. "Bob's clueless," he muttered.

But Harden stopped him. "Give up the rock," he said, tilting his head from Pat Bev to me.

Pat Bev fired the ball at me and stomped back to his original position, jostling against the others around the rim.

"You're supposed to miss the first shot," Harden patiently explained. "But if you wanna try to make it, move back."

I took two steps back.

"Farther."

I took two more steps back, now outside my range.

"If you make this one," he said, "we'll count it."

I'd made this shot at home in Cottage Park with a wooden backboard and a friendly rim, but I had serious doubts about making it with a hyper-fiberglass backboard and tight rim. Still, I thought it might go in if I could sling the ball close to the rim.

I jumped off my left foot to shoot a long layup, aiming at the shooter's square. As the ball left my fingers, I steered and dialed it back like a ship captain.

It went in.

The Harden Set complained again.

"We're not counting that BS," LBJ said. "You didn't call bank."

"But that's what I meant to do," I said. "I swear."

Westbrook gripped the ball tightly, hexed, and squibbed it back to me so I had to move my feet.

"Fine," Harden said. "Now you shoot free throws. You get three shots if you can make them all. Or if you wanna be a baller, you can choose to make three farther-away shots in a row."

I grabbed the ball. As my fingers stroked the pebbled surface, I focused on the sequence of shooting a free throw. First, I squared my feet at the free-throw line.

"I'll shoot the free throws, if you don't mind."

The Harden Set groaned.

I made all three.

Harden passed the ball back after the third make. "Now, you take another three-pointer," he said. "Or bring it down into the jungle, wherever you like."

Since no one came out to guard me, I shot again from the top of the key and scored. I'm automatic from that spot.

"You're at seven," Harden said. He passed me the ball. "Take your three free throws."

I made the first two, but missed the third. Then the real game began.

Harden rebounded and scored. Eventually, everyone scored. And I learned Hustle the hard way.

Out of bounds? Not when Curry stepped around me and outside the baseline on a layup.

Fouls? Not when Westbrook slaughtered me on a wide-open three-pointer.

I learned a harsh lesson after missing a free throw, and my score settled on 11.

"Poison points," Pat Bev said. "Back to zero."

We played on. At one point, Harden tried to jinx me. "Fury or Wilder?" he challenged right before my release.

I caught myself and froze.

"The fight is coming up on December first," Harden continued. "Who you got your money on?"

"He's rooting for the white boy," LBJ said. "Even though he knows white boys can't fight."

"I don't know boxing," I said. "Or Ultimate Fighting. I've never been in a fight. In my hometown, there was nothing to fight about, so I never even saw a fight. And my dad doesn't let us watch that junk on TV. Besides, any fighting makes me sick to my stomach."

Westbrook couldn't believe what he was hearing. "Your *real* dad?" he said. "Fighting's the first thing a real dad teaches his crumb crusher. Least mines did. Reason being, you have to fight on North. This life is straight-up, one-hundred-percent fighting or fucking."

"And don't forget spreading love," Harden said, "like butter."

Westbrook sidestepped to his backpack and unzipped it. He brought out two pairs of black leather Ultimate Fighting Championship gloves. He grinned as he prepared to launch one pair at me. A large hole interrupted the gleam where his right front tooth should have been, sending a warning.

I held up my hand to stop him. "Thanks, but no," I said. "Seriously, I can't fight."

"Can't or won't?" Westbrook said.

"Both," I said.

"You're soft," Westbrook said. "You can't be soft on North. Being soft here will get you eaten alive."

Soft. Was that all he saw? A white boy who didn't belong, couldn't fight, and couldn't survive in their world? I wanted to prove him wrong, but I didn't know how.

"We hoopin' at the moment," Harden told Westbrook. "Can we finish our game?"

Westbrook grudgingly returned the gloves to his backpack and returned to the court.

I steadied myself again and made the first free throw, then the next two. But again, no one came out to guard me as I readied my next shot. They thought I would miss, but I kept racking up points until I captured the lead again.

The next time I went to the free-throw line, I interrupted Harden before he could jinx me again. I wanted to show him I was beyond head games.

"Who do *you* like in the fight?" I said.

"We're straight up for Wilder," Harden said. "Fat-Boy Fury isn't in good enough shape to hang with Wilder. He'll be knocked out, no doubt."

"Wilder will seriously murder that white boy," Westbrook said. He smashed his right hand hard against his left hand. A jack-o'-lantern smile stretched across his face.

I made all three of my free throws. My score was now 16. If I made my next three free throws, I would have 19, setting myself up for the win on the next two-point shot.

I sank the free throws.

This time, as soon as Harden rolled the ball to me, the Harden Set's best defensive stopper, Curry, followed behind. Before I could grab on, Curry swiped a hand to knock the ball to the court. I picked up the ball on the dribble, angled in, and shot as Pat Bev came to help Curry.

The ball bounced off the rim far enough for LBJ to trampoline from a running jump and flush it. His takeoff was a reminder that even when things seemed unreachable, there was always a way to rise above. He hung on the rim afterward, muscles fisting and rippling like steel cords above his shoulders and near his neck, where I had none.

He checked where to land in the splash zone, then let himself fall from the sky. After returning to earth, he slicked down his heavy mustache and goatee and smiled like a cat that had devoured a delicious mouse.

"I tipped your ass," he said, striding to the line to shoot free throws. "Tip-ins put you back to nothing. You're nothing."

"Nothing is never nothing," Harden said. "Nowhere. No how. No nothing."

"Man," LBJ said. "School's out. You tell us what he's got."

"My man is at zero," Harden said. "The big O. He's waiting. Depending on where he puts himself, he can use that zero to make any number infinitely bigger or smaller. Put zero before a number with a decimal point or after any number, and see if I'm lying."

Harden glanced my way as I recognized what might have been a compliment. I beamed on the inside, but played like I had been there before on the outside.

We played another couple of possessions before I remembered the time and my responsibilities at home. In a break after Curry scored, I announced, "Sorry. I gotta go home and make supper."

"You can't leave now," Harden said. "I'm finally getting hot. Supper for who?"

"My dad and big brother," I said. I edged away to retrieve Hawk.

"Why can't they feed themselves?" Pat Bev said.

"A long story," I said. "But my little family will starve to death if I don't go home and make them supper."

"Where's your ma?" LBJ said. "Can't she fix supper for them?"

"No," I said. "Another long story . . . She's gone. Passed in August."

The silence that followed was the kind that makes you think that no one will ever speak again. But I was wrong.

"That's not a long story," LBJ said. "That's the Northside story."

The Harden Set agreed. Each muttered sympathy.

"Is your brother a hooper?" Harden said. "He's a big white boy."

"One more long story," I said, "with a not-so-happy ending. I'll save it for next time."

I collected Hawk and took one dribble before Westbrook attacked me from behind. Locking his arms around my neck and the back of my head, he squeezed both arms hard.

"Welcome to a rear naked chokehold," he stated, cold-blooded.

I struggled, but Westbrook only held tighter and choked harder. I couldn't breathe.

"Prepare to meet your maker," he said.

He wasn't joking.

I considered digging my fingernails into his arm, but it would only enrage him and hurry my suffocation or broken neck. Instead, I fake-flopped dead and hung limp in his arms, at his mercy. I was running out of time.

Westbrook held me upward and swept me from side to side like a broom.

The other Harden Set members, especially Harden, appealed for my release.

"Dayum," Pat Bev said. "You realize how long you'll be in prison for killing a white boy?"

"He didn't do nothing to you," Curry said. "It takes twelve seconds to cut off oxygen to his brain. Let him go."

"This is some sorry-ass shit," LBJ said. "A cop choked me once like that and just about killed me. They gave him an award afterward."

"He'd a been promoted if he killed you," Pat Bev said.

But Westbrook only intensified the chokehold. My head was about to pop like a champagne cork.

"What you don't know," Westbrook said to the rest of the Harden Set, "and what he don't know is he *is* a fighter. Right now, I can feel his body doing all it can to live. We all fight to live. He's just a shitty fighter. Another fifteen seconds, and he for sure won't ever have to fight again."

"You made your point," Harden said. "Now let go."

Harden stepped in and yanked Westbrook's arm from my throat. Curry, LBJ, and Pat Bev helped pry him away.

"But he never tapped out," Westbrook said as he let go, and I slipped from his hold.

He joined the rest of the Harden Set as they eased me to the court. On my hands and knees, I heaved in air and grounded myself on the white asphalt until it mirrored back a thousand tiny shimmering diamonds.

"You guys are letting him off easy," Westbrook said, towering over me. "You're not doing him any favors. We can tell him about fighting, or we can show him and let him experience it for himself. Which way you think he'll learn faster? Which way is gonna save his life?"

I rotated my head up. Westbrook grinned down at me.

My eyes landed on Hawk, sitting on the out-of-bounds line. I crawled to him. Finally, the spinning slowed enough that I could hold Hawk and use him to defy gravity, pushing up to stand.

"You okay?" Harden said, helping me up.

I lifted a hand as high as I could before it hurt. That was the only answer I could provide.

"He's fine," Westbrook said with confidence. "He'll shake it off."

My head continued to throb as I took my first steps home. My neck stiffened and ached, hopefully not broken but only strained. I held Hawk for stability and forced myself to focus on the rhythm of my steps and on my duties at home: fixing supper, cleaning, and schoolwork. My headache wasn't just from the chokehold—it was from the burden of everything I didn't know and couldn't say. I was out of place. On North, even breathing was a fight I didn't know how to win.

"Get ready," Westbrook yelled, his grin sharp and near homicidal. "Next time, I'll show you how to escape a rear naked chokehold. If you survive, that is." Their basketball dribbled again.

I only looked ahead. I didn't know if I could look back.

Nor did I want to find out.

— CHAPTER ELEVEN —

Over and Back

That night, I feared I'd dream about Westbrook and his rear naked chokehold. Instead, I dreamed about Pa Dao. In my dream, she fed me a feast, building me up to prepare for a mission to meet Mom.

In the dream, we walked together along southbound Highway 169, carrying water in our cupped hands as cars and trucks zoomed by us. The passing *whoosh* of semi-trucks knocked us off our stride, but we kept going. We were the eye of a storm. The mashing of our tennis shoes against the shoulder's dry gravel was the only sound between us. The road was as straight as a railroad track, and I knew where it would take us. Still, I was relieved Pa Dao was there, guiding us through danger. With her beside me, the unknown was less a threat and more a promise.

When I awoke the next morning, I followed Pa Dao through all my morning classes, but this time it was in a daydream. At lunch, I eagerly waited in the cafeteria for her. Many minutes passed. Finally, I heard her before seeing her.

"Sorry, I'm late!" she called from behind me.

My neck still hurt, so seeing her meant turning my whole body around. I truly was a Frankenstein, like Harden had said the week before.

Pa Dao was dressed in Thomas Jefferson–gray sweatpants and a red school badminton team T-shirt. She hustled to the table and set five hot Tupperware containers along with spoons and forks before me.

"My chemistry teacher let me use her microwave so I wouldn't have to stand in a line down here," she explained as she opened the Tupperware bowls and set out plates. "*Wb noj mov.*" She laughed as if enjoying an inside joke. "What does *wb noj mov* mean?"

"'Let's eat,'" I replied.

"'Let's eat *rice.*'" She directed me to a container with a red lid. "Sticky rice. It's the most popular dish for Hmong in Laos, usually steamed for the best taste. But my rice cooker makes it nice and fresh in twenty minutes. Still tastes good!"

I opened the lid to the sweet, nutty aroma of glistening white rice clumped together in a mini mountain.

"Use your hands to take your half," Pa Dao said.

I scooped my portion of the rice, warm and alive, like a baby bunny.

"I signed you up for Asian Club," Pa Dao said. "It's the best way to meet Hmong kids here at school, and it looks great in the extracurriculars section of your Common App for college. We meet every Wednesday for an hour after school until a week before Thanksgiving. Then we meet every day to plan for Hmong New Year. We put on the show right before Christmas break."

"Oh," I said. "I won't be able to join that group. I've got basketball after school, and that's the time I get supper ready for Puff and John."

"You have to come to Asian Club," Father said from the other end of the table. "I write a play for the Hmong New Year, and we never have enough guys. You'll be perfect for the role I'm writing for you."

"Come on," Mother said. "You can do it. We'll teach you how to manage your time better."

Pa Dao took the rest of the rice, then produced two brightly colored Tupperware bowls alongside our plates.

"Bitter beef soup," she announced. She lifted the lid from another container to reveal thinly sliced hunks of chewy beef intestine, liver, heart, and rib meat simmering in broth. "It's a reminder that life is bitter but nourishing. Just like family."

"Mom used to make this," I said as Pa Dao filled my bowl with meat, vegetables, and broth.

"Right," she said. "Your mouth tastes this Hmong food, your stomach craves it, but Mai wants your head and heart to connect to *know* it. We serve bitter beef soup at Hmong funerals—and other dishes I'll bring each day."

"Father is a Vang," Pa Dao said, nodding to the other end of the table. "Her younger sister is named Mai Vang, too, just like your mom. Mai means 'beloved, dear daughter.' It's a common name. I bet there are at least eight Mai Vangs here at Thomas Jefferson."

"Don't sleep on my May Vangs either," Father said. "The May Vangs are pretty much the same as the Mai Vangs. You'll hear the names pop up in conversations or during attendance."

I nodded thanks.

Now Pa Dao studied me. "You've never been to a Hmong funeral?"

"No," I answered.

"Well," Father said. "We'll take you to one. We all go to one at least once a month or so. Here's the best way I can put it: It's a festive show. Not the happy type, of course. But there's a little acting, lots of crying and wailing, music and songs, and endless eating and drinking for two to three days straight—twenty-four hours per day."

Pa Dao said, "Everyone needs good food so they'll have the strength and energy to help the dead stay dead." She paused, startled. "Michael, you're staring at me, not eating. Eat."

I returned to my food, and Pa Dao returned to her lesson.

"When a Hmong person dies," she said, "their family doesn't let them go alone. We dress them in their finest clothes and sing them home. The family convinces you to say your goodbyes, take your leave, and return to your birthplace. It's not just a funeral. It's a journey." She paused again, her eyes connecting to mine. "Mai deserved that journey."

I dived back into the soup, achingly familiar, bitter, and delicious. And so much simpler than all this talk about funerals.

"Mai says she wanted a Hmong funeral," Pa Dao said matter-of-factly.

"No one had any idea."

"She wanted to return to her homeland, her birthplace, far beyond the mountains of Laos, to reunite with her ancestors."

"But we don't know where she was born in Laos," I said. "John and I would ask her about it, but she'd just stare back at us—through us."

"Oh, she remembers," Pa Dao said. "But it's best not to touch a hot stove."

An impatient wall clock showed that only twenty-one minutes remained.

"Did any of your Mai's relatives come to her funeral?" Pa Dao asked.

"No," I said. "I called them, but nobody showed up."

"Who did you talk to?"

"Grandpa Vang, through one of my cousins, I think. I invited them all to the funeral, but maybe not in the right way."

Pa Dao stared into her soup. "*No* Hmong came to Mai's funeral . . ." she said to herself.

"Nope." I put down my spoon. "Only *meka*. We had a wake with a rosary the night before. At ten the next morning, people came and knelt and prayed around her open casket. At eleven, we had a funeral Mass, buried her, then came back to the church basement for a potluck the Catholic Daughters had arranged for us. But no—no Hmong came. It was only locals and Puff, John, and me. We're just a little family."

"No, you're not. You've got a big Hmong family too. Mai's family is your big family. Repeat after me: *your* big family." She waited for me to respond.

"*My* big family," I said.

"It can get too big," Sister called out. "Too many Hmong in one zip code."

The rest of Dysfunctional Family agreed.

"Almost as bad as too many Hmong is too big a family in a small house," Brother said. "No space, no privacy, no quiet."

"We Hmong are one big family," Pa Dao said. "And you can never be without your big family. Without your big family, you couldn't exist." She shuddered at such a possibility. "We need to help you and Mai—and your dad and brother—reconnect to that big family."

I grimaced. "I don't know if that's possible." The idea of connecting with a family I'd never known was like breathing underwater.

"Even families that have fallen apart come together when their beloved dies," Pa Dao said. "People show up and make amends. They must be there to pay their respects. If you ever feel alone, go to a Hmong funeral. You'll be surrounded by so many people."

We chewed our rice and sipped Hi-C Blazin' Blueberry.

"Something must have gone wrong between Mai and her family in Saint Paul," Pa Dao said, deep in thought. Her fingertips tapped her juice box. "Do you have any idea what?"

"Maybe . . ."

I pictured the few bits I knew and tried to connect the puzzle pieces. But I wasn't even sure if they were all from the same puzzle. I sighed.

"Or maybe not, no," I clarified. "At this point, I don't need or want to know. I don't like to make waves."

Pa Dao laughed. "Toughen up. Mai is perfectly fine with us finding out what happened to her."

I shot another glance at the clock and willed it to speed up.

"I keep telling you, Mai won't leave on her journey," Pa Dao said. "I've done all I can. I've tried to ignore her. I've pleaded with her. I've burned joss paper. But she won't listen. Now I have two moms—one who wakes me every morning by whispering stories in my ear, and another who nags me for the rest of the day to be a good daughter. It's too much." Pa Dao let out a long exhale. "Your mom is undeniably OG. Do you know what that means?"

"Old-school?"

"Yeah. You can say that. It stands for 'older generation,' 'old guy,' 'original gangster.' It all means the same. Mai is traditional. She wants things done a certain way and insists upon it."

She stared at me hard. Even the lazy left eye was locked in.

"Mai insists her little family needs her now more than ever. She says she won't go until you are safely on your journey. She's holding on to so much. But it's not right for her to linger around. I've told her that it might bring bad luck to your little family. She insists that the good she's doing to keep her little family safe overrules any bad luck."

John's injury came to mind.

Pa Dao sat back. "We need to help Mai move along, to make up for what she lost by not having a Hmong funeral. I'll do my part, but you and your little family must do yours. Have you thought about what I told you yesterday about being Hmong?" When she asked this, her voice was calm but firm.

I shifted in my seat. "What do you mean?"

"You have to do more than say you're Hmong. It's something you are, but more importantly, something you do. Your past, your future, and your mother demand that you honor your Hmong heritage."

My chest tightened. *Hmong.* The word was foreign, but it was the thread connecting me to Mom.

"Honestly, I'm trying to figure out who I am," I said. "I don't even know where to start."

Pa Dao was silent for a long moment, her gaze piercing me until I looked away. "But who you are is already written, Michael. You are Hmong. Accept it."

My stomach lurched as if Pa Dao had wrapped a frayed bungee cord around us both and leaped headfirst into drama.

Pa Dao produced a ripe mango and a Swiss Army knife from her grocery sack. She peeled back the mango's skin, exposing a fleshy, dripping, orangish-yellow pulp, then she cut slices for us.

"We need to prepare for our work ahead," she said, raising a slice like a cup in a toast. "Eat."

I raised my slice back to hers. Juice dripped down my wrist, sticky and sweet. We slurped the pieces into our mouths and laughed as the juice ran down our faces.

Before I could clean myself, Pa Dao took a paper towel and wiped my face, pinching my lips and nose between stiff fingers to ensure I was spotless. I flinched. Her paper towel scratched and hurt like Mom's wet washrag when she cleaned me as a toddler.

"We'll keep going tomorrow," Pa Dao said. "We'll solve this mystery and help Mai on her way."

Then she stood. Dysfunctional Family stood as well and surrounded her, bumping and holding one another as they began their way out of the cafeteria.

"But it's not just about Mai," Pa Dao said, looking back at me. "It's about you too. Finding where you belong."

Her words lingered as a challenge and a promise all at once.

"*Sib ntsib dua*, Hmong Boy."

It was the Hmong phrase for "See you later." And *Hmong Boy*. Once again, the title was strange, unfamiliar, but also a key to a door I hadn't yet opened. I didn't know what lay on the other side of that door. But for the first time, I wanted to find out.

— CHAPTER TWELVE —

Fouled Out

In the cafeteria, I opened the Friday, September 28, *Star Tribune* to the article "One More Mauer Record—He Broke Killebrew's Twins Mark for Getting on Base." The night before, in Detroit, Joe Mauer had hit an opposite-field single, surpassing Harmon Killebrew's Twins record. Joe Mauer had safely reached base 3,073 times during his fifteen-year career. In that same game, he also earned a walk plus got another hit, upping his total to 3,075.

"Hmong Boy," Pa Dao said, dropping her grocery sack on the table. "What did I say about your dopey newspaper?" She peered over the paper at the headline. "Who is Joe Bauer? One of your basketball guys?"

"It's Joe *Mauer*," I said. "He's a Minnesota Twins *baseball* guy. But he's more than that to my little family."

I folded up the paper and set it aside. Pa Dao was oblivious to my words, preoccupied instead with our meal prep as she pulled out place settings and Tupperware containers.

"I have a treat for you today," she said. "Traditional beef soup—made with oxtails and tripe. Bet you don't know what that is."

Mom had spent all day cleaning and cooking tripe. She'd mix in beef chunks, basil, lemongrass, and ginger root from her garden.

"Tripe is a cow's stomach," I said. "Mom made this soup too. Puff used to ask her to clean the crud off the linings and intestines, but she'd say, 'That's the best part.'"

"*Wb noj mov*," Pa Dao said, her voice warm and inviting.

The Hmong phrase and the steam rising from the bowls whispered of home. It reminded me of the Hmong traditions that bound us together, especially when everything else was falling apart.

Pa Dao filled our bowls with rice and arranged it with stir-fried pumpkin leaves and broth. Brother passed her tray for a serving as well. Then Pa Dao filled two glasses with ice cubes and added gooey green pulp mixed with sugar and water.

"Cucumber juice," I said, demonstrating my knowledge.

Pa Dao sat to eat but hadn't taken more than a few bites before beginning our next lesson.

"We're never ready when a loved one dies. So, relatives come as a matter of duty to join the immediate family a few weeks before the funeral. *Zov hmo* means 'to watch and guard the night.' The main purpose is to help the family get ready for the funeral. There are many responsibilities. But in the process, the relatives show empathy, help the family grieve, and make sure they're not scared of death. Grief is too heavy to carry alone. Death is also a gut check for the living to remind one another that life, even in its darkest moments, is worth living."

I chewed and took a quick sip of cucumber juice. "A bunch of Puff's relatives—the Moriaritys—never showed up for Mom's funeral," I said. "They live all over the country. Those that came flew to Des Moines or Minneapolis, rented a car, and drove to Cottage Park." I sat back in my chair, remembering. "But Holy Trinity did the most work for the funeral and helped us to our feet again."

Pa Dao blew steam from her bowl, giving me time to continue. Instead, I gestured for her to keep going.

"I remember my first night watch," she added. "One of my aunties passed away. At night watch, everyone is more at ease, consoling one another. We eat, the men drink, and we stay until the last person leaves—sometimes not until sunrise."

"Mom was Catholic," I said. "But looking back, she still had one foot in the Hmong world. Now I know why she wanted a Hmong funeral. Everybody should have that much attention on them when they die."

"By the time of the funeral," Pa Dao said, "we've cleansed the loved one's smell of decay, wiped tear stains from their face, and dressed them in their finest Hmong clothing for the journey through the spirit world. We place burnt joss paper inside their clothing so they have money, and we tuck rice into a pouch sewn on their shirt so they have food. Some Hmong clans rip their clothing, a tradition that goes back to the time when the Chinese desecrated our graves. Grave robbers won't disturb a grave with torn clothing."

Pa Dao was as matter-of-fact about grave robbers as she was about the ingredients in Hmong dishes.

"One family member sits close to the loved one to ensure their safety, keep flies away, and ensure their face and body stay straight. That helps the loved one feel comfortable in their eternal bed as we work to guide them everywhere they've lived—and beyond. We lead them across the big river, on dangerous paths, through valleys, and up mountains with snakes and other dangers, until they reach their birthplace."

Pa Dao's hands mimed her words.

"An experienced man, a *txiv xaiv*, chants directions with a clear voice to help the loved one take their first steps on their journey. A nearby rooster's head also points in the direction, along with a cow we slaughtered and a symbolic horse for the loved one to ride. Sound is everywhere. No Hmong funeral can take place without a *qeej* and a gong. The *qeej* is the sacred musical instrument that guides the spirit from the physical to the spiritual world. The gong scares away evil spirits and reminds the soul to move along. The loved one appreciates the *qeej* and the gong, their last music before eternal silence. We kneel to thank all who came to honor the loved one and to help with the funeral work."

I shook my head, hearing all these complex details. "Did Mom actually think my little family could organize a Hmong funeral?"

Pa Dao shook her head back at me. "No. That's what Hmong families are for. She was always planning to come back to her big Hmong family."

Sister snooped around the food Pa Dao had spread around us. She turned her nose up at the options until Pa Dao pulled out mini boxes of DOTS and set them before her. Sister snatched a box, opened it, and tipped it until three DOTS fell into her mouth. She talked while chewing.

"We're like those fish that come back upstream before they die," Sister said, her voice a mix of pride and gloom. "No matter how far we leave, we always find our way back home. It's wired in our blood."

Sister chewed vigorously, then pulled out another DOT and prepared to toss it into my mouth. When I declined, Pa Dao tossed me a whole box of DOTS—and an invitation.

"A bunch of us are meeting at the football game after school tonight," she said. "Wanna go?"

I hesitated.

"The weather will be perfect," she added.

"I hear we're not that good," I said.

"We don't care about the game—except when the coach puts in a Hmong guy."

"I'll see . . ."

"In Hmong, that means no," Pa Dao said. "I play football too—flag football on Saturday mornings with all the Hmong girls. Come watch us. I'll text you when we play." She pulled out her phone and prepared to input my phone number.

"I don't have a phone," I said.

"Then give me your landline number."

"But I sleep in on Saturday mornings . . ."

"I can wake you," she said. "Let it happen, Captain."

Pa Dao's eyes, voice, and persistence were drawing me toward yet another journey. This time, a journey into Thomas Jefferson and the Northside. A journey I wasn't ready to begin.

"Fine," I said, hoping I sounded convincing.

I wasn't sure whether I was agreeing to the football game or surrendering to the pull of Pa Dao's world. Either way, I was sure there was no turning back.

"My number is four-eight-eight, eight-eight—"

"Quit playing," she chided, cutting me off. "That's Pizza Hut."

I gave her a sheepish smile and my actual phone number.

With a sigh, Pa Dao pulled a sack of Reese's mini peanut butter cups from her grocery sack.

"Grab a handful," she said.

I did.

"And think about meeting at the football game after school, okay?" she said.

I did think about it. I thought about it all the way to Mandarin class. With each step, I warmed to the possibility of getting to know Pa Dao and her Hmong friends better. By the time I took my seat, I was excited.

But as the bell rang, Harden burst into the room. We all looked up in surprise, but no one was as surprised as me. He ran to my desk, sweating, and his eyes grew large as he spoke.

"Your brother is going wacko," he said. "Let's go, Empty."

A moment later, the school secretary's methodical voice broadcast over the intercom: "Teachers, please close and lock your doors. Any students still in the hallways must report to the Citizenship Room immediately."

Shrieking and shouting reverberated in the hallway outside our classroom. It was the sound that typically accompanied a massive fight.

I froze to my seat.

"C'mon, man," Harden said, waving for me to join him. "I'm telling you, your brother pissed himself. Hallway aides tried to hogpile him, but he busted them straight off. He's a Marvel movie. He's the Hulk."

Our teacher, Ms. Yang, came over. "I'll find out what happened to your brother once we start class," she said calmly, setting a hand on my desk. She turned to scold Harden. "You go on to the Citizenship Room."

Harden headed for the doorway but stopped to make one last appeal. "He needs you. He snatched Williams right off his back and swatted him against the lockers."

Harden acted out the sequence of Williams flying across the hallway into steel lockers. His rendition drew fireworks-style "oohs" and "aahs" from classmates. The response continued even after Harden left the room and closed the door behind him. I would have been entertained, too, if John hadn't been the villain in his little play.

Ms. Yang waited for attention before beginning her lesson. At the same time, a key slid into the door handle, and the door sprang open.

Williams scanned our faces before settling on mine. He pointed at me. "He needs to come with me."

As Ms. Yang signaled for me to leave, Zheng Xi, our Chinese foreign exchange student who sat behind me and had given herself the American name of Leslie, spoke in Mandarin: *"Mai ke, qing man man zou. Wo men dou xi wang ni gege jiankang pingan."* (Michael, please go slowly. We all wish your brother good health and well-being.)

I took my books and left with Williams, who closed the door behind me. Harden stood in the hallway, waiting for us.

"Man," Williams said. He brought an arm around me and urged me forward as he and Harden started jogging down the hallway. "We're lucky no one got hurt today from all this mess."

There was an edge to his usually mellow voice. I sensed that this was not the end of something ominous, but the beginning.

"Does your brother have epilepsy?" Williams asked.

"No," I said.

"You need to speak up if you have any idea about what's going on," Williams said, already breathless and sweating. He slowed to a stop and waved us on. "You two go. I'll catch up."

Harden accelerated to the stairs. He took the steps two at a time until he could launch himself onto the landing. He repeated the same sequence with the ease of someone who'd done it a hundred times before, until we reached the first floor.

There, five adults were gathered around John, who lay on the floor in restful sleep. His head and shoulders rested on his backpack in the school nurse's arms. She had moonlit skin and white hair pulled back in a bun. Silver glasses magnified glowing blue eyes.

She motioned me down to her level, where she dabbed blood from John's nostrils. The bloody streaks stood out against his pale, freckled skin, a reminder of how fragile he'd become.

The nurse chirped into her phone, "The father is on his way to HCMC?"

"Yes," the school secretary's voice announced on the other end. "We're holding door 1 and the elevator open for the EMTs. I hear the sirens. It should be any moment."

The nurse gazed down at John. "Your brother, Michael, is here to help us go to the hospital. You're doing fine." She grasped and patted his hand. "Looking good. Keep relaxing." She then turned to me. "You're as surprised as we are. He's in a postictal period—half asleep."

A hand rested on my back—Harden's.

"I came across your brother while walking to class," he said. "I stopped and asked him if he hooped. But before he answered, he went stiff as a board and fell backward. He started convulsing. I've seen guys seize at the rec center—my pops had us all CPR trained, and I knew to dodge around him to break his fall. Dude damn near broke my back. He a beast."

"Thanks," was all I could say.

"Your brother started shivering and got white," Harden continued. "Whiter," he corrected. He stopped to search for a more fitting descriptor. "Pale."

Williams had finally caught up to join us. He bent over and placed his hands on his knees, partly out of respect for the solemn scene but mainly to catch his breath.

"Williams and I tried to calm and cradle him," Harden said, "so he wouldn't hurt himself. That's when he went all Hulk on us. But after we calmed him, he drifted off like a baby."

We all looked up again. Four EMT staff casually walked toward John. The school nurse moved closer to me to give them room. They grunted on a three-count, lunged John onto a gurney, then wheeled him to the ambulance at the school entrance.

The school nurse motioned for Harden, Williams, and me to join the procession alongside the gurney.

"We'll send you with John downtown to HCMC," she said. "Your dad is bringing John's medication to the hospital. Do you know what medication it is?"

"We call them horse pills," I said. "He doesn't always take his medication, unless I'm there to watch him."

With much effort, the EMTs heaved the gurney inside the ambulance—in the same way the pallbearers shoved Mom's casket into the hearse for her short drive to Resurrection Cemetery. I hopped into the ambulance and strapped myself into a seat alongside John.

"We'll pass through this," Harden said, stepping up to the edge of the ambulance.

From anyone else, the words would have sounded like a wish. From Harden, they were a promise, a guarantee. He slipped a $20 bill into my palm, closed it into a fist, and palmed it like a basketball.

"You a baller. You the man now. Be strong, Empty."

Those were the last words from anyone at Thomas Jefferson before the door closed behind me. The last sight through the back window was of the school nurse, Williams, and Harden waving goodbye as we drove away.

"Your brother is *built*," an EMT said with admiration.

I hummed a "mm-hmm" in agreement. Whoever said "He ain't heavy—he's my brother" had never lifted my brother, never carried the weight of his struggles. His body had grown heavier with each recent medical setback. With the siren wailing and the horn bellowing, we split traffic in two, leaving a wake behind us. We cleared our way east on 44th Avenue, heading toward Interstate 94, which would take us into downtown Minneapolis.

I hoped someone or something would clear the way for John as well, so he could resume his life and go wherever he wanted, and as fast as he wanted.

"Can I hold his hand?" I asked the EMT.

He approved.

I took John's right hand. It was cool and heavy. It flapped over my hand like a first baseman's mitt.

We rocked back and forth as the ambulance sped to merge onto the interstate.

"You can do this," I said, pumping John's hand.

I didn't believe it, though. John was at the mercy of the forces that kept slamming him to the ground, and I couldn't "do this" or "pass through this" or anything else to help him.

Now the ambulance slowed, exiting off the interstate and merging onto the downtown streets. Bells clanged from the light rail, even louder than the sirens. The clangs were followed by a short horn burst as the engine and cars coasted by us.

John's hand warmed. "Mom . . . ?" he mumbled. His eyes were closed, but his lifelessness was easing into tranquility. "Mom," he said a second time, with certainty.

I held John's hand until we arrived at Hennepin County Medical Center. Puff awaited us as the EMTs lifted John from the ambulance. He took John's other hand as they wheeled him down the hall. We stayed with John until the staff directed us to the lobby, where they pushed him into a room for observation.

Puff and I found a family waiting room, its walls a sterile white, and sank into soft, plush chairs shaped like boxes, seeming to swallow us whole. The cutting, sterile odor of antiseptic reminded us of where and why we were there.

"The school nurse said he's in a postictal period," I told Puff. "Like you're groggy. On the way here, he kept calling for Mom."

Puff sighed. "Here we go again."

After a while, a nurse directed us to John's room. Puff handed me a rosary. But he didn't have time to even kiss the feet of Jesus on the crucifix and recite the Apostles' Creed before medical staff started asking us questions. They wanted to know John's medical background so they could identify the seizure's trigger. We were under observation as much as John, with nurses, doctors, physician's assistants, and specialists asking the same questions.

"Has John ever had a seizure?"

"Were there any indicators that he might have seized before?"

"How did he feel before the seizure?"

"What do you think triggered his seizure?"

"Was he sick before the seizure? Did he have diarrhea?"

Puff let me do the talking. I answered the medical staff the way I answered the Thomas Jefferson staff.

"Until the tornado," I said, "John was the strongest person we knew. We were as surprised as anyone at what happened today."

I also repeated Harden's account of being with John during the seizure and breaking his fall.

Eventually, a nurse wheeled John out of the room to perform an EKG test, CT scan, and blood work while we stayed behind.

Puff let out a long exhale. "Your great-grandma Moriarity said, 'Troubles come in threes.' We've survived a tornado, Mom's death, and John's health problems. Dear God, let today be the last trouble." He thought for a moment. "But I guess Grandma Moriarity also said, 'God never gives us a cross we can't carry.'"

"But why does he have to give us a cross in the first place?"

Puff called a thirty-second timeout "He doesn't *give us* a cross as much as he *doesn't stop us from carrying* a cross," he finally said. "He lets life happen to us. That's the hardest discipline in the world for a parent. And I can't do it."

He hitched a thumb out toward the hallway.

"I should be the one in that bed, unconscious, getting tested— not John. But be careful what you wish for. Free will is a gift that can also be a curse." He ran his hands over his face. "Anyway, there's not much we can do right now."

Puff collected the TV remote on the table and pressed buttons until the Twins game materialized.

"We play a doubleheader today—remember?" he said. "Against my old club, the Sox. Game one is a makeup for a game we canceled back in April due to . . ." He waited for me to respond.

"Rain?"

"Snow," Puff said as though I should have remembered.

He adjusted the volume, then sat back in his chair.

"I watched the game earlier today," he said. "Joe Mauer hit right away in the first inning—around the time I answered the call from school. Joe Mauer's hitting the ball hard now."

With that, Puff instantly escaped HCMC for Target Field. He wanted me to go with him, but I couldn't escape. The dreary little room's walls were closing in on me.

"Berríos is on today," Puff said. "And when he's grooving it, you're not gonna beat him, especially at home."

The game played in and to silence—the only sound was the faint hum of hospital machines. Before the announcer called the leadoff hitters for the bottom of the sixth, Puff leaned forward, his eyes glued to the screen.

"This is it," he said as if the outcome could change the game as well as our crisis in the hospital. After hearing the names, though, he groaned. "How can we win games with Jake Cave coming to bat or Willians Astudillo?"

"Willians is hitting the ball," I said.

"Maybe. But you can't play in the league carrying that much weight. Someday he'll regret not taking better care of himself."

Despite Puff's protests, Cave outlived a full count, Willians sacrificed him home, and we went up 2 to 1.

About that time, they wheeled John back in. He was awake but still groggy. An ongoing EEG test with connected sensors strapped across his head measured brain activity, and a nurse set him up for a urine sample.

More staff asked John the same questions they'd asked us. He grumbled, "Nope," "None," "Fine," "Dunno," and "Some."

"That's his natural disposition," Puff said, assuring the staff that a brain injury hadn't caused John's lethargic responses.

As hospital staff observed John, Puff and I observed Joe Mauer from the sixth inning until the end of the game. He slugged two nice hits, and we won.

John ate a hospital supper plus one of the large pizzas Puff had delivered for us. Then Puff sat back and prepared to watch Joe Mauer's second game.

"We won't lose at home if we stop them in the first inning," he said. "And if Joe Mauer leads off our side with a single and makes it around the bases and scores."

We scored two runs that inning. But John wasn't happy.

"I hate this place," he kept saying, his voice strained. "I'm out." His words were sharp, yet they betrayed fear, as if he were pleading for someone to tell him it would all be okay.

"We're waiting for one more neurosurgeon—Dr. Mendoza," I said. "He's reviewing your MRIs."

"He can look at them all he wants and call us when he knows what's wrong with me," John said. "I've had enough. I'm going home. Now."

"I'll make you a deal," Puff said, leaning toward John. "We'll stay until the prep football highlights end, at eleven. If Dr. Mendoza doesn't arrive by then, we'll leave." He sat back. "You can do this. Hold on a little longer, and we'll stop for wings on the way home."

John had removed the EEG sensors and left his bed by the time Dr. Mendoza entered the room at 11:11 p.m. Under his buttoned white coat, Dr. Mendoza wore a blue formal dress shirt and striped necktie. He introduced himself, stood alongside us, and regarded John, who climbed back into bed.

Dr. Mendoza cleared his throat and enunciated each word with a slight Spanish accent. "Mr. Moriarity, this seizure was a blessing in disguise. It forced us to look deeper, and now we know what we're up against."

Puff's eyes widened. He scrutinized me, then John. *"Blessing?"*

Dr. Mendoza paused, his gaze steady but heavy with the weight of his words. "Today's seizure forced us to take a closer look at John's brain. It also compelled us to take a closer look at his medical records from Mayo. Our MRI confirmed what we suspected after today's incident—it wasn't just a shadow but a tumor, a large one."

His breathless words closed and locked doors around us.

"Wait a minute," Puff said. "Are you sure? Couldn't this possibly be something else?"

"I am sensitive to your concerns," Dr. Mendoza said. "But we've ruled out all the other possibilities. It's not a bruise. Not a parasite. Nor is it TB, AIDS, or another disease."

Dr. Mendoza stretched his hand wide enough to span from his right eye, under his ear, to the back of his skull.

"A tumor this size is pressing directly behind John's right optic nerve, shifting his brain. The pressure poses an immediate threat. If we don't take the tumor now, the tumor will take John." His tone was professional but urgent. "Time is not on our side. Today's seizure was like a pressure valve blowing."

My mouth dried. I couldn't swallow.

Dr. Mendoza moved his hand away from his head and balled it into a determined fist. "We now know the enemy, and we must attack it with all our energy and resources. That means immediate surgery—early Monday afternoon—to remove the tumor. It's a formidable operation that takes ten to twelve hours. Down the road, we'll follow with radiation and chemotherapy." He took a quick breath. "Questions?"

There are no questions after such an announcement. It was checkmate. Dr. Mendoza had suffocated all ideas and any words that might spring from them.

We waited for Dr. Mendoza to continue, but he waited for us to go first.

"I'm going home," John said.

"Under no circumstances can you go home now or for the next several nights," Dr. Mendoza said.

Puff leaned over in his chair and ground the heels of his palms into his scalp as if trying to hold his head together. A low groan escaped him. "This can't be happening," he muttered. "Not to my boy."

I chewed my bottom lip. My heart pounded like a bass drum, each beat driving fear deeper into my chest. It was a rhythm I couldn't escape, a reminder of how fragile everything had become.

Dr. Mendoza turned to John and again waited. After a long silence, he placed a hand on John's left foot under the bedsheet and the thin hospital blanket.

"You must have questions," Dr. Mendoza said. "Not one?" He lightly squeezed John's toes. "This is your life we're talking about. What can I do to help you? We can't do anything without your involvement."

But John just seven-mile-stared at the TV, which was now replaying the day's first Twins game. After a few moments, he turned to me.

I couldn't speak for him—or for me. My throat tightened. Words stuck there like a fish bone, impossible to swallow or dislodge.

Finally, John slumped into his bed. "I don't have words for cancer."

"A lot is happening here in a hurry," Dr. Mendoza said. "Your seizure today was a message from the tumor. It's telling us that it isn't going to slow down, that there's no more room in your head for it to grow. Now we have to bring you up to speed—your growing tumor's speed."

John looked at me again. "What should we do, Michael?"

"Can we get a second opinion?" I said.

"Yes, of course," Dr. Mendoza said. "I can give you doctors' names and send them John's MRI images. Honestly, though, they'd agree with everything I've told you. And more importantly, you'd lose precious time. We're here late on a Friday night"—he checked his watch—"on almost a Saturday morning. We must plan the operation for Monday afternoon."

Puff sat back, sniffled, and cleared his eyes like waking from a nap. "All this talk, but we're not getting at why this tumor grew in the first place." His voice was broken down, defeated. "It's the tornado all over again—no warning, no reason, just destruction. When does it stop?"

I remembered Pa Dao's premonition in the cafeteria: "A spirit that lingers near the family is bad luck."

"It's doubtful we'll ever discover the cause," Dr. Mendoza said, "whether it's genetics, environment, or a combination of both. For all our research, we still can't say what causes or awakens cancer."

"Maybe that blow to the head from the tornado?" Puff said. "John Kruk was playing first base for the Phillies when a ball hit him so hard it busted his cup, and he ended up with testicle cancer."

"I recall that story," Dr. Mendoza said. "But people forget that the injury from the ball didn't cause the cancer. Rather, the injury prompted an exam, which revealed the testicular cancer that was already there. In other words, the injury saved Kruk's life. He was lucky in the same way John was lucky with his seizure."

Puff's face flushed in disbelief and anger. "I don't feel lucky."

Dr. Mendoza bowed his head. "I mean no disrespect. The tumor, the cancer, the suddenness of it all—this is bad luck. But that John seized into friendly arms and not in the shower or into a busy street is good luck. That he seized at all, giving us a reason to do an MRI and discover the tumor in time to operate, is good luck."

Puff's anger faded to a pout. "Yeah, well, do we *have* to operate? Can't we try a new diet? Or pills that attack only cancer? Can't we wake up his immune system and let it kill this cancer itself? I mean, look at him." He pointed to the bed. "Big Bad John is as strong as a horse."

Dr. Mendoza cupped his chin. "We don't have any data that diet makes a difference. And this isn't the type of cancer that responds to pills or immunotherapy. Our best proven treatment in this situation is surgery to remove the tumor and then radiation and chemotherapy to finish anything else."

Puff despaired. "We tried to fight my mom's cancer fifty years ago with radiation and chemotherapy. We lost. Are you telling me this is all we've got since then?"

Dr. Mendoza shook his head in sympathy. "Fifty years ago, radiation and chemo were much less effective than today. We've gotten much better at focusing radiation and chemotherapy on stopping cancer."

"Who's to say it won't come back?" Puff shot back. "We'll keep having to repeat the operation, radiation, and chemotherapy again and again whenever it returns."

Before Dr. Mendoza replied, I spoke up. "What about side effects from the surgery?"

Dr. Mendoza breathed deeply, like we'd hit the bull's-eye.

"I've operated on hundreds of brain tumors, and the fatality risk is low—less than five percent. That said, this will be a difficult operation due to the size and position of the tumor. We must prepare for side effects. John might lose a degree of lateral vision."

To illustrate, he again stretched his hand from his right eye to the back of his head.

Puff paled as he mulled over how John would hold runners on base without that field of vision. John's pitching ability was nearly as important as his life.

Dr. Mendoza interrupted Puff's mental pitching accommodations. "Surgery is necessary. Without it, another seizure or pressure from this growing tumor will kill John. As I said, the risk of death during the surgery is five percent, compared to a one-hundred-percent certainty of death without surgery."

I forced a breath.

Puff groaned.

John stared at the dry-erase board, which was blank except for the name Joan, his assigned night nurse, a name he didn't yet know.

"This is the path I would take for my own son," Dr. Mendoza said, looking at John, then Puff.

It was another checkmate.

In the silence that followed, Dr. Mendoza unbuttoned and buttoned his white coat. After a moment, he glanced at the TV. "You guys follow the Twins?"

Puff cleared his throat but never spoke. It was the only time he'd ever failed to talk up Joe Mauer and the Twins.

"We follow Joe Mauer more than the Twins," I said, pinch-hitting.

"I like Joe Mauer," Dr. Mendoza said. "I guess everybody in Minnesota does. What's not to like about Joe Mauer? How's he doing?"

At last, Puff composed himself. "The Twins mess with him in the batting order. He needs to bat third," he said. "I have a rotten suspicion he's going to retire."

Dr. Mendoza took a few steps toward the door. "I want to leave you with hope. You're correct that John is young and as strong as a horse. That's the primary indicator that he'll succeed. He *can* recover from this and live a long life. I've seen it happen. On that good news, I wish you a good night."

Puff breathed out as Dr. Mendoza left the room. He never breathed back in—but he kept going.

— CHAPTER THIRTEEN —

Swish

That weekend, the hands circled the clock like I circled the bases. But slowliness was not holiness in this case.

All day Saturday and Sunday morning, little was spoken in John's hospital room, besides the occasional snippet of encouragement. We tried to assure John he would emerge from his surgery stronger than ever, but the greeting-card positivity had no effect.

No matter what we said, he countered with the opposite. If I said "We'll get through this," he replied "Then something worse will happen." If Puff said "This, too, will pass," He replied "I, too, will pass, away."

By the time the Twins game started, I had nothing else to offer. Hawk and I itched to work on my game. I headed toward the door.

"I'll be back tomorrow," I said. "I still got to put up five hundred shots today."

Even as I said it, the guilt pressed down on me. How could I think about basketball when John was lying there in the hospital bed, facing the fight of his life?

"No way," Puff said, rising from his chair. "Stay and watch Joe Mauer with us. This is what families do." He sat on the edge of John's bed, then offered one other word he rarely said: "Please."

I sagged back down into the soft vinyl chair beside John's bed. We positioned in a row like we sat in Puff's favorite Target Field cheap seats—uppermost deck, right behind home plate.

No one spoke, and tension built—not about what was happening in that cramped hospital room but about what was happening a mile away, at Target Field. Rumors had spread that this game, the season's last, would be Joe Mauer's final game in the big leagues.

It wasn't until Joe Mauer's little daughters galloped out upon the field and hugged him, right before the game started, that the crowd at Target Field—and the crowd gathered in John's hospital room—recognized that we truly were watching Joe Mauer's last hurrah. Everyone rose to give him an ovation when he led off the bottom of the first inning.

My mood changed too. I hollered with Puff and John as loudly as anyone in the stands. Who cared who won the game? I wanted Joe Mauer to hammer a hit—one hit to go out on.

When Joe Mauer let the count go to one ball and two strikes, the TV commentators blathered on about how he'd judged the pitches. But John and I only listened to Puff, who cautioned us not to worry.

"Joe Mauer is the best two-strike hitter in baseball," he said. "Pay attention to how he hits this next pitch."

But on that fourth pitch, Joe Mauer drilled a ground ball to the second baseman for an easy out.

"In his senior year of 2001," Puff said, "he was the number one pick in the baseball draft *and* the number one football recruit in America. And I thought he was better at basketball than any other sport."

When Joe Mauer came up to bat again, two innings later, with us down 2 to zip, he drilled another hard grounder to the shortstop to end the inning.

Finally, in the fifth inning, Joe Mauer hit a towering fly ball to center left field. I yelled, "Yard!" the code word for a home run.

Puff, too, coaxed the ball to keep flying over the fence. "Come on, baby!" he shouted.

Instead, it popped and fizzled out. Two away.

Puff left his chair to pace back and forth. He froze and held his breath on every pitch.

Our Twins had managed a 5-to-4 margin by the seventh inning. Joe Mauer batted second with no one on base and worked the count to full.

"God bless Joe Mauer," John and I chanted.

As John continued the chant, I turned to Puff. "Breathe, Daddyup," I said. "Seriously."

He finally took a breath, rolled his eyes, and joined us.

We kept chanting as the pitcher fired toward the plate. The bat cracked the ball. My little family held our breath.

The looper dropped between right and center field.

We cheered, way too loudly for a hospital, as Joe Mauer raced to second base and slid, eluding the second baseman's swipe at his leg for the tag.

A nurse poked her head into our room and motioned for us to lower our volume.

Puff waited until Joe Mauer's signal for a timeout was approved before turning to high-five John and me. "We did it," he said during the replay. "That was Joe Mauer's four hundred and twenty-eighth double in a fifteen-year career."

Next, Joe Mauer advanced to third on a passed ball. But that's as far as he got before the Sox retired the side.

The Twins were still leading 5 to 4 by the top of the ninth. But no one came out of the Twins' dugout to take the field.

Then Joe Mauer emerged by himself, wearing catcher's gear, his mask snug over his face.

The crowd stood and roared again. Joe Mauer would end his career where he had started it, behind home plate.

"The first catcher to win three batting titles," Puff said, his voice cracking.

He ground fists into his eye sockets to keep tears and memories of Joe Mauer from escaping, then dropped his hands to his sides again so he wouldn't miss Joe Mauer's triumphant lap around the infield, waving goodbye to fans, teammates, the Sox, and us.

One pitch later, they took Joe Mauer out to another standing ovation.

Joe Mauer left the field, left baseball, and left us to face our continuing challenges, alone.

— CHAPTER FOURTEEN —

Tip-Off

With surgery scheduled for two o'clock, Puff said I could take Monday off from school. I decided to go in for a few hours, though. Partly to avoid all the pre-op jitters at the hospital and partly to avoid Mr. Lane chewing me out for missing another class.

As I walked into first hour, Harden came over and clapped me on the back. He asked about John, how he was doing, and what, if anything, he could do to help.

"You be sure and tell him, 'Big ups, and don't let yourself get down,'" Harden said. "We got his back out here on North. People he don't even know have him in their hearts, for sure."

The hours flew by. For the first time since I'd enrolled at Thomas Jefferson, I was happy. Lunch with Pa Dao was the highlight of my day.

I filled her in on everything while she put together two plates of *larb*—tender beef strips seasoned with cilantro, mint, green onions, and roasted rice powder. As I described our calamity, she nodded knowingly.

"They say John will be 'fine,'" I said, gesturing air quotes. "But Puff is a train wreck, and I'm trying to hold myself and my little family together." I sat back, studied her expression, and forced a smile. "But I get the sense that you knew all this already." I waved my hands to mime her receiving this very information through the spirits around us.

She jutted her chin at me. "Yes, but I wanted you to say it. Speaking your story gives you power."

I held my teacup to my nose, breathing in the steamy aroma. "Lemon," I said. "But what's that other smell?"

"Ginger. Niam slices it into the tea. She believes it can boost your immune system by fighting bacteria in your stomach." She pointed to my plate. *"Wb noj mov."*

I picked up my fork but stopped, suddenly overloaded by the food and kindness Pa Dao shared with me.

"I'll say it again—you don't need to do this for me," I said.

Before Pa Dao replied, Mother chimed in from the end of the table. "Michael, don't you know by now why Pa Dao's feeding you?"

Mother came over to fill her tray, but Pa Dao playfully elbowed her away.

"I just need a taste," Mother said. "Then I'll leave you two alone."

Once Pa Dao shared a serving, Mother returned to Dysfunctional Family and portioned off some *larb* to each member.

"I'm a health freak," Pa Dao said, adding a pork egg roll and a big clump of sticky rice to my plate. "The foods I eat have to be cleaned right. Better to rely on yourself than anyone else."

We were quiet as we took our first bites.

Mom wasn't a big egg roll person. She thought they were an extravagance. But she knew that we loved them. It was a big deal when she made them for us on birthdays.

"I miss Mom," I said. "Is it possible that I'm holding on to her and keeping her from beginning her journey?"

"No," Pa Dao answered with a dismissive wave. She kept eating.

"Can you ask Mom a question for me?"

"You want winning Powerball numbers?" Pa Dao teased.

"I'm more interested in John and Puff's future."

Pa Dao eyed me. "Only *their* future? Don't you want to know your own?"

I slowly shook my head. "I'm better off not knowing my future."

"Well, either way, Mai can't foresee the future. But I can." She took another forkful of *larb* and spoke between chews. "Your brother and your dad will keep going. Other people won't."

Her words barely sank in before she flowed into her next lesson.

"The best way to answer your questions about your little family and Mai is to understand the word *Hmong*. It means 'free people.' All we ask is the freedom to hunt and fish, live our culture, and practice our religion. But people won't leave us alone. That's why we're a people on the move. We even move around this country. We end up in the mountains, where no one else will go. But they keep pushing us farther up the mountain until we can't retreat anymore."

"Then what happens?"

"We fight." Pa Dao took a deep breath and scanned the cafeteria. "People here at Thomas Jefferson need to know that they can't punk us long before we reach that point."

"Careful," Father called out. "Here you go, instigating again. You know, it's easier to go along to get along."

"But how do you know when you've reached that point?" I said.

"You just know," Pa Dao said. "I mean, I'm not saying you should automatically fight the moment someone mean-mugs you. But you should speak up. And if you stand up for yourself and the drama still escalates, you fight. The Black kids don't take shit from anyone. Once you step out of line, they go off right away. We need to do the same."

I rubbed my neck, thinking of Westbrook.

Pa Dao waved her hands to take in the cafeteria. "We've reached that point. There's nowhere for us to flee anymore. This is the mountain we will die on."

"*Kadu* isn't going to back down if you push and shove them," Mother said.

I knew that *kadu* means "crocodile," a derogatory term for Blacks.

"You better be ready to fight everywhere, all the time, and to the death," Mother added.

The rest of Dysfunctional Family agreed.

But Pa Dao sat back and took a massive bite of *larb* and sticky rice. "Mai's a fighter who doesn't back down. We can learn a lot from her. No matter how hard I try to move her on, she dismisses me like I'm a nuisance—a fly or mosquito. I might not win a fight, but I can be a mosquito in a pup tent."

"That mosquito always gets squashed," Brother said.

"Mai would stand up for herself," Pa Dao said. "Wouldn't she? That's the question we would have asked at her Hmong funeral."

"Mom would definitely stand up for herself," I said.

Recalling all of Pa Dao's lessons, I envisioned a Hmong funeral for Mom. My big family would have arrived to help us. We would have lived at the funeral home twenty-four hours a day for three days. Bitter beef soup, *larb*, and many other Hmong foods would have been served around the clock. There would have been crying, music, and healing.

And Mom would have been at the center of it all.

As I sipped tea, I pondered how she would have taken that in. "Mom never liked attention," I said. "She never wanted people fussing over her."

"Death changes you," Pa Dao said. "But today isn't about death. It's about life. It's about John fighting to stay alive. And I have just the thing to help."

She reached into her grocery sack, and I leaned forward in anticipation.

"Here," she said, pulling out a Halloween package of KitKat Minis. "You and your dad can snack on these during John's operation."

I entered John's hospital room without knocking. He lay in bed, staring at the ceiling. Puff crouched in his chair as if preparing to diagram a basketball play on the floor. On TV, Judge Judy worked to settle a dispute between three female roommates arguing about rent money.

The wall clock ticked away ice-cold time—1:15 p.m., forty-five minutes to surgery.

I dropped two *Star Tribune*s on John's bed. The News and Sports sections displayed headlines of A MAGICAL MAUER MOMENT and SAY IT AIN'T SO, JOE.

I clicked off on the TV remote, and Judge Judy evaporated to a dull gray screen.

"You okay?" I said to John.

"Other than the brain cancer," he said, "I'm aight." He sat up and doubled up the pillows behind his back. "What's that?" He pointed to the bag under my arm.

"KitKats," I said. "My friend Pa Dao sent them. She wishes you well."

"Just my luck," John said. "I can't eat anything until after the surgery. Save me a couple."

"Harden wishes you good luck too," I added.

John blinked. "Who's Harden?"

"The guy you talked to before the seizure. He's in my classes. We hoop together. He kept you from falling backward and hitting your head on the hallway floor."

"Don't remember him," John said. "I don't remember anything right before the seizure."

"How about after?" I said. "I rode with you in the ambulance to the hospital. Do you remember anything from that ride?"

John squirmed.

"You called out Mom's name in the ambulance. Twice."

John stared straight ahead at the wall.

"Back up," Puff said. "Who's Pa Dao?"

"She's a friend I met at Thomas Jefferson," I said.

"Yeah," John said. "A friend who brings him lunch every day. Everybody talks about them."

"Aha," Puff said. "I always knew girls would throw themselves at you two."

"It's not that at all," I said. "It's different."

Puff and John awaited an explanation. I took a deep breath and started at the beginning.

"During the tornado, I died." Though I spoke to Puff, I paid attention to John. "I believe John died too. You always told us that before we die, we get one final chance to look back at our life. But it was Mom's life that passed before my eyes, starting back in Laos and Thailand—the life she never discussed. In my final look, Mom drowned in the slough. That's how I knew to find her."

"I have questions," Puff said tentatively. "First, how does all this relate to Pa Dao?"

"She's a Hmong shaman—a rising one. She's still learning the rituals. She introduced herself in the cafeteria because Mom comes to her every morning to insist that she talk to me. Mom says I'll listen better if Pa Dao feeds me Hmong food—food Mom used to cook for us."

As I spoke, I became aware of the lingering scents of *larb* on my breath.

"Mom told Pa Dao that she needed a proper Hmong funeral to set off on her spirit journey to return everywhere she ever lived—back to her birthplace in Laos. She's stuck between two worlds now. Pa Dao is trying to get Mom to move on, but Mom says she can't leave yet. She has unfinished work that she can't finish without Pa Dao."

A realization swept over me: *She can't leave because I need her to guide me, to help me find the missing part of me, my Hmong roots.*

I took another, deeper breath. "I waited for the right time to tell you so you wouldn't think Pa Dao, or I, was crazy."

"No one thinks you're crazy," Puff said.

He looked up at the TV, forgetting it was off. Then he looked at John, who was wide-eyed. Finally, he looked back at me.

"Does your mom ever talk to *you*?" he asked.

"No. Only to Pa Dao."

"How about you?" he asked John. "Does Mom ever talk to you?"

We waited.

"It's all right, Big Bad John," Puff said. "You can tell us."

John stalled, checked the time, and considered running out the clock.

"For real," I said. "Don't play."

"Give your brother time," Puff said. "Be patient. He'll talk when he's ready."

John did take his time—so long that I gave up hope he would answer. Finally, he spoke.

"Yeah," he said. "I guess so. Mom's with me whenever I can't think for myself—the tornado, Mayo, my seizure the other day." He added, "There are dreams too—Mom shows up in them to make me feel better and tell me what to do."

"And what does she tell you to do?" Puff said.

"Take care of you two," John said. "And be strong."

"So, she'll be with you during your surgery today?" Puff said.

John said, "Mom tells me I'm going to be all right. She says this isn't my time to leave. She says I'll live a long life."

"I say the same," Puff said.

No one said anything until a knock on the door introduced a middle-aged Black man in blue scrubs. He gave John a slight smile.

"I'm Dr. Shelby," he said, "your anesthesiologist. Can you tell me your name, please?"

"John Moriarity."

"And can you tell me what brings you here today?"

"To drop off a tumor," John said brusquely.

"And where is the tumor located?"

John pointed in the general direction of his head.

"Where in your head, exactly?" Dr. Shelby pressed.

"On my right side." John pointed to the area.

Dr. Shelby adjusted John's IV tubing. "This is a little champagne for the brain. It'll make you drowsy in a few minutes. After that, we'll wheel you into surgery and proceed with the operation."

A nurse arrived, her voice a sterile whisper. She folded up the sides of John's bed into a wagon. John settled back into his pillow, folded his hands across his chest, and closed his eyes.

As Dr. Shelby and the nurse prepared to push the bed away, I gripped John's hand, already wilting, and squeezed once. He did not grab back.

Puff clamped his hand over John's and mine. We let go when the nurse gathered the IV tubing and the bottle close to John's bed, a quiet signal that the real battle was just beginning.

A slight smile emerged on John's lips as they took him away.

It wasn't until after 11:00 p.m. that a nurse poked her head inside John's room.

"Mr. Moriarity?"

"Yes," Puff and I said.

"The operation has ended," she said. "Dr. Mendoza will meet with you soon."

She guided us to a bare waiting room two floors below. After a few minutes, Dr. Mendoza arrived, weary and serious but with hints of a smile. The smile reminded me of the purslane herb that grew from the cracks in the sidewalk and driveway back home—Mom's impossible delicacy that defied all odds.

"We had a successful operation," Dr. Mendoza said. "I removed as much of the tumor as I could find. I feel confident about everything with this operation." He allowed his smile to widen more. "When patients come out of anesthesia, we ask them to stick out their tongues. It's a surprisingly complex movement that tells us how the patient tolerated anesthesia and the operation. John had no difficulties whatsoever."

He stepped forward and put a hand on Puff's shoulder.

"Your son is strong. This is a journey of a thousand miles. Today we began our journey with a successful first step. We are on our way."

— CHAPTER FIFTEEN —

Pick and Roll

The first night after the operation, I stood behind John as he pushed himself out of bed and leaned on his IV pole for balance. With Puff and me at his side, he took a few wobbly steps, then stopped to rest. He was exhausted.

With our help, John shuffled outside his room and around the intensive care unit hallway. The short journey left him bushed.

Over time, he grew stronger. A physical therapist monitored his progress, noting daily his improved strength and balance. Soon, he was even climbing stairs.

A speech pathologist found no difficulties with John's speech, language, thinking, or swallowing. John enjoyed his first big meal on his second day after surgery, including the KitKat bars Puff and I had saved for him.

An occupational therapist assessed John dressing himself. She then added a note to the whiteboard in John's room: PATIENT IS UP INDEPENDENT IN THE ROOM. She also instructed him to switch from red to blue hospital socks, which allowed him to travel in the hallway without assistance. Most importantly, she noted his strong motivation to return home.

After three days in intensive care and another three days in a regular hospital room, John announced, "I'm leaving. Now."

"Stay longer," Dr. Mendoza argued. "You need time and proper care to recuperate. Patients stay up to five weeks."

"Not me," John said.

Realizing he couldn't contain John in the hospital any longer, Dr. Mendoza switched gears and encouraged John to sign up for several types of outpatient services. John agreed to do physical therapy but nuked anything else, especially counseling.

Dr. Mendoza looked at John, Puff, and me.

"To everyone's surprise, John spoke. "During the operation, Mom told me, 'Go home now.' So, I'm going home."

As John recovered at home, I had no time for anything other than attending school and caring for Puff and John. I cooked, washed dishes, and cleaned the house. Puff washed clothes and managed insurance information, appointments, and John's meds.

Once John's steroids kicked in, he couldn't stop eating. Eventually, the steroids were reduced and eliminated from his daily regimen. But his hunger level stayed the same.

We ate whenever he ate, ravaging through meals. I made all nine Hamburger Helper casseroles for Puff and John to eat while I was at school. They always requested more Deluxe Cheeseburger Macaroni.

Puff topped three hundred pounds, with John not far behind. I pushed away from the table each night long before they did. Still, the excess pounds jiggled every time I lugged over the cemetery fence.

I was carrying extra weight in many ways. When Dr. Mendoza had carved that cancer from John's brain, he'd also carved away my time. Between home and school, I was slogging through a quicksand of responsibilities.

Each night, Puff insisted I take a break. "Go to the rec center and play basketball," he'd say.

Yet each night, Hawk rested alongside Puff and John on the couch in front of the TV, disappointed that I'd ignored him.

The days passed. John's oncologist, Dr. Schneidermann, requested a meeting to discuss John's radiation sessions, which were scheduled to begin on October 15. Puff arranged the meeting for after school so I could join them without missing any more classes. We met in the runty waiting room/office in the radiation center.

Dr. Schneidermann drummed his fingers on the table and gazed just above us, unable to make eye contact. I couldn't figure out if he was tense all the time or if my little family prompted his nerves.

"How are you holding up?" Dr. Schneidermann asked John.

John grunted in reply.

Puff punctured the silence with a different question. "Do you have medical marijuana for us if Big Bad John gets nauseous?"

"No," Dr. Schneidermann said. "John shouldn't experience nausea with our treatment, so I can't prescribe medical marijuana in this situation."

"I don't believe this," Puff griped.

I couldn't believe it either. That is, I couldn't believe that Puff was asking about marijuana. He wouldn't smoke it or let us anywhere near it in a million years. It was just an excuse for him to vent at Dr. Schneidermann—and cancer.

And he had more excuses and more venting on top of that. He tilted his head like a robin searching for a worm, looking at John with one eye and Dr. Schneidermann with the other. "I still can't comprehend how the same stuff that *causes* cancer can *cure* it too. What if it weakens his immune system—the immune system that he needs to kill cancer?" Puff sat back and clenched his fingers from both hands to steeple them. "We brought Michael so you can explain it better to him than you did to us."

Once again, Dr. Schneidermann's eyes drifted up and away from ours. "Radiation works," he said. "We can demonstrate success in battling astrocytomas like John's. We don't have that same data for success with the alternative treatments and immunotherapy you discussed."

"And you determine success by quarterly MRIs?" Puff asked.

"That's one important measure, yes," Dr. Schneidermann said.

"Even though radiation will scar John's brain and make it difficult to differentiate from cancer if it comes back?" Puff said.

"We can tell the difference," Dr. Schneidermann said, but his certainty rang as hollow as a bouncing basketball in an empty gym.

"I wouldn't do it," Puff said, turning to me. "But that's why I brought you. John and I trust your judgment. What's your opinion?"

"I hear you," I said. "But this doctor and center have treated hundreds of patients with brain cancer for a long time."

"Thousands of patients," Dr. Schneidermann corrected. "We're buying time here—for hopefully a long life. I stand by our record of success."

I looked at Puff. "You always say, 'Better the devil you know than the devil you don't,'" I shrugged. "We should stick with the devil we know—radiation. They have proof that radiation works—we have no idea if John's immune system can fight this on its own. It's too much of a gamble."

Puff awaited John's response.

John's head rested on the back of his chair, and his arms flopped to his sides like he couldn't sit upright. "Can we go now?" he said.

"There's one more issue to discuss," Dr. Schneidermann said. "All our patients must wear their immobilization mask." He picked up a thermoplastic white mesh mask that had been specifically fitted for John.

Puff and I had heard about the mask and John's complaints about it when it had been created. "This contraption makes me look like Hannibal Lecter," he'd said.

And now this was our first time seeing the mask. Dr. Schneidermann turned it over and around for our review.

John was correct. He would look like Hannibal Lecter—a Star Wars version of Hannibal Lecter.

Lecter, as John called the mask, would bolt John to the table to prevent him from moving during radiation. John feared Lecter—feared being trapped inside him and bolted down to the table, unable to ever escape. I read his mind: What if they forgot and left him to rot on the table?

"I'm not wearing Lecter," John said.

"Can't you have him lie perfectly still without a mask?" Puff said.

Dr. Schneidermann shook his head. "For John's safety, we cannot perform radiation therapy unless he consents to wearing the mask as designed. That's nonnegotiable."

"Then we're done here," Puff said. He stood to leave.

"What if my dad was with John during the treatment?" I said quickly.

I first looked at Puff to coax him to sit back down. Then I looked at John to ensure he was listening. And lastly, I looked to Dr. Schneidermann to sell him on my pitch.

"Maybe my dad could help position John on the table in his mask and be nearby, somewhere close to John but still safe for my dad. When the treatment ends, he'd be right there to help John up from the table."

I looked back at John.

"Nobody will ever see you in this mask," I said. "Think of it like a catcher's mask—which you've worn a hundred times—only it's lighter and more comfortable. Come on. You can do this. The world's strongest dad will be right there, near you."

John's eyes darted to Puff. Both relaxed.

But Dr. Schneidermann tensed. "We've never done anything like that before. Parents and family must wait in the lobby for their loved ones during radiation." He drummed his fingers and eventually let out a resigned sigh. "Well, we might be able to make that work. You'd have to be outside in the hallway, and you couldn't carry on a conversation," he said, gazing above Puff's head. "But you would be nearby."

Puff and John exchanged a glance.

"That might work," Puff said.

Moments after we returned home from the meeting with Dr. Schneidermann, Mrs. Flowers knocked at our door.

Mrs. Flowers had been checking in on us every night. In the first few days, she'd arrived with a homemade gift—bread, fruit bread, cake, pie, or cookies. Recently, she'd arrived with a homemade gift and a job to do. She'd been assigned as John's homebound teacher from Thomas Jefferson. She delivered an hour of tutorial instruction per class by reviewing notes and assignments she'd received from his teachers.

Before John opened the door, I knew her gift would be a blueberry pie with berries picked up north, near the Boundary Waters. I'd seen her that day between classes, and she'd called me over to discuss this treat, even explaining how she'd prepared the crust.

"Thank you," John said as he took the pie.

"Why?" Mrs. Flowers pressed, never allowing John to get away with a simple thank-you.

"Because you spent your time preparing this pie for us," John said.

"And?"

Mrs. Flowers waited for John to continue, but he looked at her, confused. After a moment, she modeled a response, one word at a time.

"You . . . took . . . into . . . consideration . . ."

John followed her lead, speaking slowly. "I—I mean *you*—took into consideration . . ."

She spun her hand around now to reel in the full answer.

". . . the needs of the person receiving the gift," he completed.

With a big exhale, he turned to come back inside.

Mrs. Flowers cleared her throat.

John stopped and turned back toward her. "Would you like to come in and join us?"

"Thank you!" she said, her voice and manner like rhubarb jam dripping over a hot English muffin.

She removed her shoes and stepped inside the door. Once inside, she made her presence known immediately.

"Turn that monstrosity off," she announced to Puff, referring to the TV.

Her command doubled as an invitation for Puff and me to escape. I hustled to the kitchen, and he scooted out to do laundry. Only then did Mrs. Flowers sit with John and get to work. But Puff might as well have stayed because Mrs. Flowers frequently called him back to witness John's brilliance for himself.

"Are you aware of how much John is learning?" Mrs. Flowers said. "And how quickly he learns? He's incredible."

Puff reacted with the same passion as the faces on Mount Rushmore, which unraveled her.

"My goodness!"

She would say that same phrase whenever she learned that Puff had failed to lead us out to explore her bucket list of the Northside's landmarks and restaurants.

"Excuse me," Mrs. Flowers said. "I spent eight hours today working with the brightest students in the world, many college-bound, and I rank your John at the top of those students."

"He's coming around," Puff mustered. The response was enthusiastic enough to allow him to retreat once again.

Mrs. Flowers stayed longer than her assigned hour to help John. Each night, she also found ways to help my little family face the tidal wave of challenges that threatened to overwhelm us.

"Mr. Moriarity, come here," Mrs. Flowers called out again. "I have exciting news for John."

Puff trudged in, laundry basket in hand.

"You know the nature center that's just two miles away—the park area filled with exhibits and a meeting place where local wildlife groups study the Mississippi River? We can arrange for John to volunteer there a few times over the winter months, and that experience will lead to a full-time, paid job in the summer." She ended joyfully. "Isn't that wonderful?"

"John plays his baseball in the summer," Puff said flatly.

Mrs. Flowers viewed Puff in consternation but continued. "Not all day," she said. "And certainly not every day. The staff at the center can be creative in accommodating his schedule. Not to mention, it allows John to network with the Mississippi, the Northside, and a career."

She appeared to be years younger when she turned from Puff to John.

"Are you ready to take on this exciting adventure?"

"It sounds okay," John said.

High praise.

— CHAPTER SIXTEEN —

Flagrant 2 with Ejections and Suspensions

On Friday, October 19, amid the cafeteria's bedlam, Pa Dao opened a larger, longer Tupperware container as if unveiling a treasure. Inside lay a white bass, complete with head and tail, simmering atop an aluminum blanket, along with a banana leaf, cilantro, and thin lime slices. John and I call them silver bass. We would bring them home to Mom, who cooked them the same way, but without the banana leaf.

"My dad and brothers caught her in Stillwater, on the Saint Croix," Pa Dao said. "Dad calls these flat mouths, like the whitefish he used to catch in Laos. He says this fish takes him home."

She placed the fish on a plate, then poured a lemon juice mix—which included chili peppers, green onions, and sugar—into a white china bowl. Next, she filled two glasses with bubble tea from a Thermos.

"To Mom," I said, clinking my glass against Pa Dao's.

We gulped the sweet, cool bubble tea and ate silently for a few minutes.

At the other end of the table, Dysfunctional Family shared a laugh over a joke. Why couldn't I hear anything they said, yet they heard everything Pa Dao and I discussed?

As they continued to laugh, I noticed that Sister had white yarn tied around her wrist.

"What's that on Sister's wrist?" I asked Pa Dao.

"*Khi tes* string," she explained. "It helps a person heal when they're sick or depressed or beaten down. It's a connection to our ancestors, a way to heal, or a way to lift your spirit when it's heavy. One more reminder that you're never alone."

"Do they work?"

"Of course." Pa Dao cocked her head at me. "Do you imagine I conjure this up?"

"No. But if—"

Pa Dao waved me off like wiping a windshield. "I see where you're going. You're wondering about a *khi tes* for your little family and a *hu plig* and *ua neeb* for John."

"I'll be there," Brother blurted. "Where? When?"

Pa Dao waved her off too. "But I can't do any of those ceremonies without your permission. You need to invite me." She viewed me half expectantly, half impatiently.

"Would you please come help my brother . . ."

"And . . ."

". . . and my little family by performing *khi tes* and"—I hunted for the other terms—"*hu plig* and *ua neeb*?"

Now she eyed me skeptically.

"I believe in you," I said. "You can heal my little family. Will you please come help us?" I was begging—not just for John, but for all of us—for the chance to be whole again.

Pa Dao smiled. "Yes, I will."

She pulled out her phone and thumbed through the days and months in her calendar. "We should make this happen between December twenty-first and January seventh, during winter break." She pointed at me and her phone calendar. "Before or after Christmas?"

Mom had loved Christmas, decorating a living tree, wrapping presents, and making cookies. Our first Christmas without Mom would be easier if we preoccupied ourselves.

"Let's do the Saturday before Christmas," I said.

"Saturday, December twenty-second," Pa Dao said. She entered the date, then put her phone away. "You won't believe the food your family will bring." Her eyes lit up. "It's not just about the food, of course. It's about coming together to heal. This is how we fight—not just for John, but for all of us."

The food my family would bring? I knew she couldn't be referring to my little family. "Do you mean *your* family?" I ventured.

"No," she said. "I mean *your* big family—your Hmong family. You'll need your dad to invite your Grandpa Vang in Saint Paul. They'll come if he invites them properly. They'll want to oversee everything. They may insist on hosting the day at their place. Your dad must discuss the details with them, including whether they choose to invite me."

"Geez," I said. "Does it have to be Puff?"

Pa Dao nodded as she chewed.

"And what do you mean they choose whether to invite you? You *have* to be there. Can't we tell them that?"

"Your big family doesn't know me," Pa Dao said. "It's their call."

I groaned.

Pa Dao waved me off. "I know it won't be easy working with Grandpa Vang, but your dad needs to do right by Mai and John. Mai is on your side. Get it done. And my dad can help out with the meeting. Besides, your dad will do anything for you."

Pa Dao pulled a Nutella jar and a clear plastic bottle filled with honey-roasted peanuts from her grocery sack. She spooned a chocolate lump into a bowl, sprinkled it with peanuts, and shoved it before me.

I was picking up a spoon to take a bite when the racket of chairs knocking over interrupted me. Several tables away, where the Black kids sat, two guys were jostling to play-fight, though harder than usual. One had pranked the other.

The Harden Set roared in laughter, watching it unfold.

When one of the play-fighters snatched a milk carton and threatened to throw it, the crowd encouraged him. Instead, he seized a french fry and flung it at the other play-fighter's face like a skipping stone.

But the fry-flinger immediately recognized he'd gone too far, so he ran away, darting by our table. He zigged just as a flurry of revenge fries zagged, missing him but pelting everyone at our table.

Pa Dao's friends cursed in Hmong and English as we brushed cold, greasy fries off us and our table.

"God damn *kadu* ruin everything," Brother said.

"Especially the underclassmen," Sister said.

Pa Dao and I used napkins to dab at the stains on our clothing. Brother signaled Williams over to help. As he approached our table, Brother pointed to the fries on the table and the floor, then at the Harden Set.

"We got fry-bombed again by those rejects," Brother said. "They think it's funny."

"I'll handle it," Williams said firmly. He moved toward the Black kids' tables, his presence alone enough to de-escalate the situation.

I was uneasy, my stomach twisting in knots. The Harden Set hadn't thrown the fries. Pa Dao made no distinction between the real culprits and the Harden Set, and she wasn't in the mood for corrections. I chose not to upset her further.

But that choice had a trade-off. By not correcting Pa Dao, I'd allowed her to wrongly ID the Harden Set for trouble they didn't start. That was a serious offense around here. Every day at Thomas Jefferson was like sitting on a powder keg. The tension was always just below the surface, ready to explode at the slightest spark.

Thankfully, Williams passed Harden's table and made a beeline to the true mass fry-thrower.

Pa Dao scowled. "Those little punks," she muttered, her voice calculating and dangerous. "They're not going to stop until we throw those fries right back at them."

For a moment, I thought she might do it. Instead, she brushed two more fries off the table.

"I'm done for today," she said. "I've lost my appetite."

As Pa Dao packed her Tupperware, a voice called out, "Empty!"

The Harden Set had gathered close behind me. They encircled Harden like the president's Secret Service security detail. LBJ even surveyed the scene behind sunglasses.

"Where you been at night?" Harden said. As he stepped forward, LBJ and Westbrook stepped backward. "You still hoopin' or what? And what's up with your bro?"

Pa Dao sprang from her seat to stand between me and Harden. "Little shits," she said, one hand clenched in a fist. "Why did you fry-bomb us?"

Dysfunctional Family stood as well. Brother edged toward Pa Dao to restrain her.

"Whoa," Harden said. "My guys and I threw nothing. The only time we bomb is on the court. You're standing strong before the wrong people. Now, I don't know you or your crew. And clearly, you don't know me. But you're not going to step to me. My ignore game is only so strong."

"And his name is Michael," Pa Dao said. "Call him by his name." Now she balled both fists. "You're not gonna bully us."

"Better move on outta my face," Harden said. "Step back!" His words were a hard frost in the tropical cafeteria. "You're in my space, and I don't play that."

But Pa Dao held her ground.

"You be dippin', China Girl," he said.

That was the worst insult Pa Dao could receive. She bit hard on her lower lip, slowly circling Harden. Brother grabbed onto Pa Dao's arm, but the unborn baby jerked away.

"Let it go, Pa Dao," Father called out, leading the rest of Dysfunctional Family toward her. "He's not worth the trouble."

Pa Dao inched closer to Harden.

Dysfunctional Family pressed behind Pa Dao, all seeking to pull her back while she glared at Harden, mean-mugging, waiting for him to make the first move.

"Nasty lil' B, please," Harden said, shaking his head casually.

Lionesses leaped from their seats at the Black kids' tables and bounded to Harden's side, eager to show allegiance to him and eager to rip Pa Dao's face off. They lined in tightly behind Harden, even crowding out the rest of the Harden Set.

My eyes darted from Pa Dao and Dysfunctional Family to Harden and his girl-fighter posse. Williams, having successfully calmed the original fry-bombing situation, was now stationed at the cafeteria's exit, totally unaware of the new combustible activity happening at the core of the lunchroom.

Harden downplayed the confrontation by looking away—but then he instantly brought his right hand around with fury, stopping an inch from Pa Dao's face. He was "stealing on" her, warning her how close she was to becoming a casualty or fatality.

But at Thomas Jefferson, once you swing a fist—whether you follow through with a punch or not—you should plan on getting into the blender and mixing it up.

Pa Dao recognized that fist as a declaration of war. She tucked her face behind tiny fists, ready to battle like the Notre Dame Leprechaun.

The crowd surged. Mad hands grabbed, shoved, and pulled. Bodies collided, tumbling to the floor in a heap. The scrum spiraled until everyone fell into and upon one another.

Losing my balance, I plowed into Harden and draped around him. Once in that position, I maneuvered behind him to lock my arms under his armpits in a full nelson. I held onto him as we fell to the floor in the middle of the chaos.

Black and brown kids with bright white eyes fell lengthwise to the floor, shouting and screaming, throbbing like dominoes, not showing numbers but color and ethnic affiliations. The Hmong guys shot out like they were yellow jackets or pit bulls, with two or three jumping on each member of the Harden Set. The good news: Black students forgot their longstanding feuds and reunited for the first time since forever. The bad news: They reunited for a common cause—to fight the Hmong.

"Knock this shit off!" police shouted. The air burned with the sting of Mace that sought the eyes and noses of the tangle of bodies. They sprayed more Mace, like lasers, directly into fighters' eyes. The fighters scrambled to their feet and sprang away from the poison, rushing to grab milk cartons and flush their faces in a cooling milk wash.

Pa Dao lay on the concrete not far from us. A wiry Black girl straddled her. Pa Dao had her hands locked tightly over her face. With one hand, the Black girl desperately tried to pry Pa Dao's hands away; with her other, cocked in a hard fist, she prepared to land a knockout punch onto Pa Dao's delicate butterfly nose.

All the while, Harden lay lightly in my arms. His bones were hollow, like a bird's, which explained how he could fly like one.

Mona Harris, from our geometry class, held her palms out to stop Thomas Jefferson's police liaison—who the Black students had nicknamed Officer Friendly—as he charged toward us, bristling. He had an Irish last name, O'Toole, but was light-skinded. Harden labeled him American Indian.

"Hold on!" Mona said. "No one did nothing!"

But another policeman blindsided Mona to the floor and wrestled her until she lay on her stomach. She struggled while he jerked her arms backward.

"Empty!" Harden said, flailing his hands. "For real—let go!"

But I did not let go, even when Officer Friendly towered over us.

Back in Cottage Park, we'd never noticed our one cop, Old Sheriff Huffman. He stayed out of sight unless Puff needed him to umpire a game. That's why I assumed Officer Friendly would kindly ask me to release Harden and follow that with a gracious offer to help us to our feet.

Instead, he shook a small can until it rattled, casually aimed, and shot Mace into Harden's eyes.

I would later learn that Officer Friendly was a thumper—a police officer who'd bullied and abused suspects as a street cop and had been sent to Thomas Jefferson, hoping he would improve. But he frequently tased, maced, and choked students at Thomas Jefferson, even while we cursed him out, filmed his psychotic reactions, and shouted at him about our rights. Harden and Black students radared police like Officer Friendly, inheriting fear of him in their blood and bones.

"Let go!" Harden screamed at me and gasped as the Mace blasted him. He twisted, howling in pain. "Let go!"

When I couldn't hold him any longer, Harden kicked to his feet and bolted away. I also turned to scramble up and away, but Officer Friendly kicked my legs out from underneath me and pounced on my back. His heavy knee mashed my shoulder blades onto the concrete, knocking the air out of me. I gasped for one good breath, failed, and prepared to die.

"Don't resist," Officer Friendly said. His order hinted at a hope that I would.

He knelt with both knees on my back, yanked my hands behind, and snapped handcuffs around my wrists. While I lay there, gasping for breath, he left to break up other fights, which were so intense that no one had noticed or cared about his presence.

I lunged in the slime, heaving until my lungs uncrinkled. My lips on the concrete, I swallowed in as much air as possible, sucking oxygen under a veil of Mace.

My khakis were a mess—streaked with milk, smeared with ketchup, and splashed with blood and grime. I even recognized Nutella stains.

When the bell rang, the building shuddered. The students who had circled around to watch the fights now surged to the doors, their footsteps sounding like a stampede. I stayed on the floor; my breath came in gasps. Blood and Mace mixed to pierce my tongue.

The fight was over, at least in the lunchroom. But the chaos continued elsewhere, like a tornado.

— CHAPTER SEVENTEEN —

Picking Teams

The brawl lasted four minutes, a lifetime in the routine chaos of Thomas Jefferson.

"Teachers, please lock your doors," the school secretary's curt voice broadcast across the intercom. "Any students still in the hallways must report to the Citizenship Room." She repeated the announcement.

Janitors reassembled the cafeteria. They wiped down, swept, and mopped around us—including me, sprawled on the floor. I could barely lift my arms, let alone stand.

As the janitors maneuvered around us, I ear-hustled the chatter from their walkie-talkies. The school nurse requested extra staff to handle the fallout: asthmatic attacks from the Mace, and swollen hands and heads needing ice packs.

Old Parrothead huddled with her two assistant principals, her voice commanding. She barked orders about hallway monitors, suspensions, and how to handle teachers calling in fights from their classrooms.

Eight Hmong students, including Pa Dao, initially lined up behind Old Parrothead, waiting while a policeman positioned at the cafeteria doors kept an eye out for flare-ups. But when Old Parrothead headed my way, those Hmong students, except for Pa Dao, vanished, merging into the mass of humanity in the halls. Dysfunctional Family was long gone, having done the same earlier. Escape was easy, with zero worries of ever being tracked down by a bounty-hunter-like hall monitor.

Pa Dao could also have easily roamed away, but she held her place in line for me. She sobbed into the sleeve of her Thomas Jefferson badminton hoodie.

When Old Parrothead reached me, she gazed down and mulled over what to do with me. "Whose side were you on?" she demanded.

"No one's," I explained calmly. "I restrained another student from fighting. I just need a pass to class."

"Who did you restrain?" she said.

"Harden."

Her head snapped up. "He restrained a guy named Harden," she called out to her assistant principals.

"Those two kicked off the riot," one of them answered.

"Come with me," she ordered.

Still handcuffed, I struggled to roll over, squirming and flopping like a carp. Officer Friendly had to position me so I could genuflect to my feet. I joined Pa Dao, and we trailed Old Parrothead out of the cafeteria. Along the way, Old Parrothead walkied the school secretary to report the Code Red lockdown message.

Seconds later, the intercom crackled to life. "Teachers, please close and lock your doors. Students still in the hallway must report immediately to the Citizenship Room. We are in a Code Red lockdown. I repeat, we are in a Code Red lockdown. All afterschool activities and evening events are canceled. Students leaving classrooms or the school from this point on will be suspended for three days."

When the intercom went quiet, the walkie chatter picked up again, describing groups and individuals running the halls, looking to fight, throwing punches, and moving on.

Pa Dao and I were escorted into Old Parrothead's office and told to sit at her long conference table. After a few minutes, the assistant principals brought Harden into the office and directed him to sit opposite us.

Harden's eyes, swollen and bloodshot, peered downward from slits he dabbed with a tissue. He slumped against his arm, a pillar propping a heavy head.

Pa Dao mean-mugged him, ready to resume where she'd left off. But Harden kept his head down, staring at his lap.

The school secretary knocked on the door to announce that parents—except for Puff—were on their way.

Old Parrothead hit redial on her desk phone to try our home number again.

"He's still at radiation with my brother," I explained.

Officer Friendly checked in. "The fighting's died down," he reported. "There'll be additional squads around the school and neighborhood until the buses leave." He eyed us. "Do I need to take these three downtown?"

Old Parrothead waved him off, and he removed my handcuffs. I feared my numb hands might snap off with the cuffs. Free from the steel blades that had strangulated my chubby wrists, I pumped my hands until feeling returned to my fingertips.

Officer Friendly sat at the table with a fermenting just-try-me attitude.

The school secretary knocked again. "Jerome Vaughn's father," she announced, stepping aside for Coach to enter.

Until then, I had never heard Harden called by his real name.

Coach sat next to Harden, who sat up straight. His eyes rose to his father's, flickered recognition and shame, then sank again.

Coach covered his face in his hands. He adjusted and squirmed in his chair. At last, he dropped his hands to his sides. "Can we get a compress for my son's eyes?"

Old Parrothead walkied for the school nurse to bring ice to her office.

None ever came.

Next, Pa Dao's parents arrived with Thomas Jefferson's Hmong family liaison. Pa Dao's father wore a lime-green polyester-mesh safety vest with reflective silver tape over a MnDOT windbreaker. He also wore a blue baseball hat with the words Vietnam Veteran embroidered in gold across the front.

Pa Dao's father was much older than her mother, who was dressed professionally in a skirt and satin blouse. She and Pa Dao occasionally spoke to each other in Hmong under their breath.

Old Parrothead picked at a hangnail. Her patience wore thin as she tapped the redial button on her desk phone to contact Puff once again. When he finally answered, her voice was heavy with exasperation.

"Mr. Moriarity, you are on speakerphone," she said. "Your son, Michael, is in my office with two other students, their parents, and our school police officer. Michael started a school-wide fight today. As a result, we're suspending him. You need to come here now for an urgent meeting."

"Can't," Puff said flatly. "I'm with my son, Big Bad John. We just walked in the door from the hospital."

"Mr. Moriarity," Old Parrothead said, her tone sharpening. "We're meeting to discuss Michael's role in initiating an enormous number of fights this afternoon at Thomas Jefferson and in the community."

"Not Michael," Puff said plainly. "He doesn't fight. If you have fights there, you have a much bigger problem than my Michael."

Old Parrothead let out a sigh even Puff had to have heard. "Let's move on," she said, beginning introductions.

We introduced ourselves around the table—not so much to one another but to Puff. Everyone leaned toward the speakerphone as they spoke.

When it was Coach's turn, he slowly teetered from side to side before speaking. Hoarse, gravelly words rumbled deep from his chest.

"I'm Jerome's father—and I refuse to believe these police can't find a way to break up a fight without tasing or macing young people."

Old Parrothead hesitated blankly, then gestured for the introductions to continue. Officer Friendly introduced himself. His hand palmed his holstered Mace.

When Pa Dao's father introduced himself and her mother, the Hmong family liaison quietly translated, "Pa Dao's father, Xia Pao Xiong, and mother, Ying Her."

The interpreter mirrored the singsong quality of the Hmong dialect that Pa Dao would later identify as White Hmong.

Old Parrothead began the meeting. "I responded to an emergency call to our cafeteria to discover a terrible fight," she said. "These three students started it. At last count, we've suspended twenty-seven students."

Coach drummed his fingers on the table, eyeing us. "I want one of you to explain what happened."

Harden cleared his throat and straightened. "I went over to check in on Empty. But before I could—"

Pa Dao's hand shot up as if she was requesting permission to speak, but she stood and pointed at Harden before receiving that permission.

"Start at the beginning!" Pa Dao said. "First, you threw french fries at us. Then you walked over to gloat."

"I didn't throw any french fries!" Harden said. "I swear to God."

"I don't believe you," Pa Dao said. "But if you didn't throw french fries *today*, you threw them yesterday, the day before, or whenever. And you never try to stop your friends from throwing fries at us. Well?" Pa Dao balled her fists. Her voice shook as she sat down. "I'm done with being punked."

"Oh my God," Harden moaned. He turned to the rest of us as if we were jury members. "I swear—I never touched this little girl, even after she got in my face."

"He's right," I said, making the briefest eye contact with Pa Dao before looking at Harden and the others. "He never threw the fries. And he wasn't punking anyone. But things escalated, and we got thrown into each other. We never fought at all," I stressed, making a triangle gesture between Harden, Pa Dao, and myself.

"So," Old Parrothead said as if a timer had gone off and our speaking time had ended. She had already made up her mind. She lowered her eyeglasses and looked over the top at Harden and me. "You two will receive a five-day suspension. Furthermore, you'll be immediately expelled from Thomas Jefferson if you engage in retaliation or any other idiotic behavior."

She turned on Pa Dao. "Five days for you too. But in your case, we found a knife."

This time, Pa Dao raised her hand slowly and waited for Old Parrothead to motion for her to speak.

"You mean my little keychain Swiss Army knife?"

"Any knife is a dangerous weapon," Old Parrothead said. "After your suspension, we'll decide whether to tack on an additional five days, in which case we'll consider your expulsion from the district."

Tears filled Pa Dao's eyes as she turned to her parents and said, *"Niam thiab Txiv, kuv twb tsis ua dabtsi txhaum. Kuv noj kuv mov. Lawv thab plaub."* (Mom and Dad, I didn't do anything wrong. I was eating. They caused the problems.)

Pa Dao's parents huddled with the interpreter and urged him to speak. He did so, but shyly.

"The parents say they can't imagine this," the interpreter said. "Their daughter is small. This boy is big. How was it possible for their daughter to fight such a big boy?"

Pa Dao's parents spoke again.

"Pa Dao's older brothers and sisters graduated from Thomas Jefferson," the interpreter said. "Two graduated from college. Others still study in college. Her brothers and sisters never had a problem in school. Pa Dao has never had a problem. Pa Dao will never be a problem again."

"I appreciate their support, but rules are rules," Old Parrothead said. "And they apply to everyone without exception."

"Excuse me," Coach said sternly. "I'm not convinced anyone here ever threw a punch. These suspensions are unwarranted."

"I can assure you, they were not ballroom dancing," Old Parrothead said. "I have no patience for fighters, especially in a public venue such as a cafeteria." She sighed. "All to impress their friends." She lowered her eyeglasses to inspect us. "Well, now you can all impress your families for the next five school days at home."

"Can we at least go to tryouts next week?" Harden said. He held his breath.

"No," Old Parrothead said immediately. She cocked her head in curiosity. "What tryouts?"

"Basketball!" Harden said, with the expectation there would be an exception for such a high-priority sport.

Now Old Parrothead sat up straight, like she'd sat on a tack. "Absolutely not. First off, the suspension includes all afterschool activities. Starting now. And second, I'll personally meet with the coaches to ensure they don't allow you to participate next week or at any other time this season." She sat back in her chair and folded her arms. "You have *some* nerve. Thomas Jefferson cannot have boys who fight representing us in the community."

My heart stopped, my shoulders drooped, and my body slumped in my chair. I shrank until everyone else in the office towered above me like skyscrapers.

My one and only goal—to make varsity—and all the hours, days, weeks, and months dedicated to that goal . . . wasted.

"You're being unnecessarily punitive," Coach said. "There's no need for this. I'm going to fight you on this up the food chain."

"Go ahead and make me the bad guy," she said. "But know that everyone on the board, including the superintendent, asked me to come back from retirement to manage this school until they found a principal. They promised to support me unconditionally. I'm not the enemy here."

Did Puff, on the other end of the speaker, realize those were nearly the same words she'd told him after John's special education assessment?

Old Parrothead casually folded her hands together. "Mr. Vaughn, all this bickering will only make it worse. I suggest you focus on your son's academic performance instead."

Now Coach sank. And the lower he sank, the more his anger shifted from Old Parrothead to Harden. He knew what Old Parrothead knew.

"Do you have any idea," Coach said to everyone except Harden, "how hard you have to work to come to school every day and fail all your classes?"

I thought Harden was the smartest kid in the two classes I had with him. Everyone did. No possible way he was failing every class.

Harden sucked his lips and gummed them.

"I warned you of the consequences if you came here and started trouble," Coach growled, shifting from anger to disappointment to resignation as he looked at Harden. "I'm withdrawing you from Thomas Jefferson."

"Pops, please—one more chance. I swear," Harden pleaded.

Coach waved him off and focused on me with sympathy. "And you—you've spent all that time at the rec center, getting ready for tryouts?"

I nodded.

"All this mess blew up from a misunderstanding," Harden said quickly. "But Empty and I are cool. Aren't we, Empty?"

"No problem," I said.

"And this young woman?" Coach said, motioning to Pa Dao.

Harden tucked his chin inside his Nike T-shirt until he bit the collar and mumbled a response.

"Sit up straight and pull your shirt down," Coach said.

Harden did as instructed, though he now fingered Jesus's feet on the crucifix hanging around his neck. He peeked up at Pa Dao, speaking barely above a whisper. "My bad."

"Yeah, right," Pa Dao said. "Mind your business and leave me alone . . . forever."

"Wait, wait, wait," a metallic voice said. It was Puff, jumping into the conversation. "Did I hear correctly that Michael can't go out for basketball? He tried to protect another student. This isn't fair."

"Michael will explain our meeting to you when he gets home," Old Parrothead snapped, not trying to hide her exasperation with Puff. "You can call me with further questions. We're sending him home now."

She disconnected Puff, then stood with her back to us, looking outside onto Thomas Jefferson's front lawn. A police surveillance camera sat on a tall pole, recording the action below. Thomas Jefferson would release students for the day in nine minutes.

"You should all leave now," she said. "We're anticipating further fights from this idiocy."

After receiving our suspension forms, we were dismissed. I checked back on Pa Dao, whose parents did not acknowledge her. She peeked at me and gave me a tiny wave.

Outside, two police cars pulled onto the school lawn, under the flagpole. One car shone its red strobe lights, in stationary mode.

Coach placed a heavy arm around my shoulders. "We'd better give you a ride home," he said. "You'll be a lot safer that way. We'll meet you at door 1."

In the hallway, I met Williams, who escorted me to my locker so I could gather my books and Hawk.

"You got everything?" he said. "There's no coming back here during your suspension."

"Everything," I said, holding Hawk protectively.

We started back to door 1.

"How's your brother?" Williams said. Before I could answer, he spoke again. "Would you tell him I miss him? I don't miss sitting in the classroom with his teachers all day, though. Sitting down in the Cit Room would do them a world of good. Help them cool off. I hope you do more with all those books than carry them back and forth from school."

"I will."

Coach and Harden were already waiting at door 1.

"You taking these menaces to society off our hands for a few days?" Williams said to Coach.

Coach wearily half smiled and hugged Williams, the only man on the Northside bigger than him.

Once Coach, Harden, and I stepped outside, I couldn't help myself—I let Hawk go, dribbling him high and low, fast and slow. I was anxious to hear his thoughts and consolations.

More cars than usual lined up and down the street, with parents waiting to pick up their children. Three additional policemen clumped together and mean-mugged us. Another officer rode around the block on a police motorcycle with a sidecar.

Coach directed us across the street to his car. He motioned for me to sit in front. Harden sat in the back, hanging his head. Coach glanced at him before starting the car.

The long dismissal bell rang like the start of a horse race. Students raced out of door 1, caught sight of police, and gathered in groups by race and ethnicity: Black, Hmong, Latino, and a few Somali.

"Keep moving," the police called out to the groups. "Go home."

Fifteen Black students grouped and moved toward the Penn Avenue bus stop, a favorite spot for an after-school fight. As they passed us, Coach lowered the car windows and called them by name.

"I see you, Damian Adams," he said. "This nonsense gets squashed right now."

His voice carried low and louder than a bullhorn.

"Same goes for you, Kendrick. If you continue this foolishness, you can forget the rec center. If I don't kick your butt first, your mom or your grandma will."

Coach turned to Harden and me.

"His grandma used to do this for us—call us out like this. Back when everybody in the community took a share in raising kids."

For one block, we drove slowly behind the group, whose members periodically checked back to see Coach on their tail. Eventually, Coach drove around them, waving as we passed.

"Those guys will be all right," he said. He rechecked them in his rearview mirror one more time before focusing on Hawk and me. "What does a kid your age know about the ABA?"

"Lots," I said matter-of-factly.

"Who's your favorite ABA player?" Coach said.

"Dr. J," I said. But I corrected myself. "No, make that Connie Hawkins. He went to Iowa but never played because of a gambling scandal. And he was innocent."

Coach reacted with surprise. "Damn. *You* know Connie Hawkins?"

"He first dunked when he was eleven," I said. "He played in the ABA, NBA, and Globetrotters. I watch his YouTube videos. I named my basketball, Hawk, after him."

Coach said, "He played in Minnesota."

"Minnesota Pipers," I said.

I unzipped my backpack to show my copy of *Foul!*, the Hawkins biography.

"I love the way he palmed a basketball," I said. "It was like a baseball to him. I stretch my hands across bowls and plates so my hands will be big like his." I attempted to palm Hawk but failed. "I wear ankle weights too, to improve my vertical. I want to jump like Hawk."

Coach chuckled. "You can grab all the bowls and plates in the world and wear all the ankle weights you can fit around your legs, but you'll never grow the hands or the hops of Connie Hawkins."

Coach adjusted his rearview mirror until he found Harden.

"Your grandpa got to see Hawk play," Coach said.

I glanced back at Harden.

"You told me that story already," he said. "Grandpa's told me too."

We stopped at Penn before taking a left to go south.

"Regarding your new friend in the back seat," Coach said to me without taking his eyes off Harden, "Jerome wants to be a tough guy to impress people. But he can't fight a lick. The problem is, you can't fight on these streets if you know better—if you're brilliant."

Coach turned to me.

"You a tough guy too?"

"No way," I said. "I'm too scared." It was a response Harden would never admit. "I feel like I'm going to throw up whenever I see a fight."

Coach said, "Boys your age *should* be scared. You aren't supposed to fight. You're supposed to be soft. To fight, you need a bellyful of nothing—like I did at your age. But Jerome's never missed a meal in his entire life."

He pulled up to a stop sign and waited three seconds before proceeding.

"I poured my life into Jerome so he could skip all the drama and groove on the right track: college, a nice job, a home, a family. I fathered him so he shouldn't and wouldn't want to fight. I don't want him fighting or doing anything on these streets. These streets don't show you no love." He tapped his temple. "I want him to fight up here."

"I'm not as smart as you think," Harden said.

"You're right," Coach said. "You're *way smarter* than I can imagine. Way beyond school and this life. Beyond basketball." He viewed me. "You know that Jerome asked us for a saxophone and taught himself to play? Now he accompanies the music on the radio." He studied Harden in his rearview mirror. "You don't play basketball as much as it plays you."

Coach stopped at our house and shifted into park.

"I'll never find out the whole cafeteria story that happened today," he said. "But things happen for a reason. Here's my commitment to you: One way or another, you two will play together this year—and play on the same team." He turned and looked at Harden. "And once that happens, I'll consider letting you stay at Thomas Jefferson."

I thanked Coach as I left the car. When Harden got out to take my seat in front, I pulled *Foul!* from my backpack and handed it to him.

"For you and your dad," I said.

"Straight," Harden said. He lifted the book up and down until he found a balance. "Heavy. It might take a while to finish." He angled sideways into the car's front seat but stopped before closing the door. "You hoopin' tonight?"

"I guess so," I said.

"My right hand to God, fam," Harden said, "that's all I wanted to find out when your girl jumped me."

— CHAPTER EIGHTEEN —

Sixth Man

Puff always says, "If you crash your car into a ditch in a small town, the news of your accident gets back to town before you do." There aren't any ditches on the Northside, but it's still a small town, and news travels faster than light, especially about fights. It doesn't matter if the fight was with girls, guys, Siamese fighting fish, roosters, or dogs.

And news of a race war? That travels the fastest of all. I instantly transformed from "It's Just Lunch Guy" to "Mad Dog Moriarity," even though I couldn't punch my way out of a paper bag.

After making supper and explaining the brawl to Puff and John as best I could, I cleaned up, then headed out. As I dribbled Hawk to the rec center, I knew I'd have to fight again. It's the Northside way. I knew I'd have to throw hands before they stopped throwing them back. Best to get it over with and move on with my life.

The gym was alive with the thud of basketballs. I found my familiar rim and began my practice routine with layups while sizing up possible combatants on the sidelines, including the Harden Set, racing up and down the court.

But then, for the first time since I'd started coming to the rec center, someone other than the Black guys joined me—John. He strolled inside and positioned himself under my rim.

I froze and held Hawk close. I no longer thought about getting my ass kicked but instead worried about John's safety. Since his brain tumor diagnosis in September, he hadn't been outside the house.

"We better leave," I said.

"What?" John said. "Keep shooting."

"You shouldn't be here. You can't play." I tapped the right side of my head. "Or fight."

John motioned for me to keep shooting.

I slapped Hawk hard once to emphasize seriousness. "You take a blow to the head, and you're dead. I got myself into this mess. I can find my way out."

"I'm not gonna play," he said. "And I won't fight." He again motioned for me to shoot. "You've been there for me when I needed you. Why can't I be here for you?"

John was there to stay, so I shot Hawk up. He spun, whirled, and spun around the rim before zigzagging through the net. John swatted my rebound back, and I repeated the motions.

John, Hawk, and I settled into a give-and-go dance. But our trance was cast away when Harden's game ended.

"You're next, Empty," Harden called out from midcourt.

I looked behind me to ensure he wasn't talking to the next team waiting.

His eyes still swollen, Harden waved me out with annoyance. "Sometime today?"

I backed out toward Harden, peeling off my ankle weights and sliding them across the floor to John.

"Listen, Empty," Harden said as I met him. He took my hand and guided me through a dap handshake, holding me at the end. "My bad today. I didn't figure all that chaos would go down."

The Harden Set surrounded us. Though we'd played together before, Harden introduced his set as if I were meeting them for the first time.

"Say hello to your new teammates," Harden said. "LBJ [LeBron James], Westbrook [Russell], Curry [Steph], and Pat Bev [Patrick Beverley]." He pointed to each player as he went, waiting until I recognized each before introducing himself. "People call me Harden, after James Harden. The Beard. And the best player in the NBA."

"Yeah, but we call him No D, Harden," Pat Bev said. "Both couldn't guard a parked car."

The Harden Set chuckled.

Harden ignored the cap. "All these cats got suspended today too."

I took a deep breath. "That's on me." I offered fist bumps, but the Harden Set laughed.

"You didn't make anybody do nothing," Harden said. "They're all grown-ass men."

"Since when do fights cost a five-day outs?" Westbrook protested. "For all my fights, I got three-day outs and came right back to school."

Pat Bev said, "Old Girl told us if you fight in the cafeteria, there's more people around and a bigger chance somebody else gets hurt."

"She be illin'," LBJ said. "No one told us that new rule. I swear to God, people make shit up to push us down whenever we start to rise." He sighed.

"You're right," Harden said, dribbling as he spoke. "The rules change whenever we figure out how to play the game." He turned to me. "We call your Hmong friends H-Mob. They're sneaky AF. You notice that their asses all got away today? Well, except for your girl."

"I get it," I said.

"One thing you can bet on—*we* always get caught." Harden regarded each Harden Set member. "But we never give up. We keep on fighting. And we gotta trust that Pops is working on a bigger and better plan for us than any janky team at Thomas Jefferson." He awaited me. "He told us about it today—am I right?"

I nodded again.

"I'm just saying"—Harden eyed each Harden Set member— "from now on, Empty runs with us."

"It's good," I said.

Harden cocked his head toward John, who sat on the sideline with his back against the wall and spun Hawk on his finger. "How 'bout bro? Can he run with us?"

"He can't play until doctors clear him," I said. "He shouldn't be here. A blow to his head could kill him."

"Damn," Harden said. "Shit is fucked up. Well, I guess it's just you, then. For now." He clapped his hands and pointed to Curry.

"You're out until we score five, then you can come back in for anyone except Empty. We gots to run his slow ass into shape."

The Curry walking off the floor had nothing in common with the authentic Steph Curry except a baby face with dimples. One look at that face, and opponents assumed our Curry was a pushover. But Harden had trained him to strike first, like a pit bull, and lock on to the foe's lips or neck until the other dogs in the Harden Set finalized the attack.

Harden summed up winning defense by saying, "To kill a snake, you cut off its head."

Before each game, Harden determined the other team's best offensive player. Unless that guy was a low-post player, Harden unleashed Curry on him in the same manner as he would for a pit bull to "sic 'em." Curry played up on his man so close that their chests would touch. Puff called it belly-button-to-belly-button defense. From that position, Curry could block his man's way in any direction.

It never took long for Curry's man to lose heart, get fatigued, and quit—then get swarmed by the rest of the Harden Set. They'd chew the flesh from his bones. To avoid the inevitable, Curry's man usually quit right away. But Curry was on the sideline now. We had to take a different approach.

Harden smacked the ball to alert the opposing team. "Winners take ball," he said.

The other team called out who they would guard. The big guy called me. I refer to him as Banger. He's twice my age and embalmed with Scotch whisky. It leaks from him in fumes and sweat, making his opponents woozy.

To set up, I sprinted to the other end, where Banger delivered a forearm shiver, as they do in the NBA whenever establishing a low post. It hurt.

On the first play, I slipped away from Banger, and Harden drilled a hard pass that I caught. I head-and-shoulder-faked Banger and set myself in motion for what would have been an easy layup in Cottage Park, where the score of every basketball game was "fun to fun."

But I wasn't in Cottage Park. I was in the life-or-death drama of the Northside rec center. I wasn't playing for fun but for my place in this world. And for Mom in her place in her world.

Three guys, counting Banger—hacked me with part or all their hands on the resulting facial. The ball propelled back at me with top spin. It bounced off my head to the posterizing guy already speeding off on a three-on-one.

Down at the other end, Banger grunted and butt-shoved me backward to his preferred spot. That's why I call him Banger—whenever he gets the ball, he backs you down jackhammer-style until he posts up underneath the rim. Then he muscles his wrists, elbows, and the ball to the rim. It's not unusual for him to miss, rebound his shot, and shoot again while his defender nurses a bloody nose or adjusts a wobbly tooth.

Banger prepared to shoot. But before he jacked up a shot, Harden swooped in from his blind side to strip the ball away.

"I got ball!" Banger yelled as Harden took off on a fast break. "I got fouled!"

Play came to a halt.

"No, no, no," Harden said, running back to face Banger. "I didn't touch you, fam. That was all ball. Be real. You *cannot* call that a foul. Not here. Not on North."

"Respect the call," Banger said.

He lunged for the ball, but Harden held it in a tight headlock.

"No can do," Harden said. "You're wasting our time with this insanity. I'm for real, bro. Let's keep playing."

Banger approached Harden and reached for the ball again. This time, Harden took one step back and gripped the ball tighter. LBJ and Westbrook flanked Harden like pillars on his left and right.

"Oh," Banger said. "Am I supposed to be scared of you three little pussies?" He flexed his fists. "You can go ahead and cry to your old man too. I ain't afraid of you, him, nobody."

Harden bit hard on his lower lip and edged in the direction of Banger. "Better check yourself," he said. "Be careful what you wish for and what comes out your mouth next."

"I didn't say anything," Banger said. He swallowed. "I just said I'm not afraid."

"You wanna talk smack about Pops?" Harden said. "Then come at me, motherfucker."

"Please," Banger said. "You ain't that. I'd beat you so bad you'd shit yourself."

"I would advise against that," LBJ said to Banger with seasoned confidence, professionalism, and a genuine concern for Banger's well-being. "Move on. This conversation's done."

More reinforcements came in. John rose and edged toward the court. Curry came back onto the court, too, alongside Westbrook and LBJ.

Westbrook's nostrils flared, and he sucked down hard on his stretched lower lip. His intensity was the only characteristic he shared with the real Westbrook. Our Westbrook weighed forty pounds more than the real deal; his stocky, clumsy mix of fat and muscle made him more like Charles Barkley.

"Hey, bro," Westbrook said casually. "Maybe we should box."

Harden stepped between Westbrook and Banger.

Pat Bev came behind Banger, startling him. "Maybe if you'd shoot your sorry Black ass a normal layup and make the gimme on your first try, we'd give you the rock."

Everyone laughed except Banger and me. Banger waited for me to show the beginning of a smile. Banger was mean-mugging me. I thought he might swing, yet I looked away. For the first time, I noticed the smell of the gym—old wood and new flop sweat.

Harden backtracked to the top of the key and positioned the ball on the court, glaring at Banger. "We'll let you shoot, but from out here."

Banger stood his ground.

"Or we can let Empty shoot," Harden said, motioning to me. "He's the poor guy you've dry-humped from the jump. Either way, the ball won't lie. Pick your poison."

"Fuck you and all your moms," Banger said. "Take the ball, you sorry-ass cheaters. That's why you win all the time."

Banger jogged to the other end, and Harden directed us to follow him and set up. John retook his seat on the floor against the wall, and Curry returned to the sideline.

On the next possession, Harden faked a pass my way and instead delivered a chest pass to LBJ, alone in the corner. LBJ drove baseline, slashed through defenders, and performed a reverse layup, complete with backspin off the backboard.

"Ball don't lie," Pat Bev told Banger. "Drinks are on Bob!" he called out to the entire gym as we set up on defense.

"You don't have to guard him anymore," LBJ told me, loud enough for everyone to hear. "Nobody will pass him the ball."

He was right. From that point on, the ball never came Banger's way. I merely had to check in on him so he wouldn't sneak past me, since he ignored the three-second rule or refused to move even without the ball. I played off him enough to get myself into the passing lane and anticipate an interception.

Toward the game's end, I felt behind me to determine Banger's location. As I brushed against his sweat-soaked jersey, he swung a fist to knock me away. After a shot went up, I screened him out and crashed the boards. I pulled down the rebound, mimicked a Kevin Love pivot, and fired a pass downcourt to Harden.

That launched a fast break, with the rest of us trailing behind. Harden juked, broke ankles, planted his feet, and propelled straight up—like Jesus ascending to heaven on the funeral holy cards at Holy Trinity. He hammered a ferocious left-handed dunk to end the game, then held on and pulled himself up above the rim so he could see down through the net. All he saw was Banger.

"Look at me!" Harden yelled at Banger. Harden hung there like a mic, then dropped like one. It was a statement. In this gym, on this court, we were untouchable. Harden charged over to Banger to ensure he received the message and another one.

"That's for you and your mom," Harden said, thrusting his hand as if jamming a dagger into Banger and his mother's collective gut.

Banger glared back.

This time, the Harden Set gathered behind him, including me. I stood behind Westbrook. Banger turned, walked off the court, and left the rec center.

"He's got a gun," LBJ said. "He mighta gone and got it."

"I know," Harden said. "But he put my pops on his lips. That slick hate got into my head, and my heart spoke up. I'm already dead if I put up with his bullshit." He turned to me. "Sometimes you get to choose how you die."

"I can get mines," LBJ said, referring to his pistol, "and wait in the parking lot for him to come back."

"No," Harden said. "Not here—not anywhere around Pops. Basketball is church. Pops is God."

Harden looked over at the other team, who'd also watched the Banger drama unfold. They now awaited his reaction.

"Let's go," he said. "Next!"

As guys called out who they would guard, Westbrook leaned in toward me. "Around here," he said in a serious tone, "if dude hits you, run that back. When dude hits you, you strike back harder."

He waited for me to agree.

"Better yet, don't wait for dude to hit you," Westbrook said, placing a hand on my shoulder. "Throw the first punch. And do it right away. Whoever strikes first wins. You don't have to finish the fight. But you have to start it. We'll finish up for you, fam. Swear to God."

"I guess I'm all fought out after today," I said.

Westbrook bent over and laughed. He motioned for our teammates to join him. As they gathered, he broadcast my words and tone.

"My man Empty just said, 'I guess I'm all fought out after today.'"

I'd never heard Harden and the Harden Set fall out laughing as hard as they did for Westbrook's dead-on imitation of me. I laughed. From the sidelines, John laughed too.

Westbrook took both hands and pushed me hard. "That's good shit, man!"

It was a celebration—and an initiation.

We failed to score the first few times when we started up again. Harden encouraged me through my fumbles, missteps, and missed shots. I scored twice in the following games, which we won. Harden made everyone come out of a game for a breather except me.

That night, I learned that shooting around with the Harden Set was one thing, but playing with them in an actual game—where a guy puts a hand in your face or smacks you in the mouth—changed everything.

I also learned that I would never fight the Harden Set again, but only fight with and for them.

At 10:00 p.m., Coach cleared the gym as usual, but Harden told John and me to stay behind. While my new teammates played two-on-two, Harden took John and me to the other end to shoot around.

"All right," Harden said. "What do you think of our squad? Pretty good, huh? We've hung together since middle school, so we decided to stick together and attend Thomas Jefferson. Northside stars have never done that before. We get cherry-picked into Catholic schools and the suburbs. But you wait and see—we're going places. And now we're bringing you with us, and the whole Northside. We're the future."

"Nice," I said. I bounced the ball off the floor and up into the backboard before it died and buried through the rim.

Harden smiled. "By the way, what's the deal with your girl bringing you nice meals all the time?"

"It's a long story," I said. It wasn't the first time I'd said those words at the rec center. "You'd never believe me if I told you."

Harden focused on John. "You know the story?"

"Yes," John said.

"We got the time," Harden said back to me. "Proceed."

"First, she's not my girl. Not yet." I paused as a wicked smile teased across Harden's face. "Her name is Pa Dao."

"You talking your girlfriend, the chef?" Pat Bev said.

He'd drifted from the other end of the court to join us, and the rest of the Harden Set had followed. We all lined up for a shootaround, with John standing under the net, distributing made shots so everyone got a turn.

"Why did she choose *you?*" Pat Bev politely capped. "It wasn't for your looks. No offense, but you look like a homely-ass pit bull chewing on a porcupine."

That remark generated a laugh from everyone, including me. Pat Bev readied a follow-up joke, but Harden shot him a look.

"Not now," Harden said, his voice low. "This shit is real."

I broke the brief quiet. "A tornado took our house—and Mom— in August," I said.

"Life sucks," Harden said, "and then we die. Maybe tonight. Or maybe we'll make it to the ripe old age of twenty. Sorry your mom went faster than the rest of us." He half-hooked shots, alternating with each hand over an imaginary seven-footer. "What happened next?"

"We moved up here—and Mom came with us," I said. "I should say, her spirit did. That's what Pa Dao says. She's a Hmong shaman. A shaman helps spirits move where they're supposed to go. She says Mom's spirit should have gone back to Laos, but it couldn't. We didn't have a proper Hmong funeral for her. Now Mom appears before Pa Dao and tells her I should learn Hmong culture. Mom says I'll listen and learn better if there's food involved. And Pa Dao and I are figuring out how to help Mom get started on her journey."

"Fuck me," Westbrook said. "Goose bumps—see for yourself." He held out his arm to me, then John. "And you believe her?"

"When I was a kid," LBJ said, "my ma woke in bed one night to tell me that she didn't know what, but something terrible was happening. We found out later it was the exact moment my grandpa died in Illinois." He pronounced it *Ill-uh-noise.*

"Hold on—you dudes are Hmong?" Pat Bev said, his head swinging from John to me. "No way. Not unless Hmongs in Iowa are a different kind of Hmong."

"Mom was"—I corrected myself—"*is* Hmong. We're mixed. You have to know what it means to be Hmong to really be Hmong. I'm only now understanding what that involves."

I put the ball behind my back, eyeballed the rim, and shot, banking into the rim as easily as shooting a layup.

"Damn," Pat Bev said. "Do that again."

I repeated the same shot twice, then drew in a long breath. "Right before you die," I said, "your life passes before your eyes. In Mom's case, her life and death passed before *my* eyes."

I took the ball behind my back, eyeballed the shooter's square on the backboard, and launched a shot that twisted around the rim before squirting out.

Curry picked up the rebound and held the ball, waiting for me to continue.

"I died that night," I said. "Right after Mom. At the bottom of our house." I signaled toward John. "And underneath John. We both died. EMTs brought us back to life, but we couldn't do the same for Mom."

Curry bounced the ball toward the rim and missed badly. John tossed the ball back to me.

I moved to the rim's side and gripped the ball with both hands flanking it. "Put top spin on the ball and kiss it off the backboard," I explained. "It's as easy as making a layup after you sink a couple in a row."

I modeled as I shot the ball. It went in.

"That's cold," Curry said. "Let me try it again."

John tossed the ball to him. He practiced the new bounce shot over and over.

"It's cool your girl is connecting you to your mom and all," Harden said, "but don't let her or any other girl ever run your life. Trust me—she'll try. And more than anything else, you got to be free."

"Back to your mom," LBJ said, looking around. "Is she here now?"

The gym fell silent as I spoke. "She's still here—just not the way she used to be."

Harden's eyes narrowed—finally understanding.

I tried to lighten the mood. "Then again, she could be at home, haunting Puff."

"Who's Puff?" Pat Bev said.

"Our dad," I said. "It's his nickname. In Cottage Park, everybody had a nickname." I pointed at John. "He's Big Bad John."

Harden clapped appreciatively.

"John sees her too," I said, putting him on blast.

The Harden Set awaited confirmation from John, who collected a shot, then scooped the ball up and around for a reverse layup. He got his rebound and took a soft bank shot, missing.

Harden gathered the missed shot. "Well?" he said.

John said, "I've seen Mom whenever I've been out of it.'

"Like during your seizure?" Harden said. "While I was with you?"

"Yeah," John said, his voice steady. "She was right there. She said she wouldn't let anything bad happen to me. Mom's not just watching over me. She's watching over Puff and Michael too. She's guiding us. She wants us to stick together no matter what."

"Does Mom ever mention 'emptiness' to you?" I asked John.

He tiptoed to pinch the net's bottom loop and pulled hard. "I don't think so."

"Hold up," Harden said. "You two are just now figuring this shit out? Spill," he demanded. "We got no secrets around here."

John shook his head. "She never says anything about emptiness. She tells me I'm responsible for caring for my family and that family is everything."

"With Puff," LBJ said, "has your ma come back to him too?"

I jumped to flick one hand on the backboard's bottom. "He's not a big talker."

"You gots to ask him," Westbrook said. "And piece together all the messages."

Coach poked his head into the gym. "Closing time," he called out. "You've all had yourselves quite a day. Maybe it's true—the best fights make the best friends. But it's time for you fellas to go home and go to bed. I guess you don't have to worry about getting up early to go to school."

As we filed by Coach, Harden clapped me on the back as if to steady me for what he would say next. "You're one of us now. That means you gotta show up for work tomorrow. And the day after. We don't break. We reload."

He smiled, but there was something fierce in his eyes, something that made me believe him. I trusted him.

"And then do it all over again," he said.

— CHAPTER NINETEEN —

Make-Up Call

Puff nudged my shoulder to wake me at 8:30 a.m. on Monday, my first day of suspension.

"Phone call," he whispered, not wanting to wake John. "Probably your girlfriend from school."

I shuffled into the TV room and grabbed the phone. "Hello?"

"Next time, warn me that you have a nickname," Pa Dao said. "Just so you know, I hate it. You're Michael to me."

I cleared my throat.

"Did I wake you?" she said.

"No," I said. "I've been up for hours." It was my first lie to Pa Dao.

"I don't do sarcasm," she said. "If I woke you, sorry, but not sorry. Mai woke me again at her usual 5:00 a.m., and Niam's had me working ever since. Bathrooms today: tubs, toilets, sinks, and floors. Then it's winter prep for the garden. Suspension's no vacation. I'm in jail here—no K-dramas, no Hmong boy bands until I go back to school." She yawned. "I'm breaking out of this prison before I lose it. Meet at the library on Lowry at twelve thirty. I told Niam I have to go there for homework."

I rubbed my eyes, still half asleep.

"I hear breathing," Pa Dao said. "I know you're there."

"Twelve thirty today?"

"Yes," Pa Dao said. "And your correct answer is yes."

"Then yes," I said.

"Good. Niam says you have a good heart, a Hmong heart."

"How does Niam know—"

"No, no," Pa Dao cut in. "She's Niam to me. You call her Auntie Xia Pao."

"But isn't that your dad's name?"

"Correct. In our culture, married women are addressed by their husband's name, except when they are close in relationship to you. We have lots of naming traditions. When a married Hmong man has his first son, he receives an old-age name. Who gives the old name? Easy—the wife's parents. All of this can happen through a ritual. If you think about it, it's like receiving an adult name. Who knows? Maybe that day will come for you."

Trying to process a Hmong culture lesson before breakfast made my head throb. No wonder Mom told Pa Dao that I'd pay better attention on a full stomach.

"Auntie Xia Pao thinks I have a good heart?" I said. "Just from seeing me in Old Parrothead's office?"

"She can tell these things," Pa Dao said. "And I update her on our lunches. She asks questions. I answer them. Well, I better get back to work. See ya at twelve thirty. I'll bring snacks."

I found Pa Dao by the magazine rack at the back of the library's first floor.

"I got us a study room, where we won't be bothered," she said. "Follow me."

We walked past a row of tiny, dark-glassed cubicles and entered a brightly lit room at the end. Pa Dao then closed the door, and we sat close enough that I could see leftover dirt in her fingernails from her garden work.

"I love libraries," Pa Dao said. "I'm one of the Hmong girls who stay at the library every night after school until they kick us out. Teachers call us library rats. You should join us."

"No time," I said.

Pa Dao spread her arms to take in the room. "Privacy, quiet, and space to spread out without tripping over my brothers and sisters.

You've got it made at your place. Just John and your dad. It must be so quiet. We've got three bedrooms and two bathrooms for my parents, my grandparents, and us nine kids. You do the math."

"People sleeping on couches," I said.

"And in the basement," Pa Dao said. "People tell me I'll be grown and gone soon enough." She gazed into the future, sighed, then came back to me. "I have news for you . . ."

But instead of continuing with the news, she opened a plastic produce sack and pulled out a cluster of small golden-brown spheres the size and shape of Ping-Pong balls, their surfaces rough but thin-skinned.

"Take a handful," she said.

I pulled a few balls from the grocery sack.

"Longans—dragon eyes," Pa Dao said. "Like this." She took a ball, bit off the tip, and pinched the sides until a white pulp spurted into her mouth. "Careful of the seed."

I copied her, slurping the pulp like a skinless grape.

"Niam says you take after your mother," Pa Dao said. "And since she never met Mai, that means she thinks you look and act Hmong. My lessons are working."

"Is that the news you have for me?" I asked, spurting the contents of another longan into my mouth.

She shook her head. "No. I have real news. Big news." She leaned in. "Niam checked around to find out what happened back in the day with Mai and her family. Remember how I said Hmong know one another here? Well, people remembered. It has to do with your father."

"Puff?" I said. "You mean, with him being *meka*?"

"Being *meka* is one of the factors," Pa Dao said. "But it's more complicated." She paused as if deciding to take a new approach. "Did your father ever explain why Mai lost touch with her family?"

I nodded. "Sort of. He said a few things—never in front of Mom. He said Mom had married that older guy in the refugee camp and attended high school in Saint Paul for a year before she had to quit. Her husband lived with his mother, and Mom also cared for her. She had countless needs. Mom burned out of the arrangement and walked away. Puff said that the husband's family and Mom's family turned their backs on her after the divorce. He called it 'Hmong without a clan.' Puff told us he rescued Mom."

"Some of that is true," Pa Dao said.

I set my longan down.

"After they escaped from Laos," Pa Dao said, "Mai and her family lived in the Ban Vinai Refugee Camp. It wasn't an easy life for the Hmong, even more so for a Hmong woman. Mai got married there before they came to America. She and lots of other young Hmong wives were unhappy when they first arrived. The Hmong were happy just to survive."

"Which is why she got divorced," I said.

Pa Dao crinkled her mouth in a skeptical pucker. "According to Niam, your father caused Mai's divorce. He regularly visited the restaurant where she worked. She spent time with him there, just being friendly. But then the gossip started, and any time they spent together became too much time. Mai's husband warned them to stay away from each other, but your dad kept coming. Mai's husband beat her, but that failed to solve anything. Eventually, he divorced her. He sent her back to the Vangs, and her Vang family lost face. That's when your father married Mai the American way. On their way, they trampled over Hmong marriage rules. Mai left the Hmong community long before she and your dad moved from Saint Paul to Cottage Park."

I sat up and leaned forward. "Wait," I said. "I need to stick up for Puff—and for Mom. Puff never would have broken up Mom's marriage. And Mom never would have left a marriage unless it'd already fallen apart."

Pa Dao acknowledged me with big, appreciative *Nice try* eyes. "You and I may see it that way, but in the Hmong world, perception is truth. And their truth is that Mai and your dad stepped outside the lines. Your parents' actions shamed Mai's family and her husband's. Since the Hmong first arrived here, we've held one another dearly and held our customs even tighter. Divorce and marriage have complicated rules. Mai and your dad never respected the rules for either. That's how she ended up without a clan."

"Your mom and the people she talked to said all this?"

"Yep," Pa Dao said. "Does it matter who said what? It's all the truth."

The weight of that truth slowed me like ankle weights. This wasn't just about Mom's past. It was about me and how I fit into the Hmong culture, or didn't.

"What am I supposed to do?" I said. "I can't go back and reset the clock."

"No," Pa Dao said. "But you can repair the damage. Hmong parents bluff their kids into believing they have all the answers, and they set harsh ultimatums. But when push comes to shove, they're as confused as any other parents. Mai's family got past their shame. But Mai still carries hers, and it's backbreaking. Hmong children are way less forgiving of themselves than their parents. Mai can't move on until she lets her shame go. You have to help."

"How? What difference can *I* possibly make? Mom is supposed to return to all the places she's lived. Not me. This isn't my journey."

Puff was right. You can't go home again.

"But it's your job to bring your little family together with your big family," Pa Dao said. "Have you asked your father to contact your relatives in Saint Paul? Are your dad and John prepared for the *khi tes*?"

"They're fine with it," I said, lying to her for the second time.

"Be honest," Pa Dao fussed.

"Okay, okay—I haven't told them yet. I told them about you and Mom, but not the *khi tes*."

Pa Dao crossed her arms and leaned back in her chair.

"If John learned we were planning a healing ceremony for him," I said, "he'd jump the next freight train in any direction, with Puff right behind him."

Pa Dao waited for the correct answer.

"Fine. I'll bring it up," I said. "I promise. But it has to be the perfect time."

"Anytime is the perfect time," Pa Dao said. "Mai was your dad's wife and your brother's mom. She's counting on them to take these simple steps to heal John and your little family. And she's counting on you to make this happen. There's a reason she chose you. And me. Our mission is no-nonsense. I need you all in on everything. Now."

This was becoming a pattern: Pa Dao's voice in my ear, reminding me that Mom's future and *my* future were in my hands. But the more I listened to that voice, the less certain I became about following her path. Pa Dao sensed my doubts about plunging into the Hmong culture.

"You have to decide," Pa Dao said. "Do you want to keep being this . . . lost kid? Or do you want to be a man of the Hmong community?"

I didn't answer. Her expectations hung heavy, and I wanted to break free from them. But every time I tried, a force inside me—Mom and a growing respect for Pa Dao—snapped me back into place.

Pa Dao took my silence as a yes—or at least as not a no.

"Good," she said. "Next time we meet, bring one of your long-sleeved shirts and a pair of pants." She raised her hands to stop me. "Don't ask questions. I don't have the time or energy to answer them. Bring your clothing, okay?"

"Could I just—"

Pa Dao brought her hand to my mouth. When I tried to talk through it, she closed my lips with her fingers, pinching tighter each time I added a word.

"And yes, I do know what I'm doing," she said, anticipating my next question. "I don't ask much from you. When I do, you trust me, okay?"

She held her hand over my lips until I consented by raising my eyes up and down.

"There's a good reason for everything I do with you. I'm following Mai's direction." Pa Dao released my lips. "By the way," she continued, "I signed you up in the Hmong basketball league."

"The *what?*"

"They play on Thursday nights and Saturday mornings at Franklin Middle School—all Hmong guys. It's fun. I'm sure you'll be the best player there. You'll love it."

Pa Dao was right that I would be the best player there. The Hmong guys ran up and down the floor like rabbits, launching chaotic layup shots whenever they got near the rim. But she was wrong that I would love it—just the opposite. It would kill my game to play that way. Besides, Harden would never allow me to be away from the rec center for that much time.

I've always gone out of my way to avoid saying the word *no*. But I would have to say it regarding the Hmong basketball league. Just not now.

Pa Dao smiled, content with the deal she assumed she'd just sealed, perhaps more with Mom than with me.

I spent the next few nights at the rec center, where John kept an eye on me from the sidelines. Each night, I'd barely finish my warm-up before Harden pulled me into a game.

And each night, I played a new way of basketball.

In Cottage Park, we hooped like a marching band—everyone reading the same sheet music, moving in formation. But on North, the Harden Set, which now included me, were a jazz ensemble, all improvisation and rhythm. No sheet music. No rules. Just magic.

Harden pressed me to speed up and cut to the lane. "Keep moving," he'd bark. "Find a spot beyond the three-point line." No matter what, he'd get me the ball.

"No, man," he'd snap whenever I passed up a wide-open three-point shot to feed a teammate closer to the hoop. "*We* pass the ball to *you* to shoot. Pull the trigger. Take us to the promised land."

He was right. Even if I didn't shoot, the threat pulled my defender out to the arc, clearing the lane for him to dunk.

"All you," Harden encouraged whenever I made a good play.

He couldn't stand anyone sulking after a missed shot. "Shake it off," he'd say. "Now I'ma hit you up for damn sure the next time down. You best be ready."

Harden meant what he said. Whenever I'd miss a shot, he'd wheel and deal to feed me for the three the next time down. He believed 100 percent I would make each shot, especially after I shot a brick.

"Good shooters have bad memory," he'd say.

We lost the last game Wednesday night—the kind you carry home with you. The kind that gnaws at you until you get back on the court.

We had the ball and the lead, 11 to 10. In what should have been the final play of the game, I lingered at the top of the key, ready to get the pass, take my shot, and seal the game. But Harden called out, "Front door's closed."

That meant the back door was open.

I fake-reached for the ball, luring my defender to go for the steal. Once he committed, I snuck behind him to the basket, wide open. Harden threaded a perfect bounce pass into my hands. I received the gift and went in for a layup, left-handed, just like Luka Dončić. No way would Luka miss a gimme like that.

But I did.

The other team snatched the rebound and scored. We went back and forth for another few buckets until they took the lead for good and for the win.

We should have played next. Instead, I slogged off the court and caved in on the floor alongside John. I buried my head in my hands, chin to my chest.

"You suck," I muttered to myself.

I closed my eyes, replaying the missed layup in slow-motion auto replay, each frame a painful reminder of my failure. I believed every cruel word the announcer—me—used to describe the play. I'd failed to prove myself. I didn't belong with the Harden Set at the rec center.

I stopped the self-torment only when a hand lifted my chin. I opened my eyes and looked into Harden's. He held me until I gave up trying to turn away from him.

"Head up," Harden said. "Let go."

"How?" I blurted.

"What do you mean, 'How'?" Harden said. "How do you let go?" He glanced at John and pointed at me. "Is he for real?"

"I'm serious," I said.

Harden turned back to me. "Was there a playground in that little town you came from?"

"One," I said. "A prehistoric city park behind the library. We played there when we were little, but no one does anymore. Everything is rusted."

"Was there a slide?"

"Yeah," I said. "Petrified. And so tall that if you fell off at the top, you could kill yourself."

"Good," Harden said. "Now, what did Puff tell you before you went down that slide for the first time?"

I took a deep breath. I remembered sitting at the top of the slide, frozen stiff, holding on for life. John was right behind, nagging me to get going or let him take his turn. Puff waited at the bottom of the slide, a thousand miles below.

"He told me I could do it," I said. "He told me he would catch me."

"And I bet he said something else," Harden said. "He told you to . . ."

I looked back across time at the little boy, now the grown man, John.

"Let go," John said.

"And did you?" Harden said.

"I pushed him," John answered.

Harden smirked. "Well, either way, you had to let go, right, Empty? And once you slid to the bottom, you got your ass back up and you went again."

"True," I said. "I did go back down the slide. Just not that day."

"It's the same out here," Harden said, waving a hand at the world that was the court, the rec center, and the Northside. "You made a mistake. Now let go. I'll catch you at the bottom."

"Easier said than done," I said.

"You're too hard on yourself," Harden said. "How do you breathe? Swallow? Fall asleep? You don't stop and think about it. You let go. Here, basketball is flex for what happens next, and next is next. Next comes up fast, so move on. Get in the flow. We on the go."

He fake-punched me in the arm, then turned to John.

"How about you, Big Bad John? Did your doc say you could hoop again?"

John's eyes were locked on Coach, who was shooing the other players out of the gym while the rest of our set took their place on the court.

Suddenly, I did let go of the missed layup. Instead, I held on to the image of John running the floor and catching an elbow or fist to the temple from a headcase like Banger, who would easily interpret John's poor language skills and slow-moving gaze as mean-mugging and an immediate invitation to fight.

"His doctors ruled out sports for now," I said as John watched the other players gather their gear and head for the door. "Even pickup games."

Harden stroked a few chin hairs with his right hand. "But that doesn't mean he can't shoot around with us after Pops closes down."

He studied John and me for a moment, then sprang to his feet with a broad smile and pulled us up.

"I got myself a nice idea for next."

On Friday, the fifth and final day of suspension, Pa Dao waved me into our library study room, her expression grim.

"Did you at least bring the pants and shirt?" she said.

I handed her a crumpled grocery sack.

She pulled out the pants and held them up. They were deflated like a circus tent.

"I'm getting lean and mean for the team," I said.

"Yeah, right." Pa Dao rolled her eyes. "My friends said you skipped the Hmong basketball league last night. They were counting on you. So was I."

"It's a big commitment," I said. "The guys at the rec center count on me too."

"One night a week," Pa Dao shot back. "We're talking about Hmong guys who will appreciate you. You've got one more chance to play with them tomorrow morning. Play ball, then I'll take you to a Hmong funeral in the afternoon."

I hesitated. I was a chess piece, a pawn. I at least needed to make sure the words coming from my mouth were mine.

Next, Pa Dao tugged my long-sleeved shirt from the sack, draped it over herself, and pulled the sleeves tight. "Aren't you curious what I'll do with these?"

I head-faked a *Who cares?* look. "Figured you'd wear them. They'll fit you perfectly."

Pa Dao stuck out her tongue. "Nope. My sister Sheng will make you a Hmong outfit for special events. She'll use these for measurements."

"No way."

I reached for the clothes, but Pa Dao yanked them back and clutched them to her chest.

"Your Hmong shirt," she said, tracing her fingers across my old shirt like a weatherman mapping a storm, "will be all black. No collar. And there will be hot-pink dragon tails embroidered down the front"—she swept her hand dramatically—"from your right shoulder, down your chest, to your left hip."

"Pa Dao . . ." I started, exasperated. But I bit back the rest.

Do I even get a say in this?

Unfazed, Pa Dao continued. "A coin belt will wrap around your waist," she said, making a circle gesture with her hand. "Coins represent great wealth."

If you make me an outfit, I'll be obligated until the end of time. And I'll really have to be Hmong.

"You'll also wear two bands of solid red aprons, with two long and wide sheaves draping down to your knees, under the coin belt." She used her hands to make outlines. "The aprons symbolize blood and sacrifice."

I'm grateful, but why do I have to be a doll to dress up?

Pa Dao eyed me and said, "You know this is for your own good. You'll be happy when your outfit comes together. You can wear it to Hmong events." She added," Which you should attend with me."

"I hate dressing up for anything," I said.

"Which is why Mai directed me to do it this way. She warned me you would be difficult to dress." Her grip on the clothing tightened,

like she was trying to squeeze meaning out of them. "This isn't about
'dressing up.' Hmong outfits are about telling a story. Your clothing
says, 'I am Hmong.' It tells the world you're Hmong, even from a mile
away."

Her tone shifted to the familiar one Mom had used to order me
around.

"We're not going to argue," she said. "I won't argue. Wear the
outfit and be happy—discussion over."

I rolled my eyes.

Pa Dao stuck out her tongue again, pulled it back in, and smiled.

"Guess what?" she said. "Old Parrothead called Niam this
morning and said I can come back to school on Monday. I'm not
getting expelled. She'll be watching me, though. She'll transfer me to
another school if I even think about fighting." Her expression grew
determined. "Keep Harden away from me. I've had bad dreams about
spirits leaving him. Those spirits may try to find a home in you."

"What's that supposed to mean?"

"You let me worry about that for now. That's my job."

Pa Dao checked over her shoulder for anyone snooping on us
through the little window in the door. Seeing the coast was clear, she
reached under the table to retrieve a grocery sack filled with Tupperware containers.

One by one, she opened the containers to reveal steamed stuffed
cabbage leaves, homemade tofu that resembled brain tissue, greens in
a thin broth, two spicy Hmong sausages, and stuffed chicken wings.
Together we set out plates and silverware. Then Pa Dao opened a
container of ripe mango slices with coconut and sticky rice and
poured two bubble teas—one chocolate, the other blueberry.

"On Monday, I'll treat you to papaya," she said. "Now, *wb noj mov.*"

Back home, I held out the grocery sack like an offering.

Puff held the sack open while John pulled out the Tupperware.
They popped off the lids and scooped rice with their fingers.

I headed to the kitchen to chop vegetables, crack a dozen eggs, and prepare omelets for supper.

A few minutes later, Puff joined me, carrying the empty containers. "This food brings Mom home," he said, setting the Tupperware above the dishwasher. He tore off two paper towels from the roll near the sink.

John followed, and they sat at the kitchen table, wiping their hands and mouths with the paper towels.

"When do we meet your Pa Dao?" Puff said.

My opportunity had arrived.

"She wants to help us in December," I said. "Right before Christmas. She's arranging healing ceremonies for us."

"Us?" Puff said.

"For Mom. And John," I said, swallowing. "We need help now."

Puff fidgeted. "Pa Dao doesn't have to wait until December to meet us," he said, dodging the real topic. "She's welcome anytime."

"I'll let her know," I said.

I cracked my last egg, wiped my hands on a paper towel, then joined Puff and John at the table. "These ceremonies mean we'll have to connect to our Hmong family."

"What do you mean?" Puff said. "The Vangs in Saint Paul? Pa Kao Vang and his family? The family that disowned Mom?"

"We need to connect with the Vangs so Pa Dao can help us welcome spirits, call to our ancestors, guide Mom on her journey, and heal John."

"Pa Dao told you all that?" Puff said. "What are you getting us into? Did Pa Dao mention I'm about as popular with the Vangs as a steaming cow pie in a punch bowl? They don't want to be near me, let alone share a Hmong ceremony." He waved his hands. "Do your thing on your own. Take John if he agrees. But count me out."

"You have to be there for this to work," I said. "Pa Dao said you need to drive to Saint Paul and explain what's happening with Mom and our little family. She'll help you figure out what to say."

"Oh my God, no," Puff said, standing to leave.

"Mom's behind this," I said. "Pa Dao's following Mom's lead, and I'm following Pa Dao's. Mom wouldn't steer us wrong."

Puff sat, lowered his head into his hands, and groaned. "My worst nightmare is driving to Saint Paul to grovel before those people," he said. "My second-worst nightmare is them agreeing to help us."

He lifted his head and stared out into the distance, perhaps at the future.

"I bet they'd come from everywhere for this ceremony," he said. "You'd need the Target Center for the crowd Pa Kao Vang will bring."

"Pa Dao said the Vangs will want to host the event and handle the arrangements. She recommended that you take her dad over with you to meet with them. I have their address on Magnolia Avenue East. All you have to do is start the process." I half smiled. "You've said yourself that you can get anything you want by starting your request with the words, 'My son has a brain tumor . . .'"

Dread spread across Puff's face. "How long will this ceremony last?"

"All day. They start making food early in the morning. Then the ceremonies happen. We eat later in the afternoon."

Puff groaned again. "Do we have to stay the whole time? How many ceremonies are we talking about?"

"Yes, we have to stay all day. Pa Dao thinks there will be three ceremonies. They all require our involvement. She'll lead us on the journey to the spirit world to meet our ancestors."

Puff itched his eyes.

"Remember, this is not me," I said. "It's Mom."

"Like when she was alive," Puff said, his voice tinged with anger and awe.

"Yup." I then turned to John, who'd been sitting like a statue through the conversation. "Pa Dao knows what needs to take place so the tumor won't return."

Puff, too, focused on John. "Do you believe this Hmong healing stuff will cure you?"

I knew Puff would follow John's direction, no matter what he or I reasoned.

"It can't hurt," John said.

After I practiced with my Hmong basketball league team the next morning, I went to the Hmong funeral with Pa Dao. I estimated it would last one hour or, at the most, two. We left after five hours—and only after I told Pa Dao that I had to leave. Otherwise, we would have stayed another five hours. By the time I left the funeral, my head buzzed with drumbeats and chants.

But that night, as I finally stepped onto the rec center court, the rhythm changed—basketballs thumping against polished wood, an elevated kind of heartbeat.

Harden was waiting for me midcourt, arms crossed. He called me to stand before him, in front of the team.

"I'm going to keep it real with you," he said. "You're not that good. Not yet. And if you wanna be, your ass needs to be out here more than anyone. Otherwise, that's all you'll ever be—a wannabe. You either go all in on ball or keep playing dress-up with Sweetie. No half steppin'. Choose."

"I got it," I responded quickly, looking for the ball and hoping we would start the next game.

But Harden wasn't through. "What exactly do you got?"

"I got next."

My head-fake misdirected Harden, who let go. But I couldn't fake the reality that I had become a tug-of-war, with everyone pulling from opposite directions and everyone, especially me, losing the battle.

— CHAPTER TWENTY —

Huddle Up

The next Monday, Pa Dao and I returned to Thomas Jefferson along with the rest of the suspended students. The razor's-edge peace between the Hmong and Black students also returned. Only Harden and Pa Dao remained on the outs. Harden wanted to make amends, but Pa Dao had made up her mind never to speak with him again.

The cafeteria was a symphony of chaos—trays clattering and four hundred conversations blending into one sustained roar. Pa Dao never looked across the lunchroom at the rest of the Harden Set. Instead, she ladled a hot beef stew with bamboo and eggplant onto my plate. She also served me papaya salad, as she had promised. The aroma of fried pork and the sweet green scents of cilantro and basil mingled with the slapping sting of bleach from freshly mopped cafeteria floors and tables.

Pa Dao forked through the stew until she found soft fried pork skin. Mom had also used fried pork skin to add texture and flavor to her dishes. I was about to tell Pa Dao that, but she waved her hand to silence me.

"Listen carefully," she said. "This morning, Mai told me she's pleased with our progress. She said she'll be with you, but only if you're with her. That means you fully join your big Hmong family and community, wear Hmong clothing, and eat Hmong food."

Pa Dao examined the open containers on the table, grabbed a bowl filled with baby bok choy and pork belly, then spooned a fist-sized portion onto my plate. Finally, she added basmati rice.

She spread her hands over the food. *"Wb noj mov."*

I blew steam off each serving and dug in.

"Would you like to experience Hmong culture, clothing, and food all in one place?" Pa Dao said.

My eyebrows showed interest because my mouth was full.

"We're putting on Hmong New Year here on December 21." Her voice rose with excitement. "The show begins at seven p.m. and includes two hours of song, dance, and a play written and directed by Father." She tilted her head at Father, at the other end of the table. "She wrote me a teensy part. I'm also in a dance performance."

She paused, her fork in a holding pattern over her plate before she pointed it at me.

"And you'll be there. For Mai and for me."

Pa Dao then made a plate for herself and sat to eat.

"This show is my life," she said. "I have cousins coming for it. I know Mai will be there too. The performances will give you everything Mai wants you to know about being Hmong. She'll begin the journey to her ancestors once she sees how far you've come and where you're going."

The New Year event was another addition to the expanding list of Hmong activities Pa Dao had committed me to: funerals, weddings, Asian Club, and the Hmong basketball league. She wasn't just introducing me to Hmong culture—she was bulldozing me with it. I needed to slow her down in the same way I needed to slow down my Hmong basketball league teammates' frenzied fast breaks.

How could I explain that I was drowning in a culture I barely understood? Every event, every ceremony, every meal pulled me deeper into a culture I was supposed to belong to but didn't understand. Was I honoring Mom and her wishes, or killing time?

But instead of expressing any of this, I said, "I'll be there," between chews. Though a part of me wondered, *Are you ready for this?*

Pa Dao ignited a glowing smile. "Good," she said. "And wear your new Hmong outfit."

"Wait until you read the part of the play I wrote just for you," Father said from the end of the table.

I waved back to her with a smile. Inside, though, I was standing at the cemetery fence, questioning whether to stay put in my ways or leap over to the land of Pa Dao, Dysfunctional Family, and the Hmong.

A week later, at the rec center, Harden stopped our game earlier than usual, at 9:45 p.m.

"It's time for our team practice," he announced as he held the ball on his hip. Play stopped at once. "We'll pick up again tomorrow night," he said, fist-bumping our opponents.

As the other team headed to the far end to play half-court, Harden gathered the rest of us under the hoop and called for John to join us.

John hesitated, remaining in his usual position against the wall. But when Coach entered the gym, he went straight to John and pulled him from his sitting position. Together, they walked over to join our huddle.

"Did you say anything?" Coach asked Harden.

Harden shook his head.

Coach held out his hands, and Harden threw him the ball. Coach massaged it.

"I've assembled an AAU team for the spring," Coach said.

John and I just stood there, but everyone else, including Harden, instantly leaned into one another, punched fists into the air, and pounded fists against their hearts. LBJ and Westbrook jumped as high as possible and chest-bumped at the top.

Coach raised his hands to bring us back to attention. "Y'all are great for your age, and you'd clean up in the Under 15 Division. But I can't sign you up for that division with our big man here." He pointed at John, who'd soon turn seventeen. "If he plays, you gotta run with the bigs."

"He can stick anybody," I found myself saying. "Seriously. He can hoop for real."

"Even while he's getting chemotherapy?" Coach said. "He can get clearance from his doctor?"

I turned to John, and he gave a small wave.

All these nights at the rec center had lifted John's spirits. His color, strength, and life had returned in a week. And as John's spirits lifted, so did Puff's and mine. The sooner we could get John back to his everyday life, the sooner John and my little family would feel better.

Forget radiation and chemotherapy—John just needed to hoop again.

"I can do this," John said.

Everyone high-fived.

"So," I said, looking around at the beaming faces surrounding us, "AAU is good?"

Harden took a step back and challenged our teammates. "Man, tell these country dudes what's going on."

"It's sick," Curry said, his eyes lighting up. "A thousand times better than the team at Thomas Jefferson. Everything's first-class: the best shoes, best uniforms, and hotel rooms that don't stink like dukey. We live like pros."

The rest of the team agreed.

Coach stepped in. "Elite players choose AAU over their high school teams. You travel all over to go up against top teams. There are tournaments in Las Vegas and Kansas City."

"How much does all that cost?" I asked, channeling Puff.

Coach winced a little. "Airfare is no joke. But we'll do fundraisers—sack groceries, shovel walks. We'll make it work."

Coach scanned us one by one. His gaze lingered longer on the others than on John and me.

"I won't recruit backups," Coach said. "My team is here—my only team." He held out his arms over us. "This is all-or-nothing. If one of you can't travel with us or make a game, the rest won't be able to play. That means you need to make good grades—a minimum of a C average."

Coach again scrutinized us one by one. Except for John and me, everyone fidgeted.

"Oh God," Coach said. "That's what I suspected. Well, now it's time to crack down and get serious."

Pat Bev half raised his hand. "Teachers say we're too late to change our grades."

"I'll take care of those teachers," Coach said.

"We'll get afterschool tutoring," Harden said, speaking for our set.

"Most definitely," Coach said. "Schoolwork is a game too. Play the game and play to win. I've already hired tutors from the university to monitor your progress. You can't play ball each night until they sign off. I'll take care of supper for you after your tutoring."

Hopeful eyes flickered through the group.

"Fellas, do your part and bring in a solid GPA," Coach said. "Not just so you stay in the AAU game but so you stay in the *life* game. You can't qualify for college ball without good grades and a good ACT score."

Coach hammered the ball hard once to the floor.

"I repeat: Anyone failing even one class will not play on the AAU team, and we will cancel the season. Now—how many of you have seen the trophy case in the Thomas Jefferson auditorium?"

Coach counted hands.

"Everyone," he said. "And what do you see there?"

"Four state basketball championship trophies," LBJ said. "And your picture is on each trophy."

"Good," Coach said. "But behind those four championship trophies is another trophy with my picture. It's a consolation championship trophy for the Thomas Jefferson team I played on in eighth grade. That team was as good as any that won a championship. But three starters broke curfew the night before the championship game, and our coach benched them for the first half. I started that game—as an eighth grader—in their place."

He looked up at the hoop and drifted there for a moment before returning to us.

"We had the world at our feet, and we stomped over it wherever we wanted. All we had to do was not get in our own damn way. A lot of life is not having to beat your opponent but making sure you don't beat yourself."

Coach sighed.

"We should have won by twenty. Instead, we lost by five. But I learned more from that failed championship than from the four winning championships combined. Unfortunately, I learned to win by losing the hard way." He palmed the ball, pointing it at us. "Discipline matters. You can't mess around, cheat on yourself, cheat your teammates, and win. If you mess around, you won't play for me."

Coach reviewed each of us until we acknowledged him.

"Next year, you guys will play for Thomas Jefferson," Coach said. "And we'll put your trophies in front of mine." He breathed deeply. "Discipline is the backbone of defense—and defense is ninety percent of the formula for winning. What's the other ten percent?"

"Defense," Curry said.

"That's my boy," Coach said.

He flipped me the ball and stepped between Harden and me.

"Try to throw him the ball," Coach instructed.

Harden faked back and forth, and I snapped him the ball. But Coach knocked down the pass.

"No way I'm letting him get the ball," Coach said.

Next, he took hold of the ball and tossed it to John.

"You try to pass the ball to Jerome," Coach said to John. But this time, he stepped back and motioned to the rest of us to guard John at the same time. "You five better not let him near that ball!"

Again, Harden juked back and forth and side to side. Our team's ball-hawking arms reached out wherever he went to prevent the pass.

Finally, after five long seconds, John gave up. "I can't," he said.

"Right," Coach responded. "Real defense makes your opponent say, 'I can't.' It makes your opponent give up. Now, here's a little secret my man Curry here knows."

Coach pointed to our resident pit bull, who gave a slight bow.

"Naturally talented ballers get frustrated and quit the moment you don't let them get what they want most—the ball," Coach said. "You each pick a man to guard. But together, you're all responsible for keeping the ball from that top guy who's just ready to quit."

"Bob," Pat Bev said, naming the hypothetical player.

Coach's brow momentarily wrinkled before he remembered the alias Pat Bev created for the clueless. "Fine—'Bob.' We're here to deny the living hell out of people. Especially Bob. We press—full court, baseline to baseline. Start guarding Bob before the game starts. As soon as he comes back after a timeout. Get up on him. Front, back, sideways, and inside his head. Become his skin, so close he can't receive a pass without you stealing it—like Curry does every night. I gotta have six more Currys on this team."

Curry was rarely recognized for his defense. He pretended that this compliment meant nothing to him, but his glowing demeanor said differently.

Coach now motioned us to follow him to the top of the key.

"You gotta play defense the whole game. You only have to score once to win. But we have to change the way we score. From now on, you take only two shots. First, when we free you up, the three-ball. Then, if we can't free you right away, we take it inside and dish it off for the layup. Those are our two shots. Nothing in between. We might lose a few games starting out, but we'll beat everybody once we groove."

Coach put his right hand on my shoulder and guided me until I stood at the top of the key. Then he positioned my teammates around me, three on each side.

"Watch how Empty shoots the trey," Coach said. "Until y'all can shoot better your way, follow the leader."

I took a deep breath, wriggled my arms loose, and stretched my back forward and backward. Harden backpedaled below the net. They knew what was about to happen.

Coach fired a perfect pass that I received and adjusted so my fingers grasped into grooves among the ball's dimples. I jumped as my left hand held the ball and my right hand flicked underneath for backspin. I followed through until I pretend-reached my right hand to the net loop, and I kept my focus on that net loop even after the ball arced outside my field of vision. At its journey's end, the ball swished, and the net twerked.

Harden stood hands-on-hips as the ball jerked the net backward and backspin took effect, bouncing the ball onto the floor and right back to me.

Coach exchanged a knowing glance with Harden. They understood the how and why of my shot.

"Empty doesn't need anyone to rebound for him," Coach said. "The ball comes back to him—that's the beauty of backspin. You learn backspin, you control the ball."

"Make the ball your bitch," Harden translated.

"I need six more Emptys on our team," Coach said. "Let's see you each give it a try."

Harden motioned me to throw him the ball as I took my place to rebound. One by one, my teammates attempted the backspin trey. No one came close, not even John. Coach tracked down the errant shots bricking against the backboard or rim.

When it was my turn to shoot again, Coach put the ball on his hip and called me out.

"You can shoot treys, and you've got backspin," he said. "But good teams won't let you sit around and shoot open threes. If there's a guy all over you, create separation, freeze him, and fake him. Like The Beard."

Coach took two strong dribbles, planted his left foot, exploded backward off that foot behind the three-point line, and took his shot. It was a perfect James Harden step-back move, with one big exception—the shot fell short.

"Your turn," Coach said. He tossed me the ball and took a knee to observe. "Work your magic."

I'd practiced James Harden's step-back in my mind and alone on the court countless times. I'd imagined many imaginary defenders stumbling in the fakery. But I'd never attempted the move in front of anyone. But standing there before Coach and my team, I believed I could execute the signature step-back and make the shot.

The key is staying relaxed—don't telegraph the move. Next, you shake your defender with your dribble, left-foot jab, or shoulders.

I did all three. I jab-stepped left, shifted my weight, and planted hard. The step-back was clean. The ball arced, spinning with back-spin—nothing but net.

No one said anything as the ball rolled back to me.

I turned to John. For the first time since the tornado, there he was—the brother I remembered, the one who could still smile, something he hadn't done since the tornado.

I, too, was acting like I had before the tornado—hopeful. No matter how the world darkened around us, more and more cracks provided enough light for us to reflect that light, let it shine through us, and even make our own.

— CHAPTER TWENTY-ONE —

Stripped

Four Mead spiral notebooks sat stacked on my desk in English class. The notebooks were wide-ruled, each a different color, and each labeled with a different structural component of "The Empty Set," my personal narrative:

1) Exposition and Conflict
2) Rising Action
3) Climax and Falling Action
4) Resolution

As Mr. Lane instructed, I wrote the date—Thursday, November 15—on a blank page in the "Exposition and Conflict" notebook.

"Now get ready for speed dating," he announced.

Over a mixed chorus of snickers and groans, he told us to arrange our desks into two concentric circles, pairing desks face-to-face. He then divided our class into two equal groups. The first group would stay in their desks in the inner circle. The second group would move from one desk to the next in the outer circle. Each interval would last four minutes, and we were to ask each other five questions posted on the whiteboard:

1) What is the plot of your story?
2) Did you choose your story, or did it choose you?
3) Who narrates your story?
4) What problem do you address in your story?
5) How does your story end? How do your characters change and show growth?

Desk to desk, the scene played out the same way. First, we'd look at each other, laugh, and apologize for our perceived stupidity. But by the end of the four minutes, we'd accept praise for our brilliance. Then we summarized the dialogue notes in our notebooks.

I was in the rotating group. I followed LBJ, who in turn followed Zheng Xi—or Leslie. During one of our rotations, I noticed LBJ stroking a cell phone with a sparkly pink case—Leslie's. She'd forgotten it as she'd rotated to the next station.

LBJ's eyes darted around the room, calculating. In one motion, he slid the phone below the desk and into his pocket. My stomach churned as he then approached Mr. Lane for a bathroom pass. He left with his notebook, and when he returned without it a few minutes later, he acted like nothing had happened. But I knew better.

One of the first fats Harden had put on my head was, "Trust LBJ, but only trust him with nothing. He'll take anything—bikes, wallets, even pets. If food gets dropped on the floor, he'll eat it."

Harden told me that LBJ had been banned from the stores on Broadway, due to his frequent shoplifting. He kept returning to the same stores, though, to shoplift. The police often jailed him at the juvenile detention center downtown, or they placed him for a few nights at Saint Joe's Home for Children.

In other words, I wasn't shocked. But I did feel sick. I was learning a lesson my classmates had long since taken for granted: Our narratives, good or bad, were edited and rewritten by the Northside.

At the end of class, we hurried to return the desks to their original rows. Leslie scrambled to gather her things and make her way to her next class. LBJ never once looked in her direction.

I, too, headed for second hour. I knew I had to confront LBJ, but doing so was like skipping across a minefield. I wanted to help Leslie, but I knew LBJ's temper and his desperation. I knew better than to make a scene in front of everyone.

Near the end of second hour, with a few minutes left in Choir, Old Parrothead came on the intercom.

"Excuse me, teachers and students, for this brief interruption. I've repeatedly communicated that we cannot have a functioning school if you bring phones here. We've told you to leave them at home or lock them in your locker. We can't help you when your phone is lost or stolen. But we're making one exception today to support our foreign exchange student, Leslie, who lost or had her phone taken today. Leslie is our guest who has come from far away. At Thomas Jefferson, we treat such guests as our best friends. Leslie's phone has her contact information for China, her host family, and vital interpretations."

Old Parrothead paused. Leslie sobbed in the background.

"We need that phone returned immediately," Old Parrothead said. "No questions asked. No one will be blamed or punished. But let me be clear—this is about more than a phone. It's about who we are as a community. Do the right thing."

"Our Hmong New Year show theme," Pa Dao said, "is '1979 to 2019—the Life We Left Behind and the Life We Hold On to, from Laos to North Minneapolis.'" Her eyes lit up. "It's more than a celebration. It's a reminder of who we are, where we've been, and who we can become."

She set bowls, plates, silverware, and glasses on the cafeteria table and handed me a plastic knife.

"Cut the mango into slices and arrange them into the bowls with the sticky rice," she said, chuckling as she added, "Wow me with the presentation."

I arranged the place setting neatly. When Pa Dao reviewed my work, she smiled.

"Functional and inviting," she said. "Like our people. Those first Hmong arrived in midwinter in shorts and sandals. They couldn't comprehend winter, snow, English, or even flush toilets."

She spooned pork and chicken salad with peanuts onto our plates. Alongside the salad, she placed steamed stuffed cabbage leaves. Then she pulled a thermos from the sack.

"Thai iced coffee," she said. "Pour us each a glass."

I filled our glasses with the creamy caramel-colored drink, then lifted mine toward Pa Dao in a toast.

"To the journey," I said.

Pa Dao clinked her glass against mine.

"No immigrant community has sacrificed more for this country," she said as we sipped our coffee. "No group arrived more unprepared yet achieved so much so quickly as the Hmong. Know why?"

"Hard work," I said.

Pa Dao shook her head. "That's only part of it. The actual reason is what I've been stressing since we first met: family. Big, little, and everything in between."

Pa Dao sliced her stuffed cabbage to reveal a dull rainbow of ground pork, noodles, vegetables, herbs, and mushrooms, and brought a forkful to her mouth. She closed her eyes as she chewed.

"Perfection," she said. "How often do we ever say that word?"

She chewed in bliss for a few moments before reopening her eyes.

"We're born into families that nourish and raise us. We depend on our family, but good families raise us to be independent enough to *choose* to depend on them. For the ones that don't—and it's not just Hmong families—a hug can become a strangling. Mai had to pop out of her family to breathe. Those who pop out first are the strongest and healthiest. They make the family they leave behind stronger too. Mai's strength also made you stronger when she gave birth to you."

We ate together silently, making quick work of the feast before us. I had finished my pork and chicken salad when Pa Dao spoke again.

"Language can also make or break us."

"Language?"

"Our Hmong New Year program is written in both English and Hmong. We'll have two emcees—one for Hmong and the other for English. Each word we speak in English weakens our reliance on our Hmong family." She pointed to our fellow Hmong at the nearby tables. "We rarely speak our beautiful language anymore. Language is the direct link to our ancestors. When we lose our language, give it away, we lose a part of ourselves, the part we can't live without—our soul."

"Mom's Hmong was a hiccup that slipped out of her of something bigger she never shared with us."

Pa Dao ignored my comment. "Our music is also a language. At the New Year event, you'll hear our sacred *qeej*, which speaks to us."

"The instrument played at funerals."

She beamed like a proud teacher. "Yes! Some Hmong believe the *qeej* should only be played at funerals." Still holding her fork, she threw out both closed hands for me to guess which one held the correct response. "What should we hold on to? What should we let go of? Cut out and cut off enough parts, and we'll end up like *meka*."

I set down my fork. "I have those same questions—about holding on and letting go."

Pa Dao withdrew her hands and responded in Hmong. "*Kuv cov me tub siab zoo thiab yog neeg zoo. Tiam sis ua cas yuav tub nkeeg ua luaj.* That's what Mai told me this morning."

I gulped without choking. Mom had said those words to John and me ten thousand times—every time she fussed over our hair with her fingers.

"*Kuv cov me tub siab zoo thiab yog neeg zoo. Tiam sis ua cas yuav tub nkeeg ua luaj,*" I repeated for Pa Dao in the same loving way Mom had said it to us. "Mom said that all the time. But she never told us what it means, no matter how many times we begged her."

Pa Dao smiled. "'My dear sons are good.'"

"That's all? Mom just called us good?"

"Tell him the truth," Mother said. She had come from the end of the table, helping herself to the stuffed cabbage. Now she stood over Pa Dao, lingering to join our conversation.

Pa Dao said, "Hmong moms love their children in simple ways— patting heads, brushing hair, and calling them to eat a delicious meal. She clothed you, fed you, watched over you at school and home, and cleaned your house." Pa Dao paused. "You expected more?"

"Yes. Something more meaningful."

Pa Dao finished her coffee, her expression darkening. "I left out the last part: 'But why are they so lazy?'"

I sat back in my chair.

Pa Dao pointed toward the rest of Dysfunctional Family, who had left their seats to join Mother in the dialogue. "Ask them or any Hmong girl here or anywhere to describe a Hmong boy, and they'll say the same thing: 'Good but lazy.' Hmong boys are treated like kings—coming and going as they please and doing as they wish. They know Hmong women will be there to clean up for them afterward."

"My brothers have freedoms at home that I can only dream about," Brother said.

"I'll forever be property," Father said, "either my parents' or my husband's. It's called a patriarchy. It must have served a purpose back in the day."

"Yeah," Sister said. "To keep a boot on our necks. And that boot ain't lifting anytime soon. Not in our lifetimes."

"Which is why we Hmong girls have to work harder and longer than anyone," Brother said. "We're trapped in a system that holds us back. But we have to break through that system, even if it hurts. And that's by going to college."

"That's the Hmong girl's secret sauce recipe," Pa Dao said. "Hold on to the good things about being Hmong, but run from the bad. Unfortunately, there are a lot more bad things if you're a woman." Her weary half smile was equal parts challenge and affection. "Now that you know the truth about what we think of lazy Hmong men, you can change yourself, and the system."

When the final bell rang at the end of the day, I met LBJ at his locker.

"What you lookin' at?" he said as he closed his locker. "What's your problem?"

"Whatever it costs, I can pay you."

"Think so?" he said. "Then give me eighty dollars right now, or clear out of my face."

"I'll give it to you tonight at the rec center."

"Right," LBJ said. "You can go home and get whatever you want from your pops. Well, I don't have a pops—never had one. I don't have anyone at home waiting to help me. I don't have a home. You trying to be a hero? I'll whoop your head, boy." He mockingly clapped his hands in my face.

I backed off. "No," I said. "I just want to do the right thing."

"That Chinese girl put her phone out for everyone to take," LBJ said slowly, emphasizing each word. "It was only a matter of time before somebody snatched it. I got to it first." His scowl darkened. "Fuck you for judging. Only God can judge me. No one ever helped me after my shit got stole—and I've had more stuff stole from me than you or she will ever know."

He wasn't just defending his own actions but schooling me on the entire Northside—like lifting a rock at the slough to show me the life underneath. I didn't want to see the ugly things that grew there. But I couldn't back down, not this time.

"You're right. I'll never know what you've had taken from you," I said. "But I do know that Leslie lost everything when you stole her phone."

LBJ smirked. "All your China girl lost was a phone. I bet she ends up with an upgrade. And you—you don't know nothin'. Regrets for your ma. Regrets for the tornado, man. But you have a pops. You've got a new place. You've got a brother who lives with you. My folks are dead. My brothers and sisters live in foster homes in the burbs. And you'll leave the Northside whenever you want. I'm one of the guys who'll always be here, dead or alive."

He waved me to move out the way.

"No one gives a shit if my Black ass lives or dies. Mic check—the whole world would be happy if I died. Now make like bull shit and hit the road. Unless you have me on camera taking her phone, it didn't happen." As he stepped by me, his jaw tightened. "Same for this little talk."

"I'll tell Leslie."

He kept walking.

"I'll tell Mr. Lane," I said louder. "I'll tell Old Parrothead and Coach. I'll tell Harden."

LBJ circled back toward me and made a fist. Each knuckle displayed a crooked homemade dollar-sign tattoo. A larger, broader, professional dollar-sign tattoo shone over his right temple.

"Snitches wear stitches," he snarled.

"If I knew someone had stolen your phone," I said, "I'd do everything I could to get it back. I'd do all this for you."

None of my methods were working, so I went back to LBJ's original offer.

"All right. I'll pay you eighty dollars, and I'll give the phone back to Leslie myself. Puff can drive the money here now if you don't want to wait for the rec center. Then this all gets squashed. I'll never interfere with your business again." I raised my right arm to take an oath. "On my mom."

LBJ huffed.

The vow to Mom worked.

"Fine. Since you're such a big hero, I'll give you the phone back—but the price just went up. You owe me a hundred and twenty dollars by tonight. And if anyone ever hears about our little deal, it's double, and you're nothing."

"Done," I said.

LBJ let out a frustrated sigh. "I don't need any more drama from you, aight? I'm stressing these police, trying to lock me up for every little thing. Gangsters want to start shit with me. I'm just trying to survive out here."

He motioned to a trash can at the end of the hallway. "Dig through that for a red notebook wrapped in a rubber band."

He left.

I waited until he turned the corner and was out of sight, then I went to the trash can. Underneath the dust, loose paper, and candy wrappers lay a notebook labeled "Personal Narrative—Exposition and Conflict." I removed the rubber band, and the shiny new phone slipped into my hand.

I flipped through LBJ's notebook pages—all blank except for the page titled "Thursday, November 15." Then I dropped the notebook back inside the barrel and headed for Old Parrothead's office.

"Hurry up and sit down," Puff said when I arrived home.

He and John sat glued to Joe Mauer's retirement press conference on TV. Puff slid over so I could join him.

Throughout the conference, Puff leaned toward the TV in approval at everything Joe Mauer said, yet shook his head at the retirement news. "No! Too soon. He just needs to play on a winning team. Then he can go on for years."

When Joe Mauer noted the important role his brothers had played in his success, I half hoped he would include us Moriaritys as part of his family.

After a reporter questioned Joe Mauer on his responsibility as a role model, the future Hall of Famer explained, "You try to do your best because someone is always watching you."

My little family will always watch and watch out for Joe Mauer. But for the first time, I believed Joe Mauer was watching me back, expecting me to do the right thing—as if he had my back even when I didn't. It was a comforting thought. That gave me the courage to speak up.

I lifted the remote and turned down the volume.

"Daddyup," I said, "I'm in a jam. I need help."

Puff and John sat up from their prone positions and leaned forward to hear me.

"What kind of jam?" Puff said.

"I need a hundred and twenty bucks by tonight," I said. "If I don't come up with the money, I could be in serious trouble."

"For what?" Puff said.

"Someone stole a friend's phone today. She's helpless without it." I slowed. "I got the phone back to her, for a price. Part of the price is no questions asked. Ever. You can never repeat any of what I've said."

"I worry about you two," Puff said. He shook his head. "A hundred and twenty bucks is a lot to pay for a phone."

"It'd be a lot more than that to replace it," John said.

"You know we don't have that kind of money lying around the house," Puff said. "Can I write a check?"

"No way," I said.

"Why?" Puff pressed.

I fidgeted with the remote. "I've already said too much."

"The bank closed at five," Puff said. "The best I can do is go there first thing tomorrow morning."

"I promised my guy he'd get the money tonight," I said.

Puff grimaced. "Jeez. What kind of situation do you have yourself in?"

When his question ran headlong into my wall of silence, Puff let out a lung-emptying sigh, removed his wallet from his pocket, and opened it wide. Two twenty-dollar bills flipped from the crease. He placed them on the table.

I reached inside my front pocket for the twenty-dollar bill Harden had palmed me when I got into the ambulance to take John to the hospital. I'd kept it on me every day since. I pulled it out and unfolded it to cover the other bills.

We stared at the weak pyramid of bills. Halfway there.

"I can pick up the rest," John said. "From the gift cards the Moriaritys sent me."

John stood and walked into our bedroom. A moment later, he returned and dropped three more twenties onto the pile.

"That should cover it," John said.

"You guys just saved my life," I said. "I appreciate you, and I'll pay you back. Every penny."

John was the first to decline the offer.

"We're good," he said. "I don't need money for anything. I don't know what I ever would have used it for. I'll never spend it."

"Put the rest in a bank account," Puff said. "I don't trust having money in this house. Not in this neighborhood."

"If you need it, you can have it," John said. "It don't matter to me."

I breathed a sigh of relief as I collected the bills and carefully folded them together. I was about to place the bills in my pocket, but stopped, drawn to the motto arched over the White House.

"In God we trust," I said aloud.

"In God and Joe Mauer," Puff said.

"And don't sleep on John Moriarity," I said.

I slipped the bills into my pocket and headed for the door. Out of pure muscle memory, I almost reached for Hawk on my way out, but I jerked back at the last second. Grabbing Hawk would've given away the handoff location, if not given away that "my guy" was one of our teammates.

I threw a glance back to see if my stutter step had been spotted. Puff had the remote and was turning up the volume. John, though, had noticed. He waved me on to leave.

"I'll be back in a minute to make supper." I'd be serving Puff's favorite meal: pork chops, applesauce, baked potatoes, and Rice Krispie bars for dessert. "It's Cottage Park Night."

— CHAPTER TWENTY-TWO —

Assist

The day before Thanksgiving, Mrs. Flowers gave me a ride home after school. As we rolled up and over the curb, she asked me to help carry in food, party decorations, and books she'd picked out for John from the Thomas Jefferson library.

We had much to celebrate and be thankful for. While I'd been at school, John had gone in for his thirtieth—and final—day of radiation. *Final.* Puff had proclaimed it Ring the Hell Out the Bell Day. He had it all planned: John would finish his treatment, come out to the lobby, pause for all the cheers from the radiation staff, then recite the poem engraved on the golden plaque on the wall, near the bell.

> *Ring this bell*
> *Three times well*
> *Its toll to clearly say,*
> *"My treatment's done*
> *This course is run,*
> *and I am on my way."*

After the poem, John was to ring the bell. Three times. And loud enough for me to hear it back at Thomas Jefferson. After that, John would hand Lecter over to Puff for good.

We'd seen pictures from patients who had creatively transformed their hideous head coverings into keepsakes such as plant holders. Puff's plan was creative too. He would load us into Vicky, and then we'd drive over Lecter and back until he was a fine powder. I'd caught myself smiling throughout the day, imagining it.

"Of all your accomplishments," Puff had told John the night before, "completing your radiation program is my proudest."

John wasn't out of the woods yet, as he would now start chemo. But he was ready for next.

We all were.

"We're here," I announced as I held our front door open with one hand for Mrs. Flowers and her banana cream pie, its whipped cream frosting layered with whitecaps. I pivoted in behind her with two boxes.

We slipped off our shoes. I was about to set the boxes on the table, but Mrs. Flowers waved me over.

"Bring those boxes with you, honey," she said.

Together, we proceeded to our TV room. Mrs. Flowers handed me the pie as we stepped inside.

"Where's the party?" she asked, her eyes scanning the scene.

Velveeta cheese crumbs, Ritz crackers, and pepperoni slices were scattered across the coffee table, and Puff and John were scattered across their couches with ESPN blaring on the TV. At least they sat up in respect for Mrs. Flowers.

"Turn that noise box off," she bulldogged Puff.

"We had a lousy day," Puff groused as he searched for the remote.

As it turned out, it hadn't been Ring the Hell Out of the Bell Day but Come Back on Monday Because the Radiation Machine Is Broken Day. Puff had spent a full hour badgering the staff, insisting that they either hurry the repairman or allow Puff himself to inspect the multimillion-dollar radiation machine.

When his rants got him nowhere with the staff, Puff then grilled Dr. Schneidermann, John's oncologist, about the need for this final session. He tried to convincing Dr. Schneidermann to let John skip it.

And when that effort failed, Puff spiraled into the same argument he'd made back in early October—that radiation, not brain cancer, would kill John. He cited John's hair loss as proof.

Puff stopped only when he noted John's fatigue and hunger. Then they went home.

"And now we have to wait until *Monday*," Puff said, as if closing a radiation center over the Thanksgiving holiday was unreasonable.

"We'll celebrate the final treatment on Monday night," Mrs. Flowers said. She smiled. "And tonight, we'll celebrate the twenty-nine treatments you've already finished, okay?"

She settled onto John's couch and gestured for me to place the boxes between her and him. She pulled out three long-stemmed orange roses, their petals velvety and fragrant.

"Orange symbolizes admiration for a big accomplishment," she said as she handed them to John. "Careful—they've got thorns."

As John considered what to do with three roses, Mrs. Flowers rummaged through party favors, candies, and soda until she pulled out two books: *From Ghetto to Glory* and *Stranger to the Game*.

"You're my favorite pitcher," she said to John. "My second favorite is Bob Gibson."

"Same for me," Puff said, perking up.

John put the roses aside to look through the books. When he was done, Puff helped himself to them. He read the back covers and leafed through pages.

"I can't wait to read these," he said. "Gibson used to pitch in town ballgames back home."

Mrs. Flowers dug into her box and pulled another book, *A Sand County Almanac* by Aldo Leopold.

"Read this if you want a career in wildlife," she told John.

John browsed the first few pages. "Says he's from Iowa."

Next, Mrs. Flowers brought out stapled materials and handwritten assignments from John's teachers. She set them aside and continued digging, removing a large, thick manila folder.

"In each public speaking class I subbed today, I invited students to write you a letter. They loved the idea. Now, we'll read them together."

Mrs. Flowers gave the folder to John. He opened it and flipped through a handful of letters—the first few featured drawings. John traced the words, lips moving silently. His shoulders sank with each line. His eyes filled with tears.

"It's nice they remembered me, but I'm tired of people helping me," he said, his voice breaking. "I'm tired of being the one who needs to be saved."

Still holding the folder, he pushed himself from the couch, dragged his feet to our bedroom, and closed the door.

"My Big Bad John had a rough day," Puff said wearily. He pushed his palms backward into his scalp until his hair tightened into a ghastly fun house mirror image. "The hospital staff said that John should have a counselor for these kinds of days. We tried to get him help . . ."

Puff lowered his hands to his lap and waited for my affirmation. I nodded.

"But now here we are," Puff said. "I doubt we'll get anything out of him today. He should be better on Monday." He attempted a weak smile. "How about you come back then, at the usual time?"

"No. I'll work with John now," she demanded. "I can't wait until Monday. Michael, please go in and kindly inform John that I'm waiting out here. I'll continue to wait until he returns."

Puff fidgeted on the couch. He wanted to be the one to go back and talk to John. But he also knew that John wouldn't give in to him.

"In the meantime," Mrs. Flowers said, noting Puff's discomfort, "you can start cleaning up this floor."

I walked back to the bedroom and opened the door. John was lying on his side, his face buried in a pillow.

"Go away," he grouched.

"Mrs. Flowers said she's not leaving," I said. "If I were you, I'd come out now. She means business."

"Yeah, well, you're not me," John said. "Lucky for you. I'd trade places with you any day."

"The sooner you come back out," I said, "the sooner we can eat supper and play ball. I know Harden's counting on you." I paused. "I'll tell her you're on your way."

When I returned to the TV room, I reported that John would return.

Mrs. Flowers stood. "Please take my seat, Michael," she instructed. She moved over to the couch with Puff.

We waited a few minutes, until John returned and sat beside me. His hands were empty.

"Where did you put those letters?" Mrs. Flowers said.

"In the trash can," John said.

"In your room?" Mrs. Flowers said. She signaled to me. "Get those letters and bring them back to John."

As I stood, so did Puff. I froze, but Puff tried to dash off.

"Where are you going?" Mrs. Flowers said to him, sniffing out one of his patent escapes.

"Um . . . to get Kleenex," Puff lied.

"No," she said. "Sit." She turned to me. "Michael, bring tissues with those letters."

I hurried down the hall to retrieve the folder. We had no Kleenex, so I returned with a roll of toilet paper for each couch. I set the folder on John's lap.

Mrs. Flowers smiled as I returned, then focused on John. "What do you see in that folder?"

"Nothing," he said.

"You see letters. What do you think those letters stand for?"

"Pity." Again, his eyes welled. He blinked some tears away and pinched the ones that slipped by.

Puff made a guttural grunting sound like he might throw up. He lowered his head nearly to his knees, placed his face in his hands, and sobbed. Mrs. Flowers placed her hand on his back.

Puff's display spooked John. His eyes cleared.

"John," Mrs. Flowers said, "you will never experience pity at Thomas Jefferson. Pity is for people who've already given up. These young people? They're fighters. They've been through hell, just like you. They're fighting for you. You should fight too."

"I meant pity for myself," John said, his voice trembling. "I'm tired of my hair falling out. My scalp itching and burning. The headaches. The swishing sounds inside my head. Having to wear Lecter. I can't do it anymore. I'm tired of dying. I'm even more tired of living."

We sat in silence for a long time, stunned by John's declaration, one of the longest in his life. There was more.

"Every day," he said, "I'm stuck in the same waiting room or the same hospital room, waiting out the same stuck clock and knowing how this story ends."

His words hung in the air, heavy and unrelenting, even as the sweet smell of banana cream pie filled the room.

We waited for Mrs. Flowers.

"You're not a burden," she said firmly and gently. "You're family. And family doesn't give up on each other. My goodness." She humphed. "We love you. And love is the only way you'll survive. I know because that's how I survived when I had breast cancer," she added, her voice softening. "When I went through radiation, I nearly lost myself. It was only the love of my family and the Northside that kept me going. That's what you have here." She leaned forward. "Everything will pass. Even your radiation—on Monday."

John sniffled, blinking hard. "It doesn't matter. Monday's just another day closer."

"Closer to what?" I asked.

He didn't answer. He didn't need to.

Puff sobbed louder. This was why men from Cottage Park cried alone, behind closed doors.

"I can't lose you," he said angrily.

As Mrs. Flowers handed him their toilet paper roll, I reached for ours. I wrapped toilet paper around my hand to make a cast that I slipped off and handed to John, who pawed away his tears.

Night after night, I'd cried imagining this moment, John or Puff breaking down. But now, sitting between the two big rocks in my life—both cracked wide open—my eyes were clear and dry, and *they* were crying. I was holding my little family together.

"Everybody, catch your breath," Mrs. Flowers said.

As she had done for Puff, I put my arm on John's shoulder. He trembled. She and I steadied Puff and John, holding them.

After a few minutes, Mrs. Flowers gave John an order: "Open the folder and read a letter to us."

He lifted the folder from his lap and jiggled it until the letters sorted into order. Finally, he took out the first one. "Starting at the beginning?"

"Go in any order," Mrs. Flowers said.

John sniffed, put the letter back, and leafed through a few more. He chose a letter and began by reading it to himself. He then opened his mouth to read aloud, only to freeze.

"I can't do this."

Mrs. Flowers reached out. "You already are."

John began reading:

Juanito:

    Too bad we didn't get to hang out before you came down with the Big C. Just remember, you're bigger than any punk-ass cancer, and when you crush it and come back to school, I swear to God we'll have a good time.

    Let's hang out sometime.

    My mom makes sweet tamales every year at Christmas. I'll bring a bunch over to your house. Call me anytime you need ANYthing.

    Let's go!

    Friends for life,

    Francisco Gonzalez

John skipped a few more pages before settling on another letter:

Big Guy,

    You are so lucky to be at home chillin' like a villain and not have to be hemmed up by these teachers who, I swear to God, are getting on my last damn nerve.

    Mrs. Flowers tells us you're getting stronger and coming back to school before the end of the year. Know that you're not missing out on anything here. It's boring as a mf.

    I hope you're smoking all the medical marijuana you can get your hands on.

    What do you think of Cardi B? Drake?

*We all got your back over here, especially me—on my mom.
Call me.*

> *Peace,*
> *Jason Newman*

"Medical marijuana?" Mrs. Flowers pondered. "Would that be something worth trying? I've heard it can help with pain and nausea."

"We asked," Puff said. He cleared his throat, sat back up, then cleared his throat again. "The doctors say he won't be nauseous during his chemo, so they won't give us a prescription."

"Well, there you go," Mrs. Flowers said. "That's good news." She patted John's arm. "Keep reading."

Hearts and flowers decorated the next letter:

Sexi Boi:

> *Mrs. Flowers promised us her chocolate chip cookies if we wrote a letter to you. Here goes nothing.*
>
> *I'm in two of your classes, US History and Chemistry.*
>
> *I like the fact that you are quiet and don't shoot off your mouth like these fake-ass boys around here who are so boring. Jesus!*
>
> *Anyway, I think you are cute AF, and I want to get together with you when you get back, or I can come over to your crib. I don't want to show up at your door without an invite. Holler at your girl!*
>
> *Love you always,*
> *Brandi—*

John stopped short as he read the girl's name. It was obvious he was keeping the last name to himself. Not that it mattered. We all knew it was Powell, the largest and most prominent family on the Northside.

Mrs. Flowers grimaced. "Pass that letter here," she said firmly, reaching out a hand.

"Oh no you don't," Puff said, asserting himself for the first and only time with her. He rose to retrieve the letter. "Maybe this will produce a future daughter-in-law." Holding the letter high, he praised, "My Lord and my God—the answer to my prayers." He stuffed the letter in his back pocket.

The hint of an upward curve played at the edges of John's mouth. But when he looked back down at the letters in his lap, it disappeared.

"I expect you to read all those letters, in time," Mrs. Flowers said. "I also expect you to learn more about the challenges Bob Gibson faced." She pointed to the books. "And the challenges any of your baseball heroes are facing. Who are the big stars nowadays?"

John hoped Puff or I would respond, but we waited until he answered on his own.

"I suppose Joe Mauer," he said.

"Ask yourself what Joe Mauer would do in your situation," she said. "He's suffered hardships with . . ." As usual, she expected John to follow her prompt.

"Concussions," Puff said.

"Right," Mrs. Flowers said. "And he came back. Ask yourself, what would Joe Mauer do?"

"Let go," John said, sniffing. He wiped his nose with the tissue cast. "And hold on."

In the kitchen, I adjusted the burner for rice and preheated the oven to four hundred degrees. Next, I opened two cans of Chicken of the Sea tuna, drained them, and placed the tuna in a bowl. Then I chopped green onion into fine pieces and added them to the bowl along with two tablespoons of hamburger relish. Finally, I globbed in mayonnaise until everything was creamy.

Mrs. Flowers breezed into the room a few minutes later, carrying the roses she'd given John. She put them in a vase, then placed it on the table.

"Let me set the table for you, dear," she said.

I pointed to the cabinets containing our glasses and plates. "Thanks, but we grab our dishes from the cabinet to help ourselves. I'm the only one who eats at the table."

Mrs. Flowers responded by gasping. "Nonsense." She called out, "John, Mr. Moriarity—wash your hands and come in here to eat supper."

As I scooped the tuna mix into hamburger buns, Puff and John obeyed Mrs. Flowers's command. They shuffled into the bathroom, washed up, then sat at the table as she arranged place settings around them, including one for herself.

"From now on, you three eat at this table," she said. "Every meal, every day."

"We eat in the TV room to keep up on the games," Puff meekly countered.

"There'll always be a game," she said. "But you won't always have each other. My goodness—these boys will be up and out of this house and on their own before you know it."

She spooned store-bought cowboy-calico beans and tater tots onto each plate and placed a thin pink radish in each center. As I brought over the tuna fish sandwiches, she filled each glass with Honeycrisp apple cider, then sat with us. After I said grace, we ate.

Mrs. Flowers sipped her apple cider, watching us like a teacher. "All right—you can sit around the TV together and watch one game per year."

Puff paused, looking to us for an explanation of her proclamation.

"The Super Bowl," she said with a smile. "Everyone gathers around the TV to eat on Super Bowl Sunday. As a matter of fact, you're hereby invited to be guests at my annual Super Bowl party."

Puff grumbled, "We'll check our schedules." I laughed to myself. We never left the house for anything except groceries on that day.

But I could already see him imagining a plate full of wings at the party.

"That's why I'm telling you now," Mrs. Flowers said. "With this much notice, I'll expect you to join me and my friends. No excuses." She sliced her sandwich in half, delicately brought one end to her mouth, chewed, and swallowed. "Delicious. Who gave you this recipe?"

"Nobody," I said. "If we'd had time, I would have wrapped the sandwiches in aluminum foil and heated them."

"Such a treat," she said. "You're the main cook around here. Does that mean you'll prepare your Thanksgiving meal?"

I gave a cool thumbs-up. But inside, I'd been panicking all week about Thanksgiving. I'd found a recipe for turkey in a book from the Thomas Jefferson library. What if I messed up? What if the turkey was dry—or worse, raw?

"Have you ever prepared a Thanksgiving meal before?" she asked, sensing my unease.

I shook my head.

"Have you planned a dessert?"

"Store cookies, I guess."

Mrs. Flowers frowned.

"Pepperidge Farm Milano Dark Chocolate," I explained. "We love them."

Mrs. Flowers scowled. "Absolutely not. I'll bring you a pecan pie and whipped cream. What time will you put your turkey in the oven?"

My shoulders raised. "I guess I'll have to reread the recipe and plan backward from suppertime."

"I'll be here at nine a.m. Be ready," she said. "First Thanksgivings are challenging."

She nibbled away at her sandwich as I got up to make more for Puff and John. That was when I noticed that I'd forgotten the rice, which had cooled on the counter. I'd begun to serve rice at every meal. I'd also started to fry *zaub paj*, a green Mom used to grow in her garden, but not for this meal. I fluffed the rice and served it from the pot to each person.

Mrs. Flowers waited until I sat before saying, "Michael, how was your day? Who do you sit with at lunch?"

"Pa Dao Xiong," I said.

"His girlfriend," Puff said. His smile was as much a boast. "She makes him a nice Hmong meal every day for lunch."

"Oh, how nice," Mrs. Flowers said. "I know that young lady and her family. They have a big plot in our community garden. How did you two meet?"

I raised a finger to signal that I needed a few moments to chew and swallow rice. John and Puff set their forks down to await my response. I swallowed and inhaled.

"Mom told Pa Dao she needs to meet with me every day to teach me Hmong culture."

"Your mom, who died in the tornado?" Mrs. Flowers asked, her tone gentle but probing. There was no judgment in her voice, only a quiet curiosity that made me feel safe enough to tell the truth.

"Yes," I said. "Mom didn't die that night. Not totally." Puff hung on each word I spoke. "Pa Dao is a rising Hmong shaman. Mom visits Pa Dao so Mom can continue to help us on our way without her."

I let all that hang in the air.

Everyone quieted until Mrs. Flowers said, "We're all connected to the spirit world—through memories or the people who carry those memories forward. Your mom may not be here in body, but she's certainly with you in Pa Dao, and in your family."

We silenced again until Puff said, "I miss Mom."

"Me too," John said.

— CHAPTER TWENTY-THREE —

Pivot

A week later, John and I trekked through seven inches of drifting snow as we crossed the street to the rec center. Beneath that snow lay minuscule chunks and powder—what Puff called "the slain, insane, inhumane membrane remains" of Lecter.

Once inside the gym, I slipped off my boots and changed into my worn tennis shoes, the soles thin from all my practice time on the court. As I laced up, Harden's voice cut through the gym.

"Empty, you're in for LBJ."

Every time Harden called my name, my stomach tightened. I was unprepared for the teacher's test that I could never pass.

"All right," Harden barked, tossing me the ball with a smirk. "Empty's shooting. Or y'all pick someone else, and we can watch your guy miss." His confidence in me was unshakable. He knew what I could do, even if I didn't.

"Take the damn ball," a guy on the other team said. "But we get it next time."

Harden smiled with the confidence of an investor putting money on a sure bet.

He was still wearing that same smile at ten o'clock, when everyone else left the gym. He called his growing Harden Set to the free-throw line, a set that included me and, for the first time, John.

"Your name is Capela," Harden said, bro-hugging John.

The rest of us exchanged knowing smiles. The Houston Rockets center, Clint Capela, teamed with Harden's idol and namesake. We knew what Harden was planning.

The Beard did whatever he wanted on offense. With the ball in his hands, he'd mesmerize his defender—dribbling back and forth between his legs and eating up the twenty-four-second clock until a few ticks remained—before taking flight to the rim. If you played back off him, even a step, he'd pull up and shoot. If you played on him, he'd step around you for a layup. If you double-teamed him, he'd dish to the man you left wide open for a three-ball, or he'd toss an alley-oop that Capela flushed with a thunderous dunk.

"Capela's radiation is done," Harden said. "Let's start warming him up to play with us in our practices after the gym closes." He glanced at me and held the look until I nodded tentatively. He smiled. "Make some noise for the brother."

Harden led the cheers, then held up a hand for silence.

"Any time these two are on the floor at the same time," he said, pointing at John and me, "the rest of y'all spread out." He flicked five fingers, the new sign for our spread offense. "I don't care where you go. Just take your guy with you."

He waited for affirming eyeballs, then turned back to me.

"Empty, you take off for the right corner."

I ran to my place.

"Capela," he said next, "you come from the low post to set a pick on my guy."

John trotted to his position and waited.

Harden rehearsed the new spread play at half speed, barking instructions as he went. "Pivot right. My guy's on your back," he said, clapping as John rolled to the hoop. "One of us will be open."

Harden took three dribbles toward the rim. John followed a step behind and to Harden's left.

"If no one takes me," Harden said, "I'll go in and dunk. If Capela's guy leaves to come after me, I'll lob Capela the dunk. And if Empty's guy sags back to pick me up, I'll hit Empty in the corner." He reviewed our team. "Now, run it back."

Harden took the ball and ran back to half-court. He raised his left hand with the spread sign, and we took our positions. He then burst through the imagined pick, stopped below the rim, jumped straight up, and flushed the ball.

"Again," he bossed.

John gathered the loose ball and fired a pass to Harden, who jogged back to center court. Again, Harden dribbled to the top of the key. As John pivoted and rolled, Harden lofted a pass near the rim. John's shoulders tightened as he approached the hoop, not from effort, but from years of holding himself back. He jumped high enough but couldn't dunk or tip it in.

John shook his arms loose, curled his fingers, and examined his nails, finding refuge there. "Weird," he said, eyes downcast.

Harden clapped John on the back. "No worries. We'll get you back in basketball shape," he said. "Until then, don't worry about the dunk. Catch the pass, come down, and shoot it."

I shook my head. John's hesitation wasn't about his lack of conditioning—it was fear. Fear of failure. The fear of letting Harden and the set down was a heavy shadow that always trailed behind us. But I didn't want Harden to know that.

"It's not just about getting him back in shape," I explained. "John can dunk, but in Cottage Park, they made him pay for damages if he wrecked a rim or brought down a backboard."

"That's not how we play on the Northside. You rip that shit down," he said, pointing straight at John. "Don't hold back. Be a beast. If you're not a beast, you're the prey."

We reran the play. Harden passed the ball to me in the corner. I caught it and started to dribble.

"No!" he barked. "Stop." He glared at me. "It's catch and release. You only dribble if you're taking it to the hoop to score. You a shooter. Your dumbass dribble cost the team a three and me a dime." He pounded the ball against the floor, pacing like a coach on the sidelines. "We dribble too damn much. That slows us down. Slow is weak. It's what's for supper tonight."

Harden directed Westbrook to take my place in the corner and motioned me to follow him to midcourt.

"You be me," Harden said. He handed me the ball. "Call the play."

"Point guard?" I said. I'd never played the point.

Harden crouched to guard me. "That's what Luka plays."

I signaled the play and dribbled toward John's pick. Harden got up on me to play me tight.

"The second I bash that pick," he said, "you pull up and shoot your three."

Harden rubbed into John at the top of the key, and I let loose a three—*swish*.

We ran the play a few more times. Each time I took my shot, I scored.

"All right," Harden said. "Now LBJ's gonna guard you."

As we took our places, Harden gestured to me.

"Empty, now you drive through the pick. Watch his hips turn, and drive right into and around them. If his shoulders turn, step back and take the three."

Then Coach walked in. He stood beside Harden, and they watched LBJ hound me for three possessions. In two, I tossed lobs to John. In one, I dished off to Curry in the corner.

On my fourth possession, I dribbled lower and ran the play faster. I head-and-shoulder-faked LBJ hard before stepping back beyond the three-point line to drill a trey.

"I told you so," Harden boasted. "Empty can shoot." His head bobbled vigorously. "Nothing but net." He puffed his chest out. "*That's* my legacy."

The next night, after the others left the gym, Curry stayed behind, launching himself at the rim again and again like he did every night. Only Curry worked on elevating his jumping skills. At six feet, two inches, he already had good hops. "But good isn't good enough," he'd once told me. "In my life, I have to be the best." Curry, already our best defensive player, now worked to be our best jumper—our best dunker. Better than Harden.

He repeated the same drill every night. He'd eye the rim from beyond the top of the key and to his left, like a high jumper preparing to leap a record height. Then he'd push the ball upward, like a volleyball player setting up a spike. After the ball bounced toward the rim, he'd rock and run as fast as possible to time his jump so he and the ball would reach the rim at the same time, tapping and dunking the ball with one hand.

This night, he focused on two-handed slams, though the ball kept slipping from his grip. Still, he kept at it. I was as inspired as I was intimidated.

"What would you say to a hooper who thinks he can't jump?" I said, after I chased an errant ball and brought it to him.

"Lazy," Curry said, agitated. "You get what you put in. You think I was born doing this? Or that I think it's fun? Nah. I work for it every damn day. You want it? Earn it. If I can do it, you can too."

He took the ball, stood underneath the rim, and pointed to where he'd stood a few moments earlier, his takeoff point.

"Your turn. I'll set the ball. You come in as fast and high as possible."

I took my position and waited. In the first few tries, I took off too early or too late. On the fourth try, I came close.

Curry smiled as he collected the ball. "My turn."

I gladly stepped back. Jumping was hard work. I was drained.

Curry lofted the ball, waited, then took off. He clenched the ball at the apex and threw it against the back of the rim. The ball ricocheted to midcourt.

I ran for it and tossed it back to him. "You almost got that one."

"Yeah," he said. "But I can't live in almost-got. I got to get it. I got to feed my son—feed him food and example. My dad was never around to do that for me."

He held out his fist, where a professional tattoo of the name Frank covered the skin from his knuckles to his wrist.

"We don't die—we multiply. That's one bit of wisdom my pa told me before he went away to the feds. My dad's name is Frank. My name is Frank. And now my son's name is Frank."

Harden had told me that Curry had moved in with an older girl from Thomas Jefferson and that they'd recently had a son. Harden also said that Curry was "seeing" other girls too, all at the same time—a fact that Baby Frank's mother regularly discovered. To make it all work, Curry couch-surfed, crashing with his son and his baby mama one night, at his mom's the next, and other with girlfriends as the opportunity arose. It was easy to track Curry's love life. Every time Baby Frank's mom found out about a new girlfriend, she'd lather herself with Vaseline and fight the girl in school the next day.

Curry stood under the rim, and held the ball as if preparing for a volleyball spike. "Ready?" he said. "Go faster this time."

As he lofted the ball over the rim, I charged in and jumped as high as possible, swinging my right hand forward. My fingers grazed the rim, a butterfly kiss, and the ball dropped through. My first dunk. Barely, but it counted.

My heart pounded. I belonged here. You always remember your first kiss.

"There you go," Curry said. "Next time, reach a little farther. Reach higher. You can do it."

He started back to his spot, but held back.

"Hey, Empty." He paused. "Every time I stay with Frank, I do the normal things a dad does. I play with him, roll him a ball, and read him books. Last night, my boy struggled to fit a square block into a round hole. But he didn't give up. I won't either. I'm going to read. My boy is going to read. He's going to college for brains, not ballin'. Feel me?"

"Makes sense," I said.

"Now I'm thinking, if I want him to be a reader, a good student, and smart, I have to be all those things first. Good teachers model what they want you to learn."

He paced back to the takeoff spot. I trailed behind.

"I'm special ed—not stupid," he added quickly. "It's just, my family moved all over the place. I have"—he thought for a moment—"*holes* in my learning. I plug those holes with special ed. Reading and math. I'm an A student in special ed. In those classes, kids mess with each other. They've quit trying. They've given up their future. I earn Cs in regular classes. But teachers give me Cs because they like me."

He eyed the rim and spun the ball in his hands.

"The other day," he said, "I asked both of my special ed teachers how many of their students make it to college. Take a guess."

"None."

"Not one. They couldn't think of anyone who even went to junior college. Ever."

Curry lofted a soft shot that bounced short of the rim. He tried to jerk it up and over but caught it against the tip. He collected the miss and prepared to lift the ball for me to dunk again.

"I should be in regular classes with guys like you," he said, "but I don't know if I'm smart enough. My teachers say I'll get lost in the crowd." He shrugged. "What would you do?"

He measured me and the rim, then softly tossed the ball to a perfect height. Again, I raced to the rim to nick the ball with my middle finger. When I landed, he was waiting for me to answer his question.

I felt a tender pimple growing on my nose. "I bet Coach's tutors from the U could help. And you and I can help each other if we have classes together. So, yeah—go for it."

Coach headed our way. "Let's call it a night, kings."

Curry tossed the ball to Coach, and we gathered our gear.

"You'll only go as far as your legs will take you," Curry said as we made our way to the exit. "But they won't take you anywhere unless you work them."

"Uh-huh," I agreed, but too quickly for Curry.

"I mean every day," he said. "For the rest of your life."

LBJ and Westbrook were waiting inside the front doors, sitting on the old metal air cabinet that heated up like a burner. Once the surface became too hot, they popped off but stayed close enough to lean in and bask in the hot air that battered them. After a few moments, they sat back down again and repeated the whole process. During this on-again-off-again, they worked their phones like slot machines, trying their luck at securing a place to crash until school started the following day.

"Stay at my crib," Harden told both of them.

"We were just at your place," Westbrook said.

He snuggled headphones over his ears, pulled strings to tighten his hoodie, and snapped his windbreaker. LBJ did the same. Together, they bum-rushed outside but separated, each finding his own way to wherever home was for that night, and another three-dog night of snow and cold, gunshots and police sirens, people laughing and crying, and the mixture of all.

Harden shuffled forward in his Nike slip-on sandals, every step tentative on the icy pavement. On the court, he ran circles around Westbrook and LBJ. But here, the cold was an opponent. His stiff joints, aching from juvenile arthritis, made him wobble like a marionette with tangled strings.

Finally, he stopped and gazed at snow meandering down, floating through the soft yellow halo of the streetlight above before splintering and sprinkling like confetti in the darkness. Snow crunched beneath us as John and I circled Harden. The world stopped spinning and held its breath.

Harden shivered in his green Nike bomber jacket, which was covered in bright-white Nike checks on the front, back, and both sleeves. Dog tags dangled from the zipper, pulled high and snug.

"Empty," Harden said, "question . . . Am I too hard on you?" Before I responded, he continued. "If I am, that be sitting on my heart—on my mom. I'm trying to help you. You want to survive on the Northside? Never be fake. Be honest, even if it hurts you or a friend or family. Be quiet all you want, but when you open your piehole, say what you mean and mean what you say. That's what makes you real. I need you to be real." He bore down on me. "I can tell if you're bullshitting. Don't ever lie to me."

I placed my hand over Hawk and took an oath. "I won't."

Harden reached his hand out to John, who dapped, slapped, held on, and snapped fingertips when they pulled away.

"This brother is solid," Harden said, throwing an arm around John's shoulder. His grin was wide, but his eyes held a flicker of something deeper. Respect? Brotherhood? Or relief that he'd found someone he could rely on?

John and I stood silently, giving Harden space to gather his thoughts.

"I gotta be honest with y'all." He quickly held up his hand like he, too, was taking an oath. "Big Bad John won't repeat this. You can't either, Empty. What I'm about to say stays between us brothers."

His eyes flicked to the shadows beyond the streetlight, as if they might be ear-hustling. He dropped his hand, and his breath became visible in the frosty December-night air.

"I'm working hard, so my shadow work is in check," he said. "But bro, it ain't easy, considering I'm not who I am. I have to fight with that all the time."

Harden's words were as hollow as his bones yet heavy as iron chains. They wrapped around, pulling me deeper into a reality I wasn't ready to take on.

"My pops wants me to ghost," Harden said, shivering, his breath visible in the cold, "from Murderapolis." He paused. "And he's right. I'm sick of it—the fighting, the dying. On North, we're running out the game clock in a doom loop. When we're not boxing for real, we're swinging scared stiff at shadows—fighting ourselves, and pretending this is all there is." He looked at us. "You ever feel like it's fourth quarter all the time?"

Harden held an imaginary basketball low and away and motioned for me to reach for it. As I did, he pivoted into me until I was nearly on his back, reaching in.

"That's a game winner," he said.

He drove in for an imaginary basket and fist-bumped John on his way back to our conversation.

"Pops says it's my destiny to move on outta here and find a destination with zero drama. How about that place you're from?"

"Cottage Park," John said.

"It's truly the most boring place in the world," I said. "The big headline in the *Chronicle* last week was about someone parking their car on their front lawn."

John concurred.

"Damn," Harden said. "That's not boring. That's gangster."

"It's a ninety-year-old woman," I said, looking at John. "One of the O'Connor twins."

"Still," Harden said, imagining the scene. "How's the weather?"

"Same as here," John said.

"I'm getting out," Harden said. "Way down south. In seventh grade, Pops took Mom and me to Florida. That's where I'll live—right around Orlando, between the Gulf of Mexico and the Atlantic Ocean, surrounded by orange groves."

He inhaled deeply through his nose. John and I did the same.

"This is dead air. I can't smell nothing. In those orange groves, you're intoxicated by the fruits and flowers. I never tasted grapefruit until I picked one off a tree down there and peeled it on the spot. Damn! Sweet, tart, real. It burst in my mouth. That's where I'm supposed to be." He shook his head, almost like he could taste it again. "You dudes ever seen the ocean?"

"Lake Okoboji is the closest we've ever gotten to the ocean," I said.

"What's that?" Harden said.

"A big lake near Cottage Park," I said.

"Move to Orlando with me. Not everyone gets out of here, but we will. We're the lucky ones. We'll take Orlando in and everything else with it—Disney World, SeaWorld, Universal Studios . . ." He sighed. "But it's a long way to Orlando."

I saw that distance in miles and years as Harden looked beyond the streetlight into darkness.

"Empty, I don't care about your girl's spirits coming and going. You get one shot with your life. Don't waste it trying to be someone you're not. Stick with us. We're your family now."

I was a born-again newborn, with Pa Dao as my mother and Harden as my father. Only they didn't trust each other. They each drew strict red lines to keep me from the other, promising me the best in life and the afterlife if I didn't cross them. Yet here I was, taking my first unsteady steps, stumbling and fumbling over those lines and falling on both sides.

Coach came outside, pushing the door shut behind him until it locked. He then began making his way to their car. Harden joined him, turned back to us, and flicked his fingers in a check sign.

"I always got you, my dudes," Harden said.

His voice was confident, but his eyes looked far away. He saw something the rest of us couldn't—or took for granted. Something bigger than basketball. Bigger than all of us—a future where we weren't just surviving but thriving.

I was letting myself believe it too.

— CHAPTER TWENTY-FOUR —

Set Play

Monday, December 17, arrived with brown icicles snapping from the roof and shattering to pieces on the frozen ground below. It was also the first day of finals week—a week that could lift us up or break us down, the semester's final hurdle before our two-week holiday break. For many of us, it was the final chance to prevent an F, or Fs. As Old Parrothead's Sunday-night robocall had explained, thirty percent of our sophomore class were failing at least one class, and ten percent were failing two or more classes.

"But most of you can still pass," Old Parrothead had urged, "even at this late date, if you come to school and work hard in finals week."

For students who had no hope of passing, finals week was the last chance to settle beefs before transferring to another school. I ear-hustled plans for big fights every day.

I had a two-hour final in each class. Plus, "The Empty Set" was due on Friday, but I'd obtained permission to submit it late. I wanted to conclude it with Saturday's healing ceremony with my big family.

At the end of English class, Harden, LBJ, Pat Bev, and I bunched around Mr. Lane at his desk.

"You know," Mr. Lane said to Harden, "we teachers are intrigued about your future. Do me a favor and complete this prediction: 'Harden will be the next big . . .'"

"Lottery pick," Harden shot back.

"For what?" Mr. Lane said.

"The NBA," Harden said. "And at the rate they're going, the Timberwolves. No joke."

"Oh, brother," Mr. Lane said. "Meanwhile, you better finish your personal narrative. Are you ready to turn it in?"

"I'm so ready," Harden said. "I bet you'll sell the movie rights to my story."

"As for you, Mr. Michael," Mr. Lane said, focusing on me, not in a challenging way but more as the bearer of bad news. "You've proven to be a good student. But from day one, I told you I couldn't give you a passing grade, not with all your absences and tardies, plus those five suspension days. That's too much lost time."

Harden spoke up before I could take in what Mr. Lane was saying. "Empty *has* to pass this class. We're on a traveling AAU team together this summer."

LBJ leaned forward. "His grade shouldn't be about where he started the race but how he finished it."

"Empty's still got his personal narrative," Harden offered.

"Yeah," Pat Bev added. "This mug can tell a good story."

He and LBJ pounded the spigot of Mr. Lane's moisturizer bottle and spread generous amounts of lotion on any area of their bodies not covered by clothing, including their faces.

Mr. Lane leaned back in his chair like a crocodile submerging and narrowing his eyes before an attack.

"Writing is not storytelling," he said, his voice deliberate. "Anyone can sit on a barstool and shoot the shit to spin an engaging yarn. Writing is surgery. It hurts. It's performing an appendectomy on yourself with a butter knife. If you're lucky, what you twist and yank out is worth it. Hemingway said, 'You have to open a vein and bleed.'"

"He'll bleed all over his personal narrative," Harden said. "Trust me."

Mr. Lane slightly bowed and clasped his hands together, fingers pointing upward, thumbs close to his chest. After a moment, he thoughtfully dragged his index fingers across his lips until they opened.

"All right," he said to Harden. "I will trust you. Indeed, I'll trust you so much I'll make you a deal: If Michael's personal narrative is perfect and—I emphasize *and*, which is a coordinating conjunction connecting grammatically equal elements—*and* if you, Jerome Vaughn, edit and vouch for its perfection by literally signing off on it, I'll pass him in this class."

"What if it's not perfect?" Harden said.

"Then you'll be right there with Michael in summer school every day," Mr. Lane said matter-of-factly.

Harden's head snapped up. "Summer school? Hell no. I know for damn sure I already passed this class. I've been grinding all semester."

Mr. Lane didn't blink. "Then prove it. Make sure Michael's personal narrative is perfect, and you're free. Otherwise, consider your summer booked. To save Michael's soul, you will have to gamble losing your own." Mr. Lane sneered. "It's called a deal with the devil."

Harden's eyes awaited direction as they flitted around to each member of his set, including me. Then he settled back on Mr. Lane. "Why you gotta do me this way?"

Mr. Lane's tone and manner changed instantly. He leaned forward and reached his arms to brace Harden.

"Yes, you passed. But I'd like you to come to summer school anyway. We'll conduct an independent study to refine your personal narrative so you can utilize it for your college admission essays— same for Michael. Truth is, I was planning to talk to your dad about this anyway."

"Essays aren't due until later in our junior year," Harden protested. "I can't spend my summer in this hellhole. I need a break from school. No offense, Mr. Lane, but I need a break from you."

Mr. Lane chortled. "Let me offer a few important considerations. First, rats that are shocked frequently at uniform intervals develop fewer ulcers than rats that are shocked infrequently but at random intervals. Life is not fair in any way, shape, or form. And it never will be. Life shocks us all the time. You can count on it. Get accustomed to that reality and you'll have fewer ulcers than those who are unsuspecting. Second, ideally, you should finish your college admission essays by October of your junior year. That's coming fast. And third, there's an expression that good teachers don't smile until Christmastime, but we're close enough that I will now break that rule."

He paused to smile broadly—his first of the semester.

"From now on," he said, "you'll experience the warm, lovable side of Mr. Lane—the Mr. Lane you've only dreamt about. You'll see that I tend to grow on people. By the time summer school starts, we'll be best buds."

Harden raised a skeptical eyebrow.

"But please keep in mind," Mr. Lane said, "if—and I emphasize *if*, a subordinating conjunction indicating a conditional clause—if you help make Michael's personal narrative perfect, then we can take summer school off the table for both of you. If you hold up your end of the deal, Michael will pass the class, and you can pass on an independent study with yours truly."

Harden turned to me. "Let me see what you've got so far."

"Not much on paper," I said. "Just an outline and a lot of good ideas."

Harden glanced at Pat Bev and LBJ.

"And I've chosen a title," I said. "I call it 'The Empty Set.' My topic sentence is about letting go and holding on."

"You figure that out yet?" Harden asked.

"I'm getting close," I said.

Harden fist-bumped me, then turned back to Mr. Lane. "Aight. I'll take you up on your deal."

Mr. Lane laughed again. "Good. And no takebacks on this deal. For your information and planning purposes, summer school starts on Monday, July eighth, at seven thirty a.m. We start early in the morning here in room one thirty-nine so we can duck in and out of here before the building heats up. You two cowboys can sit on your same horses."

At lunch, Pa Dao arrived with a familiar garment bag—the kind Mom used to store her Hmong clothing. Dysfunctional Family huddled around her like a rugby scrum. Pa Dao wriggled the garment bag into my arms as if passing me a baby.

I peered inside the plastic window to view my Hmong outfit, wrapped proudly over a broad wooden hanger like a treasure to be claimed. A faint scent of incense drifted out.

"It's all there," Pa Dao said. "My sister Sheng and I checked everything: shirt, pants, coin belt, sash, hat, and silver-bar breast-plate."

I folded the bag over my left arm. The silver-bar breastplate braced against my forearm as I set the garment bag on the vacant chair beside mine.

"*Ua tsaug*," I said, the Hmong expression for "thank you."

I'm getting back what Thai bandits stole from my family—the threads of who we are. This outfit, my Hmong culture, is our real wealth. I can feel it calling me, protecting me like a suit of armor.

Dysfunctional Family took their seats at the end of the table, and Pa Dao arranged two plates with steamed cabbage rolls and sticky rice. She laid a Hmong sausage in the little uncovered space on each plate.

"Eat," she said, sliding a plate to me.

I sliced the Hmong sausage into chunks, lifted my fork, and scooped cabbage roll and rice into my mouth.

"I've spent too much time talking about how we Hmong face death," Pa Dao said. "On Friday, you'll see our joy. We'll do *pov pob*, which means 'ball toss.' Girls line up on one side, guys on the opposite side. You toss a ball back and forth with a boy you want to know better."

She bit into her cabbage roll and took her time chewing.

"You can learn all you need to know about a partner by how they toss and catch a ball," she said. "It shows how your partner handles life's ups and downs. Good couples can toss and catch the ball one-handed, which builds confidence and trust in a relationship." She added, "With your basketball hands, you should be good with a tennis ball."

I grabbed my coffee and took a big gulp, hoping it would distract from the flush in my cheeks.

Pa Dao pointed her fork at the garment bag. "By the way, try everything on as soon as you get home after school. If there's a problem, Niam can fix it, so it'll be perfect for you to wear to school on Friday."

My head popped up from my plate.

Pa Dao looked at me warily. "You *are* coming to the show Friday night, aren't you?"

"I am . . ."

"But what . . . ?" Pa Dao pressed. "Finish your sentence."

I hesitated. "It's just that I wasn't planning on wearing the outfit to school. The freshman and JV games with Central High are on Friday afternoon. But don't worry—they'll be over before the show. Puff's driving John, Harden, and me to the games at Central, then straight to the show afterward. I can get into my outfit at that point."

I wanted to see the New Year show, but I *had* to see those games. "Don't even think about missing them," Harden had said. He didn't have to twist my arm. The daily intercom announcements hyped the freshman, JV, and varsity games at Central as "the oldest and fiercest rivalry in Minnesota." I was all in.

"Michael, you're losing yourself." Pa Dao's expression darkened, and worry crept into her voice. "A stupid basketball game? That's what you're trading your heritage for? You can be . . . you *have* to be more than that."

She put her silverware on the table, closed her eyes, and massaged her temples.

"My cousins live across the street from Central," she said. "That's the most dangerous spot in Minneapolis. More shots are fired there than in any other part of the city. Those bullets don't have a name or an address on them. My cousins' house and car have been hit. It's so bad they're selling at a loss to get out of the neighborhood. Michael, you can't go. Skip the game. Stay after school and hang with us before the show."

"I don't know," I said.

"You do know," she shot back. Her eyes drilled into mine until I looked away. "You're at a crossroads. One path leads to who you are; the other to who they want you to be. You want to live your life as a mixed kid, lost between two worlds? Fine. But don't come back to me when it doesn't work out."

I shook my head. "Central's the only game I *have* to go to all year. Plus, the games are in the afternoon. And I'll be with Puff, John, and Harden."

Pa Dao took my hand. "Harden," she said, her tone softer, pleading. "Can't you see it? His spirit's slipping through his fingers, like water he can't hold on to. And if you're not careful, yours will too."

She sighed and released my hand.

"Mai told me she's almost ready to move on," Pa Dao said. "She and I made a deal. I lived up to my end by teaching you our Hmong story, and now, Mai will live up to her end by moving on. You need to come through for us."

Though Pa Dao looked at me, she gazed beyond.

"New Year is the perfect time for Mai to begin her journey."

— CHAPTER TWENTY-FIVE —

Styling, Smiling

The next night, after the rec center emptied, Coach poked his head inside the gym doorway. His voice cut through the quiet. "Office. Now." His tone was low-key, but his eyes hinted at something bigger.

"Follow me," Harden said, taking the lead.

Coach waited for us outside his locked office door.

"Fellas," he said, "I made you a promise. I said I'd give you an AAU team if you improved your grades. Your teachers and tutors say you've held up your end of the deal."

Coach unlocked the door and pushed it open.

"Have a look," he said.

The tiny office had transformed into a shrine to Nike. Boxes were stacked to the ceiling, their Swooshes gleaming under fluorescent lights and permeating rubber and fresh leather.

"This is heaven," Pat Bev said in astonishment.

Coach stepped into the cave of boxes, produced a box cutter, and sliced open a box. Inside was a bundle of jerseys.

"This is just the beginning of the well-deserved payback for all your hard work at school," Coach said. "You earned it."

He peeled off the top jersey and held it high. The front was all black with red pinstripes framing the name that Harden had chosen for our team: 4TH QUARTER, written in New York Yankees script. Below the name was a clock face numbered 1 through 4, for the four quarters. The minute and hour hands pointed at 4.

"Dope," Pat Bev said.

After savoring our oohs and aahs, Coach rotated the jersey. Across the back, in place of the player's name, were the words 4TH QUARTER.

"We're one team, with only one name: 4th Quarter," he said.

Coach flung the jersey at LBJ. "Jerome made sure you got your namesake's number, twenty-three."

LBJ gulped, brought the jersey to his chest, and hugged it. "Man, I got no words."

Coach peeled off the next jersey, number 21, and held it up for a moment, letting the fabric bask in the light. He handed it to Pat Bev with a grin. "Wear it proudly—but not so loudly that you get teched."

"I'll try," Pat Bev said.

Coach next lifted a jersey with a big 0. "Westbrook wears zero, representing a new beginning. Everything begins with zero." He flung the jersey to Westbrook.

"I won't let you down," Westbrook said.

"Jerome made an exception for this brother," Coach said, holding up a jersey for John. "Jerome says John wears his Joe Mauer jersey with the lucky number seven so much that he could be Mauer in a basketball uniform."

"But in real life, he's Capela," Harden added.

Coach grinned. "True story," he began. "Back in his senior year of '01, we beat Joe Mauer's undefeated team in the Twin Cities championship, 68 to 67." He tossed the jersey to John. "I wouldn't mind having Joe Mauer's money, though."

John caught the jersey and looked around at his teammates. "This is perfect. Thanks."

Coach eyed the next jersey in the box but waited to pull it out. "Who knows whose number Empty will wear?"

He waved his hands like a choir director, and everyone said, "Luka!"

Coach handed me the highest compliment I have ever received: a jersey with Luka's number, 77. I shook my head in disbelief, too dumbstruck to speak.

"And finally . . ." Coach's voice trailed off as he took a step toward Harden and draped a jersey over him.

Harden instantly shucked his practice jersey and wriggled into his new one. He was the last to receive but the first to shimmy into and preen in the jersey.

"I tried my best to persuade him not to take unlucky thirteen," Coach said. "But I suppose James Harden has always had good luck."

Harden wasn't listening. His fingers caressed the fabric until the jersey opened and came to life.

"Tight enough to show my muscles," he boasted. "Y'all see if yours fit too. Everybody got XLs except for Capela, who got a triple-XL."

Coach sliced into another box, revealing our warmup pants. Harden checked the waistbands before tossing each pair to the appropriate player.

"Old-school tearaways," he said. "Try them on too."

Matching black pinstriped warmup jackets with hoodies followed. As boxes piled up, Coach asked me to set the empties at the door to recycle. Once we were dressed, Coach lined us up to admire us and take our picture on his phone.

"You'll be the best-looking team at every tournament—stylin' and smilin'," he said. "Now if we can only play half as good as we look."

"Say it!" Harden said.

"But seriously . . ." Coach stopped to clear his throat. Words rumbled deep in his chest before coming out heavy and hard in a gravelly mix. "I want you all to be happy and healthy. Right now, everyone is all that. But all good things must pass. It's time for you all to go home and get your beauty sleep. See you tomorrow."

"He's teasing," Harden said, stepping behind Coach and arming himself with boxes containing Nike Precision 3 men's basketball shoes.

"Size fourteens for you two." He handed John and me each a box. Coach helped him pass out the other boxes.

I peeled back the onionskin tissue paper to discover Nike-red Swooshes, shoelaces, and soles lighting up black shoes as light as a feather. I slipped the shoes from the box, mittened them over my hands, smooched them to my cheeks, and massaged the cool circular grooves against my skin.

My first Nikes. John's too. I was stepping into a new version of myself as well as stepping into a team with long-held values I now shared.

We put on our new shoes and jumped as high as we could—instantly better players.

Once the excitement of the shoes and uniforms had settled into quiet gratitude, Coach gathered us into a tight circle. His voice, usually booming, softened as he leaned in.

"Listen up, fellas." He pondered his workman's steel-toed boots, pressed his right toe against the floor, and looked us each in the eye. "Your education should mean money to you. You earn what you learn. And you earned this!"

We hollered in agreement.

He patted his belly, Santa-style. "Merry Christmas, young kings."

"Man," Harden said, running his hands along every seam, "we gotta show these uniforms off at the Central game tomorrow." Then Harden winked at Coach.

"About the game," Coach said. "We'll meet here after school. I'll drive the van. Mr. Moriarity will take the overflow. We leave no later than three thirty."

John and I changed back into our old shoes. We wouldn't think of wearing our new Nikes out into the snow. We then loaded ourselves with empty boxes, stomped them down, and slid them into the recycling bin.

We started toward home but took only a few steps before Harden appeared beside us. He threw a glance over his shoulder and opened a pocket on his bomber's left sleeve. He hesitated, his usual swag replaced by something more solemn. From his pocket he pulled a Ziploc baggie that held a blunt and a BIC pocket lighter. He pressed it into John's hand.

"Empty told me you start your chemo pills tonight," he said. "This should help. Just take care of yourself, aight?"

"I don't know if Puff will go for this," I said, eyeing the bag.

John smiled. "He asked the doctor to prescribe me medical marijuana."

"Yeah," I said, "but I don't know how serious he was about it. Plus, that's not 'medical marijuana.'"

"Your pops needs more than you, Capela," Harden said. "It's good for all of you." He clapped John's shoulder. "I got you when you tap out."

At home, Puff was glued to the 10 p.m. sports on TV. Governor Mark Dayton had declared today, December 18, as "Joe Mauer Day" in Minnesota. The Twins also announced their plans to retire Joe Mauer's number in the summer.

John and I waited in the doorway and in our new gear until the segment ended. When Puff finally noticed us, he popped up off the couch.

"Your uniforms are here already?" he asked. He spoke slowly, like he couldn't believe it. "Finally, you two will play on the same team."

I opened my shoebox and pulled my Nikes from the crinkled tissue paper. "We got shoes too. You want us to put them on?"

Puff smiled, then shook his head. "Shoes later." He muted the TV volume and handed John a padded envelope. "This arrived in today's mail."

John noticed the medical supply company's name and return address, then dropped the envelope on my lap. I grabbed scissors, slit the envelope, and sat beside Puff.

"You're responsible for making Big Bad John take what's in there," Puff said to me. "I've got too many bad chemo memories with your grandmother."

I pulled out two tiny pill bottles. I rattled the first bottle, twisted off the cap, and sniffed. "That smell? *Vomitrocious.*" I quickly replaced the cap.

"Antinausea," I read aloud, with irony. "Take thirty minutes before bedtime."

I gave that bottle to John, then picked up and rattled the other bottle.

"And this is the chemo," I said. "You take one pill right before bed." I locked eyes with John. "I know it sucks, but taking these pills seems simple enough. One pill at a time."

"Nothing in this world is simple," Puff said. "Not one single speck."

I reopened the antinausea pills, shimmied one out, handed it to John, and read the instructions aloud: "Place pill under tongue until it dissolves."

John set the pill under his tongue.

"I remember talking to a guy at the cancer center once," Puff said. "A Gulf War vet. He said he sings a song while his chemo pill dissolves—'Lucy in the Sky with Diamonds.'"

"By who?" I said. John didn't know either.

"I've failed you two as a parent," Puff said sadly. "Ever heard of The Beatles?"

I found the remote, exited ESPN to YouTube, and typed the words LUCY IN. The full title popped up with a link. I clicked the remote, and the song played.

"Ugh," John said. He put his hand to his stomach. "I'm already queasy from that antinausea pill." He made a pukey face.

His dramatics were funny. To keep myself from cracking up, I bit my lip and pretended that a stain on the couch was the most fascinating thing in the world. I was still looking away when John produced the baggie.

"But this will make me feel better," he said.

"Give me that," Puff said, instantly yanking the baggie away. His face lit up in anger as he examined the lighter and blunt.

"You wanted Dr. Schneidermann to prescribe medical marijuana," I quickly said.

As the final notes of "Lucy in the Sky with Diamonds" faded, YouTube's algorithm took over, filling the silence with a cover version. The new voice was unfamiliar, but the melody was the same—a thread connecting us across generations and the world.

Puff stretched back in his chair, his anger already melting. "Yeah. I know. But I meant the legal stuff." He thought for a moment, sighed, then waved his hand. "Go ahead. Light up. But if Mrs. Flowers finds out, I know nothing. The last thing I need is her teasing me about breaking the law."

Puff handed me the baggie, just as he'd handed me the padded envelope. Helping John with this would be my responsibility too. Only this came with no label and no instructions. I'd never even lit a cigarette before.

I flicked the lighter until a flame emerged, then I held the blunt to the flame. "Is this right? I don't know what I'm doing."

"Give me that," Puff said.

I gladly handed it over.

Puff produced a flame and rolled the blunt tip over it until it was evenly charred.

"I've seen others do it this way," he explained. "Back in the minor leagues, before I met Mom."

He brought the blunt to his mouth, lit the end again, and inhaled. Once the tip fired up, he passed the blunt to John, who smoked it like he had been doing so all his life.

When the blunt made its way to me, I sucked in the dry, rotting smoke that reeked of grass that had been cut with an overheated mower.

When the song ended, YouTube continued on autoplay with yet another cover version.

"Elton John," Puff announced without looking at the screen.

More covers were played as we passed the blunt around. By the fourth cover, we were singing along with a group none of us knew. As the music swelled and the smoke descended around us, John's eyes closed, and a smile played on his lips.

In that moment, the weight of the world—the chemo, the team, the future—blissfully floated by and dissolved in the haze. I didn't know or care what "next" would bring. Tonight, we were just three amigos in a boat on a river, chasing tangerine dreams and following a girl I was beginning to know and possibly love.

A girl with kaleidoscope eyes.

— CHAPTER TWENTY-SIX —

Countdown

On Friday, soft cotton caressed my skin with every step as I walked into school. After a week of Pa Dao's relentless urgings, I'd finally decided to wear my Hmong outfit to school. "Wearing your Hmong outfit promotes the show and shows Hmong pride," she'd told me. And she was right. As I moved through the halls, I wasn't afraid of standing out. I stood taller. Hmong pride, long buried, sprouted from deeply buried seeds within me.

My outfit fit better than anything I'd ever worn. It was light and airy, more like pajamas. The hat fit so snugly that I forgot it was there. With every step to first-hour English, the silver coins hanging from my belt jangled like a tambourine. The outfit, the sounds it made, and my swag all boasted, *I am Hmong*.

My fellow Hmong also dressed up in their most colorful Hmong outfits. We were brightly decorated Christmas cookies. Everyone else at Thomas Jefferson wore Christmas clothing or red and green—except the Somali kids and Jehovah's Witnesses.

The school's mood was one of peace and joy, a temporary truce. Anyone who'd been itching to fight before the end of the semester had already done so or was now skipping school.

My finals all went well. I aced the English exam, especially the concluding essay question:

F. Scott Fitzgerald wrote that "The test of a first-rate intelligence is the ability to hold two opposing ideas in mind at the same time, and still retain the ability to function. One should, for example, be able to see that things are hopeless and yet be determined to make them otherwise. This philosophy fitted on to my early adult life, when I saw the improbable, the implausible, often the 'impossible' come true." List the opposing themes in your personal narrative.

I outlined how my personal narrative is about holding on and letting go. As evidence, I described how the personal narrative begins with Cottage Park and its unchanging routine. But then I described the constant change my little family faced after the tornado, where every new beginning betrayed our past.

Next, I detailed our move to the Northside, where I discovered the fragility of life, after cancer split John's head open. I also explained how my personal narrative explores how violence sucks the futures and life from children who should be dancing in the light on North instead of lying in the darkness beneath.

By the time Mr. Lane told us to put our pencils down and hand in our essays, I had captured how "The Empty Set" concludes with my dreamy childhood transitioning into the dreadful reality of adulthood and how I looked to my beacon of light in the storm: Joe Mauer.

I walked out of first hour with a confident smile that stayed with me all morning.

At lunch, Dysfunctional Family wore traditional ceremonial headdresses covered with eye-busting colors and beadwork that dangled in intricate spider webs and icicles around their heads.

Brother called me out as I walked over. "You're coming tonight," she said, her tone leaving no room for argument.

Father, Mother, and Sister awaited my answer, preparing to pounce.

"Seven o'clock," Brother continued. "And that's seven o'clock sharp. Definitely no 'Hmong time' tonight. Your special someone wants to show you off tonight. She says you're becoming a man of our people."

I gave a thumbs-up, though my stomach tightened. Tonight wasn't just a show. It was a test I hadn't prepared for.

The cafeteria fell silent as Pa Dao glided in, commanding the room. Dysfunctional Family erupted in applause. Pa Dao burst brightly in glittering fabric, and coin chains made music when her pleated white skirt swayed. A soft black turban wrapped her hair up to frame her face. Round-toed pumps added an inch to her height, making her towering and regal.

"You look nice," Pa Dao said as she made her way to our table. She spun her finger for me to turn, so I did. "It fits perfectly."

She stood close enough to me that I caught her scent—spring's first baby dandelions. "You look nice too," was all I could say.

"You have such a way with words," she said, rolling her eyes. "Try again."

I swallowed hard. "You look stunning. Unforgettable." Before I could corral safer words, the truest one dashed out: "Electrifying."

"Much better," she said.

Pa Dao pulled an assortment of Tupperware from her grocery sack—round, square, and rectangular, each a different arc of the rainbow. The smells of Asian cuisine sought me out. My stomach growled. As I positioned the place settings, she ladled head-on shrimp in coconut-cream broth alongside purple rice and stir-fried beef with bitter melon, its sharp zest complementing the richness.

"I made these myself." Pa Dao waved over my plate. "Eat."

I began eating, but Pa Dao didn't. Instead, she swirled patterns in her food with her fork. I put my silverware down.

"You're sad," I said. "What's wrong?"

"This morning . . ." Pa Dao said. She shook her head. "Mai ordered me around like Niam, insisting that I work for her. But today, she also thanked me."

"*Ua tsaug?*" I said.

"Yes. Then she added three words: 'Emptiness is everything.'"

Pa Dao inhaled deeply. After a long pause, she pointed her fork at me.

"I'm the shaman. I'm supposed to understand these things. But this one, I don't. 'Emptiness is everything.'" Her eyes searched mine for an answer. "What do *you* think her talk of emptiness means? Right now, it feels like a riddle I'm too tired to solve."

I, too, now curled a design in my food, a slowly turning yin-yang wheel dividing purple rice from white coconut cream.

Dysfunctional Family hushed, drowned out by sudden laughter from a growing crowd behind me. I turned to find LBJ, Westbrook, Curry, Pat Bev, and Harden dressed in their namesakes' NBA jerseys.

Harden carried three presents wrapped in Christmas paper. He presented me with the top two boxes, both wrapped in glossy emerald green.

"Merry Christmas," he said. "Open the top one."

I set the bottom package on my lap. It was addressed to John with a sticker featuring Santa holding a large, red bag of presents. I already knew the contents of the package: a Houston Rockets jersey, like Harden's, except this one bore number 15 and the name Capela.

The sticker on the top box featured an angel hovering in flight and holding an open scroll bearing my name, Empty. I slipped the broad red bow from the box, then tore into the wrapping paper. I crumpled it—and the angel—into a compact ball that I alley-ooped to Harden. He caught and dunked it into a nearby garbage barrel on wheels.

I also knew the present awaiting me: a Luka Dončić Dallas Mavericks jersey, no doubt in white. But as I peeled back the tissue paper, my breath caught. A different Luka beamed back—not Mavericks Luka but throwback Luka. The navy-blue jersey boasted SLOVENIJA in light-green lettering and the number 77. How had Harden found it? I breathed again as I raised the jersey from the box.

A chant arose: "Put it on!"

I removed my Hmong hat, pulled the jersey over my face, and unfurled it down my chest and back, muffling the coins hanging from my outfit. The jersey was heavier than I expected. Slipping into something new meant shedding something old.

People clapped and cheered.

"Wear it tonight," Harden ordered, "with your uniform pants."

Harden stepped around me to Pa Dao. He placed the remaining present on the table before her.

"I apologize for everything that went down in the brawl," he said. "I came over here to make peace. I hope we can kick off the New Year as friends."

Pa Dao studied the gift, Harden, then the gift again.

He smiled. "We cool?"

Pa Dao spoke deliberately. "You know, I'm not perfect either."

"Go ahead and open it," he prodded.

Pa Dao slid the red ribbon from the flat package, peeled the wrapping paper, and peered at the contents: chocolate-covered cherries.

"I love these," she said. She dug into the box, popped one into her mouth, closed her eyes, chewed, and smiled. She passed the box back to Harden.

"Take one and pass it around," she said.

The box and its chocolates quickly disappeared.

After school that day, Puff and John finished Pa Dao's leftovers while I changed from my Hmong outfit into my throwback Luka jersey and my 4th Quarter warmup jacket and pants. Once John finished eating, he also changed into his 4th Quarter jacket and pants, along with his new Capela jersey.

Puff, John, and I then crammed into Vicky. Her dashboard lit up like a Christmas tree with brightly colored warnings and maintenance reminders. As usual, Puff ignored them. But he did study Vicky's odometer, which read 339,996 miles. Our three-mile round trip to Central High School would fall short of the endurance milestone.

We drove to the rec center and pulled up alongside their van, which held Coach and the rest of our 4th Quarter teammates. Harden popped out of the van and headed toward Vicky's rear door.

I waved him to the other side. He sprinted around, opened the door, and folded himself into the back seat with me. Vicky's low ride—the result of rotten or broken tires, struts, and suspension shocks—made it a deep drop.

"That door's been frozen stuck shut since we got Vicky back from the impound lot after the snow emergency," I said.

"I feel you," Harden said. "Minneapolis will tow like a mofo. They messed up our transmission."

Harden leaned forward, elbows on knees. "Sup?" he said to Puff. "Appreciate you helping tonight."

Coach pulled onto Dowling, and we followed. Puff had set the radio to a golden oldies station. As we drove away, Puff's favorite came on: "American Pie," the song about Buddy Holly's death, outside Mason City, Iowa, not far from Cottage Park.

We idled a full minute at the Penn stoplight. When the light finally changed, Coach nearly got broadsided by a car running the red. Thankfully, Vicky doesn't have much get-up-and-go; otherwise, we would have rear-ended the van when Coach had to slam on his brakes.

"Traffic on Penn is cray," Harden said as we caught our breath and rolled forward. "People don't know where they're going, but they're in a hurry to get there."

"Maybe people are making up for lost time, lost daylight," Puff said. "Today is the shortest day of the year. Winter solstice. I checked, and the sun sets at four thirty-three."

We drove along blocks of pristine homes mixed with homes littered with yellowing, mushy community newspapers in orange plastic wrap. Satellite dishes mushroomed from many homes. Other homes wore one or two skimpy strands of Christmas lights. We passed frequent signs: BEWARE OF DOG. NOW HIRING. WE BUY HOUSES.

Coach went through a yellow light at the intersection of Penn and Broadway, but Puff couldn't cross fast enough. We stopped.

Puff looked over his shoulder at Harden. "Those big flowers over there." He pointed at the intersection's southeast corner, where five massive, radiant aluminum flowers sprouted from a bus stop fashioned into a vase. The flowers stood twenty feet high. "Do they mean anything?"

"They're the *Blossoms of Hope*," Harden said. "A big tornado came through here in 2011, when I was little. People died, houses were leveled, and trees covered the streets. No electricity. But those flowers kept standing." Harden pointed beyond the flowers to a burnt-reddish brick building. "Guess what's in that building?"

"We don't come down here much," I said.

"That's the people's station," Harden said. "The heart and soul of the Twin Cities. K . . . M . . . O . . . J. Eighty-nine point nine FM," he spit out like a disc jockey. "Pull it up so we can listen."

Puff winced as John snuffed "American Pie" before it ended and spun the tuner knob until KMOJ music pulsated through Vicky's speakers. Someone was singing about an elevator: "Are we gonna let de elevator bring us down? Oh, no, let's go!"

"His mom was a social worker at Pop's junior high school," Harden said. "My middle school too. Franklin." He paused to gauge my blank face. "Prince. The guy who's singing right now. You *do* know Prince, don't you?"

"Yeah, I know him," I said. "But I don't know all his music."

"Oh man," Harden said, shaking his head in disbelief. "Turn it up, Big Bad John."

"Let's Go Crazy" jumped from Vicky's speakers.

"Prince couch-surfed on the Northside," Harden said. He sat back in his seat like he had devoured a big meal. "Fam, when you come to my place, we bump KMOJ all day."

The light changed to green, and Vicky sputtered away, leaving a white plume of exhaust that landed upon a Nation of Islam man distributing their newspaper as he darted back and forth from the sidewalk to cars on the street.

We turned left off Penn and onto Golden Valley Road, where faint moonlight shone in the eastern sky. Then we turned again onto Morgan Avenue under an umbrella of skeletal branches. Downtown Minneapolis sparkled farther away, glowing in greens and blues like the Emerald City.

A few blocks later, we parked behind Coach's van. We got out and clustered on the sidewalk.

"Let's go," Coach said.

He and Puff led us toward the Central gym. We gathered around Harden as we walked, blowing into our cupped hands and rubbing them together like quarterbacks preparing shivery fingers to launch game-ending Hail Marys. We ignored the cars that crept by us as they searched for parking spots. We got friendly beeping hellos from other guys and long, bawdy honks from flirty girls.

"Tonight, we show folks the future," Harden said. He unzipped his coat, flashing his James Harden jersey, then he focused on me. "Tonight you make a name for yourself, Empty. Don't let anyone tell you who you are or what you should be. You're bigger than what they see."

The Central school building and freestanding gym were square brick boxes without windows. They were above-ground fallout shelters jutting from a simple locked-in neighborhood. The fortresses screamed security. But the two mounted policemen on the grassy lot outside the gym—their horses skittish, snorting, and trying to prance away—told a different story. Trouble was brewing, and the gym was anything but safe. The police patted their anxious horses to assure them, and themselves, that all would be fine.

We all got into the security line. Groups of guys and girls kept budging until Coach called them out, his eyetooth scraping against his bottom lip.

I'd never walked through a security line before. Once we made it inside the lobby, I had to be told what clothing to remove and what metal objects to place on a lunchroom tray for security staff to examine at a metal detector. Police and security staff used wands and frisked us before we could retrieve our stuff.

Coach and Puff passed first, with John and I following. Once we four made it through, we turned and waited as the police questioned Harden and the rest of the Harden Set.

"You boys smoking weed?" a policeman said.

"Nope," Harden said.

"They reek of weed," the policeman said with exasperation to anyone who would listen.

"Everybody standing in the line outside smells like weed," Coach said. "But these boys weren't the ones smoking."

The policeman rolled his eyes and waved them on.

A policeman with a German shepherd instructed me to proceed to the Thomas Jefferson side. "Don't look at the dog," the policeman said. "Act normal."

The dog followed me for a few steps, sniffed, then lost interest. The policeman and dog repeated this same perp walk with my teammates.

Finally, we were free to gather around Coach, who led us inside to the bleachers. Stepping around long legs stretched across aisle steps, we made our way to the top row, the only open spot where we could sit together. We wriggled behind families and students—all Black. Also in the top rows were a handful of stiff, balding, pencil-armed white guys holding clipboards and peering over shaded eye-glasses at the notes they'd made on the game's xeroxed program.

We removed our winter coats and set them on our laps or cushioned them against the wall behind us, then followed Harden's lead as he unzipped his 4th Quarter warmup jacket far enough to show off his NBA jersey.

"Basketball scholars take in a game from the top row," Coach said once we were settled. "It's the best place to watch plays develop."

But even from our eagle-eyed vantage point, we strained to find examples of playmaking in the ninth-grade game.

Thomas Jefferson had no inbound play—not even a pick to get a man open. Since it took over five seconds to inbound the ball, the referee took the ball from Thomas Jefferson and awarded it to Central.

On the next inbound play, Central backed off to allow the ball in, only to instantly clamp down on that Thomas Jefferson player, forcing him to fling the ball like a hot potato to an equally pitiful teammate who was surrounded. With each inbound play, panicked passes burst through greased fingers until Thomas Jefferson failed to cross half-court in ten seconds. Turnover.

Other times, Central forced a turnover by dropping their press back to half-court to trap the Thomas Jefferson point guard into holding the ball for more than five seconds. At other times, Central's defense did nothing, and Thomas Jefferson's players forfeited the ball by loitering in the lane for more than three seconds.

After Thomas Jefferson mindlessly dribbled out the first quarter—oblivious to the scoreboard, oblivious to the fans ticking off the remaining seconds, and even oblivious to the blaring horn—Harden had suffered enough.

"Oh my God," he said. "What a bunch of little clowns."

Our set agreed.

Coach leaned forward, talking around Puff to Harden. "But they're on the court and in the game. Trip on this: Ninety-nine percent of any success is showing up. The best way to show up is to steer clear of getting into trouble. No matter what, avoid getting yourself suspended and barred from school sports."

Talk of the suspension buzzkilled our vibe. Coach noticed the drooping shoulders and adjusted his message.

"Your schoolmates are just confused," Coach said, pointing to the court. "Central runs a simple little press, but your boys panic. They need a leader. How would you break this press?"

"Take a deep breath," Harden said. "Then chill and pass the ball up the middle."

"See?" Coach said. "Easy. And how would you finish the press once and for all?"

"By scoring," Harden said. "Don't wait for the defense to catch back up. Go for the jugular. Shoot the ball and score."

"And swag-walk afterward," Pat Bev said. "Show them who's boss until you *are* the boss."

"That same strategy works for life too," Coach said. He surveyed Puff. "Am I right, Mr. Moriarty?"

"Dr. Tom Davis was the winningest coach at Iowa before you boys were born," Puff said. "All he did was press. He only took it off after the other team started scoring—just like you said," he added, tilting toward Harden.

Thomas Jefferson did score in the second half. Our team's parents led us in shouting encouragement: "This isn't a library—make some noise!" "Box out your man!" "Stick your man!" "Who got shooter?"

In the final two minutes, the teams traded fast baskets back and forth like heavyweights throwing haymakers in the terminating round of a fight. Thomas Jefferson's final shot, a Hail Mary from half-court, bricked off the backboard. The ball collapsed to the floor, where it joined Thomas Jefferson's players, laid out, done in—not so much defeated as time-depleted. Central had taken the first game 60 to 54.

The Thomas Jefferson players came to their feet slowly, but only after the junior varsity teams took the floor, and only with help from the Central ninth-grade players. Those players were former class-mates and teammates from middle and grade school, and others were current Northside neighbors and lifelong friends.

As the JV teams lined up to shoot layups, the announcer said, "Thank you for joining us tonight. In accordance with fire regulations, our gym has reached maximum capacity. No one else will be allowed entry from this point." As both sides cheered, the announcer added, "Now give it up for our drumline battle between Thomas Jefferson and Central! We'll kick off with our guests from Thomas Jefferson."

Thomas Jefferson's drumline—six guys and one girl, seated five rows beneath us—banged away with a hip-hop beat on different-sized drums. On the other side of the gym, Central countered. Back and forth, they taunted and teased each other, playing to cheers from both sides.

The crowd swayed with them, occasionally spitting out dancers who jumped from the bleachers to the gym floor. All the while, the JV players attempted and occasionally dunked in their own layup-line battle.

"Last minute," the announcer said.

The announcer then walked over to the Thomas Jefferson side of the gym, stretched one hand toward our drumline, and cupped his other hand to his ear, waiting for our cheers. He repeated the same ritual on the Central side.

"What can I say?" the announcer said. "We have ourselves a tie."

The crowd playfully booed but were quickly drowned out by deafening rap blasted from the loudspeakers.

"Old-school Brother Ali," Harden yelled into my ear. "'Uncle Sam Goddamn.'" Midway through the song, he recited the verses with the crowd:

Imported and tortured a work force
And never healed the wounds or shook the curse off
Now the grown up Goliath nation
Holding open auditions for the part of David, can you feel it?
Nothing can save you, you question the reign
You get rushed in and chained up
Fist raised but I must be insane
'Cause I can't figure a single goddamn way to change it
Welcome to the United Snakes
Land of the thief, home of the slave
The grand imperial guard where the dollar is sacred, and power is God

Everyone recognized the song. Most, like Harden, recited it from heart. Only my little family and the referees were listening to it for the first time.

The music quieted as the closing seconds ticked off the scoreboard before the start of the game. Both teams huddled with their coaches before running onto the floor for the opening tip-off.

Then the fight flared up.

Both coaches quickly called their players back to the bench.

Harden elbowed me and pointed to the other side of the gym. On the top row of the Central bleachers, two high school girls were screaming and gesturing frantically at each other. The surrounding students laughed—first at the girls, then at Old Parrothead and the Central principal and assistant principals, who speedwalked to break up the fight.

Before the principals got there, both girls bowed and swung windmill punches, a couple of which landed on nearby people. The crowd pushed them from all directions until the girls grappled and clung to each other, clumsily crowd-surfing down the bleacher rows.

LBJ and Westbrook stood and flexed.

"Sit down, you two," Coach barked. "This is not your fight."

LBJ and Westbrook sat back down but stayed on alert.

Whenever other students in our section stood and edged toward the brawl, Coach shouted again, "Everyone, sit tight!" They also sat.

But farther down our side, under the scoreboard, a few students left their seats and bolted for the other side. They threw punches wildly at anyone they met.

"Please take your seats!" the announcer implored. "Anyone involved in fighting will be removed from the gym and arrested."

"Sit your asses down!" Harden yelled across the gym at the fighters. He turned to us, his eyes blazing. "Shit is about to get real."

I couldn't watch or avoid the fights. Bodies dropped and were slugged and kicked until lifeless. The gym spun around me. I reached out for Harden to keep from falling down the bleachers. I swallowed hard to keep from throwing up.

A rowdy football player from the Thomas Jefferson side opened an unguarded exit door to the parking lot, and forty people rushed in. They scattered throughout the gym, traipsing over the gym floor, dragging snow wherever they went, showing off for friends, dancing, and throwing shadow punches. Others headed directly to a fight to join in, or swung their fists to start new fights.

"They've lost control," Coach said. "We have to go." He stood and ordered, "Grab your coats."

"But Pops," Harden pleaded, "it's the Central game. We been waiting for this game all year."

"There'll be other Central games," Coach said. "Ones you'll play in. Now follow me."

"We always miss out on the good stuff," Harden muttered as we stood and gathered our things. "Tough titties—the good always suffer for the bad."

Like a squadron leader, Coach held up his fist, a signal for us to hold tight. He plotted whether to take the aisle steps or climb down the bleacher benches. Both ways were clogged. Students and now adults were on their feet, soaking up the fight, calling out names, and providing play-by-play for the delivered and absorbed assaults.

Coach scanned us. "Watch your backs, stay together, and stick close to Mr. Moriarity and me." He shimmied us down the aisle steps, politely asking people to make room and clear our way.

As we squeezed down the steps, Officer Friendly and four other cops rushed onto the floor, shouting for the fighting to stop. They poked their batons at the fighters. Meanwhile, more students poured onto the floor to join the brawl, ignoring the police and their batons.

I couldn't hold back any longer. I fell to my knees, and hot puke poured from me, cascading through the bleacher floorboards to the gym floor.

Westbrook snickered. "Damn, you didn't even chew those chocolate-covered cherries at lunch! Nobody's gonna want to fight you now."

Puff crouched behind me and steadied my forehead. "You're going to be all right," he said. "But now, we have to get out of here."

I coughed the last few strands of warm spit and slime onto the floor below. After I heaved in a breath, Puff helped me to my feet.

"Can you make it now?" Puff said. As he steadied me, the Harden Set took another few steps down the bleachers.

Officer Friendly ran across the court to the scorer's table and gripped the microphone. "The games tonight are canceled! Everyone exit the gym immediately."

Most people—nearly all the high school kids—chose to do the opposite. The fight swelled as more bodies joined in.

"Idiots!" Coach's voice cut through the chaos.

Police cars wailed as they arrived outside the gym's four exits, which were now all open. Red and blue lights washed across the gym floor. Fifteen minutes earlier, the floor had been a playground of dreams and glory. Now it was a battlefield.

Harden covered his ears to block out the sirens. The shrieks of the fighters grew to howls as police entered, sprayed Mace, leaped onto fighters, and tasered them. A few fighters scrambled out the doors with police chasing them.

Down on the floor, Old Parrothead and her assistant principals tried their best to direct Thomas Jefferson students and families around the fights and out to the lobby doors. She waved her arms like a traffic cop and ignored the students challenging her for ticket refunds.

"Keep going!" she said. "Everybody out. Go right home. Let's go! Let's go! Let's go!"

A bottleneck formed as we jammed together to maneuver through Central's narrow lobby.

As we neared the doors, two gunshots fired outside, followed by another shot from a different direction. Instantly, the crowd behind us stopped pushing. Instead, the crowd ahead of us turned around and pushed us back into the gym.

"No!" a policeman shouted right behind our group. He pointed to the exit. "Do not come back into my gym! Go that way! Move!"

"They're shooting out there!" people called back.

"We're not going out into that mess!" a woman with two little kids yelled.

"I said *move!*" the policeman shouted, this time directly at our group. He set his hands, bound in tight black leather gloves, against Pat Bev's shoulders and shoved him into Harden.

"Man," Pat Bev said, leaning in to mean-mug the officer, "you better check yourself and your perverted little fingers. Somebody 'bout to be knocked out fast."

"It takes a strong hater," Harden added.

Coach spun around until he faced Pat Bev, Harden, and the officer. "It's not that we won't move," Coach said as calmly as possible. "We *can't* move, even if we wanted to." He pointed at Harden. "And you—keep your mouth shut."

Coach wrapped an arm around Pat Bev and brought him into a bear hug. Though Pat Bev struggled against Coach, he couldn't break away.

The policeman locked eyes with Pat Bev, then with Coach. "For his sake," the policeman said gruffly, "you better not let go."

"I'm filming this joint," Harden said. He reached inside his bomber jacket for his phone.

"Stop!" the policeman said. He jerked his pistol from his holster and fumbled it in Harden's direction.

The gun fired once.

It sounded more like a screen door clapping shut than an explosive. A metal casing ejected from the gun, spun, flipped over the policeman's wrist, and clunked on the floor.

Harden torqued and lunged into me, knocking me over. I caught him, and we stumbled and sank together to the gym floor.

I rolled out from under Harden, my hands jiggling as I cradled his head and back. He lay light and limp in my arms. I lurched him up and over, pulling his face inches from mine. My right hand found the back of his head, and my middle finger pressed into a dime-sized hole of sticky, warm gel. The heat and energy that always flowed from Harden withered through my fingers as the gel liquefied.

The tornado that had haunted me since August had returned, and with a vengeance.

The bullet had punctured Harden's right eye. His other eye drifted sideways, nothing but white, like a cue ball.

Harden unwound and deflated. He heaved, took a giant deep breath, spasmed huffs, gasped, and gulped for air. Then silence, everywhere. Harden went limp, life drained from him as quickly as his warm blood and urine pooled onto me and beneath us.

Everything around us froze—for one second, until the policeman spoke.

"It went off," he whimpered. He stared at his gun as if it had betrayed him. "I didn't mean to . . . It went off . . ."

Then bedlam with ear-splitting screams.

The policeman holstered his gun and bum-rushed Harden, frantically patting him down and pulling out his pockets. Harden's money clip clattered to the floor. The policeman popped up and backed away, his eyes fixed on the gaping hole in Harden's right eye.

Coach released Pat Bev to Westbrook, who wrapped him in yet another bear hug. Pat Bev tried to kick his way free, but LBJ held his legs as Westbrook constricted his chest.

"Let me go!" Pat Bev cried out.

LBJ let go as he followed Coach to Harden. Pat Bev quieted and allowed Westbrook to clutch him.

"Help!" Curry screamed. "We need a doctor!"

Coach fell to his knees. He moaned, lifted Harden's upper body from me, and cradled him. "No! Help my boy!"

Blood seeped from Harden's eyes, ears, nose, and mouth. Coach bunched his leather jacket sleeve and pressed each leak, but the blood dripped onto his hands and the gym floor. A sharp metallic smell fused with sweat and fear.

I staggered up, but my heart flopped like a carp working its way back to the water. Everything around me tilt-a-whirled until I lost my balance and careened into John. I grabbed him to keep from hurling to the ground.

When I took hold of my vision and balance, I focused on Coach, who was sopping up Harden's blood. I stripped off my coat and my more absorbent 4th Quarter warmup jacket and pushed them into Coach's hands. He pressed the jacket wherever blood dripped.

LBJ pocketed Harden's money clip from the gym floor.

Curry pulled out his phone and jabbed 911. "I'm at Central High School's gym," he said. "The police shot my friend in the head." He listened to the operator and answered her questions patiently. "Yes, the police are here. Yes, it's secure. No, we don't need anything else— only an ambulance."

"I'll be back!" Curry said, running from us.

The crowd that had been pushing us back into the gym now surrounded us. Policemen shoved through the crowd until they circled the officer who had shot Harden.

"He reached inside his pocket," the policeman said, his voice quivering. "I asked him to stop. I thought he had a gun. My gun went off by itself."

"Don't say anything," another policeman said. He quickly escorted the officer away from us. The pair was replaced by other policemen, who crowded into us.

"We've called for medical assistance," one of them said. "Everyone needs to leave the area."

Westbrook eased his grip on Pat Bev. "Careful," he warned.

Pat Bev beheld Coach and Harden, then clenched his fists and glared at the group escorting the policeman who had shot Harden.

"Fucking cowards!" Pat Bev screamed, pointing a shaking finger at the retreating officers. "You'd better run! You can't outrun truth. Never!"

His words, both challenge and curse, hung in the air as the crowd fell silent. He whirled the other way to face the swelling crowd.

"You'll never outrun the memory," he said to them. And to the police who had stayed, he pleaded, "What if this were your son?"

Pat Bev's mouth formed to speak again, but no words came out. Instead, he hunched over, wrapped his arms around his stomach, and staggered forward. Westbrook caught and held him before he fell. Pat Bev tried to push him away, but Westbrook would not let him fall.

Puff reached around and steadied John and me. Coach continued to fail to stop the bleeding from Harden's mouth and eyes.

A policeman scrambled by Pat Bev to Harden. "Do we have any pulse?" he said to Coach. He put his fingers to Harden's throat and held them. "No pulse." He added, "Do we have an open airway? Is he breathing?"

Coach wailed. "No breath. Only bleeding everywhere." He once again pressed my warmup jacket around Harden's eyes, ears, and mouth. "And he's cold." Coach ripped his jacket off and wrapped it around Harden, whose skin color had changed from cinnamon brown to ashen gray.

Curry squeezed through the crowd, returning with a plastic case containing a defibrillator. "Can I try this, Coach?" Curry said. "Please."

Coach and the policeman eased Harden onto the gym floor, opened the defibrillator's plastic casing, and pushed a button on its panel. A robotic voice provided instructions. The policeman pulled off Harden's bomber jacket, then used sharp scissors from a pouch in the defibrillator's casing to cut down the middle of Harden's jersey until it slipped off to his sides, revealing once-bursting abs and pecs that now wilted and sagged. The policeman then connected the pads and applied the electrical charge. He tried again.

Harden lay limp.

"My God," Pat Bev groaned, backing away from the surrounding crowd. He knelt, sobbing.

John whispered, "God bless Joe Mauer. God bless Joe Mauer." His voice trembled as he pleaded. "God bless Joe Mauer."

Joe Mauer didn't show up, but he got Mom to. John saw her first. Then Puff and I did too.

"Mom," John said out loud.

Mom didn't look our way. Instead, she knelt alongside Harden, looking at him, her face serene, waiting. It was time to let go.

I wanted the world to remember Harden as invincible. Not as a statistic or a victim but the victor who soared, who led with smirk and swag, who made us believe we were more than the Northside, more than this life. Harden was that fallen crow in Mr. Hatch's driveway, the one the other crows had surrounded and killed. Crows want the world to believe they're invincible. We all do. But the truth is we're not. On North, we're all one misstep from being in the wrong place at the wrong time.

"Head up," I whispered to Harden. "Let go." The same words he'd said to me that October night at the rec center when I'd missed an easy layup and lost us a game.

With the defibrillator failing to revive Harden, the policeman started mouth-to-mouth resuscitation. As that effort also failed, Coach's arms slipped from lifting to grounding Harden.

Maybe it was just hope playing tricks on me, but Harden stirred before lying still once again.

But then his spirit moved. He rose with Mom. Together they drifted through the chaos and the furious crowd, toward the lobby. I wanted to call out, to stop them, but I didn't.

"He's gonna be okay, right?" a cheerleader asked, her eyes wide with both hope and dread.

No one answered her. Their silence was answer enough.

Some wailed, "No!" or "No, no—this isn't happening! Not again!" Others despaired, "This can't be possible!" "This isn't happening!" "Why?" and "When will this ever stop?"

More police pressed us toward the gym doors and sealed off gym sections with yellow crime-scene tape. A team of EMTs arrived and wheeled a gurney near Harden. They checked his vital signs, discovering none. They then wrapped him in a blanket and lifted him onto the gurney, which we followed to the ambulance.

Coach entered the ambulance with Harden. LBJ ran up to Coach and handed him Harden's money clip before the ambulance siren pealed and its back door slammed shut.

I froze like I did on a hot day last summer, when I'd startled a roosting wake of turkey vultures in a big pine tree, causing them to explode in flight. But when LBJ, Westbrook, Curry, Pat Bev, and John each placed a hand on the back window, I, too, reached out and touched the glass separating us from Harden. We followed behind the ambulance as it slowly pulled away. We let go only after it rolled off the curb onto the parking lot and sped away to HCMC.

Like startled sparrows, the other Harden Set members scattered in flight, northward, ignoring Puff's pleas to come home with us. Puff gathered John, and we ran from the parking lot to Vicky, ducking at the sound of gunfire in the distance.

The Hennepin County Medical Examiner's Office listed Harden's time of death as 17:35. I'd marked the time of his departure earlier, even before my little family had watched him leave with Mom; Harden had left us when I encouraged him to let go.

Harden's got next.

— CHAPTER TWENTY-SEVEN —

Loss

Back home, I found freckles of Harden's blood splattered across my coat. I left them but showered away the blood that had dried into scabs on my hands and wrists.

After cleaning up, I dressed in my Hmong outfit, complete with hat, and lay on my bed, unable to sleep or move. I stirred only enough to cocoon myself deep inside the covers. I waited to become a red admiral butterfly and fly far away from the Northside—so far I could go back in time. The transformation never came.

I stared at the ceiling, a blank canvas that my mind emptied into. My eyes never closed, not even a blink. But after some time had passed, I began to see death. Not Harden's but mine. I saw myself strapped into an electric chair—half of me in my new Hmong outfit, the other half in my Nike gear, all the way down to my Precision 3s, which anchored me down. A noose yanked me up. Screams and sirens echoed while I waited for the switch to be thrown.

Puff knocked and stepped into our bedroom before any harm could come to me. "We should get moving," he said. "It's late. The show started at seven."

I lay motionless, barely breathing.

"You promised your Pa Dao," Puff said. "We have to go."

I finally closed my eyes, sighed, then reopened them. I swung my legs off the bed, both asleep, and tottered like an old man from the bedroom to the hallway and outside into the slicing night air. Puff and John waited for me in Vicky with the engine running.

Puff couldn't find a parking spot near Thomas Jefferson. We parked two blocks away and penguin-walked on slick streets, nearly falling on thick, hard ice.

At the entrance to Thomas Jefferson, the perpetually broken electronic marquee scrolled the wrong date, April 15, and listed back-to-school events from August 2017. But the time, 8:07 p.m., was accurate. So was the temperature reading of –7, unless wind chill was factored. That would have sunk the reading to –25 degrees.

We made our way to the darkened auditorium. Sprawling Hmong families with teens, toddlers, babies, and grandparents filled all the seats. We stood in the back.

Two Thomas Jefferson Hmong emcees introduced the next act, switching between Hmong and English. The dance group Blooming Flowers consisted of seven Hmong girls and one Black girl. They wore traditional white pleated skirts, satin beaded blouses, coin vests, and belts. They also wore black turbans like Pa Dao had worn at lunch. But while Pa Dao had wrapped her hair into her turban, these girls let their long braided ponytails flop freely from theirs and bounce off their waists.

Each girl placed her hands on her hips and swayed to the music. The girls then opened their hands and arms to mimic a harvest as they twirled into a group and circled the stage. Broad smiles beamed throughout their performance.

The stage lights faded to black for the final act, and a red velvet curtain opened to darkness. Slowly, a dim spotlight shone on Tong, a guy in my geography class. He lay on his back, his *qeej* draped across his chest. Dressed in black pants and a black shirt, he was blanketed in darkness except for his bare face and feet. Neon-green glow sticks, attached to his back and front, illuminated a skeleton pattern. Glow sticks also shone on the ribs of his *qeej*, which hopped and twirled with him as he rose to his feet and bowed.

Though I couldn't see his fingers stroking and pressing against the hollowed bamboo pipes, the *qeej* called out, a cross between an accordion and a bagpipe. Tong spoke music. The notes clung to him as he rocked back and forth and spun in circles. After a few minutes, he slowed, and the broad loops he traveled in around the stage shortened. Bursts from the *qeej* blended into mournful melodies that lingered into even more somber melodies.

When he finished, Tong sidestepped behind a swooshing curtain.

That was also the end of the show.

The emcees asked us to remain seated so that elders could leave first for the cafeteria banquet that followed. My little family quietly slipped into the open seats the elders had vacated. Families with little kids followed the elders. Lastly, alumni and our fellow students filed by until only my little family remained.

"You came," Pa Dao called out, breaking the auditorium silence.

She emerged at the entrance and scooted down the aisle in her heels. Coins jangled as she side-shuffled to where we sat. She wore her Hmong outfit, though I knew she'd also worn a special dance outfit when her group had performed earlier in the show. I had missed her performance.

I stood, and Pa Dao leaned to hug me. "We heard what happened to Harden."

I held her so hard that I lifted her. She squeezed back. After a moment, I set her down and stepped back.

Pa Dao looked over my little family. "It's a sad tragedy."

She said the word *sad* like it was rat poison, but said the word *tragedy* as if it were expected, like a blizzard in 'Sota. Respecting Harden's life meant continuing ours and waiting for the Northside's next inevitable senseless tragedy.

Pa Dao paused, her eyes searching ours. "And Mai?"

"We saw her go," John said.

"Her love for all three of you was strong," Pa Dao said. She stopped to consider. "No, *fierce*."

For a few moments, none of us said anything.

Then Pa Dao took my hand, her grip firm but gentle. "Tomorrow," she said, resolute despite tears in her eyes, "we'll honor her, grieve her, and remember her. And in remembering, we'll keep her alive."

No one in my little family slept that night. After the madness and sadness of Harden's death and the gladness of the Hmong New Year festivities, we returned home, numb, too tired to go to bed.

Instead, we gathered around ESPN to watch meaningless college basketball highlights of powerhouse programs crushing what Puff called "Little Sisters of the Poor" teams. Iowa State blew out Eastern Illinois. Gonzaga routed Denver. None of it mattered. We were just going through the motions, in slow motion, trying and failing to fill the silence that Harden had left behind.

When the phone rang and Coach lifelessly relayed details of Harden's funeral plans, Puff could do little more than sadly interject, "Okay . . . Okay . . . Okay . . ." Eventually, he signed off with a long "I'm so sorry."

After Puff hung up and John swallowed his chemo pills, we buried ourselves under more blankets and ESPN analysis of NBA recaps and NFL previews. No one spoke a word until Puff suddenly muted the TV during a commercial.

"What if that policeman had shot one of you?" he said. He stared at the TV, but his eyes looked farther into the screen, where imagined horrific scenes played out. "You two are the only reason I live. If I lost you—" He sniffed and swiped his eyes. "Promise me you'll never die before me," he challenged.

John agreed immediately. I hesitated.

"Michael?" Puff's voice sharpened. "I'm serious."

"I'd rather have you live," I said, "than have me live and not want to live."

Dropping the blanket covering him, Puff rose and stood before me. "Promise me now."

"I promise," I said, but didn't mean it. When Puff remained in front of me, I sighed. "All right. I promise. For real this time."

Puff returned to his couch and covered himself in the blanket again.

"Mom's genes and my genes didn't create you two. Our dreams did. You're supposed to finish everything we dreamed of but couldn't finish in our lifetimes."

"We will," John said.

"I know you will," Puff said to him. "Not so sure about your little brother." He focused on me. "I don't give a crap whether you want to or not—you're going to complete our dreams. You have no more choice in it than you do in changing any of your genes. That's the way it has to be. You complete our dreams, then you can live your own dreams and leave a few leftovers for your own boys."

"What are your dreams?" I said to Puff.

Puff's bloodhound eyes—black, dark, and baggy—searched ours. "I don't know anymore," Puff said. "But I got one job: Keep you safe." His voice trembled. "We can't go back to the past, but we also can't go forward to the future. Not here, anyway. It's time we leave the Northside."

I couldn't disagree. The Northside had taken Harden's life, and he had taken the life of the Northside. It didn't matter where I lived or where I died. Harden had become the heartbeat of our little family. Now, we had no pulse.

Puff was scared. We were all scared. And scarred.

— CHAPTER TWENTY-EIGHT —

Deep Bench

"Take a right at the Hmong grocery store on the corner," Puff told Pa Dao's father before Siri offered the same command from Pa Dao's iPhone from the backseat. "That's Magnolia," Puff added from the passenger seat.

These were the only human words spoken during the half-hour trip from the Northside of Minneapolis to the East Side of Saint Paul.

Three weeks earlier, Puff had come to this neighborhood with Pa Dao's father, Xia Pao, to negotiate the day's scheduled events. Now Pa Dao sat in the back seat of a Toyota minivan, along with her mother, Auntie Xia Pao. I was crammed in the wayback bench seat with John, Pa Dao's sister Sheng, and Pa Dao's shaman materials: a bench, her clothing, and her instruments. Rattles shook whenever we hit a pothole. And in Saint Paul, there are a lot of bone-jarring potholes.

One other person was crammed in the van with us, on us, heavy on our hearts and minds. Though he never said a word, Harden cried out to be with us on our journey.

I kept my eyes closed, but the ache behind them refused to go away. The cold water I'd splashed on my face that morning had done little to rejuvenate the exhaustion etched into my skin. My eyes were soupy. The weight of the past few days had settled into the creases around them.

When I finally cracked open my eyes, I observed that the quiet Saint Paul neighborhood could have been airlifted from Cottage Park.

All the homes were two stories, draped unevenly in gowns of broad asbestos-shake siding in dull, worn colors.

"Last house on the left, if you recall," Puff told Xia Pao. "If you get to the park, you've gone too far."

His directions went unheard, though. Pa Dao was loudly calling out house numbers and listening to Siri's instructions. When Siri finally announced, "Arrived," Pa Dao called for her father to pull the minivan to the curb.

Grandpa Vang's house was a patchwork of moss-green siding and a rising dough of build-ons and bump-outs, each sided with shakes of slightly different shades, textures, and vintages. Some had weathered to a dull gray. A US flag hung limply from a sagging three-season porch that leaned to the right. A life-sized plastic Santa, his rosy cheeks worn to white, stood guard over a spindly hip-high plastic fence pretending to guard a ten-foot front lawn adorned with a dark-green EAST SIDE PRIDE sign. It wasn't a house as much as a collection of this and that—like Puff's billfold.

A steady stream of little Hmong kids—bundled, booted, and roly-poly—emerged from the front door and plodded down the porch steps like wood ducklings under the watchful eyes of older cousins escorting them to the park. The children hardly noticed us as we stepped out of the minivan, but our arrival sparked a flurry of activity among the adults inside the house.

My stomach squiggled. I was about to meet my big family—Grandpa Vang and my Hmong cousins, aunties, and uncles—for the first time and immerse myself in the spirits of my ancestors.

While my little family gathered at the back of the minivan, waiting for Pa Dao to tell us what to bring inside, Puff directed my attention to the matter of most importance to him.

"See that backstop for the baseball field?" He pointed to an area at the park's edge. "Under that snow is the only ballfield I've ever seen that has no trace of basepaths or a pitching mound. No one's played ball there for decades."

Xia Pao left us to greet Grandpa Vang's family and ensure the day got off to a good start. He was there to smooth the way for Pa Dao, but also for us.

"All right, men," Pa Dao said, standing by me. "Let's begin." She clicked a button on the key fob, and the hatch lifted. "Michael, you and your father carry in my shaman bench."

As Puff and I gripped the bench, she tapped my shoulder with the firm but guiding touch of a Hmong farmer urging a water buffalo to plow a rice field.

"Be careful," she said. "My father made this bench from solid oak. It's heavy. Use your legs, not your back."

We grunted and pulled the bench from the minivan, and Pa Dao set the others to work. She had her mother and sister carry in the outfits and had John carry in the vase of white roses, a gift from Mrs. Flowers to represent reverence for my big family.

Gripping the bench, Puff and I shuffled across the quiet street. After a few moments, he needed to set down his end and catch his breath. But before we could pick it up again, two men hustled from the house and took our places. Both were barrel-chested and built like the beefy Maplewood Toyota mechanics in *Hmong Times* ads. Puff called their type "super Hmong." Perfect offensive tackles.

"Long time," Puff said. He turned to the one wearing heavy winter boots, a camouflage coat, and a worn San Francisco 49ers cap. "You still out west?"

"Fresno," the man said.

Puff pivoted to me. "These are your uncles, Zong Yia and Cha Ying."

Both men scanned me and huffed, but Uncle Zong Yia's eyes smiled.

Uncle Cha Ying eyed me sharply. "Who are you?"

"I am Michael," I said. "Mai's son." Remembering what Pa Dao had taught me, I added, "And I am Hmong."

"Good," Uncle Cha Ying replied. "Then you know how to work."

"And know that you can never run out of work," Uncle Zong Yia said. "If you think you're done working, make more work." He gestured to the house. "Come on in. You have a lot of relatives in there— at least fifty. They're waiting to meet you."

We followed them as they lugged the bench toward the house. When they'd passed through the front door and I stepped inside, six women, all aunties, cried as they hugged us. In between the sobs, a wave of their names rolled at and over me. Thankfully, Pa Dao was remembering all of them.

To each auntie, I responded, "I am Mai's son, Michael. And I am Hmong."

Each acknowledged me and told me her relationship to Mom. I knew there was one more auntie, Mom's oldest sister. When the other aunties stepped back and turned to the dining area, she called out to me.

"I'm your Auntie Chong," a heavyset woman in her seventies called out in a voice sharp but tinged with longing. She sat alone at a long table, her heavy frame draped in layers of fabric and a heavy sweater. "Aren't you going to greet me?" She gestured for me to hurry her way.

I knelt alongside her legs—solid, fleshy posts with buried knees and calves that covered her ankles and protruded into chunky leather orthopedic tennis shoes with Velcro straps for laces. Her hair was gray and unkempt. Though she was a mass of soft, pillowy skin, she held me so tightly it hurt. She had Mom's cheekbones and motherly love, a love she'd waited years to give Mom but now gave to me.

Puff sidestepped in our direction. "You remember me—I'm Patrick Moriarity," he said reassuringly. "This is my son Michael."

Auntie Chong ignored him. She pulled me close and pressed padded fingertips into my cheeks.

"No," Auntie Chong said, her eyes darting around my face. "This is my little sister Mai. These are her cheekbones, her eyelashes, and her eyebrows." She ran her fingers through my hair. "Mai's hair!"

"You're going to frighten the boy," Uncle Zong Yia said.

"I don't need you or anyone else to tell me what to do about anything," she said. She stared down Uncle Zong Yia until he looked away.

"It's been too many years since you've been away," Uncle Zong Yia said to Puff. "Let's go outside and start you with a beer."

When they left, Auntie Chong surveyed me again. "Mai is inside this boy!" she wailed. She pulled me close again and patted my hair. "I love you so much. I fought with the family about abandoning you.

After you left us, I tried to find you. No one would tell me where you'd gone."

It took a moment to realize that Auntie Chong was not talking to me but to Mom. I took her hand and held it to my cheek to reassure her. She let out another high-pitched wail—whether laughter, grief, or joy, I couldn't tell. With Auntie Chong, they all sounded the same. Her expressions were also the same, so strained that her eyes creased and she panted, out of breath.

"I will call you Chi," she said. "*Chi* means 'to shine.' Mai shines from you. Now bring your brother to me."

I called to John, who was still in the entryway with the other aunties. Pa Dao came to his rescue and led him over. She introduced him in Hmong and used dramatic up-and-down tones and lively gestures to explain his brain surgery, radiation, chemotherapy, and even the tornado.

Auntie Chong pulled John close. Her hands went to pat his head but stopped once she noticed his thinned hair. Instead, she patted his back, smushed her face into his chest, and sobbed. After several seconds, she pulled him away.

"You have Mai's eyes," she said to John. "She looks out from you and for you. She lights the way. I will call you Teng, which means 'light.'"

By this point, the other aunties had gathered around us. Auntie Sai, Mom's youngest sibling, spoke up in Hmong. The rest of the women laughed, including Auntie Chong, who displayed a silver front tooth.

"I said you inherited your red hair from the Hmong," Auntie Sai told John.

Auntie Chong let us go so the rest of our aunties could question us about Cottage Park, the Northside, Thomas Jefferson, and John's cancer. Pa Dao smiled at us, then joined Sheng and Auntie Xia Pao in the kitchen to prepare vegetables.

The chatter stopped when Grandpa Vang came in from the backyard, where he'd been overseeing the meat preparation. He was short but solid, in his late eighties, and dressed in a big, puffy down winter jacket that covered him from head to knees. He also wore a thick Minnesota Vikings stocking cap pulled down over his ears and rubber boots extending to his knees. Grandpa Vang looked just like General Vang Pao holding a book in the READ poster at Thomas Jefferson.

"*Nyob zoo, Yawm Txiv,*" I said.

My rough-accented Hmong caught Grandpa Vang's attention. He walked toward me until we stood face-to-face. "Ah," he muttered. "*Me tub, zoo li kuv twb yuav paub koj na. Koj puas txawj hais lub hmoob? Koj puas tau taub lus Hmoob?*"

I blinked and scratched my head.

Grandpa Vang chuckled. "You speak Hmong a little?"

My thumb and finger separated to show a pinch.

Grandpa Vang clenched my upper arm. "Strong," he said. His face broke into a thousand wrinkles and one smile. "Such a big boy."

He turned to inspect John and asked us to stand back-to-back to measure us. We did, and he stared in disbelief.

"And an even bigger brother!" he said.

"Someday, I'll catch up to him," I said.

Grandpa Vang shook his head and grinned. "Brothers."

He turned to First Grandma Vang and said a few words in Hmong. Based on his gestures toward the door, I interpreted it to mean that he was returning to the backyard.

"Could John and I join you?" I said.

He smiled again and motioned for us to follow him.

Nothing had ever been thrown away at Grandpa Vang's—only relocated to the backyard. Old, broken bicycles with rusted chains leaned against a chain link fence. A plastic playhouse sat alongside a wooden sandbox that leaked sand from a corner where the boards had come apart. There were bare motors long since separated from their original homes, and motors exposed but encased in a washer, a dryer, two lawnmowers, and a tiller.

Grandpa Vang led us into the garage. Inside were two large coolers filled with Budweiser and Bud Light, propane tanks, outdoor cookware, and massive aluminum pots like the one Mom had kept on our stovetop in Cottage Park. Heavy smoke billowed from a propane grill, filling the wintry air with the pungent fragrance of beef.

Dressed in plastic aprons and standing at eight-foot-long folding tables lined with plastic sheets, the Vang men piled raw meat onto handcrafted butcher-block boards. There they chopped the meat into smaller pieces and placed them into large stainless steel bowls. They were as efficient as a three-man weave passing drill in basketball. And all the while, they drank beer. Cans and hands were smeared with blood.

Uncle Zong Yia surprised Puff with a second beer. Puff accepted it, then raised an eyebrow. "Kind of early for all this beer, isn't it?"

"You're working," Uncle Zong Yia said. "You can drink and work at the same time. Plus, it's never too early to honor a Hmong woman who loved her family."

Puff cracked open the second can, raised it in a silent toast, and took a long swig.

Beside Uncle Cha Ying, Grandpa Vang watched John and me watching the men. After a few moments, he made eye contact and motioned us over.

"You know how to cut? Cut meat?" he said.

John and I shook our heads.

Grandpa Vang's mouth and eyes opened like the letter *O*. The sound came a few seconds later. "Ohhh . . ."

The uncles and their sons nearby let out low chuckles, which embarrassed John and me.

"*Txiv*, they're part *meka*," Uncle Cha Ying said. "They don't know."

"They should learn," Grandpa Vang said. "Grab an apron."

John and I stepped toward the pile of aprons at the end of the table, only to stop when Grandpa Vang said something in Hmong to Uncle Cha Ying. We understood the tone, though not the words. It was an order. Grandpa Vang pointed to the back door, then to John.

Uncle Cha Ying gestured for John to follow him. They went inside, but only Uncle Cha Ying returned.

"Grandpa Vang said that John is healing and should not be working," Uncle Cha Ying explained to me. "He asked me to take John inside, where it is warm and comfortable. He's in the living room with Auntie Chong now. As for you, I will show you how we work."

He handed me an apron, a cutting board, and a Hmong knife. When I held the knife, I thought of Mom cooking for us in the kitchen. Uncle Cha Ying handed me a large chunk of meat and modeled chopping the meat and bone, like chopping wood with an axe. Sweat dripped down my brow. Mom must have built a lot of stamina cooking for us over the years. The thought made me work even harder.

We'd been working for an hour when Auntie Sai came outside and complimented me on my effort. "You fit right in," she said. "Like you've been doing this work all your life."

I noticed the cold for the first time and also missed John and Pa Dao.

"Pa Dao told us about your tragedy yesterday," Auntie Sai added, placing a hand on my shoulder. "We don't know how many of your spirits were lost with your friend last night, but the *hu plig* will call those spirits back and many others. We'll bless your family and ensure that Mai continues her journey. We should head inside for the *hu plig* soon. Then we'll do the *ua neeb* and *khi tes* later this afternoon."

Puff and I followed Auntie Sai back to the house, stepping over a mountain of shoes and snow boots at the back door. Fifteen women were crammed inside the tiny kitchen, mostly gathered at the table. Other women washed and dried dishes around the sink while others stood at the counter, preparing greens and other vegetables.

No one was ready to join us for the *hu plig*, the soul-calling ritual. The women were too busy preparing tasty food and sharing tasty gossip. Some of the aunties complained about how disobedient children are these days. Others agreed, mimicking their children's tantrums. Without any transition, the conversation moved on to juicy news about an impending divorce in the community.

"Have you heard what happened to *Txiv Hlob* Cha Seng and his wife?" asked one woman with a stuffed-up nose and a hoarse voice. She looked over her shoulder as she washed veggies in the sink.

"Oh yeah, everybody knows," gasped another.

"I'll tell you what happened," said Auntie Pahoua, her slender arms shaking angrily as she chopped lemongrass. "He left her for a younger woman. It's so sad. They'd been married for fifteen years and have six children." She shook her head wearily. "Men . . ."

The other women also shook their heads from side to side—a sign of agreement and distress. They traded scandalous details about the affair and separation until First Grandma Vang, sitting quietly at the table, spoke up.

"You're always talking about other people's lives," she said with a sour face. "Focus on your own!"

The women paused.

First Grandma Vang's granddaughter, Mee, was the first to respond. "Okay. We'll stop." She picked a safer subject: the weather. "I don't ever remember such a fierce winter."

The others agreed. And the conversation flowed from winter to springtime to gardening. They discussed plans to plant new vegetables and fruit trees: red cherry, pear, and plum. They also discussed building a small greenhouse to cultivate exotic herbs and plants such as pink frost, white mugwort, and bloodleaf.

When First Grandma Vang stepped out of the kitchen, the women switched topics yet again. This time, they bickered about Auntie Chong, who sat out of earshot, in the living room with John. She had many health concerns. And she smoked whenever she talked on her phone, which was all the time. Though her siblings had each invited her to stay with them, Auntie Chong lived alone. She'd buried husbands in two countries, Laos and America. Grief and time had blurred the differences between countries, cultures, and the things she should and shouldn't say.

A few moments later, Auntie Chong called out for me. "Chi, can you bring me a bowl of candy?"

Everyone paused, speculating whether she'd somehow sensed the conversation or even whether she'd been within earshot after all.

I stepped toward Auntie Chong, with Auntie Sai close behind. Auntie Sai answered in a firm but gentle voice before I responded.

"No," Auntie Sai said. "Candy is high in sugar, and you know what that does to your blood. You've got diabetes. You—we—cannot ignore that." She crossed her arms, but her tone softened. "Chi can bring you another snack—something healthier that won't send you to the hospital. How about some nuts, seeds, or cheese?"

"Ick," Auntie Chong said, turning to John and scrunching her face like she had caught a whiff of a hog-confinement barn in Cottage Park. She turned back to her sister. "Excuse me, but I was talking to Chi. Besides, my doctor said I could have small amounts of candy—I just can't overdo it."

"I'll bring you a glass of spring water," Auntie Sai said, ushering me back to the kitchen.

In the time I'd stepped away to the kitchen, the dining room had been transformed. The aunties draped white linen tablecloths over long tables stretching from the dining room to the living room. Each table had flowers, but the center table featured a magnificent centerpiece: a fountain flowing with brightly colored fruit, flowers, dozens of boiled eggs, and vanilla and strawberry sugar wafer cookies scaffolding around a banana fortress. To top it off, hundreds of strands of thin white yarn for the *khi tes* covered the fountain like snow.

The little kids returned from the park as the last tablecloth was smoothed into place. One group chased another upstairs and downstairs, ignoring the warnings not to enter the bedroom closet that held the pull-down ladder leading to the attic. Another group darted and crawled under the tables.

While the aunties scolded the little kids, Auntie Chong motioned for me to join her and John. When I reached her side, she defiantly pushed her glass of spring water aside and magically produced a package of Starburst candies. She flung each piece into her mouth the second she unwrapped it, making no effort to share.

"Maybe now," she said as she chewed, "I can tell you two boys my story of winning a thirty-thousand-dollar jackpot playing bingo at Mystic Lake a few years ago."

"That's a true story," Auntie Sai said. She was right behind me again. "But it's a story that requires—and deserves—enough time to tell it properly, and this is the time for the *hu plig*."

"Listen," Auntie Chong said. "I won't take part in any spiritual ceremonies today. I've become a Christian."

"I know," Auntie Sai said with indifference. "You're free to do as you wish."

Auntie Sai waved to Pa Dao, Sheng, and Auntie Xia Pao, who were standing near the front door with Pa Dao's ritual tools and items.

"You can go ahead," Auntie Sai said. "We'll continue to work around you and check in on you occasionally."

To my surprise, my big family left us, heading to work or play in different areas of the house. Even Auntie Chong hobbled off to find a new place to rest. Only my little family and Pa Dao's little family huddled in the living room like we were about to play in a championship game.

Pa Dao stood barefoot, her black pants and teal blouse shimmering with intricate Hmong embroidery. Under the dining room chandelier, the delicate patterns around her wrists and neckline pulsed like they were breathing. She tapped her gong three times while chanting in Hmong. To her left was a cardboard box holding a live rooster and hen, bound with twine. In front of her was a stool sitting a small bowl of rice, three incense sticks, and three eggs.

This wasn't just a ritual. Pa Dao was building a bridge between two worlds, and we were about to cross it.

Pa Dao chanted, sprinkling John's name throughout her petition. John sat before her on a folding chair, eyes closed, in deep thought or the early stages of a nap. Puff, though, was hyperalert, expecting something bad to happen.

Pa Dao took out her *txiab neeb*—a circular steel wire with steel rings that resembled a tambourine—and roughly shook it a few times. After removing a black headscarf from her canvas bag, she handed the bag to Auntie Xia Pao, who stood behind her.

"Spirits might not respond to me without shaman clothes," Pa Dao announced. "I wear a black headscarf to show that my shaman gift passed through generations. My dialogue with the spirits will be in Hmong."

Pa Dao pointed to a pig's head nestled on a plastic sheeting on the floor. Sitting on the same sheeting was a cow's head. Two sets of glassy eyes gazed at Pa Dao's low wooden bench, a few feet away.

"This is my horse," Pa Dao said, gliding her fingers across the bench. "I'll ride it later this afternoon, during the *ua neeb*. It'll take me into the spirit world to meet your ancestors." She looked at me. "You know, every Hmong shaman has shaman guides. They are the main reason why we can perform shamanism. Our shaman guides oversee everything we understand about the spirit realm. These chickens are examples of spirit guides. They help guide my way."

Pa Dao crouched beside the chickens, murmuring to them in Hmong. As she did, Sheng whispered an interpretation.

"I am grateful for your presence today. Your lives will be cut short because your mighty souls will bring John Moriarity home. When you have completed your task, your work will be recognized, and you will resurrect as humans in the next life."

I shivered as Pa Dao's voice burrowed so far into my head that I also heard Mom, longing for Hmong traditions. I understood why she'd wanted me to learn these rituals. It wasn't just about culture. It was about connection.

"Pa Dao is asking the chickens to guide John's spirit back," Sheng explained as Pa Dao continued talking to the chickens. Her voice softened as she turned to John. "When the tornado struck, pieces of your spirit were scattered. We should have called them back then, but today, we'll make it right."

After Pa Dao finished with the chickens, Auntie Xia Pao lifted her arm and signaled to the kitchen. On cue, Uncle Cha Ying's two teenage daughters came into the living room, pulled the chickens from their box, and carried them outside.

"We sacrifice the chickens for the same reason we sacrificed the cow and pig," Sheng explained. "The chickens are for John. They guide his spirit. You will eat the chicken later, after the *khi tes*. The sacred cow, pig, and chicken all guide spirits back to protect us."

Pa Dao reached into her bag and pulled out a pair of black bull horns, their surfaces glistening like polished stone. She moved to the front door, marking each side with the horns in a ritual as old as the Hmong. This was a gesture, an invitation, a call to the ancestors to join us in the day's activities. As Pa Dao worked, they intermingled, waiting and watching.

Then she tossed the horns on the floor.

"Both glistening sides face upward," Sheng said, eyeing the horns' placement. "That's a sign that John's spirit has returned."

Pa Dao picked up the horns and tossed them a second time.

"Glistening sides up again," Sheng said, pointing to the horns. "These horns were taken from a black bull. Shamans toss horns three times to identify the spirit. If the glistening side shows each time, the spirit joining us is the real deal. But if the results aren't consistent, the spirits are lying, and the shaman will move on. No spirits can lie when it comes to the black bull horns. They're lie detectors."

John opened his eyes and leaned forward as Pa Dao tossed the horns a third time.

"Glistening sides up," Sheng said with a satisfied exhale.

My little family breathed a sigh of relief.

The arrival of John's spirit marked the end of the *hu plig*. Pa Dao and her family began preparing for the next ceremony, the *ua neeb*.

Preparations were continuing in the kitchen as well. Mothers called out for their daughters to help. The daughters—who'd been watching Hmong dance and music videos in an upstairs bedroom— groaned as they dragged down the steps. They complained that their mothers enslaved them while their brothers were free to play *Mario Party 4* in the adjacent bedroom.

Once again, only my little family joined Pa Dao, Sheng, and Auntie Xia Pao at the temporary altar near the front door. Pa Dao took her place alongside her low wooden bench and fitted herself with four finger bells—one on each thumb and one on each index finger. She lit candles on the temporary altar and muttered a few Hmong words. After sipping from a cup of water, she stomped her foot and spat the water around the bench.

"She's cleansing the area before she starts," Sheng said as Pa Dao raised her voice and walked around her bench. "No spirits can distract or interfere once she trances."

Pa Dao circled the bench again, chanting until she returned the cup to the temporary altar, then lowered her veil. She clapped and clanged the finger bells while her mother struck the gong, producing a loud, steady tempo. Pa Dao shook and trembled as her finger bells rang.

My little family gathered around her.

"She's shaking," Sheng whispered, her eyes fixed on Pa Dao. "Soon, she'll mount her winged horse and journey to the spirit world, where your ancestors are waiting."

Auntie Xia Pao continued the steady beat on the gong as Pa Dao bowed on the bench, chanted, and rattled her *txiab neeb*.

"The *txiab neeb* alerts the spirits of Pa Dao's arrival," Sheng whispered. "The ring of rattles captures spirits. Pa Dao has mounted her horse and is leaving us, going higher and beyond, into the spirit world, one step at a time."

Auntie Xia Pao moved behind Pa Dao, put her hands on Pa Dao's shoulders, and steadied her. In Hmong, Auntie Xia Pao relayed each step of Pa Dao's progress to Sheng, who relayed it to us in English.

"First step . . . second step . . . third step . . ."

At the twelfth step, Pa Dao reached her destination. The gong quieted, but Pa Dao kept chanting.

"She's calling for Mai and your ancestors to meet her," Sheng whispered, her voice barely audible over the chanting. A chill ran down my spine as Pa Dao's chanting grew louder, more insistent. Mom was with us.

Pa Dao stepped up and down from the bench several times before calling out to Auntie Xia Pao, who relayed another message.

"We need to burn one hundred sheets of joss paper," Sheng said.

She picked up a steel pail holding a stack of joss paper sheets and ushered my little family away from Pa Dao and Auntie Xia Pao. We followed her to the back door, squeezing through the women and their daughters in the kitchen. Once outside, we made our way to the fire pit, near a plastic table with chairs.

"Whenever we go to the spirit world," Sheng said as she set the pail on the crusty, snow-covered lawn, "we must never go empty-handed. Once the shaman arrives at the destination, she must offer joss paper to the guards as a sign of respect and to obtain permission to pass through. We will burn the paper, but first, we must fold it into coin strands."

We sat at the plastic table, and Uncle Zong Yia and Uncle Cha Ying joined us as Sheng carefully unfolded the stack of joss paper. Each sheet was a tapestry of symbols—white borders, yellow rectangles, and red squares—heavy with the weight of tradition.

"Go ahead and start," Sheng told my uncles, distributing half of the paper stack to them. "I'll show the Moriaritys."

My uncles immediately went to work, expertly folding one sheet of joss paper after another. It reminded me of origami or paper airplanes.

"It's pretty simple," Sheng said. She took a piece and folded it this way and that, manipulating it into two coin-like strands. "You want me to do it again?"

"Yes," my little family replied.

Again and again, Sheng repeated the process, patiently explaining each step. Eventually, we each took a piece and followed her lead. Slowly, the process became more familiar.

Minutes passed in quiet concentration, the only sound the rustle of paper and an occasional murmur of instruction from Sheng. Then Uncle Zong Yia set down his stack and rose, moving to the fire pit. The embers glowed faintly. But as he fed them slender branches, the flames leaped to life.

"It's time," Sheng announced. "Bring your coins to the fire."

The six of us approached the fire pit, each taking turns to drop the paper strands into the flames. The fire devoured the paper. Ash rose in delicate strands that twisted and danced like snakes and dragons. They crawled over one another as they wriggled and shed their skin. As the flames caught the edges, the smoke curled upward to reach the spirit world. I hoped that Harden's spirit, too, might find its way home over that bridge.

Once the coins were burned, Sheng led us back inside, my uncles trailing behind. The sweet aroma of incense greeted us at the door, mingling with the low murmur of Pa Dao's chanting.

Auntie Xia Pao called out in Hmong to Sheng, who waved back.

"Pa Dao has come back," Sheng announced, her voice carrying through the room.

Pa Dao stilled. Her hands steadied as she lifted her veil. She arranged her *txiab neeb*, divining horns, and other ritual tools on the temporary altar. Each item had a purpose to help Pa Dao connect to the spirits.

"We thank Pa Dao for meeting and negotiating with the spirits," Uncle Zong Yia said. "Please bow."

We followed his lead, as did the few relatives who had taken a break from their preparations to join us.

Auntie Xia Pao used a dish towel to pat the sweat from Pa Dao's neck, forehead, and cheeks. Pa Dao took the towel, opened it, and pressed her whole face into it. She returned the towel to her mother, then stepped over to the temporary altar and collected the horns. After rolling on the floor, the horns landed upright again.

John's spirit was reunited with him.

After a few moments, Pa Dao motioned for John, Puff, and me to gather around her. Behind her, at the temporary altar, thin white smoke curled from an incense stick.

"I met with Mai, her parents, and her grandparents," Pa Dao said, focusing on Puff. "There is good news—you and your family will enjoy a safe and healthy year, and many more healthy and happy years to come."

"What about Harden?" I said. "Is he with Mom?"

"Mai and Harden have begun their journey back to wherever they have lived," Pa Dao answered. "Their journey began together last night on the Northside."

Puff scanned John, Pa Dao, and me. "Any bad news?" He sighed. "We're used to getting bad news with good news."

Pa Dao smiled. "There is no bad news. After Mai died, some of John's spirit left him to be with her and his ancestors. That's why John became sick. Today we remembered and honored those ancestors, helping them find peace and make their way home." She turned to John. "Your spirit came back to you today. Your spirit and good health won't leave again."

"But the doctors told us the cancer *will* come back," Puff said. "They said we're only buying time."

"They don't know about spirits," Pa Dao said. She gestured to the altar. "Spirits eat, drink, and spend money as we all do. They deserve honor. Take care of the spirits, and they'll safeguard you."

She waved for Auntie Sai to come forward with her teenage daughter. Auntie Sai opened her purse and pulled out a laminated photo, which she presented to Puff.

"This is Mai's picture from her junior year," Auntie Sai said, "the only year she attended school in America. My daughter, Mee, is a senior at Harding High School, where Mai and I also attended. She found this photo in the old yearbooks in the library and made a copy. Please take this photo to honor Mai."

Puff received the photo and stared at it for several seconds. Then he handed the picture to John, who held it gingerly and tilted it in my direction. I leaned over to view it.

In the photo, Mom wore a simple white blouse with no jewelry. Her hair flowed below her shoulders, longer than I'd ever seen it. Her expression was neither happy nor sad, but clear-eyed determination.

"Mom never smiled for a picture," I said.

"OGs don't smile for pictures," Pa Dao said. "It doesn't mean they're not happy. Mai was happy then. She is happy now." She thought for a moment. "As happy as she can be. Spirits come to us from time to time in dreams, but we are constantly in their dreams. We are their dreams. They are frustrated that they cannot help us with our struggles."

"What do you mean by 'OGs'?" Puff said.

"Old guys," Pa Dao said, keeping it simple for him. "It's a compliment." She smiled. "Let me change, and when I come back, we'll begin the *khi tes*. Once we finish, you can eat. Remember, I promised you a feast!"

As Pa Dao left us, Auntie Sai guided us away from the temporary altar to the main table, where she presented our seating arrangement.

"The eggs are delicacies to the spirits," she said, pointing to the elaborate centerpiece. "We've worked to welcome them here. Today this house contains many blessings."

When Pa Dao returned, she had changed into her third outfit of the day: a sleek black dress adorned with pearls, paired with a soft pink sweater that glowed against her skin. She bridged "elegant" to "everyday."

Mee tapped Pa Dao's shoulder from behind. "We boiled the rooster and chicken. What's next?"

"Set it in a tray or bowl and place it by the front door," Pa Dao said. "I'll make another calling before bringing the boiled chicken to the table."

Mee headed back to the kitchen.

I stepped toward Pa Dao just as one of our guy cousins came bounding down the stairs, calling for John and me.

"Come up and play *Mario* with us!"

I looked to Pa Dao.

She smiled. "Go. You have time before the *khi tes*."

Upstairs, John and I discovered that our cousin Kub, a seventh grader from La Crosse, had brought a gym bag full of gaming hardware with him. He'd connected the cable cords from Grandpa Vang's TV to a classic Nintendo GameCube. We'd take turns with the four controllers.

Twelve of us crowded around the TV. As Kub loaded us into *Mario Party 4*, another cousin cranked the Blackbird Elements, a Hmong hip-hop group, on his phone. We jammed to lyrics about real-world mayhem and murder in Minneapolis–Saint Paul while our cartoon characters scrambled to escape manic circumstances in the Mushroom Kingdom.

My cousins had mastered every trick to the minigames we played. They were generous with their patience and advice to one another, especially to John and me, who forgot their advice amid the chaos of bright colors, sped-up electronic Mardi Gras music, and silly characters racing across the screen.

Avalanche! was my favorite minigame. Thanks to my cousins, I now know that the three rocks and two ramps are in the same position. I also know that I'll never win the most coins when I play with the Vangs, but I will be the funniest, and John will be the one they cheer the hardest for.

And I learned that Puff was wrong about no baseball being played on Magnolia Avenue East. When we finished our game of

Mario Party 4, we Vangs played *Mario Superstar Baseball* for forty minutes. We would have played all night if Auntie Sai hadn't called us down for the *khi tes* at sunset.

Auntie Sai also called the men from outside and the women from the kitchen. The shapeless crowd shifted into a neat line. Little kids emerged from their hiding spots and popped up alongside their parents.

Pa Dao positioned my little family as if taking our picture with the centerpiece as a backdrop. She signaled to Auntie Sai, who summoned a few other women and headed for the kitchen. Moments later, the women reappeared, carrying plates, silverware, and glass bowls. Auntie Sai set a tray with the boiled chickens in front of Pa Dao.

Auntie Xia Pao and Pa Dao smiled at both pairs of the chickens' feet, curled inward—more proof of the spirit's return. Pa Dao's journey had been a success.

"Please examine the chickens," Pa Dao said, holding the tray before Puff. "*Nws puas zoo nkauj?*" she announced to everyone. "Is it pretty?" she whispered to Puff. "Say it's pretty." Pa Dao cupped her hands over her mouth, modeling how Puff should project his findings for all to hear.

"Very nice," Puff said loudly.

"This chicken is the best," Pa Dao said in Hmong, just as loudly. She turned to John. "We'll prepare the chicken for you to enjoy later."

Pa Dao returned the tray to Auntie Sai, who whisked it back into the kitchen. Pa Dao arranged and opened our outstretched hands— me, John, and Puff. Back from the kitchen, Auntie Sai scooped three eggs from the centerpiece and plopped one into each left hand.

"Eat those when the *khi tes* is done," Pa Dao said. "They unite us with fortune and prosperity."

Next, Grandpa Vang chanted a blessing in Hmong over the *khi tes* strings atop the centerpiece. Pa Dao stepped behind us and whispered the translation: "Tonight is a good night. We celebrate the return of strength and good health to the Moriaritys. With the assistance of many spirits, we took away all the bad things and anything else that could hurt or worry us. Now we can celebrate our good health and long lives."

When Grandpa Vang finished, he directed us to form one long line—elders first, then young parents holding infants, followed by young people and children. The line wrapped around the long table and out to the kitchen. Older people sat at tables, waiting for the line to shorten.

Responding to a cue I couldn't see or hear, Tou—the cousin who'd interpreted for Grandpa Vang when I invited the Vangs to Mom's funeral—approached the centerpiece, collected *khi tes* strings, and counted off three strings for each person. Tou was a student at the University of Minnesota. My teenage cousins leaned against the walls, eyes glued to their phones.

Pa Dao initiated the *khi tes* blessings by resting three delicate white strings on my right wrist while her polished fingernails separated them and pulled one away. Her fingers, light as feathers, brushed against my skin as she threaded the one string in elaborate knots on my left wrist. The knots were as thoughtful as the words she spoke.

"Michael," Pa Dao said. "Being Hmong—becoming Hmong—is hard. I've also been hard on you. But you don't have to do this alone. I won't ever leave you alone. We Hmong say, 'The mouth tastes food; the heart tastes words.' I wish my words will mend and feed your broken heart until you never hunger or ache again. And I hope you will see I am not above or below you, but beside you. I've learned I can't control you, but I'm getting better at understanding you." She closed my fingers around the egg still in my left hand. "Okay?"

My heart raced, and my head spun. My ears burned red.

Pa Dao pulled another string from my right wrist, placed it on John's left wrist, and tied detailed knots. "You are the biggest man, bigger than any house. I wish for you—and I promise you—a mountain's strength and long life. No person and no illness can ever cross over you. It can only go around."

"I appreciate you," John told her. He looked shyly at his feet.

Pa Dao eased away toward Puff and placed her third string around his wrist. She smiled as she tied the string into sturdy knots.

"Mr. Moriarity," she said, "the Hmong say, 'If you see the oxen, you will see horns. As you see sons, you will see the father.' I wish you a window to see the strength you have brought into the world through your sons. I hope that window turns into a mirror, so that you can see those strengths in yourself."

Puff bowed. "Thank you for your blessing and everything else today."

Pa Dao then headed for the back of the line, and Grandpa Vang stepped forward with three strings in his hand.

One by one, every person in this long line of Vangs was about to offer a blessing and tie a string for John, Puff, and me. I looked throughout the line for Mom. She needed to be here with us. Mom and our little family were becoming one big family. We were becoming Hmong.

Grandpa Vang delivered the first of my big family's blessings in Hmong. I couldn't understand his words, but I understood his blessing. He studied me as he twisted the soft, fuzzy string into a beaded rope on my left wrist.

The oldest family members followed next. Their delicate white strings were heavy with painstaking, sometimes tearful, Hmong-spoken hopes, which others translated. There were wishes for a long life, a happy marriage, and a large family blessed with children, grandchildren, and great-grandchildren.

The younger generations tied strings and uttered simple blessings in Hmonglish or English: "Peace and joy." "I hope you find a home in Minneapolis." "I hope you find love with a wife and raise a happy family." "I wish you good grades, a good college, and a good job." "I hope nothing bad comes to you and you live long, healthy, and free."

By the end, my big family had covered my wrist and arm in a sleeve of yarn and had covered my heart with love and blessings. Puff and John flexed their arm muscles until the strings tightened together into a shield.

After the final string was tied, Pa Dao solemnly stepped forward.

"Keep the strings on your arms for three days," she said. "Then, if you want, you can cut most of them off—but you must leave at least three on until they break or fall off."

Auntie Sai then escorted Puff to his seat of honor, in front of the centerpiece. She directed John and me to sit on each side of him. Next, she waved for Grandpa Vang to take his seat.

"*Txiv, los zaum ib sab ntawm John nov,*" she said. She leaned into John. "That means, 'Grandpa, come sit with John.'"

Grandpa Vang stepped over and greeted John with a quick smile. "*Nyob zoo tub. Hnub no peb hu plig rau koj es txhob txhawj nawb mog. Peb ua ntawm no tiav ces koj yeej yuav zoo xwb mog.*"

Tou interpreted for Grandpa Vang. "He said, 'Today we performed this soul calling for you. Do not worry. Soon enough, you will be well again.'"

John closed his eyes and bowed an inch.

Auntie Sai delivered a glass bowl to Puff filled with American dollar bills—ones, fives, tens, and a few twenties. "Your Vang family gives you this little money as a gift with our hopes for John's long and prosperous life."

Puff handed the bowl to John.

John's eyes darted around the room, then at Puff. "I . . . uh . . ."

Puff signaled for him to accept the money.

After a long breath, John bowed again. "Thank you. You considered my needs," he said, no doubt recalling Mrs. Flowers's prompts.

While John gathered the bills and smoothed them into stacks, Auntie Sai motioned for Pa Dao to sit alongside me. Pa Dao's mother, sister, and father sat near us. Auntie Chong was the only other woman allowed to eat with the men.

The room quieted as Grandpa Vang spoke in Hmong. Pa Dao interpreted.

"The old year is passing, and New Year is arriving. We do not sweep away good luck, prosperity, riches, or wealth. Instead, we sweep away illnesses, bad luck, and omens to vanish with the old year, so your eyes will never see and your ears will never hear them again. From now on, you will only receive good blessings."

Grandpa Vang now spoke to Pa Dao in Hmong and passed her an envelope. She bowed, took the envelope, and replied in Hmong. Setting the envelope on the table, she leaned over to interpret for us.

"He said, 'We thank you for performing these ceremonies. We have nothing to show you for our gratitude but this money to appease your shaman spirit.' And I said, 'There is no need to thank me. I have come here to heal John so he will no longer have to endure any more illness.'"

Grandpa Vang raised his can of Budweiser to prepare a toast in Hmong.

"He says," Pa Dao whispered, "'I thank you, the shaman; your mother, the assistant; your father, sister, and your spirit guides. For this drink, we will do two lips.'" She added, "Now follow Grandpa Vang's lead. When he drinks, you drink. When he stops, you stop. But he's going to lead you to finish in two lips. Two chugs, that is."

We raised our drinks into the air. All of us at the table had Budweisers, even John and me. We drank as long as he did.

"That was the first lip," Pa Dao said. "He'll call for the second one before we eat."

A few moments later, Grandpa Vang stood again and announced the second lip. *"Peb sawv daws haus."*

We raised our drinks again and chugged until we finished our cans. Anyone who did not empty their drink was "punished" with another can of Budweiser. John and I smiled for having chugged our first beers. Puff nodded in pride.

"Los sawv daws, los peb noj mov," Grandpa Vang announced. He sat.

I reminded Puff and John that Mom said it the same way: "Let's eat rice."

Grandpa Vang's announcement caused a flutter of activity. Women emerged from the kitchen, bearing deep bowls and long trays filled with boiled chicken, boiled-pork-and-greens soup, bitter beef soup, beef *larb*, and pork *larb*.

"No fruit will be served at this table," Pa Dao said. "It's bad luck for Vang men to eat fruit with their meal. But the women might eat it in the kitchen."

Uncle Cha Ying brought out a clear glass decanter. "The first of our Hmong wine," he said as he poured Puff a small glass. "Brother, it has been too many years since you've been away. Let us drink to your return!" He set the decanter on the table.

Puff lifted his glass to his lips, then hesitated. He took a slow, deliberate sniff. "Did you say this is *wine?*" He frowned, swirling the liquid. "It's clear. And it doesn't smell like any wine I've ever had."

Before Uncle Cha Ying could answer, Grandpa Vang stood to speak again, with Pa Dao translating. "He says, 'The full moon we see is the same moon every Hmong sees around the world—in California, Arkansas, France, Australia, Laos, and Vietnam. That moon calls us to be full of food and family. It shines brightest and longest tonight, leading us beyond darkness to each other. The same moon leads Mai back home to our village in Laos. I will soon join her there. But tonight, I am with my family, and my family is everywhere. We are one. We are free. We are Hmong."

My big family sat at the long tables and ate, drank, and talked for hours—in English and sometimes in Hmong or Hmonglish, depending on the speaker.

"Does anyone else here think that Trump will follow through with shutting down the government tonight at midnight?" Auntie Chong said. "They've given that poor man such a hard time. He only wants what's best for this country."

The comment floated, then evaporated. No one wanted to talk politics at a family gathering.

As chatter about vacations and kids resumed around us, Puff took the last sip of his Hmong wine, then set the glass on the table with a pointed thud.

"I'm telling you," he said, "that's not wine. That's whiskey. And as a Moriarity, I know my whiskey."

Uncle Cha Ying translated for Grandpa Vang, who gave a sly smile. He stood, left for the kitchen, and returned with a bottle of Jameson. He pointed to the bottle, to Puff, then back to the bottle.

Puff grinned. "Yes. That's what I'm talkin' about, right there!"

Grandpa Vang handed the bottle to Puff, and he shared it with the other men. Puff even poured John and me a small amount of the Hmong wine and then the Jameson so we could do a taste test.

By nine o'clock, the *khi tes* celebration wound down. The house buzzed with laughter and goodbyes. It was then that we noticed that

Sweet Flower, our four-year-old cousin with Down syndrome, was missing. She had a mischievous grin and a love for hide-and-seek.

Grandpa Vang ordered everyone to search every spot Sweet Flower could fit into. My big family searched and called her name gently so we wouldn't frighten her.

After fifteen minutes—and right before Sweet Flower's mother dialed 911—Sweet Flower's father found her curled up in deep slumber under Grandpa Vang's bed. He scooped her into his arms, covered her in her jacket as well as his own, then carried her to their car. She never woke.

With Sweet Flower found, the little families resumed their departures. They put on coats and boots, bundled kids, packed cooking materials into their cars, returned to say their last goodbyes, and drove off to their homes.

My little family and Pa Dao's family saw them off in waves. Thankfully, my uncles had already loaded the shaman bench into the minivan. We had only a few boxes, bags, and outfits to carry out now.

Before loading up with an armful, I went to Auntie Chong to say goodbye.

"I never had a chance to tell you my story about winning the jackpot," she said, clenching my arm. "Can I tell you now?"

"Is it possible," I said, "you could tell me one quick story about Mom instead?"

"Could you tell me one quick story about the sun?" she answered.

She soaked in my silence.

"I can't tell you one story about Mai," she continued. "But I can tell you a thousand. Or five thousand. Or thirty thousand. Or however many thousand stories for however many thousand times Mai rose like the sun in the morning and went about her day. Mai said and did what was on her mind. She lit the way for me, her older sister, to do the same. At sunset, she slept too. My little Mai was the sun. I am only a cloud. Clouds fly over and leave. But the sun"—she patted my head and combed my hair with her fingers like Mom did—"will always be here to guide us."

I forced a smile, but Auntie Chong saw through it. I wanted stories—real moments of Mom's life that I could hold on to, something to make her feel less a memory and more a person.

"I'll tell you more stories," Auntie Chong said. "And you should tell me stories too. I expect you to visit more often now that you know where we live. We've lived far apart. Now we are near. Remember, family is everything. Don't ever give up on your family. Never let go of us."

"Yes, Auntie Chong," I said to the gentle reprimand disguised as an invitation.

After our final goodbyes with Grandpa Vang, we headed out to the minivan. Sheng, Auntie Xia Pao, Uncle Xia Pao, Puff, and John were ahead, with Pa Dao and I following behind. Each person carried something.

I carried Pa Dao's box of instruments. But it was nothing compared to the heaviness of Harden's passing, a burden I could not set down. He lived in the ache of my chest, in the space where his laughter used to reside.

"Harden's funeral will be next Saturday," I said. "It's at Holy Family. Harden's dad said it's a big church, but it's still too small for everyone who wants to attend. Reservations are required. Would you join us?"

Pa Dao leaned into the open back of the minivan and laid her armload of clothing over her shaman bench. Once I added the box I was carrying, she lowered the hatch. Taking a step back, she cupped her hands, blew air into them, then jammed them deep into her parka pockets.

"No," she said. "Funerals can be risky places. Bad spirits can lurk, and good spirits can leave. I didn't relate to Harden in the way that you did, so I can't go with you. You can go, but be careful."

"All right," I said, though nothing was right.

"Remember when I told you that I changed my name to avoid becoming a shaman?" she said. "I didn't choose to be a shaman. It chose me. It's not an easy life. And not just for me but for those who choose to support me."

She trapped me in her eyes.

"Besides," she said, taking a breath, "we're not done with helping Mai. I must visit her resting place to check that it hasn't been disturbed. Then I'll carve a door outline in the earth above her so her graveside spirit can enter and leave as it pleases. After that, we'll present food and water for the graveside spirit. Where's her resting place?"

The *khi tes* strings bundling my left arm tightened. "You mean where she's buried? That's not possible. Puff said we can never go home again."

"Then I'll go with Niam *thiab* Txiv," Pa Dao said, nodding to her parents. "Maybe the Vangs will want to come with us. But I have to go. I've put too much into helping Mai—and I care too much for her—not to finish the remaining steps. I'll give you Saturday for Harden's funeral, but I'll visit Mai's graveside spirit on Sunday, one way or the other, with or without you. I hope your father, John, and you will join me."

She lasered in on my eyes.

"Your hometown is in Iowa, right? What's the town?" She pulled out her phone to map the directions.

I looked over my shoulder for reinforcements, but John and Puff were arranging themselves in the minivan, searching for seatbelts. I was on my own.

Identifying the town would allow Pa Dao to visit Mom's graveside spirit and free Mom for eternity. But it could also entangle my little family in strings. Not delicate *khi tes* strings. More like heavy-duty twine or steel wire that could pull us back to Cottage Park—as well as tie me in complicated knots to my big family, to the Hmong, and to Pa Dao's heart and soul. Perhaps for the rest of my life. Perhaps far beyond the rest of my life.

So many emotions surged. I couldn't process even one. Pa Dao shifted impatiently, working to get warm.

"Cottage Park, Iowa," I said. "Just off Highway 169, on 360th Street, coming into town, you'll see it—Resurrection Cemetery."

"What do you mean, '*you'll* see it?'" she said.

"*We'll* see it. Together," I clarified. "My little family and I will take you there on Sunday. I'll show you. I'll tell Mom how much I love

her and want to hold her, and I'll tell her I have to let her go so we can
be free."

— CHAPTER TWENTY-NINE —

Crossover

On Saturday morning, Puff checked his Family Dollar digital wristwatch so often that I finally had to speak up.

"Harden's funeral is at eleven," I said, "and it's a ten-minute drive. Why do we have to leave at nine forty-five?"

"We're not taking any chances," Puff said.

I was surprised. We were rarely on time for anything.

John and I stood at attention at our front door, where Puff reviewed us. We wore stiff, formal church clothes: white dress shirts, ties, black pants, and polished black wingtip shoes. Puff stepped in front of me, tightened my tie, and centered it over my shirt buttons. He did the same for John before giving us a thumbs-up.

As Puff and John headed outside, I paused before the mirror by the door. I centered my belt buckle over my zipper, tugged my tie downward to cover it, and gazed into the mirror. Beyond my reflection, a lonesome Hawk sat on a couch pillow, waiting to join me. I grabbed him, and we joined my little family outside.

Puff and John were patiently waiting when Hawk and I hopped into Vicky. Puff drove south on Penn toward Holy Family Catholic Church. Harden's family worshiped at a tiny Baptist church by Olson Middle School. But that church only sat a hundred members—way too small for the expected crowd. Harden's pastor, Reverend Price, agreed to move the funeral to Holy Family, a much larger church a few miles away.

On Broadway, John switched on KMOJ, and Cardi B's new song, "Money," came on. It sounded the same as all her other songs. I wasn't trying to hear any music, though. John wasn't either. He turned it off, and for once, Vicky drove without music. Tires pummeled snow against her floorboard, drumming out her coughs and hiccups.

Out the window, a mother hovered over a daughter struggling to pedal a tricycle on the ice covering a cracked storefront sidewalk. Two boys rode Sting-Ray bikes like Harleys and popped wheelies over snow clusters and tree roots that buckled a stretch of cement.

"Look out for that guy," John warned, pointing to a jaywalker.

Puff swerved to avoid the man, who was feeling himself, talking, singing, dancing, and shivering as he dodged cars and crisscrossed from scruffy shops on Broadway's north and south sides. Other people, a few wearing camouflage clothing, darted in and out of aluminum bus shelters like bees, searching for their tardy Metro Transit bus.

John nodded ahead. "You see this?"

Bus shelters and billboards had been graffitied with the phrase JUSTICE FOR JEROME. That was the work of out-of-towners who didn't know him. The Northsiders who knew him, including me, had scrawled JUSTICE FOR HARDEN!

Those who didn't know him met those of us who did at the vigil Mrs. Flowers maintained at the entrance of the Central gym. She had arranged a quilt of memories: crib-to-casket photos, personal artifacts, and mounds of fresh flowers surrounded by a whispering candle fence. The out-of-towners, long-term protesters from around the country, had set up tents at the Fourth Precinct, barricading Plymouth Avenue. We helped them learn who Harden really had been.

As we approached Holy Family, its towering steeple came into view. Pulling into the parking lot, there were more steeples—the antennas mounted on local TV news vans.

We parked, then climbed the wide granite steps into the church. Its bells proclaimed the time across the Northside as 10:00 a.m.

Inside, a white marble Communion railing separated the congregation from the sanctuary. At the center, in a break in the railing,

Harden lay in an open, black-glazed casket. Puff led us to him. Harden wore a black suit and gray tie printed with tiny black stars. He lay on a billowing white satin liner.

Puff and John eased onto the kneeler. They prayed silently, blessed themselves, then stood.

It was my turn. I knelt before Harden, too scared to look at his face—afraid he wasn't dead, that he'd sit up quickly and go off on me for believing he could die. Instead, I eye-hustled his hands, large enough to palm a basketball, now resting across his stomach and bound in his Dodger-blue crystal rosary. Diamonds glistened in the white gold ring on his right pinky finger. Over his left wrist, his yellow-gold diving watch still proclaimed the time of noon and midnight.

My gaze crept from his hands to his tie, too tight around his neck, like mine. Harden's collar, also tight, didn't cover his gold chain.

Curiosity blocked out my fear, and my eyes darted across Harden's face. His few fuzzy chin hairs—which he'd called The Beard and had stroked when deep in thought—had been first-shaved away. His gold-and-diamond stud glinted in his left ear. A tiny pimple tipped his nose. His hair, freshly cut, was sharp and angular.

I breathed in, expecting to smell him, his Polo cologne, his sweat. But I caught only the faint bouquets of the flowers surrounding him—not sweet, but alive like the greens that embraced me whenever I entered Orlowski's Family Grocery.

I listened to Harden's stillness.

I knew I should pray, but my mind went blank—except for an Act of Contrition. But a memorized prayer wasn't right. Black people's prayers originated from their hearts, not their memory.

I looked behind. Only Puff and John were close enough to hear me.

I didn't pray for Harden but rather for the right words to say to him. While I waited for God to answer my prayer, Pa Dao filled my heart. Then I spoke.

"Pa Dao says I should talk to you like you're alive," I whispered. "I should remind you that you're dead and encourage you to move along to everywhere you've ever lived. Your spirits will live on forever.

And everywhere on North. And here inside me, wherever I go. My spirits must have gone into you. I was supposed to die in August. I'm supposed to be in that casket. I should have left with Mom on Friday night." I gave Harden one last long look, a look that will last my lifetime. "I'll never stop seeing you. Safe travels home until we meet again."

I crossed myself, kissed my pointer and middle fingers like Harden used to, and pressed those fingers against the glossy finish of the casket. Then I pushed myself away from Harden to rejoin Puff and John.

Harden's parents and grandparents had formed a receiving line on the other side of the casket. John and I followed Puff in line, which began with Harden's mom, Mrs. Vaughn. She was a tulip blowing in the wind, dropping petals.

"You have our deepest sympathies," Puff said. "My boys played basketball with Jerome."

"Oh my," Mrs. Vaughn said, drenching us in attention. "Harden called you two horses." She reached out with cold hands and pulled John and me toward her. "Our God punishes those He loves the most. He sacrificed his son too, though I don't know why."

She held our forearms like guardrails. Her voice trembled.

"Thank you for helping us carry Jerome." She pointed to the front right pew. "You'll sit there. After the service ends, Reverend Price will give you a signal. Then you'll come out to carry Jerome to the hearse."

We nodded, and Puff and John moved down the line to talk to Coach.

"We'll pass through this," I said, trying to move on.

But Mrs. Vaughn fixed on me and reached out her arms. "Come here, child." She hugged me, squeezing hard at the end. "What are we going to do?" she whispered in my ear.

I hunched my shoulders. "Pray and stick together. We have to be strong for each other."

"Well," Mrs. Vaughn said, "you and your brother can work as a pair at the rear of the casket when you carry Jerome from the church to the hearse and from the hearse to the cemetery plot."

She reached for John to relay the same instructions, but Coach gently took her hands instead.

"They'll work all that out," he said. Dark circles shadowed his eyes.

"Come back here for the repast afterward," Mrs. Vaughn said. "We'll have wonderful food, and we can better get to know each other."

Coach lifted her hands and placed them in the waiting hands of the person behind me. He turned to Puff, who waited with hand outstretched.

"A father should never have to bury his son," Puff said.

"Bless you," Coach said.

Puff hesitated to say something else but shook his head and moved on.

John followed next. He went to shake Coach's hand, but Coach hugged him, heartily patting John's back before letting him go.

As I stood before him, Coach reached into his coat pocket and pulled out Harden's money clip, thick with cash tucked inside an Andrew Jackson cover. Coach pressed the clip into my hand.

"Jerome's mom and I don't need any reminders that he's gone," he said. "But we do need reminders that he lives on in others. Letting everything go is the only way we'll move on."

I thanked Coach and put the clip in my front pocket, like Harden had. I'll keep it there for life.

We spoke with Harden's grandparents for a while—lifelong Northsiders—until a man from the funeral home directed John and me to sit in the front pew with the other pallbearers: Curry, Pat Bev, Westbrook, and LBJ. They wore school clothes: brightly colored pants, Christmasy Nike pullovers or full-zip hoodies, and new white Nike kicks. LBJ sank into a pillowy black down Nike jacket that he never unzipped. His jacket was the only piece of clothing close to the dark-gray-and-black funeral gear Puff had forced John and me to wear.

"I'll come get you at the end of the service," the man from the funeral home said. He handed each of us a program and left.

On the front of the program, the words IN LOVING MEMORY were scripted underneath a golden eagle soaring through sunshine and snowy-white clouds. Sunrays shone onto a school portrait of Harden giving a huge, toothy smile.

"Oh my God," Westbrook said. "Harden hated this picture."

"Didn't he destroy all these photos?" I asked.

I remembered the day we'd received our photo packages and Harden first laid eyes on that smile. He'd immediately ripped and mutilated every photo in the package. "If anyone ever sees this, my career in the rap game is ghost," he said, wiping paper dust off his hands and into the trash can, where the photos lay dismembered.

"The school sent a new copy to Harden's folks after he got shot," Pat Bev said. "Coach likes it. It's the only photo he's letting them use for T-shirts and the media."

Harden's name, JEROME KING VAUGHN, headlined below the photo, above SUNRISE: MARCH 4, 2004 and SUNSET: DECEMBER 21, 2018. At the bottom of the page, the service details were listed.

The program's inside page listed the ORDER OF SERVICE, beginning with a musical prelude of "His Eye Is on the Sparrow," "Precious Lord, Take My Hand," and "Amazing Grace." I looked up from the program in surprise, suddenly aware of the music that had been filling the church for some time. A Black soloist and a choir of a dozen members dressed in flowing red robes swayed along with a Black piano player, each note accompanied by a rollercoaster of background music—strands of dance and march woven together with grief.

As the last verse of "Amazing Grace" trailed off, the man from the funeral home somberly approached the casket. He motioned for Coach to join him. Coach reached inside the casket to remove the material objects most precious to Harden, his jewelry. After Coach finished, the man from the funeral home closed the casket cover for the final time, bowed, and left for the back of the church.

Coach came to us with his hands full. He gave Harden's watch to Westbrook, his stud earring to Pat Bev, his pinky ring to LBJ, his white-gold Cuban neck chain to Curry, and his rosary to John.

"Jerome would want you kings to remember him," Coach said. He turned to Westbrook. "I set your watch so you'll know what time it is." He walked back across the aisle to Mrs. Vaughn.

At 11:15, Reverend Price stood from his chair in the sanctuary and shuffled to the casket, leaning on his cane. He was in his eighties or nineties, with gray-speckled white hair. Thick, dark glasses magnified colorless eyes. His trembling hand steadied as he lifted it to speak.

"We celebrate the fire of young life, now cold in ash, whose memory will burn on in our consciousness and light the way for the path we must take—the journey we must make. Before we can begin on that path, we must grieve."

He lowered his hand.

"There is a time for everything. Today we cling to our faith's central tenet: We will rise again in our resurrection. Everything awaits us after this life. We are a temporary spark in eternal life and joy with Jesus in heaven. Today we celebrate and mourn Jerome King Vaughn. We find him and salvation with the guidance of holy scripture, song, and his story we will tell."

Reverend Price settled into a large, soft chair.

I turned to the inside of the program, and Curry tapped the bold header SCRIPTURE. Underneath was the name MARGARET VAUGHN (AUNTIE POOG).

Auntie Poog rose from her pew and walked with Harden's parents to the pulpit. She dabbed her eyes with a tissue as she delivered the Call to Worship with the first three verses of Psalm 45.

"God is our refuge and strength, an ever-present help in trouble. We will not fear, though the earth gives way, and the mountains fall into the heart of the sea, though its waters roar and foam, and the mountains quake with surging."

As Auntie Poog returned to her seat, Curry walked to the pulpit, where he found his place in the Bible, took in the mourners, then recited Psalm 31 from memory: "Be merciful to me, Lord, for I am in distress; my eyes grow weak with sorrow, my soul and body with grief."

Westbrook followed, reciting the first six verses of John 14, which ended with Jesus's assurance to anxious disciples: "I am the way, and the truth, and the life. No one comes to the Father except through me."

Next, the choir sang "Soon and Very Soon," and we clapped along. The song reminded us, "Should there be any rivers we must cross, should there be any mountains we must climb, God will supply all the strength that we need. Give us grace 'till we reach the other side."

The funeral program included a full-page collage of color photos. There were photos of Harden in Folwell Park Board baseball, football, and basketball uniforms. There were three photos of the Franklin Middle School Fabulous Five (Harden, Curry, Westbrook, LBJ, and Pat Bev), their gangly arms boosting a huge championship trophy. In two other pictures, Harden and Uncle Walter Vaughn hoisted overloaded stringers of fish. In one, they strained to lift two huge northern pikes.

That same uncle, Walter, left his seat with Harden's parents to take the pulpit and read the ACKNOWLEDGMENTS, CARDS & CONDOLENCES from the program. While he was reading, his phone rang. At first, I thought he had forgotten to silence it, but he calmly pulled it from his suit pocket, checked the number, then held the speaker to the microphone.

A professional-sounding woman in a voice template said, "This call will be recorded and monitored. I have a prepaid phone call from the name . . . James Vaughn, an inmate at the Minnesota Correctional Facility at Stillwater. This phone call will end in one minute and thirty seconds."

A man's voice called out from the speaker: "Walter?"

"Welcome, James," Walter said reassuringly. "We're all here. Go ahead."

"Jerome . . ." James said.

A long silence followed, as if that had been the entirety of his message. But then he spoke again.

"I'm sorry I couldn't be there for you today—or any day of these past eleven years. Today everyone else will talk up your accomplishments. But I want to go back to that magical time before I caught myself getting locked up—when I first met you, my first nephew. You weren't a week old when I first held you, beaming light and a bundle of possibilities, generating hope."

"One minute remaining," the woman's voice interrupted.

James rushed. "You latched on my finger, and I told your dad that hand would grab the rungs of life, climb them hard and fast, and raise you to worlds we only imagined. Your mom and dad did everything right. They positioned you to bust through to life beyond walls."

"Thirty seconds remaining," the woman's voice said.

James picked up the pace even more. "I haven't been there for you, but you've been here for me. Pictures, homework assignments, and anything else your dad sent over the years surrounds my cell. It keeps these prison walls from falling on me. You opened those walls to my future, to hope. And when I'm out, if I'm lucky enough, I'll find a woman as good as your mom who can give me a son who will take after you. And if your folks agree, I'm for damn sure going to—"

The call cut off.

Walter pulled his phone away from the microphone, tapped the screen to end the call, and pocketed the phone. He looked out over us. "On behalf of the Vaughn family and all those living and dead who couldn't be here today in person, I thank you for joining us." He left the altar and returned to his seat, beside Harden's parents.

Fingers dancing across the keyboard, the piano player improvised a meandering introduction that sounded more like harp than piano. The choir assembled around him and launched "Total Praise," a simple but majestic song.

When the choir concluded, Reverend Price rose, shuffled back to the pulpit, and lifted the microphone from its stand. "Our holy scriptures and songs tell the story of our loved ones who passed. But we must also make time to listen to our own Jerome stories. We need to hear your tributes of how Jerome touched you, in the hope that we can share those stories with those who can't be with us today and those who are yet to come. I ask friends and family who want to share stories to form a line and come to the microphone. Please, keep your story to two minutes."

A line of a dozen people quickly formed. I recognized them as Harden's friends, classmates, and teachers. I thought about saying how grateful I was that Harden had taught me about basketball, but I chickened out.

Mrs. Flowers was first in line. Reverend Price handed her the microphone. She looked out over the audience. The microphone wobbled in her hands.

"I'm sorry for Jerome's passing. I'm sorry about a lot of things these days." She cleared her throat. "I'm too old to stand up here and cry. We old people are supposed to have all the answers. But the older I become, the fewer answers I have. What can I say?"

Then Ms. Flowers did cry. A churchwoman approached with a box of tissues, and Mrs. Flowers helped herself to a handful. She mopped the tears away with the tissues. Words leaked through with tears.

"We plant the seeds. Nurture them. Water them with tears. They grow." Her voice faltered. "But here we are again, mourning another deadly harvest. Why?" She caught her breath. "This young man would have changed us—changed everything. We would have celebrated him one day. He'll still change us, but not how we hoped. And that hurts. That really hurts."

Mrs. Flowers presented the microphone back to Reverend Price and hugged him. She held tissues to her face and compassed back to her seat.

Next, Mona Harris trudged to the microphone. Her words rolled from her uphill.

"I have a vision of my life I'm trying to escape," she said.

She spoke to the church—its stained-glass windows, stone tiles, overflowing pews, and gigantic wooden doors. But she never looked at the mournful faces.

She brought her hands together to welcome Harden. "Shared fate, freight, boxed in a crate, shipped third rate."

She swept her hands down the front of her white T-shirt, which read REST IN POWER and featured Harden's photo. Then she turned around to show the back of the shirt, with the words IN LOVING MEMORY and a heart punctured in thorns, bleeding tears, and blood. JEROME was inscribed across the heart with his death date. Words at the bottom wept YOUR WINGS WERE READY, BUT OUR HEARTS WERE NOT.

Scattered, muffled clapping supported Mona as she completed her rotation. The applause stopped as she reached her hands around the collar and yanked it hard. Her shirt split down the middle, but the collar remained intact. She clasped a fistful to bring both sides together and cover herself.

"I got a closet full of these nightmares," she said, her fists shaking the torn pieces of the shirt. "Don't anyone here try to paste a happy face on me and tell me about your God. If there is one, I hate him and his wolf tickets about a heaven. I pray to myself—me—for the end of my never-ending death and the demise of the other sorry lives of those who still hold on." Mona trembled. She sniffed loudly as she focused on Harden's family. "My condolences."

She thrust the microphone to Reverend Price and left for her seat, her fists balled and shoulders shaking with silent sobs.

Each speaker stepped from the line to take the microphone. No one spoke for only two minutes. Those who vowed not to cry always did, often as soon as the vow left their mouths. A few cried so hard they needed help getting back to their seats.

Mr. Lane shared his memories of teaching Coach until he graduated, in 2001, and his initial excitement to continue with Harden.

"The world has changed," Mr. Lane said. "Yet I fear that in certain ways, we're not making progress. It's more of the same and worse now than ever."

The mayor promised Harden's life and tragic death would not be in vain.

Finally, Pat Bev cement-footed to the microphone. He waited, then searched out the church and us. Once he did, he turned and bowed to Reverend Price.

"Reverend, I come to challenge and instigate doubt—shout out disbelief of the thief who gives grief." Pat Bev languished in pain. "Everything's fine, really. But I'm out of place." He rolled up a shirt-sleeve to expose the skin on the back of his arm. "It's my race." He picked at his wispy hair and rubbed his lips and nose. "And my face." He extended his arms to take in the entire church. "I'm nowhere anywhere on earth or in heaven."

He pointed to a life-sized Jesus, Conan O'Brien's twin, nailed to a cross behind the altar.

"Question: Who's this pale brother of mistaken color? Born stray in the hay, probably gay, Pop's away. Stuck on a cross. Home's the boss. Such a loss. The real guy was Black. Best believe he'll be back."

He turned to his right, to another life-sized statue, the Blessed Virgin. She was whiter and fairer than Conan's twin, and her blond-highlighted strands mingled with red hair. She stood barefoot on a black snake spread across a globe, gasping its last breath. Four vases packed with pink roses surrounded her. Thirty miniature red votive candles flickered at her sides, and a golden crown rested over a North Carolina Tar Heel–blue veil.

"This version of Mom don't look nothing like mines," Pat Bev said. "I'm thinking Dee-vine is corrupt by design. I'm nowhere anywhere except for that snake. Face facts, brass tacks—we Blacks are on our backs, under attacks. Will I ever win, living in the skin I'm in? Harden lost."

Pat Bev slowed and stopped. His arms timbered to his sides before he strained to lift his right arm again, bringing the microphone to his lips.

"Now he's crossed."

Reverend Price eased toward Pat Bev, who handed the microphone to him and returned to his seat.

Reverend Price steadied himself and scanned the bereaved. "Is there anyone else who would pay tribute to Jerome today?"

Coach rose from his seat. "I need to speak."

He stepped into the aisle and made his way to the altar, where Reverend Price handed him the microphone. Coach took a deep breath and pointed to Pat Bev.

"Isiah Washington is the young man who spoke before me. Jerome loved him dearly and nicknamed him Pat Bev, after an NBA player who doesn't back down from anyone. Jerome used to tell me, 'Pops, he's not afraid to say anything to anybody.' Pat Bev, these funerals can become anesthesia that accelerates amnesia. You reminded us that this hurt should last a long time. Forever. We'll never stop feeling this hurt, which will most definitely kill me. But that's a good hurt. It guarantees we'll never let this happen again."

Pat Bev rubbed his eyes and looked up at Coach.

Coach scanned the congregation. "The world tested Jerome throughout his life. He failed and passed tests—in both cases, spectacularly. But he never quit. God will also test us." He took a long breath. "He will test us on whether we love these young men, whether they succeed or fail, whether they grow to adulthood or fall around us."

Coach focused on us pallbearers.

"Very few pursuits in life must continue regardless of tragedy. Basketball is one of those pursuits. In the dark days and weeks to come, I know one place where I'll continue to find Jerome—with his hoops team he put together. You boys will play all over America. I'll be there for every game, coaching you. And Jerome will be there with us too."

Coach took another slow, deep breath that whistled through his nostrils.

"Jerome died with his eyes wide open. We need to see the world through his eyes and resurrect him in us. Don't let my son die again when he comes to you."

He started to speak again but stopped, fixing his attention on his feet, as if praying. He returned the microphone to Reverend Price.

As Coach left the altar, LBJ entered it. At the pulpit, he adjusted the microphone, cleared his throat, and read the all-capped words from the obituary on the back page of the program.

"Jerome King Vaughn entered this world as the sun rose at six forty-four a.m. in North Memorial Hospital on March fourth, 2003. He is the only child of parents who loved and lavished him with whatever he wanted or needed. As a child, Jerome wanted dinosaurs, trucks, trains, and anything related to Egypt and the pyramids. He wouldn't let his parents give away one single toy."

LBJ's eyes froze on the words in the program. Seconds stretched into a minute—a lifetime.

When encouraging voices called out from the pews, he continued.

"As Jerome grew older, he starred in any sport with a ball: soccer, baseball, football, and basketball. Jerome teamed with the Fabulous Five at Franklin Middle School. They were undefeated in basketball during his sixth-, seventh-, and eighth-grade years. At Thomas Jefferson High School, Jerome followed in the footsteps of his hero, his father."

Again, LBJ stopped until more voices spurred him on.

"Besides sports, Jerome enjoyed spending time with his friends, playing cards and video games with his family, listening to and making music, rapping, and keeping the Nike corporation afloat."

A few smiled and chuckled, but a big tear rolled down LBJ's cheeks.

"Jerome entered eternal life on Friday, December twenty-first, at age fourteen. He rejoices in heaven with his great-grandmothers, Lenore Stewart and Ida Rice. Jerome leaves behind his parents, Derek and Asa Vaughn; his grandparents, Jeff and Cleotha Vaughn and Ronald and Jamila McGee; aunts and uncles, Pearl and Walter Vaughn, Margaret and Benjamin Vaughn, Darlene and Marcus Vaughn, James Vaughn, Josephine and Kyle McGee, Patricia and William McGee, Latoya and Desmond McGee, and Quisha McGee. Jerome's Boston terrier, Maxine, will also miss him dearly."

Once back at our pew, LBJ dropped his face into his hands. Westbrook and Pat Bev consoled him.

I wish the funeral had ended after LBJ read the obituary. I lost track of time until a single Angelus bell sounded outside, signaling noon. That was when Reverend Price rose for the eulogy.

For more than an hour, he rambled on about Paul and the Thessalonians, death, resurrection, grief, hope, sin, failure, and how to find salvation. He repeatedly said, "Hope can only be found in Jesus." He talked about everything in this world and the next—except Harden. He never mentioned his name.

Finally, he wound down and took his seat.

After a few more prayers and songs, Reverend Price signaled to the man from the funeral home. The man stood and arranged us pallbearers at the casket, with John and me at the back.

Harden's mom shrieked when we lifted the heavy wooden casket from its stand. She sobbed as the choir sang "I'll Fly Away."

We carried Harden outside the church and down the steps, then slid him into a waiting white hearse with expansive windows. John and I crowded inside beside him.

The hearse leisurely paraded from Broadway to Penn to the cemetery. There, the parade cautiously continued through two inches of overnight feathery snow covering the winding roads. Graves were marked with dead wreaths awaiting their own burials. They festered like smoldering boils on milky skin.

At last, we parked as far north as possible without coming to the fence that I jumped each day on my way to and from Thomas Jefferson. Harden's grave lay in the shadow of a tall blue-green pine tree. Across the fence stood the Thomas Jefferson football field.

"We'll wait here," the funeral director said from the driver's seat, "until everybody catches up with us. I'm in no hurry to go back outside." He coughed.

We were experiencing a polar vortex—an icy blast of air that had circulated down from the North Pole to Minneapolis. I was caught in an icy vortex of my own—falling. When and where would I land?

We waited for the long line of cars behind us to pull in and park. When they did, the funeral director said, "Time." He got out of the hearse, walked briskly to the rear, and opened the hatch. Curry, Westbrook, LBJ, and Pat Bev joined us there. Arctic wind sliced through me, biting my skin like stinging nettle.

"Work together," the funeral director said.

Pat Bev and Curry latched on to the handles and pulled the casket from the hearse. Westbrook and LBJ took hold next. Pat Bev and Curry then paused to ensure that John and I had secured a good hold in the back. My hands tightened around the cold brass handle, the weight of Harden's casket pressing into my palms.

We carried Harden to his grave, positioning his casket on a metal stand. Then we dissolved into the crowd, taking shelter among the Northside's most neglected and denied. Four Black cemetery workers emerged from the crowd, heavily bundled in layered jackets, boots, trapper hats, scarves, and big leather mittens. They stood silently near the grave, their long-handled steel shovels resting at their sides like sentinels guarding a sacred site.

Reverend Price surveyed the crowd. He wore no hat or gloves but never shivered.

"Dear God," he said, "thank you for the privilege of bowing before you once more, and thank you for the power you have given this family. Thank you for the support you have given to Jerome's friends. In this time of sorrow, give us hope to remember that you are always with us. We thank you and give you praise and glory in Jesus's name. Amen."

"Amen," the crowd murmured.

I looked at my set members. LBJ hunched his shoulders and buried his face deep into his jacket. Westbrook teetered from one foot to the other and slowly rocked his head, like his whole body was dodging punches. Pat Bev shook his head in disgust, cursing all under his breath, even God: "Man, fuck God to hell." Only Curry stood motionless and emotionless, poker-faced.

"We selfishly want to hold on to Jerome," Reverend Price said. "It brings great pain to let him go. Living in the resurrection hope of our Lord Jesus Christ, we commit his body to its rest in the trust of a loving God who promises eternal life. We will continue to mourn Jerome, who is safe and warm in God's kingdom. Dear God, we ask you to receive Jerome in your merciful arms and into everlasting peace."

For the first time that day, Reverend Price's words slowed, pulling us from our ascension to heaven's glory back to earth's monstrous slaveowner, gravity. Harden had mockingly conquered that gravity, but the force was now crushing us. We surrendered and prepared to descend with him farther beneath the ground.

Reverend Price continued. "It is my sad duty to commit Jerome's body to its final resting place—earth to earth, ashes to ashes, dust to dust. In the hope of resurrection unto eternal life, we faithfully and victoriously give him over to your blessed care through the promise of Our Lord Jesus Christ. Amen."

Mrs. Vaughn stepped forward. She held a massive bouquet of red roses wrapped in plastic bubble layers. Coach lifted the roses from her and held them before the crowd.

"We'd planned for each of you to take a rose to bury with Jerome," Coach called out to everyone. "But we can't bury such beauty. We can only give them away to you at the repast with the courage and love they manifest."

Coach stepped forward and signaled to the cemetery workers. The men waved back, quickly laid down their shovels, and positioned themselves around Harden.

"These men have a job to do," Coach told the mourners. "Let's leave so they can finish their work."

Reverend Price walked away first. Coach handed the roses to Pat Bev, then placed his arm around Mrs. Vaughn. Together, they trailed behind Reverend Price.

All around me, the crowd fell away. My set members vanished. Other people climbed into their cars. Engines stammered as if to say *I don't know . . . I don't know* before they finally turned over.

John and Puff retreated a few steps toward Vicky. But I stayed.

Puff stopped and turned to me. "We're going to the luncheon, right?"

"Definitely," I said. "But I need to make everything right before we leave."

"We can wait a few minutes," Puff said. "But don't stay much longer. You'll get frostbite."

Puff and John made their way to Vicky, and I turned back to Harden's open grave. The workers had positioned themselves two on each side of the casket. They maneuvered ropes and lowered Harden into the hole. Once he reached the bottom, they jiggled the cords free, tossed them to the side, and furiously stabbed shovels into the dirt mound abutting the grave. Clods of dirt poured over the glossy surface of the casket until that mound leveled and a newer mound rose over the grave. One man raked that new mound flat while the others collected the tarp, ropes, and shovels.

When they finished, the men jogged off to their van, leaving Harden. Alone.

I, too, was alone.

The grave was now a flat patch of dirt, a garden plot where we'd planted Harden—a holy, and wholly innocent, seed of hope buried too soon. The plot's cold soil and pine perfume whispered prayers written on hearts but never spoken.

I edged backward toward Vicky, the sole car in the cemetery, until I reached the door and hopped inside with Puff and John. Puff leaned over and gave the dash one sharp slap, making the fan blower roar to life. Blessed warmth mothered me as I leaned forward in the back seat.

"Ready to do this?" Puff said.

"We can do this," I said.

Puff revved Vicky up and down before letting her settle into a comfortable idle. He fiddled with the defroster and used his finger-nails to scrape the remaining patch of frost from the windshield.

I looked out the window at the grave—and beyond, to a pine tree, where Commander Crow and his family kept watch. I hugged Hawk, brought him to my nose, and inhaled his smoky, worn rubber grooves and paper-thin, pock-scarred, curdling skin. I closed my eyes, holding his scent a moment longer.

I spun Hawk near my ear, tapping out the backbeat to Harden's Northside rap. But then I stopped and pressed him tightly to my ear. Waves rolled through me, like the ocean trapped in a conch shell. My heartbeat and lungs grew louder until I believed they would explode.

Then I heard it. Everything—emptiness. More deafening than any noise. More articulate than any words. It all came crashing upon the shore.

I shoved Hawk aside before I shattered into pieces.

At that moment, I understood Mom's messages about emptiness and why Harden had called me Empty. I am a subset of all sets. We all are—threads in a Hmong story cloth of little families, big families, and the sprawling, chaotic story of humanity. In the emptiness left by Mom and Harden, I've become them. They live in me now. In death's vast emptiness, we become everything. Emptiness means next.

And I understood that I can choose the paths Pa Dao and Harden have laid out for me, or I can combine the best of both to make my own path. I see that path and me living successfully on it.

Puff shifted into drive and pulled Vicky onto the road.

I knew what I had to do.

"Hold on," I said. I unlatched my seatbelt, grabbed Hawk tight, and lunged toward my door.

"We should come with you," Puff said.

But I couldn't wait. I opened the door and ran with Hawk across the snow, back to Harden's grave.

Once again, I channeled Pa Dao. I remembered what she'd told me about the final ritual, the one we'd perform the next day at Mom's graveside. Pa Dao said that Mom needs a doorway so her graveside spirit can enter and leave as it pleases. Harden's graveside spirit also needs to come and go as necessary.

You gotta go down to go up. Harden, too, will come up again.

I lifted my wingtip heel over the freshly raked mound and kick-carved the outline of a door, complete with a handle.

"Front door's closed," I said.

I listened for Harden's response: *Back door's open.*

I figured that Harden's graveside spirit would be hungry, as would Commander Crow. I reached deep into my coat pocket, underneath my glove, until I found the Ziploc bag of Cheetos. I unsealed the bag and sprinkled the little orange curls over the plot.

I half genuflected, adjusting my knees until they snuggled upon the frozen ground. I twirled Hawk on my index finger. His skin had once been a bold burst of red, white, and blue. It was now a melted mix, like an American flag snow cone from the concession booth at Memorial Field in Cottage Park.

I let Hawk spin as long as he wanted before he dizzied and slipped off my finger. He fell with a thud on the spot where Harden's monument would soon stand. This time, he didn't bounce back to me.

I'd traveled "Around the World" and back home again with Hawk and Harden countless times. I understand graveside spirits, but I also believe that the spirits of Mom and Harden now reside within me. I can never let them go; I can only endure them.

Puff and John approached and knelt alongside me. They waited, ready for next. The next game, like Harden. The next pitch, like Joe Mauer.

I straightened Hawk, now heavy with sorrow, there in the dirt, with his seams aligned for Harden to shoot. Hawk was a gift. I vowed to return with another gift the next day, the day after that, and every day until I graduated.

I blessed myself and kissed my index and middle fingers to Hawk's air hole. Like me, he was freezing to the touch and holding his breath. We exhaled as I leaned away and rose.

I've learned that on North, the colder the temperature, the bluer the sky. True enough, I lifted my head to a sky of infinite, radiant robin's-egg blue, the sun a yolk of golden-white light. The darkness dogging us disappeared.

My little family headed back to Vicky for the repast at Holy Family. Afterward, we headed home.

Now I sit in my bedroom, alone, the weight of these words finally lifting from my chest to drift away in incense. It's taken me four months to write this history. But it feels more like forty years, or a lifetime. In these pages, I've buried Mom and Harden, carved doorways for their spirits, and found a way to hold on and let them go at the same time.

I am less than a victor but more than or equal to the last picked for the team. I'm a survivor. And now it's time for me to let go of "The Empty Set" and hold on for next.

Let that be all.

— AUTHOR'S NOTE —

Overtime

FROM THE EXECUTIVE SUMMARY of the United States Department of Justice Civil Rights Division and the United States Attorney's Office–District of Minnesota, Civil Division, June 16, 2023:

On April 21, 2021, the Department of Justice opened a pattern or practice investigation of the Minneapolis Police Department (MPD) and the City of Minneapolis. By then, Derek Chauvin had been convicted in state court for the tragic murder of George Floyd in 2020. In the years before, shootings by other MPD officers had generated public outcry, culminating in weeks of civil unrest after George Floyd was killed.

Our federal investigation focused on the police department as a whole, not the acts of any one officer. To be sure, many MPD officers do their difficult work with professionalism, courage, and respect. Nevertheless, our investigation found that the systemic problems in MPD made what happened to George Floyd possible.

FINDINGS

The Department of Justice has reasonable cause to believe that the City of Minneapolis and the Minneapolis Police Department engage in a pattern or practice of conduct that deprives people of their rights under the Constitution and federal law:

- *MPD uses excessive force, including unjustified deadly force and other types of force.*
- *MPD unlawfully discriminates against Black and Native American people in its enforcement activities.*
- *MPD violates the rights of people engaged in protected speech.*
- *MPD and the City discriminate against people with behavioral health disabilities when responding to calls for assistance.*

We also found persistent deficiencies in MPD's accountability systems, training, supervision, and officer wellness programs, which contribute to the violations of the Constitution and federal law.

The frustrations with MPD that boiled over during the 2020 protests were not new. "These systemic issues didn't just occur on May 25, 2020," a city leader told us. "There were instances . . . being reported by this community long before that."

I believe one such instance of MPD's unjustified deadly force is related to a Northside resident who was killed nearly fifteen years prior to the murder of George Floyd.

On July 22, 2006, a MPD officer shot nineteen-year-old Hmong American Fong Lee eight times, killing him. Police officials claimed to have found a pistol by his body, despite Lee's family and friends denying this claim and despite extensive protests after the shooting.

In 2009, documents revealed that the pistol claimed to have been on Fong Lee had been in police possession since 2004, when police recovered the weapon after it had been reported stolen.

Fong Lee lives on as long as we remember him, say his name, and tell his story. His story is best told in the following spoken word piece by Tou SaiKo Lee (next page), one of ten performances by Twin Cities Hmong emcees in Blackbird Elements in 2009.

Many thanks to Tou SaiKo Lee for permission to share this piece.

—Tommy Murray

— IN THE MEMORY OF INJUSTICE —

by Tou SaiKo Lee

In the Memory of Injustice
In the Memory of Fong Lee,
In the memory of all victims of police brutality,
In the memory of a tragedy translated to travesty
In the memory of a planted gun, conspiracies and sons lost under the
    sun,
The Videotape was lost and they thought it was all done. They were
    wrong:
3 shots running away. 5 shots on the ground. One son down bleeding
    all around
His generation are the grandsons of a secret army that sacrificed to
    save backs of soldiers.
and shooting teenagers in the back would never achieve a medal of
    bravery
unless they thought the person they shot was seen as a Refugee from
    Southeast.
The Police pull over Civics and Toyotas at the rate of heartbeats
of Hmong kids that get beat down at the side of small streets.
But Fong Lee was on a bike unarmed, before his life was stolen and
    broken with bullet holes.
As the spokes of his bicycle spun in circles, we have spoken up to
    break the cycle of this circus.
This case makes me believe that these cops perceive us as less than
    human beings and worthless.

In the Memory of Injustice

In the Memory of Fong Lee,

In the memory of all victims of police brutality,

In the memory of a tragedy translated to travesty

In the memory of a planted gun, conspiracies and sons lost under the
sun,

The Videotape was lost and they thought it was all done. They were
wrong:

We will never forget that messed up shoot out in North Minneapolis,

When cops raided the wrong house by mistake, and put little Hmong
kids' lives at stake,

And still got a medal from the station for being brave, give me a break

It makes me wonder what it takes for men with badges to earn a
medal of valor these days.

We don't feel protected and safe from Policemen with Swine-Pen
mentalities,

think outside the fence,

instead of doing dirt with blood stains on shirts that leave family
casualties.

But you know what's really corrupt? When the police chief cooperates
to cover it all up.

We scream for justice with enough evidence to force the whole force
to give it up.

The Department is Responsible, for those accountable we demand
FIRE.

Those exposed should go to prison haunted by the guilt of blood spilt
spirits for the rest of their lives.

In the Memory of Injustice

In the Memory of Fong Lee,

In the memory of all victims of police brutality,

In the memory of a tragedy translated to travesty

In the memory of a planted gun, conspiracies and sons lost under the
sun,

The Videotape was lost and they thought it was all done. They were
wrong:

For those that judge Fong Lee for possibly being down with gangs like
    his life was worth less
like a racist radio show host that wants attention or people that
    misunderstand with ignorance,
I was a former gang member, so that kid could've been me.
My last name is Lee too and I'm lucky enough to still breathe and if
    this happened to me,
I would've never had the chance for this passion to give back to
    community.
More than ever, open up arms to outreach and unite movements
    together
for every community that's had their hearts ripped open from the
    core,
by wild boars in blue uniforms, with no conscience this nonsense of
    violence,
we will not be silent to sirens of cyanide on our side of the city.
Cause it's not injustice for just us, there's a whole history of
    conspiracy.
Stand with me 'cause the next tragedy could be in your family so we
    suffocate from this case,
skeptical to breathe and only Justice will give us the oxygen to be
    treated as Human Beings.
This is a moment of our Existence, centuries since we have survived
    under oceans, it's time
to rise above tidal waves of broken hope that leave these memories of
    Injustice just floating.

—Tou SaiKo Lee, April 24, 2009

— ACKNOWLEDGMENTS —

I wish to thank the following professional editors who made each edit less a correction and more an invitation to greatness:

Scott Edelstein has stood by *The Empty Set* and me since he first took on this project in 1982. He is my brother who was always there to collect my ashes and fashion them into a phoenix so I could soar again.

Angela Wiechmann at A. M. W. Editing drove *The Empty Set* home late at night under a huge moon shining brighter than the sun, with me asleep in my pajamas in the wayback.

Kris Kobe did the final proofread, designed the cover and interior layouts, and converted the text into an ebook, making me and my story look good, on the shelf or otherwise.

In my little family, my wife, Mary Ann, proofread and offered ideas for scenes and more suitable words for description and dialogue.

The Empty Set sat in a closet box from 1985 until 2018, when my son John encouraged me to take out the typewritten pages and input them into our computer. In addition to story development, he also offered this sage advice: "After you write the opening sentence, make sure each following sentence is stronger than the previous one."

I received technical support from my other son, Joe, and daughters, Danielle and Christina.

My sister Ann Baker is a fabulous proofreader. Who knew that the Mall of America didn't have a JCPenney?

My friend Blong Yang, the most honest man I know, helped me find God in both the details of writing and Hmong culture.

There are countless other family and friends I wish I had the time and space to thank for helping me on my journey. I could write a book about them—the big family who ensured I had the time and support I needed to write *The Empty Set*.

— ABOUT THE AUTHOR —

Tommy Murray is a retired teacher who worked in the Minneapolis Public Schools district.

Murray is married to Mary Ann and resides in Shoreview, Minnesota. They are the parents of four adult children who dominated the Minnesota Knights of Columbus Free Throw Championship in their middle school years.

— A NOTE ON THE TYPEFACES —

The Empty Set is set in Iowa—and so is the typeface in the print edition. The bulk of the text is set in Iowan Old Style, a typeface rooted in the history of early Venetian printing and the sign-painting traditions of eastern Iowa. Designed by John Downer and released by Bitstream in 1991, the font blends classical beauty with a distinctly regional soul, just like the story it tells.

Each chapter begins in Schoolbell, a typeface that mimics the clumsy scrawl of Michael Moriarity's handwriting—a young man who never mastered cursive, yet wrote his narrative with urgency—imperfect, personal, honest, and alive with memory.